THE KNIFE OF NEVER LETTING GO

"Furiously paced, terrifying, exhilarating and heartbreaking, it's a book that haunts your imagination."
Sunday Telegraph

"Original, powerful and steeped in literary richness."
The Times

"Powerful and provocative… A major new talent."
Daily Mail

"Darkly imagined and brilliantly created, the painful dystopian setting of a world full of noise in which all thoughts can be heard as if spoken is the background to this tense coming of age story."
Guardian

"Imagine a world where the thoughts of men and boys are broadcast for all to hear, good and bad. Ness's novel is at once a breakneck thriller and a fable about fear, love and redemption."
Independent on Sunday

"A sophisticated, complex novel."
Sunday Times

"Ness moves things along at a breakneck pace, and Todd's world is filled with memorable characters and foul villains."

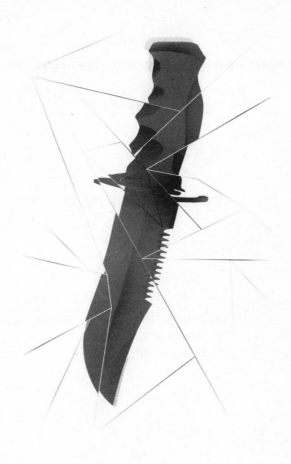

ALSO IN THE CHAOS WALKING TRILOGY

The Ask and the Answer

Monsters of Men

ALSO BY PATRICK NESS

The Crane Wife

A Monster Calls

Topics About Which I Know Nothing

The Crash of Hennington

CHAOS WALKING
BOOK ONE

THE KNIFE OF NEVER LETTING GO

PATRICK NESS

WALKER
BOOKS

First published 2008 by Walker Books Ltd
87 Vauxhall Walk, London SE11 5HJ

This edition, including *The New World*, published 2013

2 4 6 8 10 9 7 5 3

Text © 2008, 2009 Patrick Ness

The right of Patrick Ness to be identified as the author of this work has been asserted by him in accordance with the Copyright, Designs and Patents Act 1988

This book has been typeset in Fairfield and ITC Tiepolo

Printed and bound in Great Britain by Clays Ltd, St Ives plc

British Library Cataloguing in Publication Data:
a catalogue record for this book is available from the British Library

ISBN 978-1-4063-4446-2

www.walker.co.uk

For Michelle Kass

IF WE HAD A KEEN VISION and feeling of all ordinary human life, it would be like hearing the grass grow and the squirrel's heart beat, and we should die of that roar which lies on the other side of silence.

George Eliot, *Middlemarch*

PART I

1

THE HOLE IN THE NOISE

THE FIRST THING you find out when yer dog learns to talk is that dogs don't got nothing much to say. About anything.

"Need a poo, Todd."

"Shut up, Manchee."

"Poo. Poo, Todd."

"I said *shut it*."

We're walking across the wild fields south-east of town, those ones that slope down to the river and head on towards the swamp. Ben's sent me to pick him some swamp apples and he's made me take Manchee with me, even tho we all know Cillian only bought him to stay on Mayor Prentiss's good side and so suddenly here's this brand new dog as a present for my birthday last year when I never said I *wanted* any dog, that what I *said* I wanted was for Cillian to finally fix the fissionbike so I wouldn't have to walk every forsaken place in this stupid town, but oh, no, happy birthday, Todd, here's a brand new puppy, Todd, and even tho you don't want him, even tho you never asked for him, guess who has to feed him and train him and wash him and take him for walks and listen to him jabber now he's got old enough for the talking germ to set his mouth moving? Guess who?

"Poo," Manchee barks quietly to himself. "Poo, poo, poo."

"Just *have* yer stupid poo and quit yapping about it."

I take a switch of grass from beside the trail and I swat after him with it. I don't reach him, I don't *mean* to reach him, but he just laughs his little barking laugh and carries on down the trail. I follow after him, switching the switch against the grass on either side, squinting from the sun, trying not to think about nothing at all.

We don't need apples from the swamp, truth to tell. Ben can buy them at Mr Phelps's store if he really wants them. Also true: going to the swamp to pick a few apples is not a job for a man cuz men are never allowed to be so idle. Now, I won't *officially* become a man for thirty more days. I've lived twelve years of thirteen long months each and another twelve months besides, all of which living means I'm still one month away from the big birthday. The plans are being planned, the preparayshuns prepared, it will be a party, I guess, tho I'm starting to get some strange pictures about it, all dark and too bright at the same time, but nevertheless I will become a man and picking apples in the swamp is not a job for a man or even an almost-man.

But Ben knows he can ask me to go and he knows I'll say yes to going because the swamp is the only place anywhere near Prentisstown where you can have half a break from all the Noise that men spill outta theirselves, all their clamour and clatter that never lets up, even when they sleep, men and the thoughts they don't know they think even when everyone can hear. Men and their Noise. I don't know how they do it, how they stand each other.

Men are Noisy creachers.

"Squirrel!" Manchee shouts and off he goes, jumping off the trail, no matter how loud I yell after him, and off I have to go, too, across the (I look round to make sure I'm alone) *goddam* fields cuz Cillian'll have a fit if Manchee falls down some *goddam* snake hole and of course it'll be my own *goddam* fault even tho I never wanted the *goddam* dog in the *goddam* first place.

"Manchee! Get back here!"

"*Squirrel!*"

I have to kick my way thru the grass, getting grublets stuck to my shoes. One smashes as I kick it off, leaving a green smear across my trainers, which I know from experience ain't coming out. "*Manchee!*" I rage.

"Squirrel! Squirrel! Squirrel!"

He's barking round the tree and the squirrel's skittering back and forth on the tree trunk, taunting him. **Come on, Whirler dog,** says its Noise. **Come on, come get, come on, come get. Whirler Whirler Whirler.**

"Squirrel, Todd! Squirrel!"

Goddam, animals are stupid.

I grab Manchee by the collar and hit him hard across his back leg. "Ow, Todd? Ow?" I hit him again. And again. "Ow? Todd?"

"Come *on*," I say, my own Noise raging so loud I can barely hear myself think, which is something I'm about to regret, you watch.

Whirler boy, Whirler boy, thinks the squirrel at me. **Come get, Whirler boy.**

"You can eff off, too," I say, except I don't say "eff", I say what "eff" stands for.

And I really, really shoulda looked round again.

Cuz here's Aaron, right here, rising outta the grass from nowhere, rising up and smacking me cross the face, scratching my lip with his big ring, then bringing his hand back the other way, closed as a fist, catching my cheekbone but at least missing my nose because I'm falling into the grass, trying to fall away from his punch, and I let go of Manchee's collar and off he runs back to the squirrel, barking his head off, the traitor, and I hit the grass with my knees and my hands, getting grublet stains all over everything.

And I stay there, on the ground, breathing.

Aaron stands over me, his Noise coming at me in fragments of scripture and of his next sermon and **Language, young Todd** and **the finding of a sacrifice** and **the saint chooses his path** and **God hears** and the wash of pictures that's in everyone's Noise, of things familiar and glancing flashes of–

What? What the forsaken–?

But up flies a loud bit of his sermon to block it out and I look up into his eyes and suddenly I don't wanna know. I can already taste the blood where his ring cut my lip and I don't wanna know. He *never* comes out here, men *never do*, they have their reasons, men do, and it's just me and my dog only ever but here he is and I don't don't don't wanna know.

He smiles down at me, thru that beard of his, smiles down at me in the grass.

A smiling fist.

"Language, young Todd," he says, "binds us like prisoners on a chain. Haven't you learned anything from yer church, boy?" And then he says his most familiar preaching. "If one of us falls, we all fall."

Yes, Aaron, I think.

"With yer mouth, Todd."

"Yes, Aaron," I say.

"And the effs?" he says. "And the geedees? Because don't think I didn't hear them as well. Your Noise reveals you. Reveals us all."

Not all, I think, but at the same time I say, "Sorry, Aaron."

He leans down to me, his lips close to my face, and I can smell the breath that comes outta his mouth, smell the weight of it, like fingers grabbing for me. "God hears," he whispers. "God *hears.*"

And he raises a hand again and I flinch and he laughs and then he's gone, like that, heading back towards the town, taking his Noise with him.

I'm shaking from the charge to my blood at being hit, shaking from being so fired up and so surprised and so angry and so much hating this town and the men in it that it takes me a while till I can get up and go get my dog again. *What was he effing doing out here anyway?* I think and I'm so hacked off, still so raging with anger and hate (and fear, yes, fear, shut up) that I don't even look round to see if Aaron heard my Noise. I don't look round. I don't look round.

And then I do look round and I go and get my dog.

"Aaron, Todd? Aaron?"

"Don't say that name again, Manchee."

"Bleeding, Todd. Todd? Todd? Todd? Bleeding?"

"I know. Shut up."

"Whirler," he says, as if it don't mean nothing, his head as empty as the sky.

I smack his rump. "Don't say that neither."

"Ow? Todd?"

We keep on walking, staying clear of the river on our left. It runs down thru a series of gulches at the east of town, starting way up to the north past our farm and coming down the side of the town till it flattens out into a marshy part that eventually becomes the swamp. You have to avoid the river and especially that marshy part before the swamp trees start cuz that's where the crocs live, easily big enough to kill an almost-man and his dog. The sails on their backs look just like a row of rushes and if you get too close, *WHOOM!* – outta the water they come, flying at you with their claws grasping and their mouths snapping and you pretty much ain't got no chance at all then.

We get ourselves down past the marshy part and I try to take in the swamp quiet as it approaches. There's nothing to see down here no more, really, which is why men don't come. And the smell, too, I don't pretend it don't smell, but it don't smell nearly so bad as men make out. They're smelling their memories, they are, they're not smelling what's really here, they're smelling it like it was then. All the dead things. Spacks and men had different ideas for burial. Spacks just used the swamp, threw their dead right into the

8

water, let 'em sink, which was fine cuz they were suited for swamp burial, I guess. That's what Ben says. Water and muck and Spackle skin worked fine together, didn't poison nothing, just made the swamp richer, like men do to soil.

Then suddenly, of course, there were a whole lot more spacks to bury than normal, too many for even a swamp this big to swallow, and it's a ruddy big swamp, too. And then there were no live spacks at all, were there? Just spack bodies in heaps, piling up in the swamp and rotting and stinking and it took a long time for the swamp to become swamp again and not just a mess of flies and smells and who knows what extra germs they'd kept saved up for us.

I was born into all that, all that mess, the over-crowded swamp and the over-crowded sematary and the not-crowded-enough town, so I don't remember nothing, don't remember a world without Noise. My pa died of sickness before I was born and then my ma died, of course, no surprises there. Ben and Cillian took me in, raised me. Ben says my ma was the last of the women but everyone says that about everyone's ma. Ben may not be lying, *he* believes it's true, but who knows?

I am the youngest of the whole town, tho. I used to come out and throw rocks at field crows with Reg Oliver (seven months and 8 days older) and Liam Smith (four months and 29 days older) and Seb Mundy who was next youngest to me, three months and a day older, but even he don't talk to me no more now that he's a man.

No boys do once they turn thirteen.

Which is how it goes in Prentisstown. Boys become men and they go to their men-only meetings to talk about who knows what and boys most definitely ain't allowed and if yer the last boy in town, you just have to wait, all by yerself.

Well, you and a dog you don't want.

But never mind, here's the swamp and in we go, sticking to the paths that take us round and over the worst of the water, weaving our way round the big, bulby trees that grow up and outta the bog to the needly roof, metres and metres up. The air's thick and it's dark and it's heavy, but it's not a frightening kind of thick and dark and heavy. There's lots of life here, loads of it, just ignoring the town as you please, birds and green snakes and frogs and kivits and both kinds of squirrel and (I promise you) a cassor or two and sure there's red snakes to watch out for but even tho it's dark, there's slashes of light that come down from holes in the roof and if you ask me, which you may not be, I grant you that, to me the swamp's like one big, comfy, not very Noisy room. Dark but living, living but friendly, friendly but not grasping.

Manchee lifts his leg on practically everything till he must be running outta pee and then he heads off under a bush, burbling to himself, finding a place to do his other business, I guess.

But the swamp don't mind. How could it? It's all just life, going over itself, returning and cycling and eating itself to grow. I mean, it's not that it's not Noisy here. Sure it is, there's no escaping Noise, not nowhere at all, but it's quieter than the town. The loud is a different kind of loud, because swamp loud is just curiosity, creachers figuring out who you are and if yer a threat. Whereas the town knows all about you already and wants to know more and wants to beat you with what it knows till how can you have any of yerself left at all?

Swamp Noise, tho, swamp Noise is just the birds all thinking their worrisome little birdie thoughts. **Where's food? Where's home? Where's my safety?** And the waxy squirrels, which are all little punks, teasing you if they see you, teasing themselves if they don't, and the rusty squirrels, which are like dumb little kids, and sometimes there's swamp foxes out in the leaves who you can hear faking their Noise to sound like the squirrels they eat and even less often there are mavens singing their weird maven songs and once I swear I saw a cassor running away on two long legs but Ben says I didn't, says the cassors are long gone from the swamp.

I don't know. I believe me.

Manchee comes outta the bushes and sits down next to me cuz I've stopped right there in the middle of a trail. He looks around to see what I might be seeing and then he says, "Good poo, Todd."

"I'm sure it was, Manchee."

I'd better not get another ruddy dog when my birthday comes. What I want this year is a hunting knife like the one Ben carries on the back of his belt. Now *that's* a present for a man.

"Poo," Manchee says quietly.

On we walk. The main bunch of apple trees are a little ways into the swamp, down a few paths and over a fallen log that Manchee always needs help over. When we get there, I pick him up around his stomach and lift him to the top. Even tho he knows what I'm doing, he still kicks his legs all over the place like a falling spider, making a fuss for no reason at all.

"Hold still, you gonk!"

"Down, down, down!" he yelps, scrabbling away at the air.

"Idiot dog."

I plop him on top the log and climb up myself. We both jump down to the other side, Manchee barking "Jump!" as he lands and keeping on barking "Jump!" as he runs off.

The leap over the log is where the dark of the swamp really starts and the first thing you see are the old Spackle buildings, leaning out towards you from shadow, looking like melting blobs of tan-coloured ice cream except hut-sized. No one knows or can remember what they were ever sposed to be but best guess by Ben, who's a best guess kinda guy, is that they had something to do with burying their dead. Maybe even some kind of church, even tho the spacks didn't have no kind of religion anyone from Prentisstown could reckernize.

I keep a wide distance from them and go into the little grove of wild apple trees. The apples are ripe, nearly black, almost edible, as Cillian would say. I pick one off the trunk and take a bite, the juice dribbling down my chin.

"Todd?"

"What, Manchee?" I take out the plastic bag I've got folded in my back pocket and start filling it with apples.

"Todd?" he barks again and this time I notice how he's barking it and I turn and he's pointed at the Spackle buildings and his fur's all ridged up on his back and his ears are flicking all over the place.

I stand up straight. "What is it, boy?"

He's growling now, his lips pulled back over his teeth. I

feel the charge in my blood again. "Is it a croc?" I say.

"Quiet, Todd," Manchee growls.

"But what is it?"

"*Is* quiet, Todd." He lets out a little bark and it's a real bark, a real dog bark that means nothing but "Bark!" and my body electricity goes up a bit, like charges are going to start leaping outta my skin. "Listen," he growls.

And so I listen.

And I listen.

And I turn my head a little and I listen some more.

There's a hole in the Noise.

Which can't be.

It's *weird*, it is, out there, hiding somewhere, in the trees or somewhere outta sight, a spot where your ears and your mind are telling you there's no Noise. It's like a shape you can't see except by how everything else around it is touching it. Like water in the shape of a cup, but with no cup. It's a hole and everything that falls into it stops being Noise, stops being *anything*, just stops altogether. It's not like the quiet of the swamp, which is never *quiet* obviously, just less Noisy. But this, this is a shape, a shape of *nothing*, a hole where all Noise stops.

Which is impossible.

There ain't nothing but Noise in this world, nothing but the constant thoughts of men and things coming at you and at you and at you, ever since the spacks released the Noise germ during the war, the germ that killed half the men and every single woman, my ma not excepted, the germ that drove the rest of the men mad, the germ that spelled the end for all Spackle once men's madness picked up a gun.

13

"Todd?" Manchee's spooked, I can hear it. "What, Todd? What's it, Todd?"

"Can you smell anything?"

"Just smell quiet, Todd," he barks, then he starts barking louder, "Quiet! Quiet!"

And then, somewhere around the spack buildings, the quiet *moves*.

My blood-charge leaps so hard it about knocks me over. Manchee yelps in a circle around me, barking and barking, making me double-spooked, and so I smack him on the rump again ("Ow, Todd?") to make myself calm down.

"There's no such thing as holes," I say. "No such thing as nothing. So it's gotta be a something, don't it?"

"Something, Todd," Manchee barks.

"Can you hear where it went?"

"It's quiet, Todd."

"You know what I mean."

Manchee sniffs the air and takes one step, two, then more towards the Spackle buildings. I guess we're looking for it, then. I start walking all slow-like up to the biggest of the melty ice cream scoops. I stay outta the way of anything that might be looking out the little bendy triangle doorway. Manchee's sniffing at the door frame but he's not growling so I take a deep breath and I look inside.

It's dead empty. The ceiling rises up to a point about another length of me above my head. Floor's dirt, swamp plants growing in it now, vines and suchlike, but nothing else. Which is to say no *real* nothing, no hole, and no telling what mighta been here before.

It's stupid but I gotta say it.

I'm wondering if the Spackle are back.

But that's impossible.

But a hole in the Noise is impossible.

So something impossible has to be true.

I can hear Manchee snuffling around again outside so I creep out and I go to the second scoop. There's writing on the outside of this one, the only written words anyone's ever seen in the spack language. The only words they ever saw fit to write down, I guess. The letters are spack letters, but Ben says they make the sound es'Paqili or suchlike, es'Paqili, the Spackle, "spacks" if you wanna spit it, which since what happened happened is what everyone does. Means "The People".

There's nothing in the second scoop neither. I step back out into the swamp and I listen again. I put my head down and I listen and I reach with the hearing parts of my brain and I listen there, too, and I listen and listen.

I listen.

"Quiet! Quiet!" Manchee barks, twice real fast and peels off running again, towards the last scoop. I take off after him, running myself, my blood charging, cuz that's where it is, that's where the hole in the Noise is.

I can hear it.

Well, I can't *hear* it, that's the whole point, but when I run towards it the emptiness of it is touching my chest and the stillness of it pulls at me and there's so much quiet in it, no, not quiet, *silence*, so much unbelievable silence that I start to feel really torn up, like I'm about to lose the most valuable thing ever, like there it is, a death, and I'm running and my eyes are watering and my chest is just crushing and there's no one to see but I still mind and my eyes start crying, they start crying, they start *effing crying*, and I stop for a minute and I bend over and Jesus H Dammit, you can just shut up right now, but I waste a whole stupid minute, just a whole stinking, stupid minute bent over there, by which time, of course, the hole is moving away, it's moved away, it's gone.

Manchee's torn twixt racing after it and coming back to me but he finally comes back to me.

"Crying, Todd?"

"Shut up," I say and aim a kick at him. It misses on purpose.

2

PRENTISSTOWN

WE GET OURSELVES outta the swamp and head back towards town and the world feels all black and grey no matter what the sun is saying. Even Manchee barely says nothing as we make our way back up thru the fields. My Noise churns and bubbles like a stew on the boil till finally I have to stop for a minute to calm myself down a little.

There's just no such thing as silence. Not here, not nowhere. Not when yer asleep, not when yer by yerself, never.

I am Todd Hewitt, I think to myself with my eyes closed. *I am twelve years and twelve months old. I live in Prentisstown on New World. I will be a man in one month's time exactly.*

It's a trick Ben taught me to help settle my Noise. You close yer eyes and as clearly and calmly as you can you tell yerself who you are, cuz that's what gets lost in all that Noise.

I am Todd Hewitt.

"Todd Hewitt," Manchee murmurs to himself beside me. I take a deep breath and open my eyes.

That's who I am. I'm Todd Hewitt.

We walk on up away from the swamp and the river, up the slope of the wild fields to the small ridge at the south of town where the school used to be for the brief and useless time it existed. Before I was born, boys were taught by their ma at home and then when there were only boys and men left, we just got sat down in front of vids and learning modules till Mayor Prentiss outlawed such things as "detrimental to the discipline of our minds".

Mayor Prentiss, see, has a Point of View.

And so for almost half a stupid year, all the boys were gathered up by sad-faced Mr Royal and plonked out here in an out-building away from the main Noise of the town. Not that it helped. It's nearly impossible to teach anything in a classroom full of boys' Noise and *completely* impossible to give out any sort of test. You cheat even if you don't mean to and *everybody* means to.

And then one day Mayor Prentiss decided to burn all the books, every single one of them, even the ones in men's homes, cuz apparently books were detrimental as well and Mr Royal, a soft man who made himself a hard man by drinking whisky in the classroom, gave up and took a gun and put an end to himself and that was it for my classroom teaching.

Ben taught me the rest at home. Mechanics and food prep and clothes repair and farming basics and things like that. Also a lot of survival stuff like hunting and which fruits you can eat and how to follow the moons for direkshuns and how to use a knife and a gun and snakebite remedies and how to calm yer Noise as best you can.

He tried to teach me reading and writing, too, but Mayor Prentiss caught wind of it in my Noise one morning and locked Ben up for a week and that was the end of my book-learning and what with all that other stuff to learn and all the working on the farm that still has to be done every day and all the just plain surviving, I never ended up reading too good.

Don't matter. Ain't nobody in Prentisstown ever gonna write a book.

Manchee and me get past the school building and up on the little ridge and look north and there's the town in question. Not that there's all that much left of it no more. One shop, used to be two. One pub, used to be two. One clinic, one jail, one non-working petrol stayshun, one big house for the Mayor, one police stayshun. The Church. One short bit of road running thru the centre, paved back in the day, never upkept since, goes to gravel right quick. All the houses and such are out and about, outskirts like, farms, *meant* to be farms, some still are, some stand empty, some stand worse than empty.

And that's all there is of Prentisstown. Populayshun 147 and falling, falling, falling. 146 men and one almost-man.

Ben says there used to be other settlements scattered around New World, that all the ships landed about the same time, ten years or so before I was born, but that when the war started with the spacks, when the spacks released the germs and all the other settlements were wiped out, that Prentisstown was nearly wiped out, too, that it only survived cuz of Mayor Prentiss's army skills and that even tho Mayor Prentiss is a nightmare coming and going, we at least owe him that, that cuz of him we survive alone on a whole big empty womanless world that ain't got nothing good to say for itself, in a town of 146 men that dies a little more with every day that passes.

Cuz some men can't take it, can they? They off themselves like Mr Royal or some of them just plain disappear, like Mr Gault, our old neighbour who used to do the other sheep farm, or Mr Michael, our second best carpenter, or Mr Van Wijk, who vanished the same day his son became a man. It's not so uncommon. If yer whole world is one Noisy town with no future, sometimes you just have to leave even if there ain't nowhere else to go.

Cuz as me the almost-man looks up into that town, I can hear the 146 men who remain. I can hear every ruddy last one of them. Their Noise washes down the hill like a flood let loose right at me, like a fire, like a monster the size of the sky come to get you cuz there's nowhere to run.

Here's what it's like. Here's what every minute of every day of my stupid, stinking life in this stupid, stinking town is like. Never mind plugging yer ears, it don't help at all:

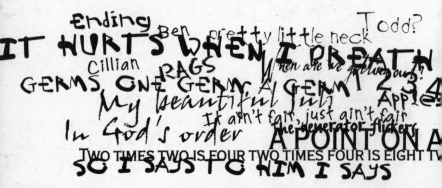

20

a shoulda seen the pair A germ *Ending*
Please help Tomas, God used to know a man from the space
You, boy! you there apples
A disease Ending ONE MONTH'S TIME
Apples APPLES Rags A SINGLE CIRCULAR BREATH
Take you by the back of yer neck Quiet, Todd?
Oh my Lillian my Karen Oh my precious pearl OH M.
Oh my Julie
YOU EVEN UP THERE? TODD?
There's only enough for my family, not a whit more.
Effing spacks and their effing germs
That small, small, that precious and tasty
No More Spackle left to kill
TS AND BRUISES AND CUTS AND BRU
the barrel but keep the oil free from the stock winning they'll be men
What I wouldn't give for a real beefburger
What if he asks about the sheeps! I AM AND ALL IS IN GOD'S ORDER
IE YER HANDS TOGETHER WITH SOME ROPE
ease don't let the fever take my Justin Apples
n my Esther my Esther oh my beautiful girl
ONE MONTH Prentiss I'll have the first go
How are we ever getting outta here you space!
tow are we ever getting outta there?
HAT HAVE WE DONE, OH, MY LORD? Todd?
ll kill him, I will that A disease, a germ from the spacks
ow are we ever getting outta here? Ending
AM A POINT AND THE POINT IS ME I'll just have the one more and go! Cillian
Ten rows One hundred nineteen days without rain
LOOK AT THE TINY HANDS ourse not Apples
er a liar, sir A 3 2 1 OH MY NORM
When are, sir A 3 4 1 you to yer tail
I'VE FORGOTTEN HER FAC.
HOLD YER THOUGHTS IN A LINE, A LINE, A LINE a germ, remember
ONE MONTH'S TIME NOTHING BUT BEASTS
Keep the boy from their hands somehow God Rags
THE WOOD IN MY HANDS
the holiness of the silence the day Oh My Kelly
and found OH MY JADE
CIRCLE ON A POINT ON A CIRCLE
MES EIGHT IS SIXTEEN CUTS AND BRUISES AND CUT
THAT HEW IT BOY Todd?
THE ANTS GO MARCHING TWO
the way she used to

1 2 3 4 4 3 2 1
ILLET BEFORE WINTER
SE GOD,
DISCIPLINE, MEN!
SHS
A holy Sacrament, found and unfound
oh my Carla
TEN STRIKES THE HOUR THE HOUR PLUS TEN
Two times sixteen is thirty-two two times thirty-two is so
our
NO PAINKILLERS LEFT WE'LL RUN
hold you AND I hold you THERE
AND I TOLD YOU the neck, yer neck
approaches SHUT IT UP

And them's just the words, the voices talking and moaning
and singing and crying. There's pictures, too, pictures that
come to yer mind in a rush, no matter how much you don't
want 'em, pictures of memories and fantasies and secrets
and plans and lies, lies, lies. Cuz you can lie in the Noise,
even when everyone knows what yer thinking, you can bury
stuff under other stuff, you can hide it in plain sight, you
just don't think it clearly or you convince yerself that the
opposite of what yer hiding is true and then who's going to
be able to pick out from the flood what's real water and
what's not going to get you wet?

Men lie, and they lie to theirselves worst of all.

In a for instance, I've never seen a woman nor a Spackle
in the flesh, obviously. I've seen 'em both in vids, of course,
before they were outlawed, and I see them *all the time* in
the Noise of men cuz what else do men think about except
sex and enemies? But the spacks are bigger and meaner
looking in the Noise than in the vids, ain't they? And Noise
women have lighter hair and bigger chests and wear less

clothes and are a lot freer with their affecshuns than in the vids, too. So the thing to remember, the thing that's most important of all that I might say in this here telling of things is that Noise ain't truth, Noise is what men *want* to be true, and there's a difference twixt those two things so big that it could ruddy well kill you if you don't watch out.

"Home, Todd?" Manchee barks a bit louder down by my leg cuz that's how you gotta talk in the Noise.

"Yeah, we're going," I say. We live on the other side, to the north-east, and we're going to have to go thru the town to get there so here it comes, as fast as I can get thru it.

First up is Mr Phelps's store. It's dying, the store is, like the rest of the town and Mr Phelps spends all his time despairing. Even when yer buying stuff from him and he's polite as can be, the despair of him seeps at you like pus from a cut. **Ending,** says his Noise, **Ending, it's all ending** and **Rags and rags and rags** and **My Julie, my dear, dear Julie** who was his wife and who don't wear no clothes at all in Mr Phelps's Noise.

"Hiya, Todd," he calls as Manchee and I hurry by.

"Hiya, Mr Phelps."

"Beautiful day, ain't she?"

"She sure is that, Mr Phelps."

"Beaut!" barks Manchee and Mr Phelps laughs but his Noise just keeps saying **Ending** and **Julie** and **rags** and pictures of what he misses about his wife and what she used to do as if it's sposed to be unique or something.

I don't think anything particular in my Noise for Mr Phelps, just my usual stuff you can't help. Tho I must admit I find myself thinking it all a little bit louder to cover up

23

thoughts about the hole I found in the swamp, to block it out behind louder Noise.

Don't know why I should do this, don't know why I should hide it.

But I'm hiding it.

Manchee and me carry on walking pretty fast cuz next is the petrol stayshun and Mr Hammar. The petrol stayshun don't work no more cuz the fission generator that made the petrol went kerflooey last year and just sits there beside the petrol stayshun like a hulking ugly hurt toe and no one'd live next to it except Mr Hammar and Mr Hammar's *much* worse than Mr Phelps cuz he'll aim his Noise right at you.

And it's *ugly* Noise, *angry* Noise, pictures of yerself in ways that you don't want pictures of yerself, violent pictures and bloody pictures and all you can do is make yer own Noise as loud as you can and try to sweep up Mr Phelps's Noise in it, too, and send it right back to Mr Hammar. **Apples** and **Ending** and **fist over hand** and **Ben** and **Julie** and **Peavt, Todd?** and **the generator is flickering** and **rags** and **shut up, just shut up** and **Look at me, boy**.

And I turn my head anyway even tho I don't want to but sometimes you get caught off guard and so I turn my head and there's Mr Hammar in his window, looking right at me and **One month,** he thinks, and there's a picture from his Noise and it involves me standing on my own but somehow even more alone than that and I don't know what it means or if it's real or if it's a purposeful lie and so I think about a hammer going into Mr Hammar's head over and over and he just smiles from his window.

The road curves round the petrol stayshun past the clinic, which is Dr Baldwin and all the crying and moaning men do to doctors when nothing's really wrong with 'em. Today it's Mr Fox complaining about how he can't breathe which would be a pitiable thing if he didn't smoke so much. And then, as you pass the clinic, God Almighty, you get the bloody bloody pub which even at this hour of the day is just a howl of Noise because what they do there is turn the music up so loud it's meant to drown out Noise but that only works partway and so you get loud music and loud Noise and worse, *drunk* Noise, which comes at you like a mallet. Shouts and howls and weeping from men whose faces never change and just horrorpilashuns of the past and all the women that used to be. A whole *lot* about the women that used to be but nothing that makes any sense, cuz drunk Noise is like a drunk man: blurry and boring and dangerous.

It gets hard to walk around the centre of town, hard to think about the next step cuz so much Noise is weighing on yer shoulders. I honestly don't know how men do it, I don't know how *I'm* going to do it when I become a man 'less something changes on the day that I don't know about.

The road bears up past the pub and to the right, going by the police stayshun and the jail, all one place and in use more than you might think for a town so small. The sheriff is Mr Prentiss Jr who's barely two years older than me and only been a man for a short while but who took to his job right well and quick and in his cell is whoever Mayor Prentiss has told Mr Prentiss Jr to make an example of this week. Right now it's Mr Turner who didn't hand over enough of his corn yield to "the good use of the whole town", which just means he didn't give no free corn to Mr Prentiss and his men.

So you've gone thru the town with yer dog and you got all this Noise behind you, Mr Phelps and Mr Hammar and Dr Baldwin and Mr Fox and the extra extra Noise from the pub and Mr Prentiss Jr's Noise and Mr Turner's moaning Noise and yer still not done with the Noise of the town cuz here comes the Church.

The Church is why we're all here on New World in the first place, of course, and pretty much every Sunday you can hear Aaron preaching about why we left behind the corrupshun and sin of Old World and about how we'd aimed to start a new life of purity and brotherhood in a whole new Eden.

That worked out well, huh?

People still go to church tho, mainly cuz they have to, even tho the Mayor hisself hardly ever bothers, leaving the rest of us to listen to Aaron preach about how we're the only thing each of us have out here, us men together, and how all of us have gotta bind ourselves in a single community.

How if one of us falls, we all fall.

He says that one a lot.

Manchee and me are quiet as possible going past the front door of the Church. Praying Noise comes from inside, it's got a special feel to it, a special purply sick feel like men are bleeding it out, even tho it's always the same stuff but the purply blood just keeps on coming. *Help us, save us, forgive us, help us, save us, forgive us, get us outta here, please, God, please, God,*

please, God, tho as far as I know no one's never heard no Noise back from this God fella.

Aaron's in there, too, back from his walk and preaching over the prayers. I can hear his voice, not just his Noise, and it's all **sacrifice** this and **scripture** that and **blessings** here and **sainthood** there and he's going on at such a rattle his Noise is like grey fire behind him and you can't pick out anything in it and he might be up to something, mightn't he? The sermon might be covering for something and I'm beginning to wonder if I know what that something is.

And then I hear **young Todd?** in his Noise and I say, "Hurry up, Manchee," and we scoot our way along right quick.

The last thing you pass as you crest the hill of Prentisstown is the Mayor's House which is the weirdest and hardest Noise of all cuz Mayor Prentiss–

Well, Mayor Prentiss is different.

His Noise is awful clear and I mean awful in the awful way. He believes, see, that order can be brought to Noise. He believes that Noise can be sorted out, that if you could harness it somehow, you could put it to use. And when you walk by the Mayor's House, you can hear him, hear him and the men closest to him, his deputies and things, and they're always doing these thought exercises, these counting things and imagining perfect shapes and saying orderly chants like **I AM THE CIRCLE AND THE CIRCLE IS ME** whatever that's sposed to mean and it's like he's moulding a little army into shape, like he's preparing himself for something, like he's forging some kind of Noise weapon.

It feels like a threat. It feels like the world changing and leaving you behind.

1 2 3 4 4 3 2 1 I AM THE CIRCLE AND THE CIRCLE IS ME 1 2 3 4 4 3 2 1 IF ONE OF US FALLS WE ALL FALL

I will be a man soon and men do not run in fear but I give Manchee a little push and we walk even a little faster than before, giving the Mayor's House as wide a curve as possible till we're past it and on the gravel path that heads on towards our house.

After a while, the town disappears behind us and the Noise starts to get a little bit quieter (tho it never never stops) and we can both breathe a bit easier.

Manchee barks, "Noise, Todd."

"Yesiree," I say.

"Quiet in the swamp, Todd," Manchee says. "Quiet, quiet, quiet."

"Yes," I say and then I think and I hurry and say, "Shut up, Manchee," and I smack him on his rump and he says, "Ow, Todd?" but I'm looking back towards the town but there's no stopping Noise once it's out, is there? And if it was something you could see, moving thru the air, I wonder if you could see the hole in the Noise floating right outta me, right outta my thoughts from where I was protecting it and it's such a small bit of Noise and it'd be easy to miss in the great roar of everything else but there it goes, there it goes, there it goes, heading right back towards the world of men.

3

BEN AND CILLIAN

"AND JUST WHERE do you think you've been?" Cillian says as soon as Manchee and I come into view off the path. He's lying down on the ground, deep into our little fission generator, the one outside the front of the house, fixing whatever's gone wrong with it this month. His arms are covered in grease and his face is covered in annoyance and his Noise is buzzy like mad bees and I can already feel myself getting angry and I haven't even properly got home yet.

"I was in the swamp getting apples for Ben," I say.

"There's work to be done and boys are off playing." He looks back into the generator. Something makes a clunk inside and he says, "Dammit!"

"I said I wasn't playing, if you'd ever listen!" I say but it's more like a shout. "Ben wanted apples so I was getting him some ruddy apples!"

"Uh-huh," Cillian says, looking back at me. "And where might these apples be then?"

And of course I'm not holding any apples, am I? I don't even remember dropping the bag I'd started to fill but of course I must have when–

"When what?" Cillian says.

"Quit listening so close," I say.

He sighs his Cillian sigh and here we go: "It's not like we ask you to do so much around here, Todd" – which is a lie – "but we can't keep this farm running by ourselves" – which is true – "and even if you ever finish all yer chores, which you don't" – another lie, they work me like a slave – "we'd still be playing a catch-up to nothing, now wouldn't we?" – and this is true, too. The town can't grow no more, it can only shrink, and help ain't coming.

"Pay attenshun when I talk to you," Cillian says.

"Tenshun!" Manchee barks.

"Shut up," I say.

"Don't talk to yer dog that way," Cillian says.

I wasn't talking to my dog, I think, loud and clear enough to hear.

Cillian glares at me and I glare back and this is how it always is, our Noise throbbing with red and hassle and irri-tashun. It's never been so good with Cillian, not never, Ben's always been the kind one, Cillian's always been the other one, but it's got worse as the day approaches when I'll finally be a man and won't have to listen to any more of his crap.

Cillian closes his eyes and breathes loudly once thru his nose. "Todd–" he starts, his voice a bit lower.

"Where's Ben?" I say.

His face hardens a little more. "Lambing starts in a week, Todd."

All I do to this is say again, "Where's Ben?"

"You get the sheep fed and into their paddocks and then I want you to fix the gate to the east field once and for all, Todd Hewitt. I have asked you at least twice before now."

I lean back on my heels. "'Well, how was your trip to the swamp, Todd?'" I say, making my voice go all sarcastic. "'Well, it was fine and dandy there, Cillian, thank you for asking.' 'Didja see anything interesting out there in the swamp, Todd?' 'Well, funny you should ask, Cillian, cuz I sure did see something interesting which might explain this here cut on my lip that you ain't asked about but I guess it'll have to just wait till the sheep are fed and I fix the *goddam fence!*'"

"Watch yer mouth," Cillian says. "I don't have time for yer games. Go do the sheep."

I clench up my fists and make a sound that sounds like "awwghgh" which tells Cillian that I just can't put up with his non-reason not for one second longer.

"Come on, Manchee," I say.

"The sheep, Todd," Cillian calls as I start walking away. "The sheep first."

"Yeah, I'll do the ruddy sheep," I mutter to myself. I'm walking away faster now, my blood jumping and Manchee's getting excited from the roar of my Noise. "Sheep!" he barks. "Sheep, sheep, Todd! Sheep, sheep, quiet, Todd! Quiet, quiet in swamp, Todd!"

"Shut up, Manchee," I say.

"What was that?" Cillian says and there's something in his voice that makes us both turn around. He's sitting up by the generator now, his full attenshun on us, his Noise coming right at us like a laser.

"Quiet, Cillian," Manchee barks.

"What does he mean 'quiet'?" Cillian's eyes and Noise are searching me all over.

"What do you care?" I turn again. "I got ruddy sheep to feed."

"Todd, wait," he calls after us but then something starts beeping on the generator and he says "Dammit!" again and has to go back to it tho I can feel all kinds of asking marks in his Noise following me, getting fainter as I head out to our fields.

Blast him, blast him and all, I think, in more or less those words and worse as I stomp across our farm. We live about a kilometre north-east of town and we do sheep on one half of the farm and wheat on the other. Wheat's harder, so Ben and Cillian do most of that. Since I was old enough to be taller than the sheep, that's who I've taken care of. Me, that is, not me and Manchee, tho another one of the false lying excuses why he was given to me was that I could teach him up as a sheep dog which for obvious reasons – by which I mean his complete stupidity – hasn't worked out to plan.

Feeding and watering and shearing and lambing and even castrating and even butchering, I do all these things. We're one of three meat and wool providers for the town, used to be one of five, soon be one of two because Mr Marjoribanks oughta be dying from his drink problem any day now. We'll fold his flock into ours. I should say *I'll* fold his flock into ours, like I did when Mr Gault disappeared two winters ago, and they'll be new ones to butcher, new ones to castrate, new ones to shear, new ones to put in pens with ewes at the right times, and will I get a thank you? No, I will not.

I am Todd Hewitt, I think, the day just keeping on not making my Noise any quieter. *I am almost a man.*

"Sheep!" say the sheep when I pass their field without stopping. "Sheep!" they say, watching me go. "Sheep! Sheep!"

"Sheep!" barks Manchee.

"Sheep!" say the sheep back.

Sheep got even less to say than dogs do.

I've been listening out for Ben's Noise over the farm and I've tracked him down to one corner of one of the wheat fields. Planting's done, harvest is months away, so there's not so much to do with the wheat at the minute, just make sure all the generators and the fission tractor and the electric threshers are ready to start working. You'd think this would mean I'd get a little help with the sheep but you would be wrong.

Ben's Noise is humming a little tune out near one of the irrigashun spouts so I take a turn and head across the field towards him. His Noise ain't nothing like Cillian's. It's calmer and clearer and tho you can't see Noise, if Cillian's always seems reddish, then Ben's seems blue or sometimes green. They're different men from each other, different as fire and water, Ben and Cillian, my more or less parents.

Story is, my ma was friends with Ben before they left for New World, that they were both members of the Church when the offer of leaving and starting up a settlement was made. Ma convinced Pa and Ben convinced Cillian and when the ships landed and the settlement started, it was my ma and pa who raised sheep on the next farm over from Ben and Cillian growing wheat and it was all friendly and nice and the sun never set and men and women sang songs together and lived and loved and never got sick and never never died.

That's the story from the Noise anyway so who knows what it was actually like before? Cuz then of course I was born and everything changed. The spacks released their woman-killing germ and that was it for my ma and then the war started and was won and that was it for pretty much the rest of New World. And there's me, just a baby, not knowing nothing bout nothing, and of course I'm not the only baby, there're loads of us, and suddenly only half a town of men to take care of all us babies and boys. So a lot of us died and I was counted among the lucky cuz it was only natural for Ben and Cillian to take me in and feed me and raise me and teach me and generally make it possible for me to go on being alive.

And so I'm kinda like their son. Well, more than "kinda like" but less than actually being so. Ben says Cillian only fights with me all the time cuz he cares about me so much but if that's true I say it's a funny way to show it, a way that don't seem much like caring at all, if you ask me.

But Ben's a different kind of man than Cillian, a *kind* kind of man that makes him not normal in Prentisstown. 145 of the men in this town, even the newly made ones just past their birthdays, even Cillian tho to a lesser degree, they see me at best as something to ignore and at worst as something to hit and so I spend most of my days figuring out ways to be ignored so as I won't get hit.

'Cept for Ben, who I can't describe much further without seeming soft and stupid and like a boy, so I won't, just to say that I never knew my pa, but if you woke up one day and had a choice of picking one from a selecshun, if someone said, here, then, boy, pick who you want, then Ben wouldn't be the worst choice you could make that morning.

He's whistling as we approach and tho I can't see him yet and he can't see me, he changes the tune as he senses me coming to a song I reckernize, Early one mo-o-rning, just as the sun was ri-i-sing, which he says was a favourite of my ma's but which I think is really just a favourite of his since he's whistled and sang it for me since I can remember. My blood is still storming away from Cillian but I immediately start to feel a little calmer.

Even tho it *is* a song for babies, I know, shut up.

"Ben!" Manchee barks and goes running around the irrigashun set-up.

"Hello, Manchee," I hear as I round the corner and see Ben scratching Manchee twixt the ears. Manchee's eyes are closed and his leg is thumping on the ground with pleasure and tho Ben can certainly tell from my Noise that I've been fighting with Cillian again, he don't say nothing but, "Hello, Todd."

"Hi, Ben." I look at the ground, kicking a stone.

And Ben's Noise is saying Apples and Cillian and Yer getting so big and Cillian again and itch in the crack of my arm and apples and dinner and Gosh, it's warm out and it's all so smooth and non-grasping it's like laying down in a brook on a hot day.

35

"You calming down there, Todd?" he finally says. "Reminding yerself who you are?"

"Yeah," I say, "just, why does he have to come at me like that? Why can't he just say hello? Not even a greeting, it's all 'I know you done something wrong and I'm gonna keep at you till I find out what it is.'"

"That's just his way, Todd. You know that."

"So you keep saying." I pick a blade of young wheat and stick the end in my mouth, not quite looking at him.

"Left the apples at the house, didja?"

I look at him. I chew on the wheat. He knows I didn't. He can tell.

"And there's a reason," he says, still scratching Manchee. "There's a reason which ain't coming clear." He's trying to read my Noise, see what truth he can sift from it, which most men think is a good enough excuse for starting a fight, but I don't mind with Ben. He cocks his head and stops scratching Manchee. "Aaron?"

"Yeah, I saw Aaron."

"He did that to yer lip?"

"Yeah."

"That sunuvahoor." He frowns and steps forward. "I just might have to have words with that man."

"Don't," I say. "Don't. It'll just be more trouble and it don't hurt that much."

He takes my chin into his fingers and lifts my head so he can see the cut. "That sunuvahoor," he says again, quietly. He touches the cut with his fingers and I flinch away.

"It's nothing," I say.

"You stay away from that man, Todd Hewitt."

"Oh, like I went running to the swamp *hoping* to run into him?"

"He ain't right."

"Well, holy crap, thanks for that bit of info, Ben," I say and then I catch a bit of his Noise that says **One month** and it's a new thing, a whole new bit of something that he quickly covers up with other Noise.

"What's going on, Ben?" I say. "What's going on with my birthday?"

He smiles and for a second it's not an entirely true smile, for a second it's a worried smile, but after that it's a smile true enough. "It's a surprise," he says, "so don't go looking."

Even tho I'm nearly a man and even tho I'm nearly getting on up to his height now, he still bends down a little so his face is level with mine, not too close to be uncomfortable, just close enough so that it's safe and I look away a little bit. And even tho it's Ben, even tho I trust Ben more than anyone else in this crappy little town, even tho it's Ben who saved my life and who I know would do it again, I still find myself reluctant to open up my Noise about what happened in the swamp, mainly cuz I can start to feel it pressing on my chest again whenever the thought gets near.

"Todd?" Ben says, looking at me closely.

"Quiet," Manchee barks softly. "Quiet in swamp."

Ben looks at Manchee, then back at me, his eyes going all soft and asking and full of concern. "What's he talking about, Todd?"

I sigh. "We saw something," I say. "Out there in the swamp. Well, we *didn't* see it, it hid, but it was like a rip in the Noise, like a tear–"

I stop talking cuz he's stopped listening to my voice. I've opened up my Noise for him and am remembering it as truthfully as I can and he's looking at me something fierce and from way behind me I can hear Cillian coming and he's calling "Ben?" and "Todd?" and there's concern in his voice and in his Noise and Ben's is starting to buzz a little, too, and I just keep thinking as truthfully as I can about the hole we found in the Noise but quietly, too, quietly, quietly, so as to keep the town from hearing if I can and here comes Cillian still and Ben's just looking at me and looking at me till finally I have to ask.

"Is it spacks?" I say. "Is it the Spackle? Are they back?"

"Ben?" Cillian's yelling it now as he's coming across the fields.

"Are we in danger?" I ask Ben. "Will there be another war?"

But all Ben says is, "Oh, my God," real quiet like, and then he says it again, "Oh, my God," and then, without even moving or looking away, he says, "We have to get you outta here. We have to get you outta here *right now*."

4

DON'T THINK IT

CILLIAN COMES RUNNING UP but before he says anything to us, Ben cuts him off and says, "Don't think it!"

Ben turns to me. "Don't you think it neither. You cover it up with yer Noise. You hide it. You hide it as best you can." And he's grabbing my shoulders as he's saying it and squeezing tight enough to make my blood jump even more than it already is.

"What's going on?" I say.

"Did you walk home thru town?" Cillian asks.

"*Course* I walked home thru town," I snap. "What other effing way is there to get home?"

Cillian's face tightens up but it's not with being pissed off at me snapping, it's tightening up with fear, fear I can hear loud as a shout in his Noise. They don't yell at me for "effing" neither, which makes it all somehow worse. Manchee's barking his head off by this point, "Cillian!

Quiet! Effing! Todd!" but nobody's bothering to tell him to shut up.

Cillian looks at Ben. "We're gonna have to do it now."

"I know," Ben says.

"What's going on?" I say again, all loud like. "Do *what* now?" I twist away from Ben and stand looking at them both.

Ben and Cillian take another look at each other and then back at me. "You have to leave Prentisstown," Ben says.

My eyeballs go back and forth twixt theirs but they're not letting nothing go in their Noise 'cept general worry. "What do you mean I have to leave Prentisstown?" I say. "There ain't nowhere else on New World *but* Prentisstown."

They take yet *another* look at each other.

"Stop doing that!" I say.

"Come on," Cillian says. "We've already got yer bag packed."

"How can you already have my bag packed?"

Cillian says to Ben, "We probably don't have much time."

And Ben says to Cillian, "He can go down by the river."

And Cillian says to Ben, "You know what this means."

And Ben says to Cillian, "It doesn't change the plan."

"WHAT THE EFF IS GOING ON?" I roar, but I don't say "eff", now do I? Cuz it seems the situashun calls for something a little stronger. "WHAT EFFING PLAN?"

But they're still not getting mad.

Ben lowers his voice and I can see him try to get his Noise into some kinda order and he says to me, "It's very, very important you keep what happened in the swamp outta yer Noise as best you can."

40

"Why? Are the spacks coming back to kill us?"

"Don't think about it!" Cillian snaps. "Cover it up, keep it deep and quiet, till yer so far outta town no one can hear you. Now, come on!"

And he takes off back towards the house, running, actually *running*.

"Come on, Todd," Ben says.

"Not till someone explains something."

"You'll get an explanashun," Ben says, taking me by the arm and pulling me along. "You'll get more than you ever wanted." And there's so much sadness to him when he says it that I don't say nothing more, just follow along running back to the house, Manchee barking his head off behind us.

By the time we make it back to the house, I'm expecting–

I don't know what I'm expecting. An army of Spackle coming outta the woods. A line-up of Mayor Prentiss's men with guns at the ready. The whole house burning down. I don't know. Ben and Cillian's Noise ain't making much sense, my own thoughts are boiling over like a volcano, and Manchee won't stop barking, so who can tell anything in all this racket?

But there's no one there. The house, *our* house, is just as it was, quiet and farm-like. Cillian busts in the back door, goes into the prayer room which we never use, and starts pulling boards up from the floor. Ben goes to the pantry and starts throwing dried foods and fruit into a cloth sack, then he goes to the toilet and takes out a small medipak and throws that in, too.

I just stand there like a doofus wondering just what in the effing blazes is going on.

I know what yer thinking: how can I *not* know if all day, every day I'm hearing every thought of the two men who run my house? That's the thing, tho. Noise is *noise*. It's crash and clatter and it usually adds up to one big mash of sound and thought and picture and half the time it's impossible to make any sense of it at all. Men's minds are messy places and Noise is like the active, breathing face of that mess. It's what's true and what's believed and what's imagined and what's fantasized and it says one thing and a completely opposite thing at the same time and even tho the truth is definitely in there, how can you tell what's true and what's not when yer getting *everything*?

The Noise is a man unfiltered, and without a filter, a man is just chaos walking.

"I ain't leaving," I say, as they keep doing their stuff. They don't pay me no mind. "I ain't leaving," I say again, as Ben steps past me into the prayer room to help Cillian lift up boards. They find what they're looking for and Cillian lifts out a rucksack, an old one I thought I'd lost. Ben opens the top and takes a quick peek thru and I can see some clothes of mine and something that looks like–

"Is that a book?" I say. "You were sposed to burn those ages ago."

But they're ignoring me and the air has just stopped right there as Ben takes it outta the rucksack and he and Cillian look at it and I see that it's not quite a book, more a journal type thing with a nice leather cover and when Ben thumbs thru it, the pages are cream-coloured and filled with handwriting.

Ben closes it like it's an important thing and he wraps it inside a plastic bag to protect it and puts it in the rucksack.

They both turn to me.

"I ain't going nowhere," I say.

And there's a knock on the front door.

For a second, nobody says nothing, everyone just freezes. Manchee's got so many things he wants to bark that nothing comes out for a minute till he finally barks "Door!" but Cillian grabs him by the collar with one hand and by the maul with the other, shutting him up. We all look up at each other, wondering what to do next.

There's another knock and then a voice comes thru the walls, "I know yer in there."

"Damn and blast," Ben says.

"Davy bloody Prentiss," Cillian says.

That's Mr Prentiss Jr. The man of the law.

"Do you not think I can hear yer Noise?" Mr Prentiss Jr says thru the door. "Benison Moore. Cillian Boyd." The voice makes a little pause. "Todd Hewitt."

"Well, so much for hiding," I say, crossing my arms, still a little annoyed at it all.

Cillian and Ben look at each other again, then Cillian lets go of Manchee, says "Stay here" to both of us and heads for the door. Ben shoves the sack of food into the rucksack and ties it shut. He hands it to me. "Put this on," he whispers.

I don't take it at first but he gestures with a serious look so I take it and put it on. It weighs a ton.

We hear Cillian open the front door. "What do you want, Davy?"

"That's Sheriff Prentiss to you, Cillian."

"We're in the middle of lunch, Davy," Cillian says. "Come back later."

"I don't think I will. I think I need to have a word with young Todd."

Ben looks at me, worry in his Noise.

"Todd's got farmwork," Cillian says. "He's just leaving out the back. I can hear him go."

And these are instructions for me and Ben, ain't they? But I ruddy well want to hear what's going on and I ignore Ben's hand on my shoulder trying to pull me towards the back door.

"You take me for a fool, Cillian?" Mr Prentiss Jr says.

"Do you really want an answer to that, Davy?"

"I can hear his Noise not twenty feet behind you. Ben's, too." We hear a shift in the mood. "I just want to talk to him. He ain't in no trouble."

"Why you got a rifle then, Davy?" Cillian asks and Ben squeezes my shoulder, probably without even thinking.

Mr Prentiss Jr's voice and Noise both change again. "Bring him out, Cillian. You know why I'm here. Seems like a funny little word floated outta yer boy into town all innocent-like and we just want to see what it's all about, that's all."

"'We'?" Cillian says.

"His Honour the Mayor would like a word with young Todd." Mr Prentiss Jr raises his voice. "Y'all come out now, you hear? Ain't no trouble going on. Just a friendly chat."

Ben nods his head at the back door all firm like and there ain't no arguing with him this time. We start stepping towards it slowly, but Manchee's kept his trap shut for just about as long as he can bear and barks, "Todd?"

"Y'all ain't thinking about sneaking out the back way, are ya?" Mr Prentiss Jr calls. "Outta my way, Cillian."

"Get off my property, Davy," Cillian says.

"I ain't telling you twice."

"I believe you've already told me about three times, Davy, so if yer threatening, it ain't working."

There's a pause but the Noise from them both gets louder and Ben and I know what's coming next and suddenly everything's moving fast and we hear a loud thump, followed quick by another two, and me and Ben and Manchee are running to the kitchen but when we get there, it's over. Mr Prentiss Jr is on the floor, holding his mouth, blood already coming from it. Cillian's got Mr Prentiss Jr's rifle in his hands and is pointing it at Mr Prentiss Jr.

"I said get off my property, Davy," he says.

Mr Prentiss Jr looks at him, then looks at us, still holding his bloody mouth. Like I say, he ain't barely two years older than me, barely able to even get a sentence out without his voice breaking, but he's had his birthday to be a man so there he is, our sheriff.

The blood from his mouth is getting on the little brown hairs he calls a moustache and everyone else calls nothing.

"You know this answers the asking, doncha?" He spits some blood and a tooth onto our floor. "You know this ain't the end." He looks right at my eye. "You found something, dincha, boy?"

Cillian aims the rifle at his head. "Out," he says.

"We got plans for you, boy." Mr Prentiss Jr smiles bloodily at me and gets to his feet. "The boy who's last. One more month, ain't it?"

I look to Cillian but all he does is cock the rifle loudly, getting his point across.

Mr Prentiss Jr looks back at us, spits again, and says, "Be seeing you," trying to sound tough but his voice squeaks and he takes off as fast he can back to the town.

Cillian slams the door behind him. "Todd's gotta go *now*. Back thru the swamp."

"I know," Ben says. "I was hoping–"

"Me, too," Cillian says.

"Whoa, whoa," I say, "I ain't going back to the swamp. There's Spackle there!"

"Keep yer thoughts quiet," Cillian says. "That's more important than you know."

"Well, since I don't know nothing, that ain't hard," I say. "I ain't going nowhere till someone tells me what's going on!"

"Todd–" Ben starts.

"They'll be coming back, Todd," Cillian says. "Davy Prentiss will come back and he won't be alone and we won't be able to protect you from all of them at once."

"But–"

"No arguing!" Cillian says.

"Come on, Todd," Ben says. "Manchee's gonna have to go with you."

"Oh, man, this just gets better," I say.

"Todd," Cillian says and I look at him and he's changed a little. There's something new in his Noise, a sadness, a sadness like grief. "Todd," he says again, then suddenly he grabs me and hugs me to him as hard as he can. It's too rough and I bash my cut lip on his collar and say "Ow!" and push him away.

"You may hate us for this, Todd," he says, "but try to believe it's only cuz we love you, all right?"

"No," I say, "it's not all right. It's not all right at all."

But Cillian's not listening, as usual. He stands up and says to Ben, "Go, run, I'll hold 'em off as long as possible."

"I'll come back a different way," Ben says, "see if I can throw 'em off the trail."

They clasp hands for a long minute, then Ben looks at me, says "Come on" and as he's dragging me outta the room to get to the back door, I see Cillian pick up the rifle again and he glances up at me and catches my eye and there's a look to him, a look written all over him and his Noise that this is a bigger goodbye than it even seems, that this is it, the last time he ever expects to see me and I open my mouth to say something but then the door closes on him and he's gone.

5

THE THINGS YOU KNOW

"I'LL GET YOU TO THE RIVER," Ben says as we hurry across our fields for the second time this morning. "You can follow it down to where it meets the swamp."

"There ain't no path that way, Ben," I say, "and there's crocs everywhere. You trying to get me killed?"

He looks back at me, his eyes all level, but he keeps on hurrying. "There's no other way, Todd."

"Crocs! Swamp! Quiet! Poo!" Manchee barks.

I've stopped even asking what's going on since nobody's seeing fit to tell me nothing so we just keep on moving past the sheep, still not in their paddocks and now maybe never getting there. "Sheep!" they say, watching us pass. On we go, past the main barn, down one of the big irrigashun tracks, turning right on a smaller one, heading towards where the wilderness starts, which pretty much means the beginning of the rest of this whole empty planet.

Ben don't start talking again till we get to the treeline.

"There's food in yer rucksack to last you for a bit but you should make it stretch as far as you can, eating what fruit you find and anything you can hunt."

"How long do I gotta make it last?" I ask. "How long till I can come back?"

Ben stops. We're just inside the trees. The river's thirty metres away but you can hear it cuz this is where it starts rushing downhill to get to the swamp.

Suddenly it feels like just about the loneliest place in the whole wide world.

"You ain't coming back, Todd," Ben says, quietly. "You can't."

"Why not?" I say and my voice comes out all mewing like a kitten but I can't help it. "What'd I do, Ben?"

Ben comes up to me. "You didn't do anything, Todd. You didn't do anything at all." He hugs me real hard and I can feel my chest start to press again and I'm so confused and frightened and angry. Nothing was different in the world this morning when I got outta bed and now here I am being sent away and Ben and Cillian acting like I'm dying and it ain't fair and I don't know why it ain't fair but it just ain't fair.

"I know it ain't fair," Ben says, pulling himself away and looking me hard in the face. "But there *is* an explanashun." He turns me round and opens my rucksack and I can feel him taking something out.

The book.

I look at him and look away. "You know I don't read too good, Ben," I say, embarrassed and stupid.

He crouches down a bit so we're truly face to face. His Noise ain't making me comfortable at all.

"I know," he says, gentle-like. "I always meant to try and spend more time–" He stops. He holds out the book again. "It's yer ma's," he says. "It's her journal, starting from the day you were born, Todd." He looks down at it. "Till the day she died."

My Noise opens wide.

My ma. My ma's own book.

Ben runs his hand over the cover. "We promised her we'd keep you safe," he says. "We promised her and then we had to put it outta our minds so there was nothing in our Noise, nothing that would let anyone know what we were gonna do."

"Including me," I say.

"It had to be including you. If just a little bit got into yer Noise and then into the town…"

He don't finish.

"Like the silence I found in the swamp today," I say. "Like that getting into town and causing all this havoc."

"No, that was a surprise." He looks up at the sky, like he's telling it just how completely a surprise it all was. "No one woulda guessed that happening."

"It's *dangerous*, Ben. I could feel it."

But all he does is hold out the book again.

I start shaking my head. "Ben–"

"I know, Todd," he says, "but try yer best."

"No, Ben–"

He catches my eyes again. He holds 'em with his own. "Do you trust me, Todd Hewitt?"

I scratch my side. I don't know how to answer. "Course I do," I say, "or at least I *did* before you started packing bags I didn't know about for me."

He looks at me harder, his Noise focused like a sun ray. "Do you trust me?" he asks again.

I look at him and yeah, I do, even now. "I trust you, Ben."

"Then trust me when I say that the things you know right now, Todd, those things ain't true."

"Which things?" I ask, my voice rising a little. "Why can't you just tell me?"

"Cuz knowledge is dangerous," he says, as serious as I've ever seen him and when I look into his Noise to see what he's hiding, it roars up and slaps me back. "If I told you now, it would buzz in you louder than a hive at honey-gathering time and Mayor Prentiss would find you fast as he could spit. And you *have* to get away from here. You have to, as far away as you can."

"But where?" I say. *"There ain't nowhere else!"*

Ben takes a deep breath. "There is," he says. "There's somewhere else."

I don't say nothing to that.

"Folded in the front of the book," Ben says, "there's a map. I made it myself but *don't look at it*, not till yer well outta town, okay? Just go to the swamp. You'll know what to do from there."

But I can tell from his Noise that he's not at all sure I'll know what to do from there. "Or what I'm gonna find there, do you?"

He don't say nothing to that.

And I'm thinking.

"How did you know to have a bag already packed?" I say, stepping back a little. "If this thing in the swamp is so unexpected, why are you so ready to chuck me out into the wilderness today?"

"It was the plan all along, ever since you were little." I see him swallow, I hear his sadness everywhere. "As soon as you were old enough to make it on yer own–"

"You were just gonna throw me out so the crocs could eat me." I'm stepping back further.

"No, Todd–" He moves forward, the book still in his hand. I step back again. He makes a gesture like, okay.

And he closes his eyes and opens up his Noise for me.

One month's time is the first thing it says–

And here comes my birthday–

The day I'll become a man–

And–

And–

And there it all is–

What happens–

What the other boys did who became men–

All alone–

All by themselves–

How every last bit of boyhood is killed off–

And–

And–

And what actually happened to the people who–

Holy crap–

And I don't want to say no more about it.

And I can't say at all how it makes me feel.

I look at Ben and he's a different man than he always was, he's a different man to the one I've always known.

Knowledge is dangerous.

"It's why no one tells you," he says. "To keep you from running."

"You wouldn't've protected me?" I say, mewing again (shut up).

"*This* is how we're protecting you, Todd," he says. "By getting you *out*. We had to be sure you could survive on yer own, that's why we taught you all that stuff. Now, Todd, you have to go—"

"If that's what's happening in a month, why wait this long? Why not take me away sooner?"

"We can't come with you. That's the whole problem. And we couldn't bear to send you off on yer own. To see you go. Not so young." He rubs the cover of the book with his fingers again. "And we were hoping there might be a miracle. One where we wouldn't have to—"

Lose you, says his Noise.

"But there ain't been no miracle," I say, after a second.

He shakes his head. He holds out the book. "I'm sorry," he says. "I'm so sorry it has to be this way."

And there's so much true sorrow in his Noise, so much worry and edginess, I know he's speaking true, I know he can't help what's happening and I hate it but I take the book from him and put it back in the plastic and into the rucksack. We don't say nothing more. What else is there to say? Everything and nothing. You can't say everything, so you don't say nothing.

He pulls me to him again, hitting my lip on his collar just like Cillian but this time I don't pull away. "Always remember," he says, "when yer ma died, you became our son, and I love you and Cillian loves you, always have, always will."

I start to say, "I don't wanna go," but it never comes out.

Cuz *BANG!!* goes the loudest thing I ever heard in Prentisstown, like something's blowing right up, right on up to the sky.

And it can only be coming from our farm.

Ben lets me go right quick. He ain't saying nothing but his Noise is screaming Cillian all over the place.

"I'll come back with you," I say. "I'll help you fight."

"No!" Ben shouts. "You have to get away. Promise me. Go thru the swamp and *get away*."

I don't say nothing for a second.

"*Promise me*," Ben says again, demanding it this time.

"Promise!" Manchee barks and there's fear even in that.

"I promise," I say.

Ben reaches behind his back and unclasps something. He wriggles it for a second or two before it comes unlatched completely. He hands it to me. It's his hunting knife, the big ratchety one with the bone handle and the serrated edge that cuts practically everything in the world, the knife I was hoping to get for the birthday when I became a man. It's still in its belt, so I can wear it myself.

"Take it," he says. "Take it with you to the swamp. You may need it."

"I never fought a Spackle before, Ben."

He still holds out the knife and so I take it.

There's another *BANG* from the farm. Ben looks back towards it, then back to me. "Go. Follow the river down to the swamp and out. Run as fast as you can and you'd better damn well not turn back, Todd Hewitt." He takes my arm and grips it hard. "If I can find you, I'll find you, I swear it," he says. "But you keep going, Todd. You keep yer promise."

This is it. This is goodbye. A goodbye I wasn't even looking for.

"Ben—"

"Go!" he shouts and takes off, looking back once as he runs and then racing off back to the farm, back to whatever's happening at the end of the world.

6

THE KNIFE IN FRONT OF ME

"C'MON, MANCHEE," I say, turning to run, tho every bit of me wants to follow Ben as he's running across the fields a different way, just like he said, to confuse anyone out looking for Noise.

I stop for a second when I hear a bunch of smaller bangs from the direkshun of the house which gotta be rifle shots and I think of the rifle that Cillian took from Mr Prentiss Jr and all the rifles that Mayor Prentiss and his men have locked away in the town and how all those guns against Cillian's stolen rifle and the few others we got in the house ain't gonna be much of a fight for very long and it gets me to wondering what the bigger bangs were and I realize they were probably Cillian blowing up the generators to confuse the men and make everyone's Noise so loud they can't hear even the whisper of mine way out here.

All this for me to get away.

"C'mon, Manchee," I say again and we run the last few

metres to the river. Then we take a right and start following the river downhill, keeping away from the rushes at the water's edge.

The rushes where the crocs live.

I take the knife from its sheath and I keep it in my hand as we move along fast.

"What's on, Todd?" Manchee keeps barking, which is his version of "What's going on?"

"I don't know, Manchee. Shut up so I can think."

The rucksack's banging into my back as we run but we keep going as best we can, kicking thru river shrubs and jumping over fallen logs.

I'll come back. That's what I'll do. I'll come back. They said I'd know what to do and now I do know. I'll go to the swamp and kill the Spackle if I can and then I'll come back and help Cillian and Ben and then we can all get away to this somewhere else Ben was talking about.

Yeah, that's what I'll do.

"Promised, Todd," Manchee says, sounding worried as the ridge we're going along is getting closer and closer to the rushes.

"Shut up," I say. "I promised to keep on going but maybe keep on going means coming back first."

"Todd?" Manchee says and I don't believe it either.

We've gotten outta hearing distance from the farm and the river veers away east a little before it enters the top of the swamp so it's taking us away from the town, too, and after a minute there ain't nothing following us as we run 'cept my Noise and Manchee's Noise and the sound of the running river which is just loud enough to cover the Noise of a hunting croc. Ben says that's "evolushun" but he says not to think about it too much around Aaron.

I'm breathing heavy and Manchee's panting like he's about to keel over but we don't stop. The sun is starting to set, but it's still light as you please, light that don't feel like it's going to hide you. The ground is flattening out and we're getting down closer to river level as it all starts turning to marsh. Everything's getting muddier and it's making us slow down. There's more rushes, too, can't be helped.

"Listen for crocs," I say to Manchee. "Keep yer ears open."

Cuz the water from the river is slowing and if you can keep yer own Noise quiet enough you can start to hear them out there. The ground's got even wetter. We're barely making walking pace now, sloshing thru mud. I grip the knife harder and hold it out in front of me.

"Todd?" Manchee says.

"Do you hear them?" I whisper, trying to watch my step and watch the rushes and watch out for Manchee all at the same time.

"Crocs, Todd," Manchee says, pretty much as quiet as he can bark.

I stop and I listen hard.

And out there in the rushes, out there in more than one place, I can hear 'em. **Flesh,** they're saying.

Flesh and **feast** and **tooth**.

"Crap," I say.

"Crocs," Manchee says again.

"C'mon," I say and we start splashing along, cuz we're in muck now. My shoes start sinking with each step and water's coming up over the top of 'em and there's no way to go 'cept thru the rushes. I start swinging the knife as we go, trying to cut any rush that's in front of me.

I look ahead and I can see where we're going, up and to the right. We've made it past the town and it's the bit where the wild fields come down by the school and meet up with the swamp and if we get thru this marshy bit here we'll be on safe ground and can get onto the paths that head into the dark of the swamp.

Was it really only this morning I was here last?

"Hurry up, Manchee," I say. "Almost there."

Flesh and **feast** and **tooth** and I swear it's getting closer.

"C'mon!"

Flesh.

"Todd?"

I'm cutting my way thru rushes and pulling my feet outta mud and **flesh** and **feast** and **TOOTH**.

And then I hear **Whirler dog**—

And I know we're done for.

"Run!" I yell.

And we run and Manchee lets out a frightened yelp and leaps past me but I see a croc rear up outta the rushes in front of him and it jumps for him but Manchee's so scared he jumps even higher, higher than he really knows how, and the croc's teeth snap on empty air and it lands with a splash next to me looking mighty pissed off and I hear its Noise hiss **Whirler boy** and I'm running and it jumps for me and I'm not even thinking and I'm turning and I'm pushing my hand up and the croc comes crashing down on top of me and its mouth is open and its claws are out and I

59

think I'm about to be dead and I'm thrashing my way back outta the muck up onto the dry bit and it's on its hind legs coming after me outta the rushes and it takes a minute of me yelling and of Manchee barking his head off before I realize that it's not actually coming after me no more, that the croc's dead, that my new knife is right thru its head, still stuck in the croc and the only reason the croc's still thrashing is cuz I'm still thrashing and I shake the croc off the knife and the croc falls to the ground and I sort of just fall over too in celebrayshun of not being dead.

And it's when I'm gasping for air from the rush of my blood and Manchee's barking and barking and we're both laughing from relief that I realize that we've been too loud ourselves to hear something important.

"Going somewhere, young Todd?"

Aaron. Standing right over me.

Before I can do nothing he punches me in the face.

I fall backwards onto the ground, the rucksack digging into my back and making me look like an upturned turtle. My cheek and my eye are just singing with pain and I haven't even moved properly before Aaron's grabbing me by my shirt front and the skin beneath and lifting me to my feet. I yell out from how much it hurts.

Manchee barks an angry "Aaron!" and goes for Aaron's legs, but Aaron doesn't even look before kicking him outta the way hard.

Aaron's holding me up to look him in the face. I can only keep the one non-painful eye open to meet his.

"Just what in the name of God's bounteous, glorified Eden are you doing down here in the swamp, Todd

Hewitt?" he says, his breath smelling like meat and his Noise the scariest kinda crazy you never wanna hear. "Yer sposed to be at yer farm right now, boy."

With his free hand, he punches me in the stomach. I try to bend over with the pain of it but he's still holding on to my shirt front and the skin below.

"You gotta go back," he says. "There's things you need to see."

I'm gasping for breath but the way he says it catches my ear and some of the flickers I'm catching in his Noise make it so I can see a little bit of the truth.

"You sent them," I say. "It wasn't me they heard. It was you."

"Smart boys make useless men," he says, twisting his gripping hand.

I cry out but I ruddy well keep talking, too. "They didn't hear the quiet in my Noise. They heard it in *yer* Noise and you sent them to me to keep them from coming after you."

"Oh, no, Todd," he says, "they heard it in yer Noise. I just *made sure* they did. I made sure they knew who was responsible for bringing danger to our town." He grits his teeth into a wild smile beneath his beard. "And who should be rewarded for his efforts."

"Yer crazy," I say and boy is it ever true and boy do I wish it wasn't.

His smile falls and his teeth clench. "It's mine, Todd," he says. "Mine."

I don't know what this means but I don't stop to think about it cuz I realize instead that both Aaron and I have forgotten one important thing.

I never let go of the knife.

A whole buncha things happen at once.

Aaron hears *knife* in my Noise and realizes his mistake. He pulls back his free fist to make another punch.

I pull back my knife hand and I wonder if I can actually stab him.

There's a breaking sound from the rushes and Manchee barks, "Croc!"

And all at the same time, we hear **Whirler man**.

Before Aaron can even turn, the croc is on him, clamping its teeth onto his shoulder and grabbing him with its claws and pulling him back towards the rushes. Aaron lets go of me and I fall to the ground again, clutching at all the bruises he's left on my chest. I look up and I see Aaron thrashing in the muck now, fighting with the croc and the sails on the backs of other crocs heading his way, too.

"Outta here!" Manchee's barking, almost shrieking.

"Too effing right," I say and I stumble to my feet, the rucksack knocking me a little off balance and my hurt eye trying to peel open but we don't stop and we run and we run and we run.

We get out of the marshes and run along the bottom of the fields to the start of the swamp path and we run into the swamp along it and when we get to the log that Manchee always needs help over he just sails right over it without even stopping and I'm right behind him and we're running our way to the Spackle buildings just like we were this morning.

And the knife is still in my hand and my Noise is thudding so loud and I'm so frightened and hurt and mad that I know beyond any shadow of a thought that I am going to find the Spackle hiding in his Noise hole and I am going to kill him dead dead dead for everything that's happened today.

"Where is it?" I ask Manchee. "Where's the quiet?"

Manchee's sniffing away like mad, running from building to building, and I'm doing my best to calm my Noise but there don't seem any chance of that.

"Hurry!" I say. "Before it runs–"

And it's barely outta my mouth before I hear it. The rip in the Noise, as big and horrible as life itself, I can hear it a little bit away, behind the Spackle buildings, behind some bushes.

It ain't getting away this time.

"Quiet!" Manchee barks, all keyed up, and he runs past the buildings and into the bushes.

And the quiet moves, too, and tho I can feel the pressure in my chest again and the terrible mournful things coming into my eyes, this time I don't stop, this time I run after my dog and I don't stop and I take in my breath and I swallow away the pressure and I wipe the water from my eyes and I grip the knife and I can hear Manchee barking and I can hear the silence and it's just around this tree just around this tree just around this tree and I'm yelling and I'm going round the tree and I'm running at the silence and my teeth are bared and I'm screaming and Manchee's barking and–

And I stop.

I stop right there in my tracks.

I don't, I do absolutely *not* put down the knife.

There it is, looking back at us, breathing heavy, crouched

at the base of a tree, cowering from Manchee, its eyes practically dying from fright but still trying to offer up a pitiful threat with its arms.

And I just stop.

I hold my knife.

"Spackle!" Manchee barks, tho he's too chicken to attack now that I've held back. "Spackle! Spackle! Spackle!"

"Shut up, Manchee," I say.

"Spackle!"

"I said *shut up!*" I shout, which stops him.

"Spackle?" Manchee says, unsure of things now.

I swallow, trying to get rid of the pressure in my throat, the unbelievable sadness that comes and comes as I look at it looking back at me. Knowledge is dangerous and men lie and the world keeps changing, whether I want it to or not.

Cuz it ain't a Spackle.

"It's a girl," I say.

It's a girl.

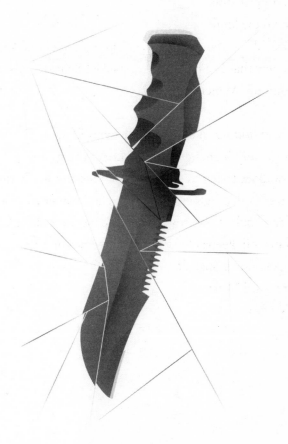

PART II

7

IF THERE WAS A GIRL

"IT'S A GIRL," I say again. I'm still catching my breath, still feeling the pressure on my chest, *definitely* still holding the knife way out in front of me.

A girl.

It's looking back at us like we're gonna kill it. It's hunched down in a little ball, trying to make itself as small as possible, only taking its eyes off Manchee to snatch quick glances of me.

Of me and my knife.

Manchee's huffing and puffing, his back fur all ridged, hopping around like the ground is hot, looking as charged up and confused as I am, tho completely hopeless about keeping in any way cool.

"What's girl?" he barks. "What's girl?"

By which he means, "What's a girl?"

"What's girl?" Manchee barks again and when the girl looks like it might be about to make a leap back over the large root where it's huddling, Manchee's bark turns into a fierce growl, "*Stay, stay, stay, stay, stay...*"

"Good dog," I say, tho I don't know *why* it's good what he's doing but what else can you say? This makes no sense, no sense at all, and everything feels like it's starting to slip, like the world is a table tilted on its side and everything on it is tipping over.

I am Todd Hewitt, I think to myself but who knows if *that's* even true any more?

"Who are you?" I finally say, if it can even hear me over all my raging Noise and Manchee's nervous breakdown. "Who are you?" I say, louder and clearer. "What are you doing here? Where did you come from?"

It looks at me, finally, for more than just a second, taking its eyes off Manchee. It looks at my knife, then it looks at my face above my knife.

She looks at me.

She does.

She.

I know what a girl is. Course I do. I seen 'em in the Noise of their fathers in town, mourned like their wives but not nearly so often. I seen 'em in vids, too. Girls are small and polite and smiley. They wear dresses and their hair is long and it's pulled into shapes behind their heads or on either side. They do all the inside-the-house chores, while boys do all the outside. They reach womanhood when they turn thirteen, just like boys reach manhood, and then they're women and they become wives.

That's how New World works, or at least that's how Prentisstown works. Worked. Was meant to, anyhow, but there ain't no girls. They're all dead. They died with their mothers and their grandmothers and their sisters and their aunties. They died in the months after I was born. All of them, every single one.

But here one is.

And its hair ain't long. *Her* hair. Her hair ain't long. And she ain't wearing no dress, she's wearing clothes that look like way newer versions of mine, so new they're almost like a uniform, even tho they're torn and muddy, and she ain't that small, she's my size, just, by the looks of her, and she's sure as all that's unholy not smiley.

No, not smiley at all.

"Spackle?" Manchee barks quietly.

"Would you effing well *shut up?*" I say.

So how do I know? How do I know it's a girl?

Well, for one, she ain't no Spackle. Spackle looked like men with everything a bit swelled up, everything a bit longer and weirder than on a man, their mouths a bit higher than they should be and their ears and eyes way, *way* different. And spacks grew their clothes right on their bodies, like lichens you could trim away to whatever shape you needed. Product of swamp-dwelling, according to another Ben-best-guess and she don't look like that and her clothes are normal and so there ain't no way she's a Spackle.

And for two, I just know. I just do. I can't tell you but I look and I see and I just know. She don't look like the girls I seen in vids or in Noise and I never seen no girl in the flesh but there she is, she's a girl and that's that. Don't ask me. Something about her shape, something about her smell, something I don't know but it's there and she's a girl.

If there was a girl, that's what she'd be.

And she ain't another boy. She just ain't. She ain't me. She ain't nothing like me at all. She's something completely other else altogether and I don't know how I know it but I know who I am, I am Todd Hewitt, and I know what I am not and I am not her.

She's looking at me. She's looking at my face, in my eyes. Looking and looking.

And I'm not hearing *nothing*.

Oh, man. My chest. It's like falling.

"Who are you?" I say again but my voice actually *catches*, like it breaks up cuz I'm so sad (shut up). I grit my teeth and I get a little madder and I say it yet again. "Who are you?" and I hold out the knife a little farther. With my other arm, I have to wipe my eyes real fast.

Something's gotta happen. Someone's gotta move. Someone's gotta do *something*.

And there ain't no someone but me, still, whatever the world's doing.

"Can you talk?" I say.

She just looks back at me.

"Quiet," Manchee barks.

"Shut it, Manchee," I say, "I need to think."

And she's still just looking back at me. With no Noise at all.

What do I do? It ain't fair. Ben told me I'd get to the swamp and I'd know what to do but I *don't* know what to do. They didn't say nothing about a girl, they didn't say nothing about why the quiet makes me ache so much I can barely stop from ruddy *weeping*, like I'm missing something so bad

I can't even think straight, like the emptiness ain't in her, it's in *me* and there ain't nothing that's ever gonna fix it.

What do I do?

What do I do?

She seems like maybe she's calming down. She's not shaking as much as she was, her arms aren't up so high, and she's not looking like she's about to run off at the first opportunity, tho how can you know for sure when a person's got no Noise? How can they *be* a person if they ain't got no Noise?

And can she hear me? *Can* she? Can a person with no Noise hear it at all?

I look at her and I think, as loud and clear as I can, *Can you hear me? Can you?*

But she don't change her face, she don't change her look.

"Okay," I say, and I take a step back. "Okay. You just stay there, okay? You just stay right there."

I take a few more steps back but I keep my eyes on her and she keeps her eyes on me. I bring my knife arm down and I slide it outta one strap of the rucksack, then I lean over and drop the rucksack to the ground. I keep the knife in one hand and with the other I open up the rucksack and fish out the book.

It's heavier than you think a thing made of words could be. And it smells of leather. And there's pages and pages of my ma's—

That'll have to wait.

"You watch her, Manchee," I say.

"Watch!" he barks.

I look inside the front cover and there's the paper folded in just like Ben said. I unfold it. There's a hand-drawn map on one side and then a whole buncha writing on the back but it's all a big block of letters which I ain't got the calmness of Noise to even try right now so I just look at the map.

Our house is right at the top and the town just below with the river Manchee and I came down off to one side leading into the swamp and that's where we are now. But there's more to it, ain't there? The swamp keeps going till it starts being a river again and there's arrows drawn along the riverbank so that's where Ben is wanting me and Manchee to go and I follow the arrows with my fingers and it leads right outta the swamp, it leads right to–

WHUMP!! The world goes bright for a second as something clubs me up side the head, right on the sore spot where Aaron punched me, and I fall over but as I'm falling I swing the knife up and I hear a little yelp of pain and I catch myself before I fall all the way down and I turn, sitting down on the ground hard, holding the back of my knife hand to the pain in my head but looking at where the attack came from and it's here that I learn my very first lesson: Things with no Noise can sneak right up on you. Sneak right up on you like they ain't even there.

The girl is on her butt, too, sitting on the ground away from me, holding on to one of her upper arms with her hand, blood coming from twixt her fingers. She's dropped the stick she hit me with and her face is all collapsed in on itself with what she must be feeling from that cut.

"WHAT THE HELL D'YOU DO THAT FOR?" I shout,

trying not to touch my face too hard. Man, am I sick of being hit today.

The girl just looks at me, her forehead still creased, holding her cut.

Which is kinda bleeding a lot.

"Stick, Todd!" Manchee barks.

"And where the hell were you?" I say to him.

"Poo, Todd."

I make a "Gah!" sound and kick some dirt at him. He scrabbles back, then starts sniffing at some bushes like there ain't nothing unusual going on in the world. Dogs got attenshun spans about as long as a matchstick. Idiot things.

It's starting to get dark now, the sun really setting, the already dark swamp getting even darker, and I still don't have no answer. Time keeps passing and I ain't sposed to wait here and I ain't sposed to go back and *there ain't sposed to be a girl*.

Boy, that cut really is bleeding on her.

"Hey," I say, my voice shaky from the charge running through me. *I am Todd Hewitt*, I think. *I am almost a man*. "Hey," I say again, trying to be a little calmer.

The girl looks at me.

"I ain't gonna hurt you," I say, breathing hard, just like her. "You hear me? I ain't gonna hurt you. As long as you don't try to hit me with no more sticks, all right?"

She looks at my eyes. Then she looks at the knife.

Is she understanding?

I lower the knife away from my face and bring it down near the ground. I don't let go of it, tho. With my free hand, I start looking thru the rucksack again till I find the medipak Ben threw in. I hold it up.

"Medipak," I say. She doesn't change. "Me-di-pak," I say slowly. I point to my own upper arm, to where the cut is on her. "Yer bleeding."

Nothing.

I sigh and I start to stand. She flinches and scoots back on her butt. I sigh again in an angry way. *I ain't gonna hurt you.* I hold up the medipak. "It's medicine. It'll stop the bleeding."

Still nothing. Maybe there ain't nothing in her at all.

"Look," I say and I snap open the medipak. I fumble with one hand and take out a styptic pad, tearing away the paper cover with my teeth. I'm probably bleeding from where first Aaron hit me and then the girl, so I take the pad and rub it over my eye and eyebrow. I pull it away and yep, there's blood. I hold the pad out to the girl so she can see it. "See?" I point to my eye. "See? It stops things bleeding."

I take a step forward, just the one. She flinches back but not as much. I take another step, then another and then I'm next to her. She keeps looking at the knife.

"I ain't putting it down, so just forget it," I say. I push the pad towards her arm. "Even if it's deep, this stitches it up, okay? I'm trying to help you."

"Todd?" Manchee barks, full of asking marks.

"In a minute," I say. "Look, yer bleeding everywhere, okay? And I can fix it, all right? Just don't get any ideas about any more ruddy sticks."

She's watching. And she's watching. And she's watching. I'm trying to be as calm as I really don't feel. I don't know why I'm helping her, not after she whacked me on the head, but I don't know what to do about anything. Ben said there'd be answers in the swamp and there ain't no answers, there's just this girl who's bleeding cuz I cut her even tho she deserved it and if I can stop the bleeding then maybe that's doing something.

I don't know. I don't know what to do, so I just do this.

The girl's still watching me, still breathing heavy. But she ain't running and she ain't flinching and then so you can hardly tell at all she's turning her upper arm towards me a little bit so I can reach the cut.

"Todd?" Manchee barks again.

"Shush," I say, not wanting to scare the girl any more. Being this close to her silence is like my heart breaking all over the place. I can feel it, like it's pulling me down into a bottomless pit, like it's calling for me to just fall and fall and fall.

But I keep my nerve, I do. I keep it and I press the styptic pad on her arm, rubbing the cut, which is pretty deep, till it closes a bit and stops bleeding.

"Ya gotta be careful," I say. "That ain't a permanent heal. You gotta be careful with it till yer body heals the rest, okay?"

And all she does is look at me.

"Okay," I say, to myself as much as anyone cuz now that that's done, what's next?

"Todd?" Manchee barks. "Todd?"

"And no more sticks, all right?" I say to the girl. "No more hitting me."

"Todd?" Manchee again.

"And obviously my name's Todd."

And there, just there, just there in the fading light, is there a little beginning of a start of a smile? Is there?

75

"Can you…?" I say, looking as deep into her eyes as the pressure in my chest allows. "Can you understand me?"

"Todd," Manchee's barking picks up a notch.

I turn to him. *"What?"*

"Todd! TODD!!!"

And then we can all hear it. Pounding thru the bushes and branches breaking and running footsteps and Noise and Noise and oh, crap, Noise.

"Get up," I say to the girl. "Get up! Now!"

I grab my rucksack and put it on and the girl's looking terrified but in a not-helpful paralysed way and I shout "Come on!" to her again and I grab her arm, not thinking about the cut now, and I try to lift her to her feet but all of a sudden it's too late and there's a yell and a roar and a sound like whole trees falling down and me and the girl can only both turn to look and it's Aaron and he's mad and he's messed-up and he's coming right for us.

8

THE CHOICES OF A KNIFE

HE'S ON US IN THREE STEPS. Before I can even try and run, he's coming at me with his hands out, grabbing my neck, smashing me back against a tree.

"You little FILTH!" he screams and presses his thumbs into my throat. I scrabble at his arms, trying to slash at him with the knife, but my rucksack has fallen and the strap has pinned my arm back against the tree so he can pretty much go on strangling me for as long as it takes.

His face is a nightmare, a horrible thing I'm not gonna stop seeing even if I ever get outta this. The crocs took his left ear and a long strip of flesh with it going right down his left cheek. You can see his teeth through the gash and it's causing his left eye to bulge forward like his head's been caught in mid-explosion. There are other gashes on his chin and neck and his clothes are torn and there's blood practically everywhere and I can even see a croc tooth sticking out of a fleshy tear on his shoulder.

I'm choking for breath but not getting any at all and you can't believe how much it hurts and the world's gone spinning and my brain's going funny and I have this stupid little thought that Aaron didn't survive the croc attack after all, that he died but he's so pissed off at me that dying didn't stop him from coming here to kill me anyway.

"WHAT ARE YOU SMILING AT?" he screams, little bits of blood and spit and flesh spraying onto my face. He squeezes my neck harder and I can feel myself throwing up but there's nowhere for it to go and I can't breathe and all the lights and colours are flowing together and I'm dying and I'm going to die.

"AAH!" Aaron suddenly jerks back, letting me go. I drop to the ground and throw up all over everywhere and take in a huge gasping breath that makes me cough in a way like I'm never gonna stop. I look up and see Manchee's snout wrapped around Aaron's calf, biting it for all he's worth.

Good dog.

Aaron slams Manchee sideways with an arm, sending him flying into the bushes. I hear a thump and a yelp and a "Todd?"

Aaron whirls around to me again and I just can't stop looking at his face, at the gashes everywhere that no one could have survived, no one, it's not possible.

Maybe he really is dead.

"Where's the sign?" he says, his torn expression changing right quick and looking around in a sudden panic.

The sign?

The—

The girl.

I look, too. She's gone.

Aaron whirls again, this way, that, and then I see him hearing it the same time I do, hearing the rustle and snap as she runs, hearing the silence as it flows away from us, and without another look at me, he takes off after her and he's gone.

And just like that, I'm alone.

Just like that, like I have nothing to do with anything here.

What a stupid day this has been.

"Todd?" Manchee comes limping outta the bushes.

"I'm okay, buddy," I try to say and get some of it out despite the coughing, even tho it ain't true. "I'm okay."

I try to keep breathing thru the coughs, forehead on the ground, dribbling spit and barf everywhere.

I keep breathing and these thoughts start coming. They come all uninvited, don't they?

Cuz maybe that could be it, couldn't it? Maybe it could be over, simple as that. The girl's obviously what Aaron wants, whatever he means by "the sign", right? The girl's obviously what *the town* wants, what with all the ruckus over the quiet in my Noise. And so if Aaron can have her and the town can have her, then that could be the end of it, right? They could have what they want and leave me alone and I could go back and everything could be like it was before and, yeah, it would probably be no good for the girl but it might save Ben and Cillian.

It might save me.

I'm just *thinking* it, all right? The thoughts rush in, that's all.

Thoughts that this could be over as soon as it started.

"Over," Manchee murmurs.

And then I hear the terrible, terrible scream that of course is the girl getting caught and that's the choice made, ain't it?

The next scream comes a second later but I'm already on my feet without even really thinking it, slipping off my rucksack, leaning a bit, coughing still, reaching for more breath, but the knife in my hand and running.

They're easy to follow. Aaron's torn thru the bushes like a bullock and his Noise is throwing up a roar and always, always, always there's the silence of the girl, even behind her screams, which somehow makes it even harder to hear. I run the best I can after them, Manchee on my heels, and it ain't more than half a minute before we're there with genius me having no idea what to do now I've got here. Aaron's chased her into a bit of water about ankle-deep and got her back up against a tree. He's got her wrists in his hands but she's fighting him, fighting and kicking for all she's worth, but her face is a thing so scared I can barely get my words out.

"Leave her alone," my voice rasps but no one hears me. Aaron's Noise is blazing so loud I'm not sure he'd hear me even if I yelled. THE HOLY SACRAMENT and THE SIGN FROM GOD and THE PATH OF THE SAINT and pictures of the girl in a church, pictures of the girl drinking the wine and eating the host, pictures of the girl as an angel.

The girl as a sacrifice.

Aaron gets both of her wrists in one of his fists, fumbles

off the cord belt of his robe, and starts tying her hands together with it. The girl kicks him hard where Manchee bit him and he hits her across the face with the back of his hand.

"Leave her alone," I say again, trying to make my voice louder.

"Alone!" Manchee barks, still limping but still ferocious. What a ruddy good dog.

I step forward. Aaron's back's to me, like he don't even care I'm here, like he don't even think of me as a threat.

"Let her go," I try and shout but it just makes me cough some more. Still nothing, tho. Still nothing from Aaron or anyone.

I'm gonna have to do it. I'm gonna have to do it. Oh man oh man oh man I'm gonna have to do it.

I'm gonna have to kill him.

I raise the knife.

I've raised the knife.

Aaron turns, not even fast like, just turns like someone's called his name. He sees me standing there, knife in the air, not moving like the goddam coward idiot I am, and he smiles and boy I just can't say how awful a smile looks on that torn-up face.

"Yer Noise reveals you, young Todd," he says, letting go of the girl, who's so tied up and beaten now she don't even try to run. Aaron takes a step towards me.

I take a step back (shut up, please just shut up).

"The Mayor will be disappointed to hear about your untimely departure from the earthly plain, boy," Aaron says, taking another step. I take another step, too, the knife in the air like it's of no use at all.

"But God has no use for a coward," Aaron says, "does he, boy?"

Quick as a snake, his left arm knocks into my right, sending the knife flying out of my hand. He hits me in the face with the flat of his right hand, knocking me back down into the water and I feel his knees land on my chest and his hands pressing down on my throat to finish the job but this time my face is underwater so it's going to be a lot faster.

I struggle but I've lost. I've lost. I had my chance and I've lost and I deserve this and I'm fighting but I'm not nearly as strong as I was before and I can feel the end coming. I can feel me giving up.

I'm lost.

Lost.

And then, in the water, my hand finds a rock.

BOOM! I bring it up and hit him on the side of the head before I can think about it.

BOOM! I do it again.

BOOM! And again.

I feel him slide off me and I lift my head, choking on water and air, but I sit up and raise the rock again to hit him but he's laying down in the water, face half-in, half-out, his teeth smiling up at me thru the gash in his cheek. I scrabble back from him, coughing and spluttering, but he stays there, sinking a little, not moving.

I feel like my throat is broken but I throw up some water and can breathe a little better.

"Todd? Todd? Todd?" Manchee says, coming up to me, all licky and barky like a little puppy. I scratch him twixt the ears cuz I can't say nothing yet.

And then we both feel the silence and look up and there's the girl standing over us, her hands still tied.

Holding the knife in her fingers.

I sit frozen for a second and Manchee starts to growl but then I realize. I take a few more breaths and then I reach up and take the knife from her fingers and cut the cord Aaron bound her wrists with. It drops away and she rubs where it was tied, still staring at me, still not saying nothing.

She knows. She knows I couldn't do it.

Goddam you, I think to myself. *Goddam you.*

She looks at the knife. She looks over at Aaron, lying down in the water.

He's still breathing. He gurgles water with every breath, but he's still breathing.

I grip the knife. The girl looks at me, at the knife, at Aaron, at me again.

Is she telling me? Is she telling me to do it?

He's lying there, undefended, probably eventually drowning.

And I have a knife.

I get to my feet, fall down from dizziness, and get to my feet again. I step towards him. I raise my knife. Again.

The girl takes in a breath and I can feel her holding it.

Manchee says, "Todd?"

And I have my knife raised over Aaron. One more time, I've got my chance. One more time, I've got my knife raised.

I could do it. No one on New World would blame me. It'd be my right.

I could just do it.

But a knife ain't just a thing, is it? It's a choice, it's

something you *do*. A knife says yes or no, cut or not, die or don't. A knife takes a decision out of your hand and puts it in the world and it never goes back again.

Aaron's gonna die. His face is ripped, his head is bashed, he's sinking into shallow water without ever waking up. He tried to kill me, he wanted to kill the girl, he's responsible for the ruckus in town, he's gotta be the one who sent the Mayor to the farm and cuz of that he's responsible for Ben and Cillian. He deserves to die. He deserves it.

And I can't bring the knife down to finish the job.

Who am I?

I am Todd Hewitt.

I am the biggest, effing waste of nothing known to man.

I can't do it.

Goddam you, I think to myself again.

"Come on," I say to the girl. "We have to get outta here."

9

WHEN LUCK
AIN'T WITH YOU

AT FIRST I don't think she's gonna come. There's no
reason for her to, no reason for me to ask her, but when I
say to her, "Come *on*," a second time more urgently and
gesture with my hand, she follows me, follows Manchee,
and that's how it is, that's what we do, who knows if it's
right, but that's what we do.

Night's well and truly fallen. The swamp seems even
thicker here, as black as anything. We rush on back a ways
to get my rucksack and then around and a little bit further
away in the dark to get some distance between us and
Aaron's body (please let it be a body). We clamber round
trees and over roots, getting deeper into the swamp. When
we get to a small clearing where there's a bit of flat land and
a break in the trees, I stop us.

I'm still holding the knife. It rests there in my hand,
shining at me like blame itself, like the word *coward* flashing again and again. It catches the light of both moons and

my God it's a powerful thing. A *powerful* thing, like I'd have to agree to be a part of *it* rather than it being a part of me.

I reach behind me and put it in the sheath between my back and the rucksack where at least I won't have to see it.

I take the rucksack off and fish thru it for a torch.

"Do you know how to use one of these?" I ask the girl, switching it on and off a coupla times.

She just looks at me, as ever.

"Never mind," I say.

My throat still hurts, my face still hurts, my chest still hurts, my Noise keeps pounding me with visions of bad news, of how good a fight Ben and Cillian managed to put up at the farm, of how long it'll take Mr Prentiss Jr to find out where I've gone, of how long it'll take him to be on his way after me, after *us* (not long at all, if he ain't already), so who ruddy cares if she knows how to use a torch. Of *course* she don't.

I get the book out of the rucksack, using the torch for a light. I open up to the map again and I follow Ben's arrows from our farm down the river and thru the swamp and then outta the swamp as it turns back into river.

It's not hard to find yer way outta the swamp. Out on the horizon beyond it, you can always see three mountains, one close and two farther away but next to each other. The river on Ben's map goes twixt the closer one and the two farther away ones and so all we gotta do is to keep heading towards that space in the middle and we should find the river again and follow it. Follow it to where the arrows keep going.

Keep going to another settlement.

There it is. Right there at the bottom of the page where the map ends.

A whole other place.

As if I don't have enough new stuff to think about.

I look up at the girl, still staring at me, maybe not even blinking. I shine the torch at her face. She winces and turns away.

"Where'd you come from?" I ask. "Is it here?"

I point the torch down at the map and put my finger on the other town. The girl don't move so I wave her over. She still don't move so I sigh and pick up the book and take it over to her and shine the torch on the page.

"I," I point to myself, "am from here." I point to our farm north of Prentisstown on the map. "This," I wave my arms around to show the swamp, "is here." I point at the swamp. "We need to go here," I point at the other town. Ben's written the other town's name underneath, but – well, whatever. "Is this where yer from?" I point to her, point to the other town, point to her again. "Are you from here?"

She looks at the map but other than that, nothing.

I sigh in frustrayshun and step away from her. It's uncomfortable being so close. "Well, I sure hope so," I say, glancing back at the map. "Cuz that's where we're going."

"Todd," Manchee barks. I look up. The girl's started to wander around in circles in the clearing, looking at stuff like it means something to her.

"What're you doing?" I ask.

She looks at me, at the torch in my hand and she points thru some trees.

"What?" I say. "We don't have time–"

She points thru the trees again and starts walking there.

"Hey!" I say. *"Hey!"*

I guess I have to follow.

"We gotta stick to the map!" I duck under branches to follow her, the rucksack getting caught left and right. "Hey! Wait up!"

I stumble on, Manchee behind me, the torch not much good against every ruddy little branch and root and puddle in a great big swamp. I keep having to drop my head and tear the rucksack free of stuff so I can barely look ahead enough to follow her. I see her standing by a fallen, burnt-looking tree, waiting for me, watching me come.

"What're you doing?" I say, finally catching up with her. "Where're you–"

And then I see.

The tree *is* burnt, *freshly* burnt and freshly knocked over, too, the unburnt splinters clean and white like new wood. And there are a buncha trees just like it, a whole line of 'em, in fact, on either side of a great ditch gouged outta the swamp, now filled with water but piled-up dirt and burnt plants all around it show that's it gotta be a new thing, like someone came thru here and dug it up in one fiery swoop.

"What happened?" I swing the torch along it. "What did this?"

She just looks off to the left, where the ditch disappears into darkness. I shine the torch down that way but it's not strong enough to see what's down there. Tho it feels like *something's* there.

The girl takes off into the darkness towards whatever it might be.

"Where're you going?" I ask, not expecting an answer and not getting any. Manchee gets twixt me and the girl, like he's following her now, instead of me, and off they go in the dark. I keep my distance but I follow, too. The silence still flows from her, *still* bothers me, like it's ready to swallow up the whole world and me with it.

I keep the torch flashing over every possible square inch of water. Crocs don't usually come this far into the swamp but that's only usually, plus there's red snakes that're poisonous and water weasels that bite and it just don't feel like luck is bothering with any of us today so if something can go wrong it's probably gonna.

We're getting closer and I shine the torch down to where we're heading and something starts glinting back, something that ain't tree or bush or animal or water.

Something metal. Something *big* and metal.

"What's that?" I say.

We get closer and at first I think it's just a big fissionbike and I wonder what kind of idiot would try and ride a fission-bike in a swamp cuz you can barely get 'em to work over flattened dirt roads much less water and roots.

But it ain't a fissionbike.

"Hold up."

The girl stops.

Whaddya know? The girl stops.

"So you can understand me, then?"

But nothing, as ever nothing.

"Well, hold up for a sec," I say cuz a thought's coming. We're still a bit away from it but I keep flicking the torch over the metal. And back over the straight line that the ditch makes. And over the metal again. And over all the burnt stuff on either side of the ditch. And a thought keeps coming.

The girl stops waiting and heads off towards the metal and I follow. We have to go round a big burnt log, still lazily smoking in one or two spots, to get to the thing and when we do it's much bigger than the biggest fissionbike and even then it looks like it's only part of an even bigger something than that. It's crumpled and burnt in most places and even tho I don't know what it looked like before it crumpled and burned, it's obviously mostly wreckage.

And it's obviously wreckage of a ship.

An air ship. Maybe even a *space* ship.

"Is this yers?" I ask, shining the torch at the girl. She don't say nothing, as usual, but she don't say it in a way that could be agreement. "Did you crash here?"

I shine the torch up and down her body, up and down her clothes, which are a bit different than what I'm used to, sure, but not so different that they couldn't have belonged to me once upon a time.

"Where'd you come from?" I say.

But of course she don't say nothing and just looks off to a place further into the darkness, crosses her arms and starts heading off there. I don't follow this time. I keep looking at the ship. That's what it's gotta be. I mean, *look* at it. A lot of it's smashed beyond recognishun but you can still see something that might be a hull, might be an engine, even something that might have been a window.

The first homes in Prentisstown, see, were made from the ships the original settlers landed in. Sure, wood and log homes got built after, but Ben says the first thing you do when you land is build immediate shelter and immediate shelter comes from the first supplies to hand. The church and the petrol stayshun back in town are still partly made outta metal hulls and holds and rooms and such. And tho this heap of wreckage is pretty pounded, if you look at it right, it might be an old Prentisstown house that fell right outta the sky. Right outta the sky on fire.

"Todd!" Manchee barks from somewhere outta sight. "Todd!"

I go running round to where the girl disappeared, round the wreckage to a bit that seems less smashed up. As I run past, I can even see a door that's been opened out the side of one wall of metal a little way up and there's even a light on inside.

"Todd!" Manchee barks and I shine the torch over to where he's barking, standing next to the girl. She's just standing there looking down at something and so I shine the torch and see that she's standing by two long piles of clothes.

Which are actually two bodies, ain't they?

I walk over, shining the torch down. There's a man, his clothes and body pretty much completely burnt away from the chest down. His face has burns, too, but not enough to disguise that he was a man. He has a wound on his forehead that woulda killed him even if the burns hadn't but it don't matter, does it, cuz he's dead either way. Dead and lying here in a swamp.

I flash the torch over and he's lying next to a woman, ain't he?

I hold my breath.

It's the first woman I ever seen in the flesh. And it's the same as the girl. I never seen a woman in real life before but if there was a real life woman, that's what she'd be.

And dead, too, of course, but nothing as obvious as burns and a gash, not even blood on her clothes so maybe she's busted up on the inside.

But a woman. An actual woman.

I shine the torch at the girl. She don't flinch away.

"That's yer ma and pa, ain't it?" I ask, my voice low.

The girl don't say nothing but it's gotta be true.

I shine the torch over the wreckage and think of the burnt ditch behind it and it can only mean one thing. She crashed here with her ma and pa. They died. She lived. And if she came from somewhere else on New World or if she came from somewhere else altogether, don't matter. They died, she lived, and she was here all alone.

And got found by Aaron.

When luck ain't with you, it's against you.

On the ground I see drag marks where the girl must have pulled the bodies out of the crash and brought them here. But the swamp ain't for burying anything but Spackle cuz after two inches of dirt you pretty much just get water and so here they sit. I hate to say it but they do smell, tho in the overall smell of the swamp it ain't as bad as you think, so who knows how long she's been here.

The girl looks at me again, not crying, not smiling, just blank as ever. Then she walks past me, walks back along the drag marks, walks to the door I saw open in the side of the wreckage, climbs up and disappears inside.

10

FOOD AND FIRE

"HEY!" I say, following her over to the wreckage. "We can't be hanging around–"

I get up to the door at the same time she pops out, making me jump back. She waits for me to step outta the way, then climbs down from the door and walks past me, carrying a bag in one hand and a coupla small packets in the other. I look back at the door and stand on tiptoes, trying to peek in. It all looks a wreck inside, as you'd expect, things tumbled everywhere, lots of busted everything.

"How'd you live thru that?" I ask, turning around.

But she's got herself busy. She's put down the bag and the packs and has taken out what looks like a small, flat green box. She sets it down on a dry-ish area of ground and piles some sticks on top of it.

I look at her in disbelief. "There ain't time to make a–"

She presses a button on the side the box and *whoosh* we've got ourselves a whole, full-sized, instant campfire.

I just stand there like a fool, my mouth wide open.

I want a campfire box.

She looks at me and rubs her arms a little bit and it's only then that I really realize I'm soaking wet and cold and achy all over and that a fire is just about the closest thing to a blessing I can think of.

I look back into the blackness of the swamp, as if I'd be able to see anyone coming. Nothing, of course, but no sounds neither. No one close. Not yet.

I look back at the fire. "Only for a second," I say.

I walk over to the fire and start warming up my hands, keeping on my rucksack. She rips open one of the packs and throws it to me and I stare at it again till she dips her fingers into her own pack, taking out what must be a piece of dried fruit or something and eating it.

She's giving me food. And fire.

Her face still has no kinda expression at all, just blank as a stone as she stands by the fire and eats. I start eating, too. The fruit or whatever are like little shrivelled dots but sweet and chewy and I've finished the whole pack in half a minute before I notice Manchee begging.

"Todd?" he says, licking his lips.

"Oh," I say, "sorry."

The girl looks at me, looks at Manchee, then takes out a small handful from her own pack and holds it out to Manchee. When he approaches, she jerks back a little like she can't help it and drops the fruit on the ground instead. Manchee don't mind. He gobbles it right up.

I nod at her. She don't nod back.

It's full-fledged night now, dark as anything outside our

little circle of light. You can only even see stars thru the hole in the treetops made by the crashing ship. I try to think back over the last week if I heard any distant booms from the swamp but anything this far out could've been drowned in the Noise of Prentisstown, I spose, and been missed by everyone.

I think of certain preachers.

Nearly everyone.

"We can't stay," I say. "I'm sorry about yer folks and all but there's others that'll be after us. Even if Aaron's dead."

At Aaron's name, she flinches, just a little. He must've said his name to her. Or something. Maybe.

"I'm sorry," I say, tho I don't know what for. I shift my rucksack on my back. It feels heavier than ever. "Thanks for the grub but we gotta go." I look at her. "If yer coming with?"

The girl looks at me for a second and then uses the tip of her boot to knock the burning sticks off the little green box. She reaches down, presses the button again and picks up the box without even burning herself.

Man, I *really* want one of those things.

She puts it in the bag she brought outta the wreckage with her and then brings the strap of the bag over her head, like her own rucksack. Like she was planning on coming with me even before now.

"Well," I say, when all she does is stare at me. "I guess we're ready then."

Neither of us move.

I look back to her ma and pa. She does, too, but only for a second. I wanna say something to her, something more, but whaddya say? I open my mouth anyway but she starts rummaging in her bag. I think it's gonna be something to, I don't know, remember her folks with or make some kind of gesture or something but she finds what she's looking for and it's only a torch. She flicks it on – so she *does* know how they work – and starts walking, first towards me, then past me, as if we're already on our way.

And that's it, like her ma and pa ain't just lying there dead.

I watch her go for a second before saying, "Oi!"

She turns back to me.

"Not that way." I point to our left. "That way."

I head off the right way, Manchee follows, and I look back and the girl's coming after us. I take one last quick look behind her and as bad as I want to stay and look thru that wreckage for more neat stuff, and boy do I, we gotta go, even tho it's night, even tho nobody's slept, we gotta go.

And so we do, catching sight of the horizon thru the trees when we can and heading towards the space twixt the close mountain and the two farther away mountains. Both moons are more than halfway to full and the sky is clear so there's at least a little bit of light to walk by, even under the swamp canopy, even in the dark.

"Keep yer ears open," I say to Manchee.

"For what?" Manchee barks.

"For things that could get us, idiot."

You can't really run in a dark swamp at night so we walk as fast as we can, me shining the torch in front of us, tripping our way round tree roots and trying not to tromp thru too much mud. Manchee goes ahead and comes back, sniffing round and sometimes barking, but nothing serious.

The girl keeps up, never falling behind but never getting too close neither. Which is good, cuz even tho my Noise is about the quietest it's been all day, the silence of her still presses on it whenever she comes too near.

It's weird that she didn't do nothing more about her ma and pa when we left, ain't it? Didn't cry or have one last visit or nothing? Am I wrong? I'd give anything to see Ben and even Cillian again, even if they were… Well, even if they are.

"Ben," Manchee says, down by my knees.

"I know." I scratch him twixt the ears.

We keep on.

I'd want to bury them, if that's what it came to. I'd want to do *something*, I don't know what. I stop and look back at the girl but her face is just the same, just the same as ever, and is it cuz she crashed and her parents died? Is it cuz Aaron found her? Is it cuz she's from somewhere else?

Don't she feel nothing? Is she just nothing at all on the inside?

She's looking at me, waiting for me to go on.

And so, after a second, I do.

Hours. There's hours of this silent night-time fast creeping. Hours of it. Who knows how far we're going or if we're heading the right way or what, but *hours*. Once in a while, I hear the Noise of a night-time creacher, swamp owls cooing their way to dinner, swooping down on probably short-tailed mice, whose Noise is so quiet it's barely like language at all, but mostly all I hear is the now-and-then fast-fading Noise of a night-time creacher running away from all the ruckus we must be making by tromping thru a swamp at night.

But the weird thing is there's still no sound of nothing

behind us, nothing chasing us, no Noise, no branches breaking, nothing. Maybe Ben and Cillian threw them off the trail. Maybe the reason I'm running ain't so important after all. Maybe–

The girl stops to pull her shoe outta some mud.

The girl.

No. They're coming. The only maybe is that maybe they're waiting till daybreak so they can come faster.

So on and on we go, getting more and more tired, stopping only once so that everyone can have a private pee off in the bushes. I get some of Ben's food outta my own rucksack and feed small bits to everyone, since it's my turn.

And then more walking and more walking.

And then there comes an hour just before dawn where there can't be no more.

"We gotta stop," I say, dropping the rucksack at the base of a tree. "We gotta rest."

The girl sets her own bag down by another tree without needing any more convincing and we both just sort of collapse down, leaning on our bags like pillows.

"Five minutes," I say. Manchee curls up by my legs and closes his eyes almost immediately. "Only five minutes," I call over to the girl, who's pulled a little blanket outta her bag to cover herself with. "Don't get too comfortable."

We gotta keep going, no question of that. I'll only close my eyes for a minute or two, just to get a little rest, and then we'll keep on going faster than before.

Just a little rest, that's all.

I open my eyes and the sun is up. Only a little but ruddy well up.

Crap. We've lost at least an hour, maybe two.

And then I realize it's a sound that's woken me.

It's Noise.

I panic, thinking of men finding us and I scramble to my feet–

Only to see that it ain't a man.

It's a cassor, towering over me and Manchee and the girl.

Food? says its Noise.

I *knew* they hadn't left the swamp.

I hear a little gasp from over where the girl's sleeping. Not sleeping no more. The cassor turns to look at her. And then Manchee's up and barking, "Get! Get! Get!" and the cassor's neck swings back our way.

Imagine the biggest bird you ever saw, imagine it got so big that it couldn't even fly no more, we're talking two and a half or even three metres tall, a super long bendy neck stretching up way over yer head. It's still got feathers but they look more like fur and the wings ain't good for much except stunning things they're about to eat. But it's the feet you gotta watch out for. Long legs, up to my chest, with claws at the end that can kill you with one kick if yer not careful.

"Don't worry," I call over to the girl. "They're friendly."

Cuz they are. Or they're sposed to be. They're sposed to eat rodents and only kick if you attack 'em, but if you *don't* attack 'em, Ben says they're friendly and dopey and'll let you feed 'em. And they're also good to eat, a combo which made the new settlers of Prentisstown so eager to hunt 'em for food that by the time I was born there wasn't a cassor to be seen within miles. Yet another thing I only ever saw in a vid or Noise.

The world keeps getting bigger.

"Get! Get!" Manchee barks, running in a circle round the cassor.

"Don't bite it!" I shout at him.

The cassor's neck is swinging about like a vine, following Manchee around like a cat after a bug. **Food?** its Noise keeps asking.

"Not food," I say, and the big neck swings my way.

Food?

"Not food," I say again. "Just a dog."

Dog? it thinks and starts following Manchee around again, trying to nip him with his beak. The beak ain't a scary thing at all, like being nipped by a goose, but Manchee's having none of it, leaping outta the way and barking, barking, barking.

I laugh at him. It's funny.

And then I hear a little laugh that ain't my own.

I look over. The girl is standing by her tree, watching the giant bird chase around my stupid dog, and she's laughing.

She's *smiling*.

She sees me looking and she stops.

Food? I hear and I turn to see the cassor starting to poke its beak into my rucksack.

"Hey!" I shout and start shooing it away.

Food?

"Here." I fish out a small block of cheese wrapped in a cloth that Ben packed.

The cassor sniffs it, bites it, and gobbles it down, its neck rippling in long waves at it swallows. It snaps its beak a few times like a man might smack his lips after he ate something. But then its neck starts rippling the other way and with a loud hack, up comes the block of cheese flying right back at me, covered in spit but not hardly even crushed, smacking me on the cheek and leaving a trail of slime across my face.

Food? says the cassor and starts slowly walking off into the swamp, as if we're no longer even as interesting as a leaf.

"Get! Get!" Manchee barks after it, but not following. I wipe the slime from my face with my sleeve and I can see the girl smiling at me while I do it.

"Think that's funny, do ya?" I say and she keeps pretending like she's not smiling but she *is*. She turns away and picks up her bag.

"Yeah," I say, taking charge of things again. "We slept way too long. We gotta go."

We get going on yet more walking without any more words or smiling. Pretty quick, the ground starts to get less even and a bit drier. The trees start to thin out some, letting the sun directly on us now and then. After a little bit, we get to a small clearing, almost like a little field that rises up to a short bluff, standing just over the treetops. We climb it and stop at the top. The girl holds out another pack of that fruity stuff. Breakfast. We eat, still standing.

Looking out over the trees, the way in front of us is clear. The larger mountain is on the horizon and you can see the two smaller mountains in the distance behind a little bit of haze.

"That's where we're going," I say, pointing. "Or where I think we're sposed to go, anyway."

She sets down her fruit pack and goes into her bag

again. She pulls out the sweetest little pair of binos you've ever seen. My old ones back home that broke years ago were like a breadbox in comparison. She holds them up to her eyes and looks for a bit, then hands 'em to me.

I take 'em and I look out to where we're going. Everything's so *clear*. The ground stretching out before us in a green forest, curving downhill into proper valleys and dales as it starts to become real land again and not just the mucky bowl of a swamp and you can even see where the marsh starts really turning back into a proper river, cutting deeper and deeper canyons as it gets closer to the mountains. If you listen, you can even hear it rushing. I look and I look and I don't see no settlement but who knows what's around the bends and curves? Who knows what's up ahead?

I look behind us, back the way we came, but it's still early enough for a mist to be covering most of the swamp, hiding everything, giving nothing away.

"Those're sweet," I say, handing her the binos. She puts them back in her bag and we stand there for a minute eating.

We stand arm's length apart cuz her silence still bothers me. I chew down on a piece of dried fruit and I wonder what it must be like to have no Noise, to *come* from a place with no Noise. What does it mean? What kind of place is it? Is it wonderful? Is it terrible?

Say you were standing on a hilltop with someone who had no Noise. Would it be like you were alone there? How would you share it? Would you want to? I mean, here we are, the girl and I, heading outta danger and into the unknown and there's no Noise overlapping us, nothing to tell us what the other's thinking. Is that how it's sposed to be?

I finish the fruit and crumple up the packet. She holds out her hand and shoves the rubbish back into her bag. No words, no exchange, just my Noise and a great big nothing from her.

Was this what it was like for my ma and pa when they first landed? Was New World a silent place all over before–

I look up at the girl suddenly.

Before.

Oh, no.

I'm such a fool.

I'm such a stupid goddam fool.

She has no Noise. And she came from a ship. Which means she came from a place with no Noise, obviously, *idiot*.

Which means she's landed here and hasn't caught the Noise germ yet.

Which means that when she does, it's gonna do what it did to all the other women.

It's gonna kill her.

It's gonna kill her.

And I'm looking at her and the sun is shining down on us and her eyes are getting wider and wider as I'm thinking it and it's then I realize something else stupid, something else obvious.

Just cuz I can't hear any Noise from her don't mean she can't hear every word of mine.

11

THE BOOK OF NO ANSWERS

"NO!" I say quickly. "Don't listen! I'm wrong! I'm wrong! It's a mistake! I'm wrong!"

But she's backing away from me, dropping her own empty packet of fruit things, her eyes getting wider.

"No, don't–"

I step towards her but she takes an even quicker step away, her bag dropping to the ground.

"It's–" I say but what *do* you say? "I'm wrong. I'm *wrong*. I was thinking of somebody else."

Which is the stupidest thing to say of all cuz she can hear my Noise, can't she? She can see me struggling to think of something to say and even if it's coming out a big mess, she can see herself all over it and besides, I surely know by now there's no taking back something that's been sent out into the world.

Dammit. Goddam it all to hell.

"Dammit!" Manchee barks.

"Why didn't you SAY you could hear me?" I shout, ignoring that she ain't said a word since I met her.

She steps back farther, putting a hand up to her face to cover her mouth, her eyes sending asking marks at me.

I try to think of something, *anything* to make it all right, but I ain't got nothing. Just Noise with death and despair all over it.

She turns and runs, back down the hill and away from me as fast as she can.

Crap.

"Wait!" I yell, already running after her.

She's going back the way we came, down across the little field and disappearing into the trees, but I'm right behind her, Manchee after me. "Stop!" I shout after her. "Wait!"

But why should she? What kind of reason could she possibly have to wait around?

You know, she's really amazingly fast when she wants to be.

"Manchee!" I call and he understands me and shoots off after her. Not that I could really lose her, any more than she could lose me. As loud as my Noise is chasing her, her silence is just as loud up ahead, even now, even knowing she's going to die, still as silent as a grave.

"Hold on!" I shout, tripping over a root and landing hard on my elbows, which jolts every ache I've got in my body and face, but I have to get up. I have to get up and go after her. "Dammit!"

"Todd!" I hear Manchee bark up ahead, outta sight. I stumble on a bit and get my way round a big mass of shrubs and there she is, sitting on a big flat rock jutting outta the ground, her knees up to her chest, rocking back and forth, eyes wide but blank as ever.

"Todd!" Manchee barks again when he sees me, then he hops up on the rock next to her and starts sniffing her.

"Leave her alone, Manchee," I say, but he doesn't. He sniffs close at her face, licks her once or twice, then sits down next to her, leaning into her side as she rocks.

"Look," I say to her, catching my breath and knowing I don't know what to say next. "Look," I say again, but nothing else is coming.

I just stand there panting, not saying nothing, and she sits there rocking till there don't seem nothing else to do but sit down on the rock myself, keeping a distance away outta respect and safety, I guess, and so that's what I do. She rocks and I sit and I wonder what to do.

We pass a good few minutes this way, a good few minutes when we should be moving, the swamp getting on with its day around us.

Till I finally have another thought.

"I might not be right." I say it as soon as I think it. "I could be wrong, you see?" I turn to her and I start talking fast. "I got lied to about everything and you can search my Noise if you want to be sure *that's* true." I stand, talking faster. "There wasn't sposed to be another settlement. Prentisstown was sposed to be it for the whole stupid planet. But there's the other place on the map! So maybe–"

And I'm thinking and I'm thinking and I'm thinking.

"Maybe the germ was only Prentisstown. And if you ain't been in the town, then maybe yer safe. Maybe yer fine. Cuz

I sure can't hear nothing from you anything like Noise and you don't seem sick. So maybe yer okay."

She's looking at me and still rocking and I don't know what she's thinking. *Maybe* probably ain't all that comforting a word when it's *maybe yer not dying*.

I keep on thinking, letting her see my Noise as free and clear as I can. "Maybe we all caught the germ and, and, and, yeah!" I get another thought, a good one. "Maybe we cut ourselves off so the other settlement wouldn't catch it! That must be it! And so if you stayed in the swamp, then yer safe!"

She stops rocking quite so much, still looking at me, maybe believing me?

But then like some doofus who don't know when to stop, I let that thought go on, don't I? Cuz if it's true that Prentisstown was cut off, then maybe that other settlement ain't gonna be too happy to see me strolling in, are they? Maybe it was the other settlement that did the cutting off in the first place, cuz maybe Prentisstown really *was* contagious.

And if you can catch the Noise from other people, then the girl can catch it from me, can't she?

"Oh, man," I say, leaning down and putting my hands on my knees, my whole body feeling like it's falling, even tho I'm still standing up. "Oh, man."

The girl hugs herself to herself again on the rock and we're back to even worse than where we started.

This ain't fair. I am telling you this ain't fair at all. *You'll know what to do when you get to the swamp, Todd. You'll know what to do.* Yeah, thanks very bloody much for that,

Ben, thanks for all yer help and concern cuz here I am and I ain't got the first clue what to do. It ain't fair. I get kicked outta my home, I get beaten up, the people who say they care for me have been lying all these years, I gotta follow a stupid map to a settlement I never knew about, I gotta somehow read a stupid book–

The book.

I slip off the rucksack and take out the book. He said all the answers were in here, so maybe they really are. Except–

I sigh and open it up. It's all written, all words, all in my ma's handwriting, pages and pages and pages of it and I–

Well, anyway. I go back to the map, to Ben's writing on the other side, the first chance I've had to look at it in something other than torchlight, which ain't really for reading. Ben's words are lined up at the top. *Go to* are the first ones, those are definitely the first words, and then there are a coupla longer words that I don't have time to sound out yet and then a coupla big paragraphs that I *really* don't have time for right now but at the bottom of the page Ben's underlined a group of words together.

I look at the girl, still rocking, and I turn my back to her. I put my finger under the first underlined word.

Let's see. *Yow*? *You*, it's gotta be *you*. *You*. Okay, me what? *M. Moo*? *Moose*? *Moosed*? *You moosed. You moosed*? What the hell does that mean? *Wuh. Wuh. Warr. Warren*? *Tuh. Tuhee*? *Tuheem. You moosed warren tuheem*? No, wait, *them*. It's *them*. Course it's *them*, idiot.

But *You moosed warren them*?

Huh?

'Member when I said Ben tried to teach me to read?

'Member when I said I wasn't too good at it? Well–

Well, whatever.

You moosed warren them.

Idiot.

I look at the book again, flip thru the pages. Dozens of them, dozens upon dozens, all with more words in every corner, all saying nothing to me at all, no answers of any kind.

Stupid effing book.

I shove the map back inside, slam the cover shut and throw the book on the ground.

You *idiot.*

"Stupid effing book!" I say, out loud this time, kicking it into some ferns. I turn back to the girl. She's still just rocking back and forth, back and forth, and I know, I know, okay, I *know*, but it starts to piss me off. Cuz if this is a dead end, I got nothing more to offer and she ain't offering nothing neither.

My Noise starts to crackle.

"I didn't ask for this, you know," I say. She don't even look. "Hey! I'm talking to you!"

But nothing. Nothing, nothing, nothing.

"I DON'T KNOW WHAT TO DO!" I yell and stand and start stomping around, shouting till my voice scratches. "I DON'T KNOW WHAT TO DO! I DON'T KNOW WHAT TO DO!" I turn back to the girl. "I'm SORRY! I'm sorry this happened to you but I don't know what to do about it AND STOP EFFING ROCKING!"

"Yelling, Todd," Manchee barks.

"Awwghh!" I shout, putting my hands over my face. I

take them away and nothing's changed. That's the thing I'm learning about being thrown out on yer own. Nobody does *nothing* for you. If you don't change it, it don't get changed.

"We gotta keep going," I say, picking up my rucksack all angry-like. "You ain't caught it yet, so maybe just keep yer distance from me and you'll be okay. I don't know but that's all there is so that's what we gotta do."

Rock, rock, rock.

"We can't go back so we gotta go forward and that's that."

Still rocking.

"I KNOW you can HEAR me!"

She don't even flinch.

And I'm suddenly tired all over again. "Fine," I sigh. "Fine, whatever, you stay here and rock. Who cares? Who ruddy cares about anything?"

I look at the book on the ground. Stupid thing. But it's what I got so I reach down, pick it up, put it in the plastic bag, back in my rucksack, and put my rucksack back on.

"C'mon, Manchee."

"Todd?!" he barks, looking twixt me and the girl. "Can't leave, Todd!"

"She can come if she wants," I say, "but–"

I don't even really know what the *but* might be. *But* if she wants to stay here and die all alone? *But* if she wants to go back and get caught by Mr Prentiss Jr? *But* if she wants to risk catching the Noise from me and dying that way?

What a stupid world.

"Hey," I say, trying to make my voice a little gentler but my Noise is so raging there's really no point. "You know where we were heading, right? To the river twixt the mountains. Just follow it till you come to a settlement, okay?"

Maybe she's hearing me, maybe she ain't.

"I'll keep an eye out for you," I say. "I understand if you don't wanna get too close but I'll keep an eye out for you."

I stand there for another minute to see if it sinks in.

"Well," I finally say. "Nice knowing ya."

I start walking away. When I get to the big stack of shrubs, I turn back, giving her one more chance. But she ain't changed, just rocking and rocking.

So that's that then. Off I go, Manchee reluctantly on my heels, looking back as much as he can, barking my name all the time. "Todd! Todd! Leaving, Todd? Todd! Can't leave, Todd!" I finally smack him on the rump. "Ow, Todd?"

"I don't know, Manchee, so quit asking."

We make our way back thru the trees to where the ground dries out, to the clearing and up the little bluff where we ate our breakfast and looked at the beautiful day and I had my brilliant deducshun about her death.

The little bluff where her bag still lies on the ground.

"Oh, god*dam* it!"

I look at it for a second and it's one thing after another, ain't it? I mean, do I take it back to her? Do I just hope she finds it? Will I put her in danger if I do? Will I put her in danger if I *don't*?

The sun's well up now and the sky as blue as fresh meat. I put my hands on my hips and take a long look round like men do when they're thinking. I look at the horizon, look back the way we came, the mist mostly burnt off by now and the whole swamp forest covered in sunlight. From the top of the bluff, you can see out over it, over where we drove our feet into oblivion by walking it all. If it were clear enough and you had powerful enough binos you could probably see all the way back to town.

Powerful binos.

I look down at her bag on the ground there.

I'm reaching for it when I think I hear something. Like a whisper. My Noise leaps and I look up to see if the girl's following me out after all. Which makes me more relieved than I want to say.

But it ain't the girl. I hear it again. A whisper. More than one whisper. Like the wind is carrying whispering on it.

"Todd?" Manchee says, sniffing the air.

I squint into the sunlight to look back over the swamp.

Is there something out there?

I grab the girl's bag and look thru it for the binos. There's all kinds of neat crap in there but I take the binos out and look thru them.

Just swamp is all I see, the tops of swamp trees, little clearings of swampy bits of water, the river eventually starting to form itself again. I take the binos away from my face and look them over. There are little buttons everywhere and I push a few and realize I can make everything look even closer. I do that a coupla times and I'm sure I can hear whispering now. I'm sure of it.

I find the gash in the swamp, the ditch, find the wreckage of her ship, but there's nothing there except what we left. I look over the top of the binos, wondering if I see movement. I look thru them again, a little nearer to us where some trees are rustling.

But that's only the wind, ain't it?

I scan back and forth, pressing buttons to get closer and farther away, but I keep coming back to those rustling trees. I keep the binos trained on a kinda open, gully-type thing twixt me and them.

I keep the binos there.

I keep the binos watching, my guts twisting as maybe I'm hearing whispering, maybe I ain't.

I keep watching.

Till the rustling reaches the clearing and I see the Mayor himself come outta the trees on horseback, leading other men, also on horses.

And they're heading right this way.

12

THE BRIDGE

THE MAYOR. Not just his son but actually the *Mayor*. With his clean hat and his clean face and his clean clothes and his shiny boots and his upright pose. We don't never actually get to see him much in Prentisstown, not no more, not if yer not in his close little circle, but when you do, he always looks like this, even thru a pair of binos. Like he knows how to take care of hisself and you don't.

I push some more buttons till I'm as close as I can get. There's five of them, no, six, the men whose Noise you hear doing those freaky exercises in the Mayor's house. I AM THE CIRCLE AND THE CIRCLE IS ME, that kinda thing. There's Mr Collins, Mr MacInerny, Mr O'Hare, and Mr Morgan, all on horses, too, itself a rare sight cuz horses are hard to keep alive on New World and the Mayor guards his personal herd with a whole raft of men with guns.

And there's Mr bloody Prentiss Jr, riding up next to his father, wearing a shiner from where Cillian hit him. Good.

But then I realize that means whatever happened at the farm is definitely over with. Whatever happened to Ben and Cillian is done. I put the binos down for a sec and swallow it away.

I put the binos back up. The group's stopped for a minute and are talking to each other, looking over a large piece of paper that's gotta be a way better map than mine and–

Oh, man.

Oh, man, you gotta be *kidding*.

Aaron.

Aaron comes walking outta the trees behind 'em.

Stinking, stupid, rutting, effing, bloody Aaron.

Most of his head is wrapped in bandages but he's pacing the ground a little way back from the Mayor, waving his hands in the air, looking like he's probably preaching even if no one looks like listening.

HOW? How could he have lived? Doesn't he ever ruddy *DIE*?

It's my fault. My stupid effing fault. Cuz I'm a coward. I'm a weak and stupid coward and cuz of that Aaron's alive and cuz of that he's leading the Mayor thru the ruddy swamp after us. Cuz I didn't kill him, he's coming to kill me.

I feel sick. I bend over double and hold my stomach, moaning a bit. My blood is charging so hard I hear Manchee creep a little ways away from me.

"It's my fault, Manchee," I say. "I did this."

"Your fault," he says, confused and just repeating what I said but right on the money, ain't he?

I make myself look thru the binos again and I see the

Mayor call Aaron over. Since men started being able to hear their thoughts, Aaron thinks animals are unclean and won't go near 'em so it takes the Mayor a coupla tries but eventually Aaron comes tromping over to look at the map. He listens while the Mayor asks him something.

And then he looks up.

Looks up thru the swamp trees and sky.

Looks up to this hilltop.

Looks right at me.

He can't see me. No way. Can he? Not without binos like the girl's and I don't see any on the men, never saw *anything* like 'em in Prentisstown. Gotta be. He can't see me.

But like a great pitiless thing he raises his arm and points, points it directly at me, like I'm sitting across a table from him.

I'm running before I can even think, running back down the bluff and back to the girl as fast as I can, reaching behind me and pulling out my knife, Manchee barking up a storm on my heels. I get into the trees and down and round the big mess of shrubs and she's still sitting on the rock but at least she looks up as I run to her.

"Come on!" I say, grabbing her arm. "We gotta go!"

She pulls back away from me but I don't let go.

"No!" I shout. "We have to go! NOW!"

She starts hitting out with her fists, clonking me a coupla times on the face.

But I ain't letting go.

"LISTEN!" I say and I open up my Noise for her. She hits me once more but then she's looking, looking at my Noise as it comes, seeing the pictures of what's waiting for us in the swamp. Check that, what's *not* waiting for us, what's making every effort to come get us. Aaron, who won't die, bending all his thoughts to finding us and coming this time with men on horseback. Who are a lot faster than we are.

The girl's face squishes up, like she's in the worst pain ever and she opens her mouth like she's going to yell but nothing comes out. Still nothing. Still no Noise, no sound, no nothing at all coming from her.

I just don't get it.

"I don't know what's ahead," I say. "I don't know nothing about nothing but whatever it is, it's gotta be better than what's behind. It's *gotta* be."

And as she hears me, her face changes. It clears up to almost blankness again and she presses her lips together.

"Go! Go! Go!" Manchee barks.

She holds out her hand for her bag. I hand it to her. She stands, shoves the binos in, loops it over her shoulder and looks me in the eye.

"Okay, then," I say.

And so that's how I set off running full out towards a river for the second time in two days, Manchee with me again and this time a girl on my heels.

Well, *past* my heels most of the time, she's ruddy fast, she is.

We go back up the hill and down the other side, the last of the swamp really starting to disappear around us and turning into regular woods. The ground gets way firmer and easier to run on and it's sloping more downhill than it is up, which may be the first piece of luck we've had. We start

117

catching the proper river in brief glances off to our left side as we go. My rucksack's bashing me in the back as I run and I'm gasping for breath.

But I'm holding my knife.

I swear. I swear right now before God or whatever. If Aaron ever comes in my reach again, I will kill him. I ain't hesitating again. No way. No how. I ain't. I swear to you.

I will kill him.

I'll ruddy well kill him.

You just watch me.

The ground we're running on is getting a bit steeper side to side, taking us thru leafier, lighter trees and first closer to the river and then away from it again and again as we run. Manchee's tongue is hanging out of his mouth in a big pant, bouncing along as we go. My heart's thumping a million beats and my legs are about to fall off my body but still we run.

We veer close to the water again and I call out, "Wait." The girl, who's got pretty far in front of me, stops. I run to the river's edge, take a swift look round for crocs, then lean down and scoop up a few handfuls of water into my mouth. Tastes sweeter than it really should. Who knows what's in it, coming outta the swamp, but you gotta drink. I feel the girl's silence lean down next to me as she drinks, too. I scoot a little ways away. Manchee laps up his share and you can hear us all taking in great raking breaths between slurps.

I look up to where we're going, wiping my mouth. Next to the river is starting to become too rocky and steep to run on and I can see a path cutting its way up from the riverbank, going along the top of the canyon.

I blink, as I realize.

I can see a path. Someone's cut a *path*.

The girl turns and looks. The path carries up and along as the river drops below it, getting deeper and faster and turning into rapids. Someone *made* that path.

"It's gotta be the way to the other settlement," I say. "Gotta be."

And then, in the distance, we hear hoofbeats. Faint, but on their way.

I don't say another word cuz we're already on our feet and running up the path. The river falls farther and farther away beneath us and the larger mountain rears up on the other side of the river. On our side there's a thick forest starting to stretch back from the clifftops. The path's clearly been cut so men would have a place to travel down the river.

It's more than wide enough for horses. More than wide enough for five or six, in fact.

It ain't a path at all, I realize. It's a *road*.

We fly along it as it bends and turns, the girl ahead, then me, then Manchee, running along.

Till I nearly bump into her and knock her off the trail.

"What're you doing?!" I shout, grabbing onto her arms to keep us both from falling off the cliff, trying to keep the knife from accidentally killing her.

And then I see what she's seeing.

A bridge, way on up ahead of us. It goes from one cliff edge to the other, crossing the river what's gotta be thirty, forty metres above it. The road or path or whatever stops on our side at the bridge and becomes rock and dense forest beyond. There's nowhere to go but the bridge.

The first shades of an idea start to form.

The hoofbeats are louder now. I look back and see clouds of dust rising from where the Mayor is following.

"Come on!" I say, running past her, making for the bridge as fast as I can. We pound down the clifftop path, kicking up our own dust, Manchee's ears flattened back, running fast. We get there and it's way more than just a footbridge, two metres wide at least. It looks like mostly rope tied into wooden stakes driven into the rock at either end, with tight wooden planks running all the way to the other side.

I test it with my foot but it's so sturdy it don't even bounce. More than enough to take me and the girl and a dog.

More than enough to take men on horseback who wanted to cross it, in fact.

Whoever built it, meant it to last.

I look back again down the river at where we've run. More dust, louder hoofbeats, and the whispers of men's Noise on its way. I think I hear young Todd but I'm only imagining it cuz Aaron'll be way behind on foot.

But I do see what I wanna see: this bridge is the only place where you can cross the river, from back where we've run to miles on farther ahead as you look.

Maybe another piece of luck is coming our way.

"Let's go," I say. We run across and it's so well-made you can't even see twixt the gaps in the planks of wood. We might as well still be on the path. We get to the other side and the girl stops and turns to me, no doubt seeing my idea in my Noise, already waiting for me to act.

The knife is still in my hand. Power at the end of my arm.

Maybe at last I can do some good with it.

I look over where this end of the bridge is tied to the stakes in the rock. The knife has a fearsome serrated edge on part of the blade, so I choose the likeliest looking knot and start sawing on it.

I saw and saw.

The hoofbeats get louder, echoing down the canyon.

But if there suddenly *ain't* no bridge–

I saw some more.

And some more.

And some more.

And I'm just not making no progress at all.

"What the hell?" I say, looking at where I been cutting. There's hardly a scratch there. I touch the serration on the knife with my finger and it pricks and bleeds almost immediately. I look closer at the rope. It looks like it's coated in some kind of thin resin.

Some kind of ruddy tough, steel-like resin that ain't for cutting.

"I don't believe this," I say, looking up at the girl.

She's got her binos to her eyes, looking back the way we came down the river.

"Can you see 'em?"

I look down the river but you don't need binos at all. You can see 'em coming with yer own two eyes. Small but growing larger and not slowing down, thundering their hooves like there's no tomorrow.

We got three minutes. Maybe four.

Crap.

I start sawing again, fast and strong as I can, forcing my arm back and forth hard as I can make it, sweat popping out all over the place and new aches forming to keep all the old ones company. I saw and saw and saw, dripping water down my nose onto the knife.

"C'mon, c'mon," I say thru my teeth.

I lift the knife. I've managed to get thru one tiny little bit of resin on one tiny little knot on one huge effing bridge.

"Goddam it!" I spit.

I saw some more and more and more. And more and more than that, sweat running into my eyes and starting to sting.

"Todd!" Manchee barks, his alarm spilling out all over the place.

I saw more. And more.

But the only thing that happens is that the knife catches and I smash my knuckles into the stake, bloodying them.

"GODDAM IT!" I scream, throwing the knife down. It bounces along, stopping just at the girl's feet. "GODDAM IT ALL!"

Cuz that's it, ain't it?

That's the end of everything.

Our one stupid chance that wasn't a chance at all.

We can't outrun the horses and we can't cut down a stupid mega-road bridge and we're going to be caught and Ben and Cillian are dead and we're going to be killed ourselves and the world is going to end and that's it.

A redness comes over my Noise, like nothing I ever felt before, sudden and raw, like a red-hot brand pressing into my own self, a burning bright redness of everything that's made me hurt and keeps on hurting, a roaring rage of the unfairness and the injustice and the lies.

Of everything coming back to *one* thing.

I raise my eyes up to the girl's and she steps back from the force of it.

"*You*," I say and there ain't gonna be no stopping me. "This is all *you*! If you hadn't shown up in that ruddy swamp, none of this woulda happened! I'd be home RIGHT NOW! I'd be tending my effing sheep and living in my effing house and sleeping in my own EFFING BED!"

Except I don't say "effing".

"But oh NO," I shout, getting louder. "Here's YOU! Here's YOU and yer SILENCE! And the whole world gets SCREWED!"

I don't realize I'm walking towards her till I see her stepping back. But she just looks back at me.

And I don't hear a goddam thing.

"You're NOTHING!" I scream, stepping forward some more. "NOTHING! You're nothing but EMPTINESS! There's nothing in you! You're EMPTY and NOTHING and we're gonna die FOR NOTHING!"

I have my fists clenched so hard my nails are cutting into my palms. I'm so furious, my Noise raging so loud, so *red*, that I have to raise my fists to her, I have to hit her, I have to beat her, I have to make her ruddy silence STOP before it SWALLOWS ME AND THE WHOLE EFFING WORLD!

I take my fist and punch myself hard in the face.

I do it again, hitting where my eye is swollen from Aaron.

123

And a third time, splitting open the cut on my lip from where Aaron hit me yesterday morning.

You *fool*, you *worthless, effing fool*.

I do it again, hard enough to knock me off balance. I fall and catch myself on my hands and spit out some blood onto the path.

I look up at the girl, breathing hard.

Nothing. Just looking back at me and nothing.

We both turn to look across the river. They've got to the bit where they can see the bridge clearly. See *us* clearly on the other side. We can see the faces of the men as they ride. Hear the chatter of their Noise as it flies up the river at us. Mr MacInerny, the Mayor's best horseman, is in the lead, the Mayor riding behind, looking as calm as if it was nothing more than a Sunday ride.

We got maybe a minute, probably less.

I turn back to the girl, trying to stand, but I'm so tired. So, so tired. "We might as well run," I say, spitting out more blood. "We might as well try."

And I see her face change.

Her mouth opens wide, her eyes, too, and suddenly she yanks her bag out in front of her and shoves her hand in it.

"What're you doing?" I say.

She takes out the campfire box, looking all around her till I see her see a good sized rock. She sets the box down and raises up the rock.

"No, wait, we could use–"

She brings down the rock and the box cracks. She picks it up and twists it hard, making it crack some more. It starts to leak some kind of fluid. She moves to the bridge and starts flinging fluid all over the knots on the closest stake, shaking out the last drops into a puddle at the base.

The riders are coming up to the bridge, coming up, coming up, coming up–

"Hurry!" I say.

The girl turns to me, telling me with her hands to get back. I scrabble back a little ways, grabbing Manchee by his scruff and taking him with me. She steps back as far as she can, holding out the remains of the box at arm's length and pressing a button on it. I hear a clicking sound. She tosses the box in the air and jumps back towards me.

The horses reach the bridge–

The girl lands almost on top of me and we watch as the campfire box falls–

Falls–

Falls–

Towards the little puddle of liquid, clicking as it goes–

Mr MacInerny's horse puts a hoof on the bridge to cross it–

The campfire box lands in the puddle–

Clicks one more time–

Then–

WHOOOOOMP!!!!

The air is sucked outta my lungs as a fireball WAY bigger than what you'd think for that little amount of fluid makes the world quiet for a second and then–

BOOM!!!!!

It blasts away the ropes and the stake, spraying fiery splinters all over us and obliterating all thought, Noise and sound.

When we can look up again, the bridge is already so much on fire it's starting to lean to one side and we see Mr MacInerny's horse rear up and stumble, trying to back up into four or five more oncoming horses.

The flames roar a weird bright green and the sudden heat's incredible, like the worst sunburn ever and I think we're gonna catch fire ourselves when this end of the bridge just falls right away, taking Mr MacInerny and his horse with it. We sit up and watch them fall and fall and fall into the river below, way too far to ever live thru it. The bridge is still attached at their end and it slaps the facing cliff but it's burning so fierce it won't be no time at all before the whole thing is just ash. The Mayor and Mr Prentiss Jr and the others all have to back their horses away from it.

The girl crawls away from me and we lay there a second, just breathing and coughing, trying to stop being dazed.

Holy crap.

"Y'all right?" I say to Manchee, still held by my hand.

"Fire, Todd!" he barks.

"Yeah," I cough. "Big fire. *You* all right?" I say to the girl, who's still crouching, still coughing. "Man, what was in that thing?"

But of course she don't say nothing.

"TODD HEWITT!" I hear from across the canyon.

I look up. It's the Mayor, shouting his first words ever to me in person, thru sheets of smoke and heat that make him look all wavy.

"We're not finished, young Todd," he calls, over the crackle of the burning bridge and the roar of the water below. "Not by a long way."

And he's calm and still ruddy clean and looking like there's no way he's not gonna get what he wants.

I stand up, hold out my arm and give him two fingers but he's already disappearing behind big clouds of smoke.

I cough and spit blood again. "We gotta keep moving," I say, coughing some more. "Maybe they'll turn back, maybe there's no other way across, but we shouldn't wait to find out."

I see the knife in the dust. Shame comes right quick, like a new pain all its own. The things I said. I reach down and pick it up and put it back in its sheath.

The girl's still got her head down, coughing to herself. I pick up her bag for her and hold it out for her to take.

"Come on," I say. "We can at least get away from the smoke."

She looks up at me.

I look back at her.

My face burns and not from the heat.

"I'm sorry." I look away from her, from her eyes and face, blank and quiet as ever.

I turn back up the path.

"Viola," I hear.

I spin around, look at her.

"What?" I say.

She's looking back at me.

She's opening her mouth.

She's talking.

"My name," she says. "It's Viola."

PART II

PART III

13

VIOLA

I DON'T SAY NOTHING to this for a minute. Neither does she. The fire burns, the smoke rises, Manchee's tongue hangs out in a stunned pant, till finally I say, "Viola."

She nods.

"Viola," I say again.

She don't nod this time.

"I'm Todd," I say.

"I know," she says.

She's not quite meeting my eye.

"So you can talk then?" I say, but all she does is look at me again quickly and then away. I turn to the still burning bridge, to the smoke turning into a fogbank twixt us and the other side of the river, which I don't know if it makes me feel safer or not, if not seeing the Mayor and his men is better than seeing them. "That was–" I start to say, but she's getting up and holding out her hand for her bag.

I realize I'm still holding it. I hand it to her and she takes it.

"We should go on," she says. "Away from here."

Her accent's funny, different from mine, different from anyone in Prentisstown's. Her lips make different kinds of outlines for the letters, like they're swooping down on them from above, pushing them into shape, telling them what to say. In Prentisstown, everyone talks like they're sneaking up on their words, ready to club them from behind.

Manchee's just in awe of her. "Away," he says lowly, staring up at her like she's made of food.

There's this moment now where it feels like I could start asking her stuff, like now she's talking, I could just hit her with every asking I can think of about who she is, where she's from, what happened, and them askings are all over my Noise, flying at her like pellets, but there's so much stuff wanting to come outta my mouth that nothing is and so my mouth don't move and she's holding her bag over her shoulder and looking at the ground and then she's walking past me, past Manchee, on up the trail.

"Hey," I say.

She stops and turns back.

"Wait for me," I say.

I pick up my rucksack, hooking it back over my shoulders. I press my hand against the knife in its sheath against my lower back. I make the rucksack comfortable with a shrug, say "C'mon, Manchee", and off we go up the trail, following the girl.

On this side of the river the path makes a slow turn away from the cliffside, heading into what looks like a landscape of scrub and brush, making its way around and away from the larger mountain, looming up at us on the left.

At the place where the trail turns, we both stop and look back without saying that we're gonna. The bridge is still burning like you wouldn't believe, hanging on the opposite cliff like a waterfall on fire, flames having leapt up the entire length of it, angry and greenish yellow. The smoke's so thick, it's still impossible to tell what the Mayor and his men are doing, have done, if they're gone or waiting or what. There could be a whisper of Noise coming thru but there could also *not* be a whisper of Noise, what with the fire blazing and the wood popping and the whitewater below. As we watch, the fire finishes its business on the stakes on the other side of the river and with a great *snap*, the burning bridge falls, falls, falls, clattering against the cliffside, splashing into the river, sending up more clouds of smoke and steam, making everything even foggier.

"What was in that box?" I say to the girl.

She looks at me, opens her mouth, but then closes it again, turning away.

"It's okay," I say. "I'm not gonna hurt ya."

She looks at me again and my Noise is full of just a few minutes ago when I *was* just about to hurt her, when I was just about to–

Anyway.

We don't say no more. She turns back onto the path and me and Manchee follow her into the scrub.

Knowing she can speak don't help with the silence none. Knowing she's got words in her head don't mean nothing if you can only hear 'em when she talks. Looking at the back of her head as she's walking, I still feel my heart pull towards her silence, still feel like I've lost something terrible, something so sad I want to weep.

"Weep," Manchee barks.

The back of her head just keeps on walking.

The path is still pretty wide, wide enough for horses, but the terrain around us is getting rockier, the path twistier. We can hear the river down below us to our right now but it feels like we're tending away from it a bit, getting ourselves deep into an area that feels almost walled, rockface sometimes coming up on both sides, like we're walking at the bottom of a box. Little prickly firs grow out of every crevice and yellow vines with thorns wrapping themselves around the firs' trunks and you can see and hear yellow razor lizards hissing at us as we pass. **Bite!** they say, as a threat. **Bite! Bite!**

Anything you might want to touch here would cut you.

After maybe twenty, thirty minutes the path gets to a bit where it widens out, where a few real trees start growing again, where the forest looks like it might be about to restart, where there's grass and stones low enough for sitting on. Which is what we do. Sit.

I take some dried mutton outta my rucksack and use the knife to cut strips for me, for Manchee, and for the girl. She takes them without saying anything and we sit quietly apart and eat for a minute.

I am Todd Hewitt, I think, closing my eyes and chewing, embarrassed for my Noise now, now that I know she can hear it, now that I know she can think about it.

Think about it in secret.

I am Todd Hewitt.

I will be a man in twenty-nine days' time.

Which is true, I realize, opening my eyes. Time goes on, even when yer not looking.

I take another bite. "I ain't never heard the name Viola before," I say after a while, looking only at the ground, only at my strip of mutton. She don't say nothing so I glance up in spite of myself.

To find her looking back at me.

"What?" I say.

"Your face," she says.

I frown. "What about my face?"

She makes both of her hands into fists and mimes punching herself with them.

I feel myself redden. "Yeah, well."

"And from before," she says. "From–" She stops.

"Aaron," I say.

"Aaron," Manchee barks and the girl flinches a little.

"That was his name," she says. "Wasn't it?"

I nod, chewing on my mutton. "Yep," I say. "That's his name."

"He never said it out loud. But I knew what it was."

"Welcome to New World." I take another bite, having to tear an extra-chewy bit off with my teeth, which catches one sore spot among many in my mouth. "Ow." I spit out the bit of mutton and a whole lot of extra blood.

The girl watches me spit and then sets down her food. She picks up her bag, opens it, and finds a little blue box, slightly larger than the green campfire one. She presses a button on the front to open it and takes out what looks like a white plastic cloth and a little metal scalpel. She gets up from her rock and walks over to me with them.

I'm still sitting but I lean back when she brings her hands to my face.

"Bandages," she says.

"I've got my own."

"These are better."

I lean back farther. "Yer…" I say, blowing out air thru my nose. "Yer quiet kinda…" I shake my head a little.

"Bothers you?"

"Yes."

"I know," she says. "Hold still."

She looks closer at the area around my swollen eye and then cuts off a piece of bandage with the little scalpel. She's about to put it over my eye but I can't help it and I move back from her touch. She don't say nothing, just keeps her hands up, like she's waiting. I take a deep breath, close my eyes and offer up my face.

I feel the bandage touch the swollen area and immediately it gets cooler, immediately the pain starts to edge back, like it's all being swept away by feathers. She puts another one on a cut I have at my hairline and her fingers brush my face as she puts another one just below my lower lip. It all feels so good I haven't even opened my eyes yet.

"I don't have anything for your teeth," she says.

"'S okay," I say, almost whispering it. "Man, these *are* better than mine."

"They're partially alive," she says. "Synthetic human tissue. When you're healed, they die."

"Uh-huh," I say, acting like I might know what that means.

There's a longer silence, long enough to make me open my eyes again. She's stepped back, back to a rock she can sit down on, watching me, watching my face.

We wait. Cuz it seems like we should.

And we should cuz after a little bit of waiting, she begins to talk.

"We crashed," she starts quietly, looking away. Then she clears her throat and says it again. "We crashed. There was a fire and we were flying low and we thought we'd be okay but something went wrong with the safety flumes and–" She holds open her hands to explain what follows the *and*. "We crashed."

She stops.

"Was that yer ma and pa?" I ask, after a bit.

But she just looks up into the sky, blue and spare, with clouds that look like bones. "And when the sun came up," she says, "that man came."

"Aaron."

"And it was so weird. He would shout and he would scream and then he'd *leave*. And I'd try to run away." She folds her arms. "I *kept* trying so he wouldn't find me, but I was going in circles and wherever I hid, there he'd be, I don't know how, until I found these sort of hut things."

"The Spackle buildings," I say but she ain't really listening.

She looks at me. "Then you came." She looks at Manchee. "You and your dog that talks."

"Manchee!" Manchee barks.

Her face is pale and when she meets my eyes again, her own have gone wet. "What is this place?" she asks, her voice kinda thick. "Why do the animals talk? Why do I hear your

137

voice when your mouth isn't moving? Why do I hear your voice a whole bunch over, piled on top of each other like there's nine million of you talking at once? Why do I see pictures of other things when I look at you? Why could I see what that man…"

She fades off. She draws her knees up to her chest and hugs them. I feel like I better start talking right quick or she's gonna start rocking again.

"We're settlers," I say. She looks up at this, still hugging her knees but at least not rocking. "We *were* settlers," I continue. "Landed here to found New World about twenty years ago or so. But there were aliens here. The Spackle. And they … didn't want us." I'm telling her what every boy in Prentisstown knows, the history even the dumbest farm boy like yours truly knows by heart. "Men tried for years to make peace but the Spackle weren't having it. And so war started."

She looks down again at the word *war*. I keep talking.

"And the way the Spackle fought, see, was with germs, with diseases. That was their weapons. They released germs that did things. One of them we think was meant to kill all our livestock but instead it just made every animal able to talk." I look at Manchee. "Which ain't as much fun as it sounds." I look back at the girl. "And another was the Noise."

I wait. She don't say nothing. But we both sorta know what's coming cuz we been here before, ain't we?

I take a deep breath. "And that one killed half the men and all the women, including my ma, and it made the thoughts of the men who survived no longer secret to the rest of the world."

She hides her chin behind her knees. "Sometimes I can hear it clearly," she says. "Sometimes I can tell exactly what you're thinking. But only sometimes. Most of the time it's just–"

"Noise," I say.

She nods. "And the aliens?"

"There ain't no more aliens."

She nods again. We sit for a minute, ignoring the obvious till it can't be ignored no longer.

"Am I going to die?" she asks quietly. "Is it going to kill me?"

The words sound different in her accent but they mean the same damn thing and my Noise can only say *probably* but I make it so my mouth says, "I don't know."

She watches me for more.

"I really *don't* know," I say, kinda meaning it. "If you'd asked me last week, I'd have been sure, but today–" I look down at my rucksack, at the book hiding inside. "I don't know." I look back at her. "I hope not."

But probably, says my Noise. *Probably yer gonna die,* and tho I try to cover it up with other Noise it's such an unfair thing it's hard not to have it right at the front.

"I'm sorry," I say.

She don't say nothing.

"But maybe if we get to the next settlement–" I say, but I don't finish cuz I don't know the answer. "You ain't sick yet. That's something."

"You must warn them," she says, down into her knees.

I look up sharply. "What?"

"Earlier, when you were trying to read that book–"

"I wasn't *trying*," I say, my voice a little bit louder all of a sudden.

"I could see the words in your whatever," she says, "and it's 'You must warn them'."

"I know that! I know what it says."

Of course it's bloody *You must warn them*. Course it is. Idiot.

The girl says, "It seemed like you were–"

"I know how to read."

She holds up her hands. "Okay."

"I do!"

"I'm just saying–"

"Well, *stop* just saying," I frown, my Noise roiling enough to get Manchee on his feet. I get to my feet as well. I pick up the rucksack and put it back on. "We should get moving."

"Warn who?" asks the girl, still sitting. "About what?"

I don't get to answer (even tho I don't *know* the answer) cuz there's a loud click above us, a loud clang-y click that in Prentisstown would mean one thing.

A rifle being cocked.

And standing on a rock above us, there's someone with a freshly-cocked rifle in both hands, looking down the sight, pointing it right at us.

"What's foremost in my mind at this partickalar juncture," says a voice rising from behind the gun, "is what do two little pups think they're doing a-burning down my bridge?"

14

THE WRONG END
OF A GUN

"Gun! Gun! Gun!" Manchee starts barking,
hopping back and forth in the dust.

"I'd quieten down yer beastie there," says the rifle, his
face obscured by looking down the sight straight at us.
"Wouldn't want anything to happen to it, now wouldja?"

"Quiet, Manchee!" I say.

He turns to me. "Gun, Todd?" he barks. "Bang, bang!"

"I know. Shut up."

He stops barking and it's quiet.

Aside from my Noise, it's *quiet*.

"I do believe I sent out an asking to a partickalar pair
of pups," says the voice, "and I am a-waiting on my
answer."

I look back at the girl. She shrugs her shoulders, tho I
notice we both have our hands up. "What?" I say back up to
the rifle.

The rifle gives an angry grunt. "I'm asking," it says, "what exactly gives ye permisshun to go a-burning down other people's bridges?"

I don't say nothing. Neither does the girl.

"D'ye think this is a *stick* I'm a-pointing at ye?" The rifle bobs up and down once.

"We were being chased," I say, for lack of nothing else.

"Chased, were ye?" says the rifle. "Who was a-chasing ye?"

And I don't know how to answer this. Would the truth be more dangerous than a lie? Is the rifle on the side of the Mayor? Would we be bounty? Or would rifle man have even *heard* of Prentisstown?

The world's a dangerous place when you don't know enough.

Like why is it so quiet?

"Oh, I heard of Prentisstown, all right," says the rifle, reading my Noise with unnerving clarity and cocking the gun again, making it ready to shoot. "And if that's where yer from–"

Then the girl speaks up and says that thing that suddenly makes me think of her as *Viola* and not *the girl* any more.

"He saved my life."

I saved her life.

Says Viola.

Funny how that works.

"Did he now?" says the rifle. "And how do you know he don't aim to just be a-saving it for himself?"

The girl, Viola, looks at me, her forehead creased. It's my turn to shrug.

"But no." The rifle's voice changes. "No, huh-uh, no, I'm not a-seeing that in ye, am I, boy? Cuz yer just a boy pup still, ain't ye?"

I swallow. "I'll be a man in 29 days."

"Not something to be proud of, pup. Not where *yer* from."

And then he lowers the gun away from his face.

And that's why it's so quiet.

He's a woman.

He's a grown woman.

He's an *old* woman.

"I'll thank ye kindly to call me *she*," the woman says, still pointing the rifle at us from chest level. "And not so old I won't still shoot ye."

She's looking at us more closely now, reading me up and down, seeing right into my Noise with a skill I've only ever felt in Ben. Her face is making all kindsa shapes, like she's considering me, like Cillian's face does when he tries to read me to see if I'm lying. Tho this woman ain't got no Noise at all so she might be singing a song in there for all I know.

She turns to Viola and pauses for another long look.

"As pups go," she says, looking back at me, "ye are as easy to read as a newborn, m'boy." She turns her face to Viola. "But ye, wee girl, yer story's not a usual one, is it?"

"I'd be happy to tell you all about it if you'd stop pointing a gun at us," Viola says.

This is so surprising even Manchee looks up. I turn to Viola with my mouth open.

We hear a chuckle from up on the rock. The old woman

is laughing to herself. Her clothes seem a real dusty leather, worn and creased for years and years with a rimmed hat and boots for ignoring mud. Like she ain't nothing more than a farmer, really.

She's still pointing the gun at us, tho.

"Ye were a-running from Prentisstown, were ye?" she asks, looking into my Noise again. There's no point in hiding it so I go ahead and put forward what we were running from, what happened at the bridge, who was chasing us. She sees all of it, I know she does, but all I see her do is wrinkle up her lips and squint her eyes a bit.

"Well, now," she says, crooking the rifle in her arm and starting to make her way down from the rocks to where we're standing. "I can't rightly say that I'm not peeved bout ye blowing up my bridge. Heard the boom all the way back at the farm, oh, yeah." She steps off the last rock and stands a little ways away from us, the force of her grown-up quiet so large I feel myself stepping back without even knowing I decided to do it. "But the only place it led to ain't been worth a-going to for a decade nor more. Only left it up outta hope." She looks us over again. "Who's to say I weren't right?"

We still have our hands in the air cuz she ain't making much sense, is she?

"I'll ask ye this once," the woman says, lifting the rifle again. "Am I gonna need this?"

I exchange a glance with Viola.

"No," I say.

"No, mam," Viola says.

Mam? I think.

144

"It's like *sir*, bonny boy." The woman slings the rifle over her shoulder by its strap. "For if yer a-talking to a lady." She squats down to Manchee's level. "And who might ye be, pup?"

"Manchee!" he barks.

"Oh, yeah, that's definitely who ye be, innit?" says the woman, giving him a vigorous rubbing. "And ye two pups?" she asks, not looking up. "What might yer good mothers have dubbed ye?"

Me and Viola exchange another glance. It seems like a price, giving up our names, but maybe it's a fair exchange for the gun being lowered.

"I'm Todd. That's Viola."

"As surely true as the sun a-coming up," says the woman, having succeeded in getting Manchee on his back for a tummy rub.

"Is there another way over that river?" I ask. "Another bridge? Cuz those men—"

"I'm Mathilde," the old woman interrupts, "but people who call me that don't know me, so you can call me Hildy and one day ye may even earn the right to shake my hand."

I look at Viola again. How can you tell if someone with no Noise is crazy?

The old woman cackles. "Yer a funny one there, boy." She stands up from Manchee who rolls back over and stares at her, already a worshipper. "And to answer yer asking, there's shallow crossings a couple days' travelling upstream but there ain't no bridges for a good distance more either way."

She turns her gaze back to me, steady and clear, a small

145

smile on her lips. She's gotta be reading my Noise again but I can't feel no prodding like I do when men try it.

And the way she keeps on looking I start to realize a few things, put a few things together. It must be right that Prentisstown was quarantined cuz of the Noise germ, huh? Cuz here's a grown-up woman who ain't dead from it, who's looking at me friendly but keeping her distance, a woman ready to greet strangers from my direkshun with a rifle.

And if I'm contagious that means Viola's probably definitely caught it by now, could be dying as we speak, and that I'm probably definitely not gonna be welcome in the settlement, probably definitely gonna be told to keep way way out and that that's probably the end of that, ain't it? My journey ended before I even found anywhere to go.

"Oh, ye won't be welcome in the settlement," the woman says. "No probably about it. But," she winks at me, actually winks, "what ye don't know won't kill ye."

"Wanna bet?" I say.

She turns back and steps up the rocks the way she came. We just watch her go till she gets to the top and turns around again.

"Ye all a-coming?" she says, as if she's invited us along and we're keeping her waiting.

I look at Viola. She calls up to the woman, "We're meant to be heading for the settlement." Viola looks at me again. "Welcome or not."

"Oh, ye'll get there," says the woman, "but what ye two pups need first is a good sleeping and a good feeding. Any blind man could see that."

The idea of sleep and hot food is so tempting, I forget

for a second that she ever pointed a gun at us. But only for a second. Cuz there's other things to think about. I make the decision for us. "We should keep on the road," I say to Viola quietly.

"I don't even know where we're going," she says, also quietly. "Do you? Honestly?"

"Ben said—"

"Ye two pups come to my farm, get some good eatings in ye, sleep on a bed – tho it ain't soft, I grant ye that – and in the morning, we'll go to the *settlement*." And that's how she says it, opening her eyes wide on it, like a word to make fun of us for calling it that.

We still don't move.

"Look at it thusly," the old woman says. "I got me a gun." She waves it. "But I'm *asking* ye to come."

"Why don't we go with her?" Viola whispers. "Just to see."

My Noise rises a little in surprise. "See what?"

"I could use a bath," she says. "I could use some sleep."

"So could I," I say, "but there's men who're after us who probably ain't gonna let one fallen bridge stop them. And besides, we don't know nothing about her. She could be a killer for all we know."

"She seems okay." Viola glances up at the woman. "A little crazy, but she doesn't seem *dangerous* crazy."

"She don't *seem* anything." I feel a little vexed, if I'm honest. "People without Noise don't seem like nothing at all."

Viola looks at me, her brows suddenly creased and her jaw set a little.

"Well, not *you*, obviously," I say.

"Every time…" she starts to say but then she just shakes her head.

"Every time what?" I whisper, but Viola just scrunches her eyes and turns to the woman.

"Hold on," she says, her voice sounding annoyed. "Let me get my stuff."

"Hey!" I say. What happened to her remembering I saved her life? "Wait a minute. We gotta follow the road. We gotta get to the settlement."

"Roads is never the fastest way to get nowhere," the woman says. "Don't ye know that?"

Viola don't say nothing, just picks up her bag, frowning all over the place. She's ready to go, ready to head off with the first quiet person she sees, ready to leave me behind at the first sweet beckoning.

And she's missing the thing I don't wanna say.

"I *can't* go, Viola," I say, low, thru clenched teeth, hating myself a little as I say it, my face turning hot, which weirdly makes a bandage fall off. "I carry the germ. I'm dangerous."

She turns to me and there's a sting in her voice. "Then maybe you shouldn't come."

My jaw drops open. "You'd do that? You'd just *leave*?"

Viola looks away from my eyes but before she can answer, the old woman speaks. "Boy pup," she says, "if it's being infeckshus yer worried about, then yer girl mate can come a-walking up ahead with ol' Hildy while ye stay back a little ways with the puppup to guard ye."

"Manchee!" Manchee barks.

"Whatever," Viola says, turning and starting to climb the rocks to where the old woman stands.

"And I told ye," the woman says, "it's *Hildy*, not *old woman*."

Viola reaches her and they walk off outta sight without another word. Just like that.

"Hildy," Manchee says to me.

"Shut up," I say.

And I don't got no choice but to climb the rocks after them, do I?

So that's how we make our way, along a much narrower path thru rocks and scrub, Viola and old Hildy keeping close together when they can, me and Manchee miles back, tripping our way towards who knows what further danger and the whole time I'm looking back over my shoulder, expecting to see the Mayor and Mr Prentiss Jr and Aaron all coming after us.

I don't know. How can you know? How can Ben and Cillian have expected me to be prepared for this? Sure, the idea of a bed and hot food sounds like something worth getting shot for but maybe it's a trick and we're being so stupid we deserve to get caught.

And there's people after us and we should be running.

But maybe there really ain't another way over that river.

And Hildy could have forced us and she didn't. And Viola said she seems okay and maybe one Noise-less person can read another.

You see? How can you know?

And who cares what Viola says?

"Look at 'em up there," I say to Manchee. "They fell together right quick. Like they're long-lost family or some-thing."

"Hildy," Manchee says again. I swat after his rump but he runs on ahead.

Viola and Hildy are talking together but I can only hear the murmurings of words here and there. I don't know what they're saying at all. If they were normal Noisy people, it wouldn't matter how far back on the trail I was, we could all talk together and nobody'd have no automatic secrets. Everybody'd be jabbering, whether they wanted to or not.

And nobody'd be left out. Nobody'd be left on his own at the first chance you had.

We all walk on.

And I'm starting to think some more.

And I'm starting to let them get a little farther ahead, too.

And I'm thinking more.

Cuz as time passes, it's all starting to sink in.

Cuz maybe now we found Hildy, maybe she *can* take care of Viola. They're clearly peas in a pod, ain't they? Different from me, anyway. And so maybe Hildy could help her back to wherever she's from cuz obviously I can't. Obviously I ain't got nowhere I can be except Prentisstown, do I? Cuz I'm carrying a germ that'll kill her, may kill her still, may kill everybody else I meet, a germ that'll forever keep me outta that settlement, that'll probably even leave me sleeping in Hildy's barn with the sheep and the russets.

"That's it, ain't it, Manchee?" I stop walking, my chest starting to feel heavy. "There ain't no Noise out here, less I'm the one who brings it." I rub some sweat off my forehead. "We got nowhere to go. We can't go forward. We can't go back."

I sit down on a rock, realizing the truth of it all.

"We got nowhere," I say. "We got nothing."

"Got Todd," Manchee says, wagging his tail.

It ain't fair.

It just ain't fair.

The only place you belong is the place you can never go back.

And so yer always alone, forever and always.

Why'd you do it, Ben? What did I do that was so bad?

I wipe my eyes with my arm.

I wish Aaron and the Mayor *would* come and get me.

I wish it would just be over already.

"Todd?" Manchee barks, coming up to my face and trying to sniff it.

"Leave me alone," I say, pushing him away.

Hildy and Viola are getting still farther away and if I don't get up, I'll lose the trail.

I don't get up.

I can still hear them talking, tho it gets steadily quieter, no one looking back to see if I'm still following.

Hildy, I hear, and girl pup and blasted leaky pipe and Hildy again and burning bridge.

And I lift my head.

Cuz it's a new voice.

And I ain't hearing it. Not with my ears.

Hildy and Viola are getting farther away, but there's someone coming towards them, someone raising a hand in greeting.

Someone whose Noise is saying Hello.

15

BROTHERS IN SUFFERING

IT'S AN OLD MAN, also carrying a rifle but way down at his side, pointing to the ground. His Noise rises as he approaches Hildy, it stays risen as he puts an arm around her and kisses her in greeting, it buzzes as he turns and is introduced to Viola who stands back a little at being greeted so friendly.

Hildy is married to a man with Noise.

A full grown man, walking around Noisy as you please.

But how–?

"Hey, boy pup!" Hildy shouts back at me. "Ye going to sit there all day picking yer nose or are ye going to join us for supper?"

"Supper, Todd!" Manchee barks and takes off running towards them.

I don't think nothing. I don't know *what* to think.

"Another Noisy fella!" shouts the old man, stepping past Viola and Hildy and coming towards me. He's got Noise pouring outta him like a bright parade, all full of unwelcome welcome and pushy good feeling. **Boy pup** and **bridges falling** and **leaky pipe** and **brother in suffering** and **Hildy, my Hildy**. He's still carrying his rifle but as he reaches me, his hand's out for me to shake.

I'm so stunned that I actually shake it.

"Tam's my name!" the old man more or less shouts. "And who might ye be, pup?"

"Todd," I say.

"Pleasedtameetya, Todd!" He puts an arm around my shoulders and pretty much drags me forward up the path. I stumble along, barely keeping my balance as he pulls us to Hildy and Viola, talking all the way. "We haven't had guests for dinner in many a moon, so ye'll have to be a-scusing our humble shack. Ain't been no travellers thisaway for nigh on ten years nor more but yer welcome! Yer all welcome!"

We get to the others and I still don't know what to say and I look from Hildy to Viola to Tam and back again.

I just want the world to make sense now and then, is that so wrong?

"Not wrong at all, Todd pup," Hildy says kindly.

"How can you not have caught the Noise?" I ask, words finally making their way outta my head via my mouth. Then my heart suddenly rises, rises so high I can feel my eyes popping open and my throat start to clench, my own Noise coming all high hopeful white.

"Do you have a cure?" I say, my voice almost breaking. "Is there a cure?"

"Now if there were a cure," Tam says, still pretty much shouting, "d'ye honestly think I'd be subjecting ye to all this here rubbish a-floating outta my brain?"

"Heaven help ye if ye did," Hildy says, smiling.

"And heaven help *ye* if ye couldn't tell me what I was meant to be thinking." Tam smiles back, love fuzzing all over his Noise. "Nope, boy pup," he says to me. "No cure that I know of."

"Well, now," Hildy says, "Haven's meant to be a-working on one. So people say."

"Which people?" Tam asks, sceptical.

"Talia," Hildy says. "Susan F. My sister."

Tam makes a *pssht* sound with his lips. "I rest my case. Rumours of rumours of rumours. Can't trust yer sister to get her own name right much less any useful info."

"But–" I say, looking back and forth again and again, not wanting to let it go. "But how can you be alive then?" I say to Hildy. "The Noise kills women. *All* women."

Hildy and Tam exchange a look and I hear, no, I *feel* Tam squash something in his Noise.

"No, it don't, Todd pup," Hildy says, a little too gently. "Like I been telling yer girl mate Viola here. She's safe."

"Safe? How can she be safe?"

"Women are immune," Tam says. "Lucky buggers."

"No, they're not!" I say, my voice getting louder. "No, they're *not*! Every woman in Prentisstown caught the Noise and every single one of them *died* from it! My *ma* died from it! Maybe the version the Spackle released on us was stronger than yers but–"

"Todd pup." Tam puts a hand on my shoulder to stop me.

I shake him off but I don't know what to say next. Viola's not said a word in all of this so I look at her. She don't look at me. "I know what I know," I say, even tho that's been half the trouble, ain't it?

How can this be true?

How can this be *true*?

Tam and Hildy exchange another glance. I look into Tam's Noise but he's as expert as anyone I've met at hiding stuff away when someone starts poking. What I see, tho, is all kind.

"Prentisstown's got a sad history, pup," he says. "A whole number of things went sour there."

"Yer wrong," I say, but even my voice says I ain't sure what I'm saying he's wrong about.

"This ain't the place for it, Todd," Hildy says, rubbing Viola on the shoulder, a rub that Viola don't resist. "Ye need to get some food in ye, some sleep in ye. Vi here says ye ain't slept hardly at all in many miles of travelling. Everything will be a-looking better when yer fed and rested."

"But she's safe from me?" I ask, making a point of not looking at "Vi".

"Well, she's definitely safe from catching yer Noise," Hildy says, a smile breaking out. "What other safety she can get from ye is all down to a-knowing ye better."

I want her to be right but I also want to say she's wrong and so I don't say nothing at all.

"C'mon," Tam says, breaking the pause, "let's get to some feasting."

"No!" I say, remembering it all over again. "We ain't got time for *feasting*." I look at Viola. "There's men after us, in case you forgot. Men who ain't interested in our well-beings." I look up at Hildy. "Now, I'm sure yer feastings would be fine and all–"

155

"Todd pup–" Hildy starts.

"I ain't a pup!" I shout.

Hildy purses her lips and smiles with her eyebrows. "Todd pup," she says again, a little lower this time. "No man from any point beyond that river would ever set foot across it, do ye understand?"

"Yep," says Tam. "That's right."

I look from one to the other. "But–"

"I been guardian here of that bridge for ten plus years, pup," Hildy says, "and keeper of it for years before that. It's part of who I am to watch what comes." She looks over to Viola. "No one's coming. Ye all are safe."

"Yep," Tam says again, rocking back and forth on his heels.

"But–" I say again but Hildy don't let me finish.

"Time for feasting."

And that's that, it seems. Viola still don't look at me, still has her arms crossed and is now under the arm of Hildy as they walk on again. I'm stuck back with Tam who's waiting for me to start. I can't say as I feel much like walking any more but everyone else goes so I go, too. We carry on up Tam and Hildy's private little path, Tam chattering away, making enough Noise for a whole town.

"Hildy says ye blew up our bridge," he says.

"*My* bridge," Hildy says from in front of us.

"She did build it," Tam says to me. "Not that anyone's used it in forever."

"No one?" I say, thinking for a second of all those men who disappeared outta Prentisstown, all the ones who vanished while I was growing up. Not one of them got this far.

"Nice bit of engineering, that bridge was," Tam's going on, like he didn't hear me and maybe he didn't, what with how loud he's talking. "Sad to hear it's gone."

"We had no choice," I say.

"Oh, there's always choices, pup, but from what I hear, ye made the right one."

We walk on quietly for a bit. "Yer sure we're safe?" I ask.

"Well, ye can't never be sure," he says. "But Hildy's right." He grins, a little sadly, I think. "There's more than bridges being out that'll keep men that side of the river."

I try and read his Noise to see if he's telling the truth but it's almost all shiny and clean, a bright, warm place where anything you want could be true.

Nothing at all like a Prentisstown man.

"I don't understand this," I say, still gnawing on it. "It's gotta be a different kinda Noise germ."

"My Noise sound different from yers?" Tam asks, seeming genuinely curious.

I look at him and just listen for a second. Hildy and Prentisstown and russets and sheep and settlers and leaky pipe and Hildy.

"You sure think about yer wife a lot."

"She's my shining star, pup. Woulda lost myself in Noise if she hadn't put a hand out to rescue me."

"How so?" I ask, wondering what he's talking about. "Did you fight in the war?"

This stops him. His Noise goes as grey and featureless as a cloudy day and I can't read a thing off him.

"I fought, young pup," he says. "But war's not something ye talk about in the open air when the sun is shining."

"Why not?"

"I pray to all my gods ye never find out." He puts a hand on my shoulder. I don't shake it off this time.

"How do you do that?" I ask.

"Do what?"

"Make yer Noise so flat I can't read it."

He smiles. "Years of practise a-hiding things from the old woman."

"It's why I can read so good," Hildy calls back to us. "He gets better at hiding, I get better at *finding*."

They laugh together yet again. I find myself trying to send an eyeroll Viola's way about these two but Viola ain't looking at me and I stop myself from trying again.

We all come outta the rocky bit of the path and round a low rise and suddenly there's a farm ahead of us, rolling up and down little hills but you can see fields of wheat, fields of cabbage, a field of grass with a few sheep on it.

"Hello, sheep!" Tam shouts.

"Sheep!" say the sheep.

First on the path is a big wooden barn, built as watertight and solid as the bridge, like it could last there forever if anyone asked it.

"Unless ye go a-blowing it up," Hildy says, laughing still.

"Like to see ye try," Tam laughs back.

I'm getting a little tired of them laughing about every damn thing.

Then we come round to the farmhouse, which is a totally different thing altogether. Metal, by the looks of it, like the petrol stayshun and the church back home but not nearly so banged up. Half of it shines and rolls on up to the sky like a sail and there's a chimney that curves up and out, folding down to a point, smoke coughing from its end. The other half of the house is wood built onto the metal, solid as the barn but cut and folded like–

"Wings," I say.

"Wings is right," Tam says. "And what kinda wings are they?"

I look again. The whole farmhouse looks like some kinda bird with the chimney as its head and neck and a shiny front and wooden wings stretching out behind, like a bird resting on the water or something.

"It's a swan, Todd pup," Tam says.

"A what?"

"A swan."

"What's a swan?" I say, still looking at the house.

His Noise is puzzled for a second, then I get a little pulse of sadness so I look at him. "What?"

"Nothing, pup," he says. "Memories of long ago."

Viola and Hildy are up ahead still, Viola's eyes wide and her mouth gulping like a fish.

"What did I tell ye?" Hildy asks.

Viola rushes up to the fence in front of it. She stares at the house, looking all over the metal bit, up and down, side to side. I come up by her and look, too. It's hard for a minute to think of anything to say (shut up).

"Sposed to be a swan," I finally say. "Whatever that is."

She ignores me and turns to Hildy. "Is it an Expansion Three 500?"

"What?"

"Older than that, Vi pup," Hildy says. "X Three 200."

"We got up to X Sevens," Viola says.

"Not surprised," says Hildy.

"What the ruddy hell are you talking about?" I say. "Expanshun *whatsits*?"

"Sheep!" we hear Manchee bark in the distance.

"Our settler ship," Hildy says, sounding surprised that I don't know. "An Expanshun Class Three, Series 200."

I look from face to face. Tam's Noise has a spaceship flying in it, one with a front hull that matches the upturned farmhouse.

"Oh, yeah," I say, remembering, trying to say it like I knew all along. "You build yer houses with the first tools at hand."

"Quite so, pup," Tam says. "Or ye make them works of art if yer so inclined."

"If yer wife is an engineer who can get yer damn fool sculptures to stay standing up," Hildy says.

"How do you know about all this?" I say to Viola.

She looks at the ground, away from my eyes.

"You don't mean—" I start to say but I stop.

I'm getting it.

Of *course* I'm getting it.

Way too late, like everything else, but I'm getting it.

"Yer a settler," I say. "Yer a new settler."

She looks away from me but shrugs her shoulders.

"But that ship you crashed in," I say, "that's way too tiny to be a settler ship."

"That was only a scout. My home ship is an Expansion Class Seven."

She looks at Hildy and Tam, who ain't saying nothing.

Tam's Noise is bright and curious. I can't read nothing from Hildy. I get the feeling somehow, tho, that she knew and I didn't, that Viola told her and not me, and even if it's cuz I never asked, it's still as sour a feeling as it sounds.

I look up at the sky.

"It's up there, ain't it?" I say. "Yer Expanshun Class Seven."

Viola nods.

"Yer bringing more settlers in. More settlers are coming to New World."

"Everything was broken when we crashed," Viola says. "I don't have any way to contact them. Any way to warn them not to come." She looks up with a little gasp. *"You must warn them."*

"That can't be what he meant," I say, fast. "No way."

Viola scrunches her face and eyebrows. "Why not?"

"What who meant?" Tam asks.

"How many?" I ask, still looking at Viola, feeling the world changing still and ever. "How many settlers are coming?"

Viola takes a deep breath before she answers and I'll bet you she's not even told Hildy this part.

"Thousands," she says. "There's thousands."

16

THE NIGHT OF
NO APOLOGIES

"THEY WON'T be a-getting here for months," Hildy says, passing me another serving of mashed russets. Viola and I are stuffing our faces so much it's been Hildy and Tam doing all the talking.

All the *a*-talking.

"Space travel ain't like ye see it in vids," Tam says, a stream of mutton gravy tracking down his beard. "Takes years and years and years to get anywhere at all. Sixty-four to get from Old World to New World alone."

"*Sixty-four years?*" I say, spraying a few mashed blobs off my lips.

Tam nods. "Yer frozen for most of it, time passing you right on by, tho that's only if ye don't die on the way."

I turn to Viola. "Yer sixty-four years old?"

"Sixty-four Old World years," Tam says, tapping his fingers like he's adding something up. "Which'd be ... what? Bout fifty-eight, fifty-nine New World–"

But Viola's shaking her head. "I was born on board. Never was asleep."

"So either yer ma or yer pa musta been a caretaker," Hildy says, snapping off a bite of a turnipy thing then giving me an explanashun. "One of the ones who stays awake and keeps track of the ship."

"Both of them were," Viola says. "And my dad's mother before him and granddad before that."

"Wait a minute," I say to her, two steps behind as ever. "So if we've been on New World twenty-odd years–"

"Twenty-three," says Tam. "Feels like longer."

"Then you left before we even *got* here," I say. "Or your pa or grandpa or whatever."

I look around to see if anyone's wondering what I'm wondering. "Why?" I say. "Why would you come without even knowing what's out here?"

"Why did the *first* settlers come?" Hildy asks me. "Why does anyone look for a new place to live?"

"Cuz the place yer a-leaving ain't worth staying for," Tam says. "Cuz the place yer a-leaving is so bad ye gotta leave."

"Old World's mucky, violent and crowded," Hildy says, wiping her face with a napkin, "a-splitting right into bits with people a-hating each other and a-killing each other, no one happy till everyone's miserable. Least it was all those years ago."

"I wouldn't know," Viola says, "I've never seen it. My mother and father..." She drifts off.

But I'm still thinking about being born on a spaceship, an honest to badness *spaceship*. Growing up while flying along the stars, able to go wherever you wanted, not stuck on some hateful planet which clearly don't want you. You could go anywhere. If one place didn't suit, you'd find another. Full freedom in all directions. Could there possibly be anything cooler in the whole world than that?

I don't notice there's a silence fallen at the table. Hildy's rubbing Viola's back again and I see that Viola's eyes are wet and leaking and she's started to rock a little back and forth.

"What?" I say. "What's wrong now?"

Viola's forehead just creases at me.

"What?" I say.

"I think maybe we talked enough about Vi's ma and pa for now," Hildy says softly. "I think maybe it's time for boy and girl pups to get some shut-eye."

"But it's hardly late at all." I look out a window. The sun ain't even hardly set. "We need to be getting to the settlement—"

"The settlement is called Farbranch," Hildy says, "and we'll get ye there first thing in the morning."

"But those men—"

"I been a-keeping the peace here since before you were born, pup," Hildy says, kindly but firmly. "I can handle whatever is or ain't a-coming."

I don't say nothing to this and Hildy ignores my Noise on the subject.

"Can I ask what yer business in Farbranch might be?" Tam says, picking at his corncob, making his asking sound less curious than his Noise says it is.

"We just need to get there," I say.

"Both of ye?"

I look at Viola. She's stopped crying but her face is still

puffy. I don't answer Tam's asking.

"Well there's plenty of work going," Hildy says, standing and taking up her plate. "If that's what yer after. They can always use more hands in the orchards."

Tam stands and they clear the table, taking the dishes into their kitchen and leaving me and Viola sitting there by ourselves. We can hear them chatting in there, lightly enough and Noise-blocked enough for us not to be able to make it out.

"Do you really think we oughta stay the whole night?" I say, keeping my voice low.

But she answers in a violent whisper, like I didn't even ask an asking. "Just because my thoughts and feelings don't spill out into the world in a shout that never stops doesn't mean I don't have them."

I turn to her, surprised. *"Huh?"*

She keeps whispering something fierce. "Every time you think, *Oh, she's just emptiness,* or, *There's nothing going on inside her,* or, *Maybe I can dump her with these two,* I hear it, okay? I hear every stupid thing you think, all right? And I understand *way* more than I want to."

"Oh, yeah?" I whisper back, tho my Noise ain't a whisper at all. "Every time *you* think something or feel something or have some stupid thought, I *don't* hear it, so how am I sposed to know any effing thing about you, huh? How am I sposed to know what's going on if you keep it secret?"

"I'm *not* keeping it secret." She's clenching her teeth now. "I'm being *normal.*"

"Not normal for here, *Vi.*"

"And how would you know? I can hear you being

165

surprised by just about everything they say. Didn't they have a school where you're from? Didn't you learn *anything*?"

"History ain't so important when yer just trying to survive," I say, spitting it out under my breath.

"That's actually when it's *most* important," Hildy says, standing at the end of the table. "And if this silly argument twixt ye two ain't enough to prove yer tired, then yer tired beyond all sense. C'mon."

Viola and I glare at each other but we get up and follow Hildy into a large common room.

"Todd!" Manchee barks from a corner, not getting up from the mutton bone Tam gave him earlier.

"We've long since took over our guest rooms for other purposes," Hildy says. "Ye'll have to make do on the settees."

We help her make up some sheets and beds, Viola still scowling, my Noise a buzzy red.

"Now," Hildy says when we're all done. "Apologize to each other."

"What?" Viola says. *"Why?"*

"I don't see how this is any of yer business," I say.

"Never go to sleep on an argument," Hildy says, hands on hips, looking like she ain't never gonna budge and would be pleased to see someone try and make her. "Not if ye want to stay friends."

Viola and I don't say nothing.

"He saved yer life?" Hildy says to Viola.

Viola looks down before finally saying, "Yeah."

"That's right, I did," I say.

"And she saved yers at the bridge, didn't she?" Hildy says.

Oh.

"Yes," Hildy says. "*Oh*. Don't ye both think that counts for something?"

We still don't say nothing.

Hildy sighs. "Fine. Any two pups so close to adulthood could maybe be left to their own apologies, I reckon." She makes her way out without even saying good night.

I turn my back on Viola and she turns her back on me. I take off my shoes and get myself under the sheet on one of Hildy's "settees" which seems to be just a fancy word for couch. Viola does the same. Manchee leaps up on my settee and curls himself by my feet.

There's no sound except my Noise and a few crackles from a fire it's too hot for. It can't be much later than dusk but the softness of the cushions and the softness of the sheet and the too-warm of the fire and I'm already pretty much closing my eyes.

"Todd?" Viola says from her settee across the room.

I swim up from sinking down to sleep. "What?"

She don't say nothing for a second and I guess she must be thinking of her apology.

But no.

"What does your book say you're supposed to do when you get to Farbranch?"

My Noise gets a bit redder. "Never you mind what my book says," I say. "That's my property, meant for me."

"You know when you showed me the map back in the woods?" she says. "And you said we had to get to this settlement? You remember what was written underneath?"

"Course I do."

"What was it?"

There ain't no poking in her voice, not that I can hear, but that's gotta be what it is, ain't it? Poking?

"Just go to sleep, will ya?" I say.

"It was *Farbranch*," she says. "The name of the place we're meant to be heading."

"Shut up." My Noise is getting buzzy again.

"There's no shame in not being able to—"

"I said, *shut up*!"

"I could help you—"

I get up suddenly, dumping Manchee off the settee with a thump. I grab my sheets and blanket under my arm and I stomp off to the room where we ate. I throw them on the floor and lay down, a room away from Viola and all her meaningless, evil quiet.

Manchee stays in there with her. Typical.

I close my eyes but I don't sleep for ages and ages.

Till I finally do, I guess.

Cuz I'm on a path and it's the swamp but it's also the town and it's also my farm and Ben's there and Cillian's there and Viola's there and they're all saying, "What're you doing here, Todd?" and Manchee's barking "Todd! Todd!" and Ben's grabbing me by the arm to drag me out the door and Cillian's got his arm round my shoulders pushing me up the path and Viola's setting the campfire box by the front door of our farmhouse and the Mayor's horse rides right thru our front door and smashes her flat and a croc with the face of Aaron is rearing up behind Ben's shoulders and I'm yelling "No!" and—

And I'm sitting up and I'm sweating everywhere and my heart's racing like a horse and I'm expecting to see the

Mayor and Aaron standing right over me.

But it's only Hildy and she's saying, "What the devil are ye a-doing in here?" She's standing in the doorway, morning sun flooding in behind her so bright I have to raise my hand to block it out.

"More comfortable," I mumble but my chest is thumping.

"I'll bet," she says, reading my just-waking Noise. "Breakfast is on."

The smell of the mutton-strip bacon frying wakes Viola and Manchee. I let Manchee out for his morning poo but Viola and I don't say nothing to each other. Tam comes in as we eat, having I guess been out feeding the sheep. That's what I'd be doing if I were home.

Home, I think.

Anyway.

"Buck up, pup," Tam says, plonking a cup of coffee down in front of me. I keep my face way down as I drink it.

"Anybody out there?" I say into my cup.

"Not a whisper," Tam says. "And it's a beautiful day."

I glance up at Viola but she ain't looking at me. In fact, we get all the way thru the food, thru washing our faces, thru changing our clothes and re-packing our bags, all without saying nothing to each other.

"Good luck to ye both," Tam says, as we're about to leave with Hildy towards Farbranch. "It's always nice when two people who don't got no one else find each other as friends."

And we really don't say nothing to that.

"C'mon, pups," Hildy says. "Time's a-wasting."

We get back on the path, which before too long recon- nects with the same road that musta gone across the bridge.

"Used to be the main road from Farbranch to Prentisstown," Hildy says, hoisting her own small pack. "Or New Elizabeth, as it was then."

"As what was then?" I ask.

"Prentisstown," she says. "Used to be called New Elizabeth."

"It never did," I say, raising up my eyebrows.

Hildy looks at me, her own eyebrows mocking mine. "Was it never? I must be mistaken then."

"Must be," I say, watching her.

Viola makes a scoffing sound with her lips. I send her a look of death.

"Will there be somewhere we can stay?" she asks Hildy, ignoring me.

"I'll take ye to my sister," Hildy says. "Deputy Mayor this year, don't ye know?"

"What'll we do then?" I say, kicking at the dirt as we walk on.

"Reckon that's up to ye two," Hildy says. "Ye've gotta be the ones in charge of yer own destinies, don't ye?"

"Not so far," I hear Viola say under her breath and it's so exactly the words I have in my Noise that we both look up and catch each other's eyes.

We almost smile. But we don't.

And that's when we start hearing the Noise.

"Ah," Hildy says, hearing it too. "Farbranch."

The road comes out on the top of a little vale.

And there it is.

The other settlement. The other settlement that wasn't sposed to be.

Where Ben wanted us to go.

Where we might be safe.

The first thing I see is where the valley road winds down thru orchards, orderly rows of well-tended trees with paths and irrigashun systems, all carrying on down a hill towards buildings and a creek at the bottom, flat and easy and snaking its way back to meet the bigger river no doubt.

And all thru-out are men and women.

Most are scattered working in the orchard, wearing heavy work aprons, all the men in long sleeves, the women in long skirts, cutting down pine-like fruits with machetes or carrying away baskets or working on the irrigashun pipes and so on.

Men and women, women and men.

A coupla dozen men, maybe, is my general impression, less than Prentisstown.

Who knows how many women.

Living in a whole other place.

The Noise (and silence) of them all floats up like a light fog.

Two, please and The way I see it is and Weedy waste and She might say yes, she might not and If service ends at one, then I can always and so on and so on, never ending, amen.

I just stop in the road and gape for a second, not ready to walk down into it yet.

Cuz it's weird.

It's more than weird, truth to tell.

It's all so, I don't know, *calm.* Like normal chatter you'd have with yer mates. Nothing accidental nor abusive.

And nobody's hardly longing for nothing.

No awful, awful, despairing longing nowhere I can hear or feel.

"We sure as ruddy heck ain't in Prentisstown no more," I say to Manchee under my breath.

Not a second later, I hear **Prentisstown?** float in from a field right next to us.

And then I hear it in a coupla different places. **Prentisstown?** and **Prentisstown?** and then I notice that the men in the orchards nearby ain't picking fruit or whatever any more. They're standing up. They're looking at us.

"Come on," Hildy says. "Keep on a-walking. It's just curiosity."

The word **Prentisstown** multiplies along the fields like a crackling fire. Manchee brings hisself in closer to my legs. We're being stared at on all sides as we carry on. Even Viola steps in a bit so we're a tighter group.

"Not to worry," Hildy says. "There'll just be a lot of people who'll want to meet–"

She stops mid-sentence.

A man has stepped onto the path in front of us.

His face don't look at all like he wants to meet us.

"Prentisstown?" he says, his Noise getting uncomfortably red, uncomfortably fast.

"Morning, Matthew," Hildy says, "I was just a-bringing–"

"Prentisstown," the man says again, no longer an asking, and he's not looking at Hildy.

He's looking straight at me.

"Yer not welcome here," he says. "Not welcome at all."

And he's got the biggest machete in his hand you ever seen.

17

ENCOUNTER IN
AN ORCHARD

MY HAND GOES right behind my rucksack to my own knife.

"Leave it, Todd pup," Hildy says, keeping her eyes on the man. "That's not how this is gonna go."

"What do ye think yer a-bringing into our village, Hildy?" the man says, hefting his machete in his hand, still looking at me and there's real surprise in his asking and–

And is that *hurt*?

"I'm a-bringing in a boy pup and a girl pup what's lost their way," Hildy says. "Stand aside, Matthew."

"I don't see a boy pup nowhere," Matthew says, his eyes starting to burn. He's massively tall, shoulders like an ox and a thickened brow with lots of bafflement but not much tenderness. He looks like a walking, talking thunderstorm. "I see me a Prentisstown man. I see me a Prentisstown man with Prentisstown filth all over his Prentisstown Noise."

"That's not what yer a-seeing," Hildy says. "Look close."

Matthew's Noise is already lurching on me like hands pressing in, forcing its way into my own thinking, trying to ransack the room. It's angry and asking and Noisy as a fire, so uneven I can't make hide nor hair of it.

"Ye know the law, Hildy," he says.

The law?

"The law is for men," Hildy says, her voice staying calm, like we were standing there talking bout the weather. Can't she see how red this man's Noise is getting? Red ain't yer colour if you wanna have a chat. "This here pup ain't a man yet."

"I've still got twenty-eight days," I say, without thinking.

"Yer numbers don't mean nothing here, boy," Matthew spits. "I don't care how many days away ye are."

"Calm yerself, Matthew," Hildy says, sterner than I'd want her to. But to my surprise, Matthew looks at her all sore and steps back a step. "He's a-fleeing Prentisstown, pup," she says, a little softer. "He's a-running away."

Matthew looks at her suspiciously and back to me but he's lowering the machete. A little.

"Just like ye did yerself once," Hildy says to him.

What?

"Yer from Prentisstown?" I blurt out.

Up comes the machete and Matthew steps forward again, threatening enough to start Manchee barking, "Back! Back! Back!"

"I was from *New Elizabeth*," Matthew growls, twixt clenched teeth. "I'm *never* from Prentisstown, boy, not never, and don't ye forget it."

I see clearer flashes in his Noise now. Of impossible

things, of crazy things, coming in a rush, like he can't help it, things worse than the worst of the illegal vids Mr Hammar used to let out on the sly to the oldest and rowdiest of the boys in town, the kind where people seemed to die for real but there was no way of ever knowing for sure. Images and words and blood and screaming and–

"Stop that right this second!" Hildy shouts. "Control yerself, Matthew Lyle. Control yerself *right now*."

Matthew's Noise subsides, sudden-like but still roiling, without quite so much control as Tam but still more than any man in Prentisstown.

But as soon as I think it, his machete raises again. "Ye'll not say that word in our town, boy," he says. "Not if ye know what's good for ye."

"There'll be no threats to guests of mine as long as I'm alive," Hildy says, her voice strong and clear. "Is that understood?"

Matthew looks at her, he don't nod, he don't say yes, but we all understand that he understands. He ain't happy bout it, tho. His Noise still pokes and presses at me, slapping me if it could. He finally looks over to Viola.

"And who might this be then?" he says, pointing the machete at her.

And it happens before I even know I'm doing it, I swear.

One minute I'm standing there behind everyone and the next thing I know, I'm between Matthew and Viola, I have my knife out pointing at him, my own Noise falling like an avalanche and my mouth saying, "You best take two steps away from her and you best be taking 'em right quick."

"Todd!" Hildy shouts.

And "Todd!" Manchee barks.

And "Todd!" Viola shouts.

But there I am, knife out, my heart thumping fast like it's finally figured out what I'm doing.

But there ain't no stepping back.

Now how do you suppose *that* happened?

"Give me a reason, Prentissboy," Matthew says, hoisting the machete. "Just give me one good reason."

"Enough!" Hildy says.

And her voice has got something in it this time, like the word of rule, so much so that Matthew flinches a little. He's still holding up his machete, still glaring at me, glaring at Hildy, his Noise throbbing like a wound.

And then his face twists a little.

And he begins, of all things, to cry.

Angrily, furiously trying not to, but standing there, big as a bullock, machete in hand, crying.

Which ain't what I was expecting.

Hildy's voice pulls back a bit. "Put the knife away, Todd pup."

Matthew drops his machete to the ground and puts an arm across his eyes as he snuffles and yowls and moans. I look over at Viola. She's just staring at Matthew, probably as confused as I am.

I drop the knife to my side but I don't let it go. Not yet.

Matthew's taking deep breaths, pain Noise and grief Noise dripping everywhere, and fury, too, at losing control so publicly. "It's meant to be over," he coughs. "Long over."

"I know," Hildy says, going forward and putting a hand on his arm.

"What's going on?" I say.

"Never you mind, Todd pup," Hildy says. "Prentisstown has a sad history."

"That's what Tam said," I say. "As if I don't know."

Matthew looks up. "Ye don't know the first bit of it, boy," he says, teeth clenched again.

"That's enough now," Hildy says. "This boy ain't yer enemy." She looks at me, eyes a bit wide. "And he's putting away his knife for that very reason."

I twist the knife in my hand a time or two but then I reach behind my rucksack and put it away. Matthew's glaring at me again but he's starting to back off for real now and I'm wondering who Hildy is that he's obeying her.

"They're both innocent as lambs, Matthew pup," Hildy says.

"Ain't nobody innocent," Matthew says bitterly, sniffing away his last bits of weepy snot and hefting up his machete again. "Nobody at all."

He turns his back and strides into the orchard, not looking back.

Everyone else is still staring at us.

"The day only ages," Hildy says to them, turning round in a circle. "There'll be time enough for a-meeting and a-greeting later on."

Me and Viola watch as the workers start returning to their trees and their baskets and their whatevers, some eyes still on us but most people getting back to work.

"Are you in charge here or something?" I ask.

"Or something, Todd pup. C'mon, ye haven't even seen the town yet."

"What law was he talking about?"

"Long story, pup," she says. "I'll tell ye later."

The path, still wide enough for men and vehicles and horses, tho I only see men, curves its way down thru more orchards on the hillsides of the little vale.

"What kind of fruit is that?" Viola asks, as two women cross the road in front of us with full baskets, the women watching us as they go.

"Crested pine," Hildy says. "Sweet as sugar, loaded with vitamins."

"Never heard of it," I say.

"No," Hildy says. "Ye wouldn't have."

I look at way too many trees for a settlement that can't have more than fifty people in it. "Is that all you eat here?"

"Course not," Hildy says. "We trade with the other settlements down the road."

The surprise is so clear in my Noise that even Viola laughs a little.

"Ye didn't think it was just two settlements on all of New World, did ye?" Hildy asks.

"No," I say, feeling my face turn red, "but all the other settlements were wiped out in the war."

"Mmm," Hildy says, biting her bottom lip, nodding but not saying nothing more.

"Is that Haven?" Viola says quietly.

"Is what Haven?" I ask.

"The other settlement," Viola says, not quite looking at me. "You said there was a cure for Noise in Haven."

"Ach," Hildy psshts. "That's just rumours and speck-alashuns."

"Is Haven a real place?" I ask.

"It's the biggest and first of the settlements," Hildy says. "Closest New World's got to a big city. Miles away. Not for peasants like us."

"I've never heard of it," I say again.

No one says nothing to this and I get the feeling they're being polite. Viola's not really looked at me since the weirdness back there with me and Matthew and the knife. To be honest, I don't know what to make of it neither.

So everyone just keeps walking.

There's maybe seven buildings total in Farbranch, smaller than Prentisstown and just buildings after all but somehow so different, too, it feels like I've wandered right off New World into some whole other place altogether.

The first building we pass is a tiny stone church, fresh and clean and open, not at all like the darkness Aaron preached in. Farther on is a general store with a mechanic's garage by it, tho I don't see much by way of heavy machinery around. Haven't even seen a fissionbike, not even a dead one. There's a building that looks like a meeting hall, another with a doctor's snakes carved into the front, and two barn-like buidings that look like storage.

"Not much," Hildy says. "But it's home."

"Not yer home," I say. "You live way outside."

"So do most people," Hildy says. "Even when yer used to it, it's nice to only have the Noise of yer most beloved a-hanging round yer house. Town gets a bit rackety."

I listen out for rackety but it still ain't *nothing* like Prentisstown. Sure there's Noise in Farbranch, men doing their usual boring daily business, chattering their thoughts

179

that don't mean nothing, Chop, chop, chop and I'll only give seven for the dozen and Listen to her sing there, just listen and That coop needs fixing tonight and He's gonna fall right off of that and on and on and on, so heedless and safe-sounding to me it feels like taking a bath in comparison to the black Noise I'm used to.

"Oh, it gets black, Todd pup," Hildy says. "Men still have their tempers. Women, too."

"Some people would call it impolite to always be listening to a man's Noise," I say, looking round me.

"Too true, pup." She grins. "But ye aren't a man yet. Ye said so yerself."

We cross the central strip of the town. A few men and women walk to and fro, some tipping their hats to Hildy, most just staring at us.

I stare back.

If you listen close, you can hear where the women are in town almost as clear as the men. They're like rocks that the Noise washes over and once yer used to it you can feel where their silences are, dotted all about, Viola and Hildy ten times over and I'll bet if I stopped and stood here I could tell exactly how many women are in each building.

And mixed in with the sound of so many men, you know what?

The silence don't feel half so lonesome.

And then I see some teeny, tiny people, watching us from behind a bush.

Kids.

Kids smaller than me, *younger* than me.

The first I ever seen.

A woman carrying a basket spies them and makes a shooing movement with her hands. She frowns and smiles at the same time and the kids all run off giggling round the back of the church.

I watch 'em go. I feel my chest pull a little.

"Ye coming?" Hildy calls after me.

"Yeah," I say, still watching where the kids went. I turn and keep on following, my head still twisted back.

Kids. Real kids. *Safe* enough for kids and I find myself wondering if Viola would be able to feel at home here with all these nice-seeming men, all these women and children. I find myself wondering if she'd be safe, even if I'm obviously not.

I'll bet she would.

I look at Viola and catch her looking away.

Hildy's led us to the house farthest along the buildings of Farbranch. It's got steps that go up the front and a little flag flying from a pole out front.

I stop.

"This is a mayor's house," I say. "Ain't it?"

"Deputy Mayor," Hildy says, walking up the steps, clomping her boots loud against the wood. "My sister."

"And *my* sister," says a woman opening the door, a plumper, younger, frownier version of Hildy.

"Francia," Hildy says.

"Hildy," Francia says.

They nod at each other, not hug or shake hands, just nod.

"What trouble d'ye think yer bringing into my town?" Francia says, eyeing us up.

"Yer town, is it now?" Hildy says, smiling, eyebrows up. She turns to us. "Like I told Matthew Lyle, it's just two pups a-fleeing for safety, seeking their refuge." She turns back to her sister. "And if Farbranch ain't a refuge, sister, then what is it?"

"It's not them I'm a-talking about," Francia says, looking at us, arms crossed. "It's the army that's a-following them."

18

FARBRANCH

"ARMY?" I say, my stomach knotting right up. Viola says it at the same time I do but there's nothing funny bout it this time.

"What army?" Hildy frowns.

"Rumours a-floating down from the far fields of an army a-gathering on the other side of the river," Francia says. "Men on horseback. Prentisstown men."

Hildy purses her lips. "*Five* men on horseback," she says. "Not an army. Those were just the posse sent after our young pups here."

Francia don't look too convinced. I never seen arms so crossed.

"And the river gorge crossing is down anyhow," Hildy continues, "so there ain't gonna be anyone a-coming into Farbranch any time soon." She looks back at us. "An *army*," she says, shaking her head. "Honestly."

"If there's a threat, sister," Francia says, "it's my duty–"

Hildy rolls her eyes. "Don't be a-talking to me about yer duty, sister," she says, stepping past Francia and opening the front door to the house. "I *invented* yer duty. C'mon, pups, let's get ye inside."

Viola and I don't move. Francia don't invite us to neither. "Todd?" Manchee barks by my feet.

I take a deep breath and go up the front steps. "Howdy, mim," I say.

"*Mam*," Viola whispers behind me.

"Howdy, mam," I say, trying not to miss a beat. "I'm Todd. That's Viola." Francia's arms are still crossed, like there's a prize for it. "There really were only five men," I say, tho the word *army* is echoing round my Noise.

"And I should just trust ye?" Francia says. "A boy who's a-being chased?" She looks down to Viola, still waiting on the bottom step. "I can just imagine why *ye* were running."

"Oh, stuff it, Francia," Hildy says, still holding the door open for us.

Francia turns and shooshes Hildy outta the way. "I'll be in charge of entry into my own house, thank ye very much," Francia says, then to us, "Well, c'mon if yer coming."

And that's how we first see the hospitality of Farbranch. We go inside. Francia and Hildy bickering twixt themselves about whether Francia's got a place to put us in for however long we might wanna stay. Hildy wins the bickering and Francia shows me and Viola to separate small rooms next to each other one floor up.

"Yer dog has to sleep outside," Francia says.

"But he's—"

"That wasn't a question," Francia says, leaving the room.

184

I follow her out to the landing. She don't turn back as she goes downstairs. In less than a minute, I can hear her and Hildy arguing again, trying to keep their voices down. Viola comes outta her room to listen, too. We stand there for a second, wondering.

"Whaddya think?" I say.

She don't look at me. Then it's like she decides to look at me and does.

"I don't know," she says. "What do *you* think?"

I shrug my shoulders. "She don't seem too happy to see us," I say, "but it's still safer than I've felt in a while. Behind walls and such." I shrug again. "And Ben wanted us to get here and all."

Which is true but I still ain't sure if it feels right.

Viola's clutching her arms to herself, just like Francia but not like Francia at all. "I know what you mean."

"So I guess it'll do for now."

"Yes," Viola says. "For now."

We listen to a bit more arguing.

"What you did back there—" Viola says.

"It was stupid," I say, real fast. "I don't wanna talk about it."

My face is starting to burn so I step back in my little room. I stand there and chew my lip. The room looks like it used to belong to an old person. Kinda smells that way, too, but at least it's a real bed. I go to my rucksack and I open it.

I look round to make sure no one's followed me in and I pull out the book. I open it to the map, to the arrows that point down thru the swamp, to the river on the other side. No bridge on the map but there's the settlement. With a word underneath it.

"Fayre," I say, to myself. "Fayre braw nk."

Which I guess is Farbranch.

I breathe loud thru my nose as I look at the page of writing on the back of the map. *You must warn them* (of course, of *course*, shut up) still underlined at the bottom. Like Viola said, tho, warn who? Warn Farbranch? Warn Hildy?

"About what?" I say. I thumb thru the book and there's pages of stuff, pages and pages of it, words on words on words on words, like Noise shoved down onto paper till you can't make no sense from it. How can I warn anybody about all *this*?

"Aw, Ben," I say under my breath. "What were you thinking?"

"Todd?" Hildy calls from downstairs. "Vi?"

I close the book and look at its cover.

Later. I'll ask about it later.

I *will*.

Later.

I put it away and I go downstairs. Viola's already waiting there. Hildy and Francia, arms crossed again, waiting, too.

"I've got to get back to my farm, pups," Hildy says. "Work to do for the good of all but Francia's agreed to look after ye for today and I'll come back tonight to see how yer a-getting on."

Viola and I look at each other, suddenly not wanting Hildy to leave.

"Thank ye for that," Francia says, frowning. "Despite what my sister may have told ye two about me, I'm hardly an ogre."

"She didn't say–" I start to say before I stop myself, even tho my Noise finishes it up for me. *Anything about you.*

"Yeah, well, that's typical," Francia says, glaring at Hildy but not seeming too put out. "Ye can stay here for the time being. Pa and Auntie are long dead and there's not too much call for their rooms these days."

I was right. Old person's room.

"But we're a working town here in Farbranch." Francia looks from me to Viola and back again. "And ye'll be expected to earn yer keep, even if it's just for a day or two while ye make whatever plans yer going to make."

"We're still not sure," Viola says.

"Hmmph," Francia hmmphs. "And if ye two stay on past this first cresting of the orchards, there'll be a-schooling for ye to do."

"School?" I say.

"School and church," Hildy says. "That's if ye stay long enough." I'm guessing she's reading my Noise again. "Are ye going to stay long enough?"

I don't say nothing and Viola don't say nothing and Franica hmmphs again.

"Please, Mrs Francia?" Viola says as Francia turns to talk to Hildy.

"Just Francia, child," Francia says, looking surprised. "What is it?"

"Is there somewhere I can send a message back to my ship?"

"Yer ship," Francia says. "This a-being that settler ship way out in the dark black yonder?" Her mouth draws thin. "With all them people on it?"

Viola nods. "We were supposed to report back. Let them know what we found."

Viola's voice is so quiet and her face so looking and hopeful, so open and wide and ready for disappointment that I feel that familiar tug of sadness again, pulling all Noise into it like grief, like being lost. I put a hand on the back of a settee to steady myself.

"Ah, girl pup," Hildy says, her voice getting suspiciously gentle again. "I'm guessing ye tried to contact us folks down here on New World when ye were a-scouting the planet?"

"Yeah," Viola says. "No one answered."

Hildy and Francia exchange nods. "Yer a-forgetting we were church settlers," Francia says, "getting away from worldly things to set up our own little utopia, so we let that kinda machinery go to rack and ruin as we got on with the business of surviving."

Viola's eyes get a little wider. "You have no way of communicating with anyone?"

"We don't have communicators for other *settlements*," Francia says, "much less the beyond."

"We're farmers, pup," Hildy says. "Simple farmers, looking for a simpler way of life. That was the whole point we were a-trying for in flying all this ridiculous way to get here. Setting down the things that caused such strife for people of old." She taps her fingers on a table-top. "Didn't quite work out that way, tho."

"We weren't really expecting no others," Francia says. "Not the way Old World was when we left."

"So I'm stuck here?" Viola says, her voice a little shaky.

"Until yer ship arrives," Hildy says. "I'm afraid so."

"How far out are they?" Francia asks.

"System entry in 24 weeks," Viola says quietly.

"Perihelion four weeks later. Orbital transfer two weeks after that."

"I'm sorry, child," Francia says. "Looks like yer ours for seven months."

Viola turns away from all of us, obviously taking this news in.

A lot can happen in seven months.

"Well, now," Hildy says, making her voice bright, "I hear tell they got all kindsa things in Haven. Fissioncars and city streets and more stores than ye can shake a stick at. Ye might try there before ye really start a-worrying, yes?"

Hildy makes an eye towards Francia and Francia says, "Todd pup? Why don't we get you a-working in the barn? Yer a farm boy, ain't ye?"

"But–" I start to say.

"All kinds of work to be done on a farm," Francia says, "as I'm sure ye know all too well–"

Chattering away like this, Francia gets me out the back door. Looking over my shoulder, I can see Hildy comforting Viola in soft words, unhearable words, things being said that I don't know yet again.

Francia closes the door behind us and leads me and Manchee across the main road to one of the big storage houses I saw when we were walking in. I can see men pulling handcarts up to the main front door and another man unloading the baskets of orchard fruit.

"This is east barn," Francia says, "where we store things ready to be traded. Wait here."

I wait and she walks up to the man unloading the baskets from the cart. They talk for a minute and I can hear

Prentisstown? clear as day in his Noise and the sudden surge of feeling behind it. It's a slightly different feeling than before but it fades before I can read it and Francia comes back.

"Ivan says ye can work in the back a-sweeping up."

"*Sweeping up?*" I say, kinda appalled. "I know how farms work, mim, and I—"

"I'm sure ye do but ye may have noticed that Prentisstown ain't our most popular neighbour. Best to keep ye away from everyone till we've all had a chance to get used to ye. Fair enough?"

She's still stern, still arms crossed, but actually, yeah, this seems sensible and tho her face ain't kind exactly maybe it sorta is.

"Okay," I say.

Francia nods and takes me over to Ivan, who looks about Ben's age, but short, dark-haired and arms like effing tree trunks.

"Ivan, this is Todd," Francia says.

I hold out my hand to shake. Ivan doesn't take it. He just eyeballs me something fierce.

"You'll work in back," he says. "And you'll keep yerself and yer dog outta my way."

Francia leaves us and Ivan takes me inside, points out a broom, and I get to work. And that's how I start my first day in Farbranch: inside a dark barn, sweeping dust from one corner to another, seeing one single stitch of blue sky out a door at the far end.

Oh, the joy.

"Poo, Todd," Manchee says.

"Not in here, you don't."

It's a pretty big barn, seventy-five to eighty metres from end to end, maybe, and about half full of baskets of crested pine. There's a section with big rolls of silage, too, packed up to the ceiling with thin rope, and another section with huge sheaves of wheat ready to be ground into flour.

"You sell this stuff on to other settlements?" I call out to Ivan.

"Time for chatter later," he calls back from the front.

I don't say nothing to this but something kinda rude shows up in my Noise before I can stop it. I hurry and get back to sweeping.

The morning waxes on. I think about Ben and Cillian. I think about Viola. I think about Aaron and the Mayor. I think about the word *army* and how it's making my stomach clench.

I don't know.

It don't feel right to be stopped. Not after all that running.

Everyone's acting like it's safe here but I don't know.

Manchee wanders in and out the back doors as I sweep, sometimes chasing the pink moths I stir from faint corners. Ivan keeps his distance, I keep mine, but I can see all the people who come to his door and drop off goods taking a deep, long look to the back of the barn, sometimes squinting into the darkness to see if they can find me there, the Prentisstown boy.

So they hate Prentisstown, I got that. *I* hate Prentisstown but I got more cause for grief than any of them.

I start noticing things, too, as the morning gets older. Like that tho men and women both do the heavy labour, women give more orders that more men follow. And with Francia being Deputy Mayor and Hildy being whoever she is in Farbranch, I'm beginning to think it's a town run by women. I can often hear their silences as they walk by outside and I can hear men's Noise responding to it, too, sometimes with chafing but usually in a way that just gets on with things.

Men's Noise here, too, is a *lot* more controlled than what I'm used to. With so many women around and from what I know of the Noise of Prentisstown, you'd think the sky would be full of Noisy women with no clothes doing the most remarkable things you could think of. And sure you hear that sometimes here, men are men after all, but more of the time it's songs or it's prayers or it's directed to the work at hand.

They're calm here in Farbranch but they're a little spooky.

Once in a while, I see if I can hear (not hear) Viola.

But no.

At lunchtime, Francia comes to the back of the barn with a sandwich and a jug of water.

"Where's Viola?" I ask.

"Yer welcome," Francia says.

"For what?"

Francia sighs and says, "Viola's in the orchards, gathering dropped fruits."

I want to ask how she is but I don't and Francia refuses to read it in my Noise.

"How ye getting on?" she asks.

"I know how to do a lot more than ruddy sweep."

"Mind yer language, pup. There'll be time enough to get ye to real work."

She don't stay, walking back towards the front, having another word with Ivan and then she's off to do whatever Deputy Mayors fill their days with.

Can I say? It makes no sense but I sorta like her. Probably cuz she reminds me of Cillian and all the things that used to drive me crazy about him. Memory is stupid, ain't it?

I dig into my sandwich and I'm chewing my first bite when I hear Ivan's Noise approaching.

"I'll sweep up my crumbs," I say.

To my surprise, he laughs, kinda roughly. "I'm sure ye will." He takes a bite of his own sandwich. "Francia says there's a village meeting tonight," he says after a minute.

"Bout me?" I ask.

"Bout ye both. Ye and the girl. Ye and the girl what escaped Prentisstown."

His Noise is strange. It's cautious but strong, like he's checking me out. I don't read no hostility, not towards me, anyway, but *something's* percolating in it.

"We gonna meet everyone?" I say.

"Ye might. We'll all be a-talking bout ye first."

"If there's a vote," I say, chomping on the sandwich, "I think I lose."

"Ye've got Hildy a-speaking for yer side," he says. "That counts for more than aught in Farbranch." He swallows his own bite. "And the people here are kind people and good. We've taken in Prentisstown folk before. Not for a while but from way back in the bad times."

"The war?" I say.

He looks at me, his Noise sizing me up, what I know. "Yeah," he says, "the war." He turns his head round the barn, casual-like, but I get the feeling he's looking to see if we're alone. He turns back and fixes his eye on me. An eye that's really looking for something. "And then, too," he says, "not all of us feel the same."

"Bout what?" I say, not liking his look, not liking his buzz.

"Bout history." He's talking low, his eyes still poring into me, leaning a little closer.

I lean back a little. "I don't know what you mean."

"Prentisstown's still got allies," he whispers, "hidden away in surprising places."

His Noise gets pictures in it, small ones, like Noise speaking just to me and I'm starting to see them clearer and clearer, bright things, wet things, fast things, the sun shining down on red–

"Puppies! Puppies!" Manchee barks in the corner. I jump and even Ivan startles and his Noise pictures fade right quick. Manchee keeps barking and I hear a whole raft of giggling that ain't him at all. I look.

A group of kids is kneeling down, peeking in thru a torn-away board, smiling, laughing with daring, pushing each other closer to the hole.

Pointing at me.

And all so small.

So small.

I mean, *look* at 'em.

"Get outta here, ye rats!" Ivan calls but there's humour

in his voice and Noise, all trace of what was before hidden again. There's squeals of laughter outside the hole in the wall as the kids scatter.

And that's it, they're gone.

Like I mighta made 'em up.

"Puppies, Todd!" Manchee barks. "Puppies!"

"I know," I say, scratching his head when he comes over. "I know."

Ivan claps his hands together. "That's lunch then. Back to work." He gives me one more important look before he heads back to the front of the barn.

"What was that all about?" I say to Manchee.

"Puppies," he murmurs, digging his face into my hand.

And so there follows an afternoon pretty much exactly like my morning. Sweeping, folks stopping by, a break for water where Ivan don't say nothing to me, more sweeping.

I spend some time trying to think about what we might do next. If it's even *we* who's doing it. Farbranch'll have its meeting about us and they'll definitely keep Viola till her ship arrives, anyone can see that, but will they want me?

And if they do, do I stay?

And do I warn them?

I get a burning in my stomach every time I think about the book so I keep changing the subject.

After what seems like forever, the sun starts to set. There's no more damn sweeping I can do. I've already covered the whole barn more than once, counted the baskets, re-counted them, made an attempt to fix the loose board in the wall even tho no one asked me to. There's only so much you can ruddy well do if no one lets you leave a barn.

"Ain't that the truth?" Hildy says, standing there suddenly.

"You shouldn't sneak up on people like that," I say. "All you quiet folk."

"There's some food over at Francia's house for ye and for Viola. Why don't ye go on there, get something to eat?"

"While you all have yer meeting?"

"While we all have our meeting, yes, pup," Hildy says. "Viola's already in the house, no doubt eating all yer dinner."

"Hungry, Todd!" Manchee barks.

"There's food for ye, too, puppup," Hildy says, leaning down to pet him. He flops right over on his back for her, no dignity whatsoever.

"What's this meeting really about?" I ask.

"Oh, the new settlers that are a-coming. That's big news." She looks up from Manchee to me. "And introducing ye around, of course. Getting the town used to the idea of a-welcoming ye."

"And are they gonna *a-welcome* us?"

"People are scared of what they don't know, Todd pup," she says, standing. "Once they know ye, the problem goes away."

"Will we be able to stay?"

"I reckon so," she says. "If ye want to."

I don't say nothing to that.

"Ye get on up to the house," she says. "I'll come collect ye both when the time is right."

I only nod in response and she gives a little wave and leaves, walking back across a barn that's growing ever darker. I take the broom back to where it was hanging, my steps echoing. I can hear the Noise of men and the silence of women gathering across the town in the meeting hall. The word **Prentisstown** filters in most heavily and my name and Viola's name and Hildy's name.

And I gotta say, tho there's fear and suspishun in it, I don't get a feeling of overwhelming non-welcome. There's more askings than there is anger of the Matthew Lyle sort.

Which, you know, maybe. Maybe that ain't so bad after all.

"C'mon, Manchee," I say, "let's go get some food."

"Food, Todd!" he barks along at my heels.

"I wonder how Viola's day was," I say.

And as I step towards the entrance to the barn I realize one bit of Noise is separating itself from the general murmuring outside.

One bit of Noise lifting from the stream.

And heading for the barn.

Coming up right outside it.

I stop, deep in the dark of the barn.

A shadow steps into the far doorway.

Matthew Lyle.

And his Noise is saying, **Ye ain't going nowhere, boy.**

19

FURTHER CHOICES
OF A KNIFE

"Back! Back! Back!" Manchee immediately starts barking.

The moons glint off Matthew Lyle's machete.

I reach behind me. I'd hidden the sheath under my shirt while I worked but the knife is definitely still there. Definitely. I take it and hold it out at my side.

"No old mama to protect ye this time," Matthew says, swinging his machete back and forth, like he's trying to cut the air into slices. "No skirts to hide ye from what ye did."

"I didn't do nothing," I say, taking a step backwards, trying to keep my Noise from showing the back door behind me.

"Don't matter," Matthew says, walking forward as I step back. "We got a law here in this town."

"I don't have no quarrel with you," I say.

"But I've got one with *ye*, boy," he says, his Noise starting to rear up and there's anger in it, sure, but that weird grief's in it, too, that raging hurt you can almost taste on yer tongue.

There's also nervousness swirling about him, edgy as you please, much as he's trying to cover it.

I step back again, farther in the dark.

"I ain't a bad man, you know," he says, suddenly and kinda confusingly but swinging the machete. "I have a wife. I have a daughter."

"They wouldn't be wanting you to hurt no innocent boy, I'm sure–"

"Quiet!" he shouts and I can hear him swallow.

He ain't sure of this. He ain't sure of what he's about to do.

What's going on here?

"I don't know why yer angry," I say, "but I'm sorry. Whatever it is–"

"What I want you to know before you pay," he says over me, like he's forcing himself not to listen to me. "What you *need* to know, boy, is that my mother's name was Jessica."

I stop stepping back. "Beg pardon?"

"My mother's name," he growls, "was Jessica."

This don't make no sense at all.

"What?" I say. "I don't know what yer–"

"Listen, boy!" he yells. "Just listen."

And then his Noise is wide open.

And I see–

And I see–

And I see–

I see what he's showing.

"That's a lie," I whisper. "That's a ruddy lie."

Which is the wrong thing to say.

With a yell, Matthew leaps forward, running towards

me the length of the barn.

"Run!" I shout to Manchee, turning and making a break for the back doors. (Shut up, you honestly think a knife is a match for a machete?) I hear Matthew still yelling, his Noise exploding after me, and I reach the back door and fling it open before I realize.

Manchee's not with me.

I turn round. When I said "run", Manchee'd run the other way, flinging himself with all his unconvincing viciousness towards the charging Matthew.

"Manchee!" I yell.

It's ruddy dark in the barn now and I can hear grunts and barks and clanks and then I hear Matthew cry out in pain at what must surely be a bite.

Good dog, I think, *Good effing dog.*

And I can't leave him, can I?

I run back into the darkness, towards where I can see Matthew hopping around and the form of Manchee dancing twixt his legs and swipes of the machete, barking his little head off.

"Todd! Todd! Todd!" he's barking.

I'm five steps away and still running when Matthew makes a two-handed strike down at the ground, embedding the tip of the machete into the wooden floor. I hear a squeal from Manchee that don't have no words, just pain, and off he flies into a dark corner.

I let out a yell and crash right into Matthew. We both go flying, toppling to the floor in a tumble of elbows and kneecaps. It hurts but mostly I'm landing on Matthew so that's okay.

We roll apart and I hear him call out in pain. I get right back up to my feet, knife in hand, a few metres away from him, far from the back door now and with Matthew blocking the front. I hear Manchee whimpering in the dark.

I also hear some Noise rising from across the village road in the direkshun of the meeting hall but there ain't time to think about that now.

"I'm not afraid to kill you," I say, tho I totally am but I'm hoping my Noise and his Noise are now so rackety and revved up that he won't be able to make any sense from it.

"That makes two of us then," he says, lunging for his machete. It don't come out first tug, or the second. I take the chance to jump back into the dark, looking for Manchee.

"Manchee?" I say, frantically looking behind the sheaves and the piles of fruit baskets. I can still hear Matthew grunting to get his machete outta the floor and the ruckus from the town is growing louder.

"Todd?" I hear from deep in the darkness.

It's coming from beside the silage rolls, down a little nook that opens up next to them back to the wall. "Manchee?" I call, sticking my head down it.

I look back real quick.

With a heave, Matthew gets his machete outta the floor.

"Todd?" Manchee says, confused and scared. "Todd?"

And here comes Matthew, coming on in slow steps, like he no longer has to hurry, his Noise reaching forward in a wave that don't brook no argument.

I have no choice. I wedge myself back into the nook and hold out my knife.

"I'll leave," I say, my voice rising. "Just let me get my dog and we'll leave."

"Too late for that," Matthew says, getting closer.

"You don't wanna do this. I can tell."

"Shut yer mouth."

"Please," I say, waving the knife. "I don't wanna hurt you."

"Do I look concerned, boy?"

Closer, closer, step by step.

There's a bang outside somewhere, off in the distance. People really are running and shouting now but neither of us look.

I press myself back into the little nook but it's really not wide enough for me. I glance round, seeing where escape might lie.

I don't find nothing much.

My knife's gonna have to do it. It's gonna have to act, even if it is against a machete.

"Todd?" I hear behind me.

"Don't worry, Manchee," I say. "It's gonna be all right."

And who knows what a dog believes?

Matthew's almost on us now.

I grip my knife.

Matthew stops a metre from me, so close I can see his eyes glinting in the dark.

"Jessica," he says.

He raises his machete above his head.

I flinch back, knife up, steeling myself–

But he pauses–

He pauses–

In a way I reckernize–

And that's enough–

With a quick prayer that it ain't the same stuff from the bridge, I swing my knife in an arc to my side, slicing right thru (thank you thank you) the ropes holding up the silage rolls, cutting the first lot clean away. The other ropes snap right quick from the sudden shift in weight and I cover my head and press myself away as the silage rolls start to tumble.

I hear thumps and clumps and an "oof" from Matthew and I look up and he's buried in silage rolls, his arm out to one side, the machete dropped. I step forward and kick it away, then turn to find Manchee.

He's back in a dark corner behind the now-fallen rolls. I race over to him.

"Todd?" he says when I get close. "Tail, Todd?"

"Manchee?" It's dark so I have to squat down next to him to see. His tail's two thirds shorter than it used to be, blood everywhere, but God bless him, still trying to wag.

"Ow, Todd?"

"It's okay, Manchee," I say, my voice and Noise near crying from relief that it's just his tail. "We'll get you fixed right up."

"Okay, Todd?"

"I'm okay," I say, rubbing his head. He nips my hand but I know he can't help it cuz he's in pain. He licks me in apology then nips me again. "Ow, Todd," he says.

"Todd Hewitt!" I hear shouted from the front of the barn.

Francia.

"I'm here!" I call, standing up. "I'm all right. Matthew went crazy–"

But I stop cuz she ain't listening to me.

"Ye gotta get yerself indoors, Todd pup," Francia says in a rush. "Ye gotta–"

She stops when she sees Matthew under the silage.

"What happened?" she says, already starting to tug away the rolls, getting the one off his face and leaning down to see if he's still breathing.

I point to the machete. "*That* happened."

Francia looks at it, then a long look up at me, her face saying something I can't read nor even begin to figure out. I don't know if Matthew's alive nor dead and I ain't never gonna find out.

"We're under attack, pup," she says, standing.

"Yer *what*?"

"Men," she says, rising. "Prentisstown men. That posse that's after ye. They're attacking the whole town."

My stomach falls right outta my shoes.

"Oh, no," I say. And then I say it again, "Oh, no."

Francia's still looking at me, her brain thinking who knows what.

"Don't give us to them," I say, backing away again. "They'll kill us."

Francia frowns at this. "What kinda woman do ye think I am?"

"I don't know," I say, "that's the whole problem."

"I'm not gonna *give* ye to them. Honestly, now. Nor Viola. In fact the feeling of the town meeting, as far along as it got, was how we were a-deciding to protect ye both from what was almost certainly a-coming." She looks down at Matthew. "Tho maybe that's a promise we couldn't keep."

"Where's Viola?"

"Back at my house," Francia says, suddenly all active again. "C'mon. We gotta get ye inside."

"Wait." I squeeze back behind the silage rolls and find Manchee still in his corner, licking his tail. He looks up at me and barks, just a little bark that's not even a word. "I'm gonna pick you up now," I say to him. "Try not to bite me too hard, okay?"

"Okay, Todd," he whimpers, yelping each time he wags his stumpy tail.

I reach down, put my arms under his tummy and hoist him up to my chest. He yelps and bites hard at my wrist, then licks it.

"It's okay, buddy," I say, holding him as best I can.

Francia's waiting for me at the doors to the barn and I follow her out into the main road.

There are people running about everywhere. I see men and women with rifles running up towards the orchards and other men and women scooting kids (there they are again) into houses and such. In the distance I can hear bangs and shouts and yelling.

"Where's Hildy?" I yell.

Francia don't say nothing. We reach her front steps.

"What about Hildy?" I ask again as we climb up.

"She went off to fight," Francia says, not looking at me, opening the door. "They would have reached her farm first. Tam was still there."

"Oh, no," I say again stupidly, like my "oh nos" will do any good.

Viola comes flying down from the upper floor as we enter.

"What took you so long?" she says, her voice kinda loud, and I don't know which one of us she's talking to. She gasps when she sees Manchee.

"Bandages," I say. "Some of those fancy ones."

She nods and races back up the stairs.

"Ye two stay here," Francia says to me. "Don't come out, whatever ye hear."

"But we need to run!" I say, not understanding this at all. "We need to get outta here!"

"No, Todd pup," she says. "If Prentisstown wants ye, then that's reason enough for us to keep ye from them."

"But they've got guns–"

"So do we," Francia says. "No posse of Prentisstown men is going to take *this* town."

Viola's back down the stairs now, digging thru her bag for bandages.

"Francia–" I say.

"Stay right here," she says. "We'll protect ye. Both of ye."

She looks at both of us, hard, like seeing if we agree, then she turns and is out the door to protect her town, I guess.

We stare at the closed door for a second, then Manchee whimpers again and I have to set him down. Viola gets out a square bandage and her little scalpel.

"I don't know if these'll work on dogs," she says.

"Better than nothing," I say.

She cuts off a little strip and I have to hold Manchee's head down while she loops it around the mess of his tail. He growls and apologizes and growls and apologizes until Viola's covered the whole wound up tight. He immediately sets to licking it when I let him go.

"Stop that," I say.

"Itches," Manchee says.

"Stupid dog." I scratch his ears. "Stupid ruddy dog."

Viola pets him, too, trying to keep him from licking off the bandage.

"Do you think we're safe?" she asks quietly, after a long minute.

"I don't know."

There's more bangs out in the distance. We both jump. More people shouting. More Noise.

"No sign of Hildy since this started," Viola says.

"I know."

Another bit of silence as we over-pet Manchee. More ruckus from up in the orchards above town.

It all seems so far away, as if it's not even happening.

"Francia told me that you can find Haven if you keep following the main river," Viola says.

I look at her. I wonder if I know what this means.

I think I do.

"You wanna leave," I say.

"They'll keep coming," she says. "We're putting the people around us in danger. Don't you think they'll keep coming if they've already come this far?"

I do. I do think this. I don't say it but I do.

"But they said they could protect us," I say.

"Do you believe that?"

I don't say nothing to this neither. I think of Matthew Lyle.

"I don't think we're safe here any more," she says.

"I don't think we're safe *anywhere*," I say. "Not on this whole planet."

"I need to contact my ship, Todd," she says, almost pleading. "They're waiting to hear from me."

"And you wanna run off into the unknown to do it?"

"You do, too," she says. "I can tell." She looks away. "If we went together…"

I look up at her at this, trying to see, trying to *know*, to know real and true.

All she does is look back.

Which is enough.

"Let's go," I say.

We pack without any more words, and fast. I get my rucksack on, she gets her bag round her shoulders, Manchee's on his feet again and walking, and out the back door we go. As simple as that, we're going. Safer for Farbranch, definitely, safer for us, who knows? Who knows if this is the right thing to do? After what Hildy and Francia seemed to promise, it's hard leaving.

But we're leaving. And that's what we're doing.

Cuz at least it's *us* who decided it. I'd rather not have no one else tell me what they'll do for me, even when they mean well.

It's full dark night outside now, tho both moons are shining bright. Everyone in town's attenshun is behind us so there's no one to stop us from running. There's a little bridge that crosses the creek that runs thru town. "How far is this Haven?" I ask, whispering as we cross.

"Kinda far," Viola whispers back.

"How far is kinda far?"

She don't say nothing for a second.

"How *far*?" I say again.

"Coupla weeks' walk," she says, not looking back.

"Coupla *weeks*!"

"Where else do we have?" she says.

And I don't have an answer so we keep on walking.

Across the creek, the road heads up the far hill of the valley. We decide to take it as the fastest way outta town then find our way back south to the river and follow that. Ben's map ends at Farbranch so the river's all we got for direkshuns from here on out.

There's so many askings that come with us as we run outta Farbranch, askings that we'll never know the answers to: Why would the Mayor and a few men go miles outta their way to attack a whole ruddy town on their own? Why are they still after us? Why are we so important? And what happened to Hildy?

And did I kill Matthew Lyle?

And was what he showed me in his Noise right there at the end a true thing?

Was that the real history of Prentisstown?

"Was what the real history?" Viola asks as we hurry on up the path.

"Nothing," I say. "And quit reading me."

We get to the top of the far hill of the valley just as another rattle of gunfire echoes across it. We stop and look.

And then we see.

Boy, do we see.

"Oh, my God," Viola says.

Under the light of the two moons, the whole valley

kinda shines, across the Farbranch buildings and back up into the hills where the orchards are.

We can see the men and women of Farbranch running back down that hill.

In retreat.

And marching over the top, are five, ten, fifteen men on horseback.

Followed by rows of men five across, carrying guns, marching in a line behind what has to be the Mayor's horses in front.

Not a posse. Not a posse at all.

It's Prentisstown. I feel like the world's crumbling at my feet. It's every ruddy man in Prentisstown.

They have three times as many people as even live in Farbranch.

Three times as many guns.

We hear gunshots and we see the men and women of Farbranch fall as they run back to their houses.

They'll take the town easily. They'll take it before the hour is thru.

Cuz the rumours were true, the rumours that Francia heard.

The word was true.

It's an army.

A whole army.

There's a whole army coming after me and Viola.

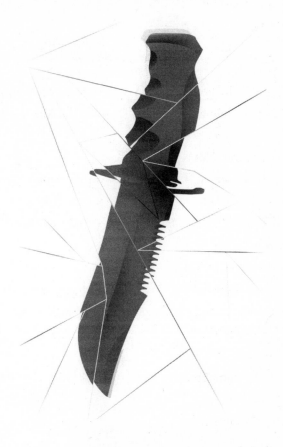

PART IV

20

ARMY OF MEN

WE DUCK BEHIND SOME BUSHES, even tho it's dark, even tho the army is across the valley, even tho they don't know we're up here and there's no way they could hear my Noise amidst all the ruckus going on down there, we duck anyway.

"Can yer binos see in the dark?" I whisper.

By way of answer Viola digs them outta her bag and holds them up to her own eyes. "What's happening?" she says, looking thru them, pressing more buttons. "Who are all those men?"

"It's Prentisstown," I say, holding out my hand. "It looks like every man in the whole effing town."

"How can it be the whole town?" She looks for a second or two more then hands the binos to me. "What kind of sense does that make?"

"You got me." The night setting on the binos turns the valley and all that's in it a bright green. I see horses galloping down the hill into the main part of town, shooting their rifles on the way, I see the people of Farbranch shooting back but mostly running, mostly falling, mostly dying. The Prentisstown army don't seem interested in taking prisoners.

"We have to get out of here, Todd," Viola says.

"Yeah," I say, but I'm still looking thru the binos.

With everything green, it's hard to make out faces. I press a few more buttons on the binos till I find the ones that take me in closer.

The first person I see for sure is Mr Prentiss Jr, in the lead, firing his rifle into the air when he don't have nothing else to shoot at. Then there's Mr Morgan and Mr Collins chasing some Farbranch men into the storage barns, firing their rifles after them. Mr O'Hare's there, too, and more of the Mayor's usual suspects on horseback, Mr Edwin, Mr Henratty, Mr Sullivan. And there's Mr Hammar, the smile on his face showing up green and evil even from this distance as he fires his rifle into the backs of fleeing women hustling away small children and I have to look away or throw up the nothing I had for dinner.

The men on foot march their way into town. The first one I reckernize is, of all people, Mr Phelps the storekeeper. Which is weird cuz he never seemed army-like at all. And there's Dr Baldwin. And Mr Fox. And Mr Cardiff who was our best milker. And Mr Tate who had the most books to burn when the Mayor outlawed them. And Mr Kearney who milled the town's wheat and who always spoke softly and who made wooden toys for each Prentisstown boy's birthday.

What are these men doing in an army?

"Todd," Viola says, pulling at my arm.

The men marching don't look none too happy, I spose. Grim and cold and scary in a different way from Mr Hammar, like they're lacking all feeling.

But they're still marching. They're still shooting. They're still kicking down doors.

"That's Mr Gillooly," I say, binos pressed to my eyes. "He can't even butcher his own meat."

"Todd," Viola says and I feel her backing away from the bushes. "Let's *go.*"

What's going on? Sure, Prentisstown was as awful a place as you could ever not wanna paint it but how can it suddenly be an army? There's plenty of Prentisstown men who're bad thru and thru but not all of them. Not *all.* And Mr Gillooly with a rifle is a sight so wrong it almost hurts my eyes just to look at it.

And then of course I see the answer.

Mayor Prentiss, not even holding a gun, just one hand on his horse's reins, the other at his side, riding into town like he's out for an evening canter. He's watching the rout of Farbranch as if it was a vid and not a very interesting one at that, letting everyone else do the work but so obviously in charge no one would even think of asking him to break a sweat.

How can he make so many men do what he wants?

And is he bulletproof that he can ride so fearlessly?

"Todd," Viola says behind me. "I swear, I'll leave without you."

"No, you won't," I say. "One more second."

Cuz I'm looking from face to face now, ain't I? I'm going from Prentisstown man to Prentisstown man cuz even if they're marching into town and are gonna find out soon enough that neither me nor Viola are there and are gonna have to come this way after us, I gotta know.

I gotta know.

Face to face to face as they march and shoot and burn. Mr Wallace, Mr Asbjornsen, Mr St James, Mr Belgraves, Mr Smith the Older, Mr Smith the Younger, Mr Smith With Nine Fingers, even Mr Marjoribanks, wobbling and teetering but marching marching marching. Prentisstown man after Prentisstown man after Prentisstown man, my heart clenching and burning at each one I can identify.

"They ain't there," I say, almost to myself.

"Who isn't?" Viola says.

"Ain't!" Manchee barks, licking at his tail.

They ain't there.

Ben and Cillian ain't there.

Which, of course, is grand, ain't it? Of course they ain't part of an army of killers. Of *course* they ain't, even when every other Prentisstown man is. They wouldn't be. Not never, not no how, no matter what.

Good men, *great* men, both, even Cillian.

But if that's true, then that means the other is true, too, don't it?

If they ain't there, then that means once and for all.

And there's yer lesson.

There ain't nothing good that don't got real bad waiting to follow it.

I hope they put up the best fight ever.

I take the binos from my face and I look down and I wipe my eyes with my sleeve and I turn and I hand Viola back the binos and I say, "Let's go."

She takes them from me, squirming a little like she's itching to leave, but then she says, "I'm sorry," so she musta seen it in my Noise.

"Nothing that ain't already happened," I say, talking to the ground and readjusting the rucksack. "C'mon, before I put us in danger any worse."

I take off up the path towards the top of the hill, keeping my head down, motoring fast, Viola after me, Manchee trying to keep himself from biting at his tail as we run.

Viola matches my speed before we get far at all. "Did you see ... him?" she says, between breaths.

"Aaron?"

She nods.

"No," I say. "Come to think of it, no, I didn't. And you'd think he'd be out in front."

We're quiet for a minute as we hurry on our way and wonder what that means.

The road on this side of the valley is wider and we're doing our best to keep to the darker side of it as it twists and turns up the hill. Our only lights are the moons but they're bright enough to cast our shadows running along the road which is too bright when yer running away. I never seen no night vision binos in Prentisstown but I didn't see no army neither so we're both crouching as we run without either of us saying that we will. Manchee's running on ahead of us, his nose to the ground, barking, "This way! This way!" as if he knows any better than us where we're going.

Then at the top of the hill, the road forks.

Which just figures.

"You gotta be kidding," I say.

One part of the road goes left, the other goes right.

(Well, it's a *fork*, ain't it?)

"The creek in Farbranch was flowing to the right," Viola says, "and the main river was always to our right once we crossed the bridge, so it's got to be the right fork if we want to get back there."

"But the left looks more travelled," I say. And it does. The left fork looks smoother, flatter, like the kinda thing you should be rolling carts over. The right fork is narrower with higher bushes on each side and even tho it's night you can just tell it's dusty. "Did Francia say anything about a fork?" I look back over my shoulder at the valley still erupting behind us.

"No," Viola says, also looking back. "She just said Haven was the first settlement and new settlements sprang up down the river as people moved west. Prentisstown was the farthest out. Farbranch was second farthest."

"That one probably goes to the river," I say, pointing right, then left, "that one probably goes to Haven in a straight line."

"Which one will they think we took?"

"We need to decide," I say. "Quickly now."

"To the right," she says, then turns it into an asking. "To the right?"

We hear a *BOOM* that makes us jump. A mushroom of smoke is rising in the air over Farbranch. The barn where I worked all day is on fire.

Maybe our story will turn out differently if we take the left fork, maybe the bad things that are waiting to happen to us won't happen, maybe there's happiness at the end of the left fork and warm places with the people who love us and no Noise but no silence neither and there's plenty of food and no one dies and no one dies and no one never never dies.

Maybe.

But I doubt it.

I ain't what you call a lucky person.

"Right," I decide. "Might as well be right."

We run down the right fork, Manchee at our heels, the night and a dusty road stretching out in front of us, an army and a disaster behind us, me and Viola, running side by side.

We run till we can't run and then we walk fast till we can run again. The sounds of Farbranch disappear behind us right quick and all we can hear are our footsteps beating on the path and my Noise and Manchee's barking. If there are night creachers out there, we're scaring 'em away.

Which is probably good.

"What's the next settlement?" I gasp after a good half hour's run-walking. "Did Francia say?"

"Shining Beacon," Viola says, gasping herself. "Or Shining Light." She scrunches her face. "*Blazing* Light. Blazing Beacon?"

"That's helpful."

"Wait." She stops in the path, bending at the waist to catch her breath. I stop, too. "I need water."

I hold up my hands in a way that says *And?* "So do I," I say. "You got some?"

She looks at me, her eyebrows up. "Oh."

"There was always a river."

"I guess we'd better find it then."

"I guess so." I take a deep breath to start running again.

"Todd," she says, stopping me. "I've been thinking?"

"Yeah?" I say.

"Blazing Lights or whatever?"

"Yeah?"

"If you look at it one way," she lowers her voice to a sad and uncomfortable sound and says it again, "if you look at it one way, we led an army into Farbranch."

I lick the dryness of my lips. I taste dust. And I know what she's saying.

"You must warn them," she says quietly, into the dark. "I'm sorry, but–"

"We can't go into any other settlements," I say.

"I don't think we can."

"Not till Haven."

"Not until Haven," she says, "which we have to hope is big enough to handle an army."

So, that's that then. In case we needed any further reminding, we're really on our own. Really and truly. Me and Viola and Manchee and the darkness for company. No one on the road to help us till the end, if even there, which knowing our luck so far–

I close my eyes.

I am Todd Hewitt, I think. *When it goes midnight I will be a man in twenty-seven days. I am the son of my ma and pa, may they rest in peace. I am the son of Ben and Cillian, may they–*

I am Todd Hewitt.

"I'm Viola Eade," Viola says.

I open my eyes. She has her hand out, palm down, held towards me.

"That's my surname," she says. "Eade. E-A-D-E."

I look at her for a second and then down at her out-stretched hand and I reach out and I take it and press it inside my own and a second later I let go.

I shrug my shoulders to reset my rucksack. I put my hand behind my back to feel the knife and make sure it's still there. I give poor, panting, half-tail Manchee a look and then match eyes with Viola.

"Viola Eade," I say, and she nods.

And off we run into further night.

21

THE WIDER WORLD

"HOW CAN IT BE THIS FAR?" Viola asks. "It doesn't make any logical sense."

"Is there another kind of sense it does make?"

She frowns. So do I. We're tired and getting tireder and trying not to think of what we saw at Farbranch and we've walked and run what feels like half the night and still no river. I'm starting to get afraid we've taken a seriously wrong turning which we can't do nothing about cuz there ain't no turning back.

"*Isn't any* turning back," I hear Viola say behind me, under her breath.

I turn to her, eyes wide. "That's wrong on two counts," I say. "Number one, constantly reading people's Noise ain't gonna get you much welcome here."

She crosses her arms and sets her shoulders. "And the second?"

"The second is I talk how I please."

"Yes," Viola says. "That you do."

My Noise starts to rise a bit and I take a deep breath but then she says, "Shhh," and her eyes glint in the moonlight as she looks beyond me.

The sound of running water.

"River!" Manchee barks.

We take off down the road and round a corner and down a slope and round another corner and there's the river, wider, flatter and slower than when we saw it last but just as wet. We don't say nothing, just drop to our knees on the rocks at water's edge and drink, Manchee wading in up to his belly to start lapping.

Viola's next to me and as I slurp away, there's her silence again. It's a two-way thing, this is. However clear she can hear my Noise, well, out here alone, away from the chatter of others or the Noise of a settlement, there's her silence, loud as a roar, pulling at me like the greatest sadness ever, like I want to take it and press myself into it and just disappear forever down into nothing.

What a relief that would feel like right now. What a blessed relief.

"I can't avoid hearing you, you know," she says, standing up and opening her bag. "When it's quiet and just the two of us."

"And I can't avoid not hearing you," I say. "No matter what it's like." I whistle for Manchee. "Outta the water. There might be snakes."

He's ducking his rump under the current, swishing back and forth until the bandage comes off and floats away. Then he leaps out and immediately sets to licking his tail.

"Let me see," I say. He barks "Todd!" in agreement but when I come near he curls his tail as far under his belly as the new length will go. I uncurl it gently, Manchee murmuring "Tail, tail" to himself all the while.

"Whaddyaknow?" I say. "Those bandages work on dogs."

Viola's fished out two discs from her bag. She presses her thumbs inside them and they expand right up into water bottles. She kneels by the river, fills both, and tosses one to me.

"Thanks," I say, not really looking at her.

She wipes some water from her bottle. We stand on the riverbank for a second and she's putting her water bottle back into her bag and she's quiet in a way that I'm learning means she's trying to say something difficult.

"I don't mean any offence by it," she says, looking up to me, "but I think maybe it's time I read the note on the map."

I can feel myself redden, even in the dark, and I can also feel myself get ready to argue.

But then I just sigh. I'm tired and it's late and we're running *again* and she's right, ain't she? There's nothing but spitefulness that'll argue she's wrong.

I drop my rucksack and take out the book, unfolding the map from inside the front cover. I hand it to her without looking at her. She takes out her torch and shines it on the paper, turning it over to Ben's message. To my surprise, she starts reading it out loud and all of sudden, even with her own voice, it's like Ben's is ringing down the river, echoing from Prentisstown and hitting my chest like a punch.

"*Go to the settlement down the river and across the*

bridge," she reads. *"It's called Farbranch and the people there should welcome you."*

"And they did," I say. "Some of them."

Viola continues, *"There are things you don't know about our history, Todd, and I'm sorry for that but if you knew them you would be in great danger. The only chance you have of a welcome is yer innocence."*

I feel myself redden even more but fortunately it's too dark to see.

"Yer ma's book will tell you more but in the meantime, the wider world has to be warned, Todd. Prentisstown is on the move. The plan has been in the works for years, only waiting for the last boy in Prentisstown to become a man." She looks up. "Is that you?"

"That's me," I say, "I was the youngest boy. I turn thirteen in twenty-seven days and officially become a man according to Prentisstown law."

And I can't help but think for a minute about what Ben showed me–

About how a boy becomes–

I cover it up and say quickly, "But I got no idea what he means about them waiting for me."

"The Mayor plans to take Farbranch and who knows what else beyond. Sillian and I–"

"Cillian," I correct her. "With a K sound."

"Cillian and I will try to delay it as long as we can but we won't be able to stop it. Farbranch will be in danger and you have to warn them. Always, always, always remember that we love you like our own son and sending you away is the hardest thing we'll ever have to do. If it's at all possible, we'll see you

again, but first you must get to Farbranch as fast as you can and when you get there, you must warn them. Ben." Viola looks up. "That last part's underlined."

"I know."

And then we don't say nothing for a minute. There's blame in the air but maybe it's all coming from me.

Who can tell with a silent girl?

"My fault," I say. "It's all my fault."

Viola rereads the note to herself. "They should have *told* you," she says. "Not expected you to read it if you can't–"

"If they'd told me, Prentisstown would've heard it in my Noise and known that I knew. We wouldn't've even got the head start we had." I glance at her eyes and look away. "I shoulda given it to someone to read and that's all there is to it. Ben's a good man." I lower my voice. "Was."

She refolds the map and hands it back to me. It's useless to us now but I put it back carefully inside the front cover of the book.

"I could read that for you," Viola says. "Your mother's book. If you wanted."

I keep my back to her and put the book in my rucksack. "We need to go," I say. "We've wasted too much time here."

"Todd–"

"There's an army after us," I say. "No more time for reading."

So we set off again and do our best to run for as much and as long as we can but as the sun rises, all slow and lazy and cold, we've had no sleep and that's no sleep after a full day's work and so even with that army on our tails, we're barely able to even keep up a fast walk.

But we do, thru that next morning. The road keeps following the river as we hoped and the land starts to flatten out around us, great natural plains of grass stretching out to low hills and to higher hills beyond and, to the north at least, mountains beyond that.

It's all wild, tho. No fences, no fields of crops, and no signs of any kind of settlement or people except for the dusty road itself. Which is good in one way but weird in another.

If New World isn't sposed to have been wiped out, where is everybody?

"You think this is right?" I say, as we come round yet another dusty corner of the road with nothing beyond it but more dusty corners. "You think we're going the right way?"

Viola blows out thoughtful air. "My dad used to say, *There's only forward, Vi, only outward and up.*"

"There's only forward," I repeat.

"Outward and up," she says.

"What was he like?" I ask. "Yer pa?"

She looks down at the road and from the side I can see half a smile on her face. "He smelled like fresh bread," she says and then she moves on ahead and don't say nothing more.

Morning turns to afternoon with more of the same. We hurry when we can, walk fast when we can't hurry, and only rest when we can't help it. The river remains flat and steady, like the brown and green land around it. I can see bluehawks way up high, hovering and scouting for prey, but that's about it for signs of life.

"This is one empty planet," Viola says as we stop for a quick lunch, leaning on some rocks overlooking a natural weir.

"Oh, it's full enough," I say, munching on some cheese. "Believe me."

"I do believe you. I just meant I can see why people would want to settle here. Lots of fertile farmland, lots of potential for people to make new lives."

I chew. "People would be mistaken."

She rubs her neck and looks at Manchee, sniffing round the edges of the weir, probably smelling the wood weavers who made it living underneath.

"Why do you become a man here at thirteen?" she asks.

I look over at her, surprised. "What?"

"That note," she says. "The town waiting for the last boy to become a man." She looks at me. "Why wait?"

"That's how New World's always done it. It's sposed to be scriptural. Aaron always went on about it symbolizing the day you eat from the Tree of Knowledge and go from innocence into sin."

She gives me a funny look. "That sounds pretty heavy."

I shrug. "Ben said that the real reason was cuz a small group of people on an isolated planet need all the adults they can get so thirteen is the day you start getting real responsibilities." I throw a stray stone into the river. "Don't ask me. All I know is it's thirteen years. Thirteen cycles of thirteen months."

"*Thirteen* months?" she asks, her eyebrows up.

I nod.

"There are only twelve months in a year," she says.

"No, there ain't. There's thirteen."

"Maybe not here," she says, "but where I come from there's twelve."

I blink. "Thirteen months in a New World year," I say, feeling dumb for some reason.

She looks up like she's figuring something out. "I mean, depending on how long a day or a month is on this planet, you might be ... fourteen years old already."

"That's not how it works here," I say, kinda stern, not really liking this much. "I turn thirteen in twenty-seven days."

"Fourteen and a *month*, actually," she says, still figuring it out. "Which makes you wonder how you tell how old anybody–"

"It's twenty-seven days till my birthday," I say firmly. I stand and put the rucksack back on. "Come on. We've wasted too much time talking."

It ain't till the sun's finally started to dip below the tops of the trees that we see our first sign of civilizayshun: an abandoned water mill at the river's edge, its roof burnt off who knows how many years ago. We've been walking so long we don't even talk, don't even look around much for danger, just go inside, throw our bags down against the walls and flop to the ground like it's the softest bed ever. Manchee, who don't seem to ever get tired, is busy running around, lifting his leg on all the plants that have grown up thru the cracked floorboards.

"My feet," I say, peeling off my shoes, counting five, no, *six* different blisters.

Viola lets out a weary sigh from the opposite wall. "We have to sleep," she says. "Even if."

"I know."

She looks at me. "You'll hear them coming," she says, "if they come?"

"Oh, I'll hear them," I say. "I'll definitely hear them."

We decide to take turns sleeping. I say I'll wait up first and Viola can barely say good night before she's out. I watch her sleep as the light fades. The little bit of clean we got at Hildy's house is already long gone. She looks like I must do, face smudged with dust, dark circles under her eyes, dirt under her nails.

And I start to think.

I've only known her for three days, you know? Three effing days outta my whole entire life but it's like nothing that happened before really happened, like that was all a big lie just waiting for me to find out. No, not *like*, it *was* a big lie waiting for me to find out and this is the real life now, running without safety or answer, only moving, only ever moving.

I take a sip of water and I listen to the crickets chirping **sex sex sex** and I wonder what *her* life was like before these last three days. Like, what's it like growing up on a spaceship? A place where there's never any new people, a place you can never get beyond the borders of.

A place like Prentisstown, come to think of it, where if you disappeared, you ain't never coming back.

I look back over to her. But she did get out, didn't she? She got seven *months* out with her ma and her pa on the little ship that crashed.

How's that work, I wonder?

"You need to send scout ships out ahead to make local field surveys and find the best landing sites," she says, without sitting up or even moving her head. "How does anyone ever sleep in a world with Noise?"

"You get used to it," I say. "But why so long? Why seven months?"

"That's how long it takes to set up first camp." She covers her eyes with her hand in an exhausted way. "Me and my mother and father were supposed to find the best place for the ships to land and build the first encampment and then we'd start building the first things that would be needed for settlers just landing. A control tower, a food store, a clinic." She looks at me twixt her fingers. "It's standard procedure."

"I never seen no control tower on New World," I say.

This makes her sit up. "I *know*. I can't believe you guys don't even have communicators between settlements."

"So yer not church settlers then," I say, sounding wise.

"What does that have to do with anything?" she says. "Why would any reasonable church want to be cut off from itself?"

"Ben said that they came to this world for the simpler life, said that there was even a fight in the early days whether to destroy the fission generators."

Viola looks horrified. "You would have all died."

"That's why they weren't destroyed," I shrug. "Not even after Mayor Prentiss decided to get rid of most everything else."

Viola rubs her shins and looks up into the stars coming out thru the hole in the roof. "My mother and father were so excited," she says. "A whole new world, a whole new beginning, all these plans of peace and happiness." She stops.

"I'm sorry it ain't that way," I say.

She looks down at her feet. "Would you mind waiting outside for a little while until I fall asleep?"

"Yeah," I say, "no problem."

I take my rucksack and go out the opening where the front door used to be. Manchee gets up from where he's curled and follows me. When I sit down, he recurls by my legs and falls asleep, farting happily and giving a doggy sigh. Simple to be a dog.

I watch the moons rise, the stars following 'em, the same moons and the same stars as were in Prentisstown, still out here past the end of the world. I take out the book again, the oil in the cover shining from the moonlight. I flip thru the pages.

I wonder if my ma was excited to land here, if her head was full of peace and good hope and joy everlasting.

I wonder if she found any before she died.

This makes my chest heavy so I put the book back in the rucksack and lean my head against the boards of the mill. I listen to the river flow past and the leaves shushing to themselves in the few trees around us and I look at the shadows of far distant hills on the horizon and the rustling forests on them.

I'll wait for a few minutes, then go back inside and make sure Viola's okay.

The next thing I know she's waking me up and it's hours later and my head is completely confused till I hear her saying, "Noise, Todd, I can hear Noise."

I'm on my feet before I'm fully awake, quieting Viola and a groggy Manchee barking his complaints. They get quiet and I put my ear into the night.

Whisper whisper whisper there, like a breeze *whisper whisper whisper* no words and far away but hovering, a storm cloud behind a mountain *whisper whisper whisper*.

"We gotta go," I say, already reaching for my rucksack.

"Is it the army?" Viola calls, running thru the door of the mill as she grabs her own bag.

"Army!" Manchee barks.

"Don't know," I say. "Probably."

"Could it be the next settlement?" Viola comes back, bag round her shoulders. "We can't be too far from it."

"Then why didn't we hear it when we got here?"

She bites her lip. "Damn."

"Yeah," I say. "Damn."

And so the second night after Farbranch passes like the first, running in darkness, using torches when we need them, trying not to think. Just before the sun comes up, the river moves outta the flats and into another small valley like the one by Farbranch and sure enough, there's Blazing Beacons or whatever so maybe there really are people living out this way.

They've got orchards, too, and fields of wheat, tho nothing looks near as well tended as Farbranch. Lucky for us, the main bit of town is on top of the hill with what looks like a bigger road going thru it, the left fork, maybe, and five or six buildings, most of which could use a lick of paint. Down on our dirt road by the river there are just boats and wormy-looking docks and dockhouses and whatever else you build on a flowing river.

We can't ask anyone for help. Even if we got it, the army's coming, ain't it? We should warn them but what if they're Matthew Lyles rather than Hildys? And what if by warning them we draw the army right *to* them cuz then we're in everyone's Noise? And what if the settlement knows we're the reason the army's coming and they decide to turn us over to them?

But they deserve to be warned, don't they?

But what if that endangers *us*?

You see? What's the right answer?

And so we sneak thru the settlement like thieves, running from dockhouse to dockhouse, hiding from sight of the town up the hill, waiting as quiet as we can when we see a skinny woman taking a basket into a hen house up by some trees. It's small enough that we get thru it before the sun even fully rises and we're out the other side and back on the road like it never existed, like it never happened, even to us.

"So that's that settlement then," Viola whispers as we take a look behind us and watch it disappear behind a bend. "We'll never even know what it was properly called."

"And now we *really* don't know what's ahead of us," I whisper back.

"We keep going until we get to Haven."

"And then what?"

She don't say nothing to that.

"That's a lotta faith we're putting in a word," I say.

"There's got to be something, Todd," she says, her face kinda grim. "There has to be *something* there."

I don't say nothing for a second and then I say, "I guess we'll see."

And so starts another morning. Twice on the road we see men with horse-drawn carts. Both times we hie off into the woods, Viola with her hand round Manchee's snout and me trying to keep my Noise as Prentisstown-free as possible till they pass.

Nothing much changes as the hours go by. We don't hear no more whispers from the army, if that's what it even was, but there ain't no point in finding out for sure, is there? Morning's turned into afternoon again when we see a settlement high up on a far hill. We're coming up a little hill ourselves, the river dropping down a bit, tho we can see it spreading out in the distance, what looks like the start of a plain we're gonna have to cross.

Viola points her binos at the settlement for a minute, then hands them to me. It's ten or fifteen buildings this time but even from a distance it looks scrubby and run down.

"I don't get it," Viola says. "Going by a regular schedule of settlement, subsistence farming should be years over by now. And there's obviously trade, so why is there still this much struggle?"

"You don't really know nothing about settler's lives, do you?" I say, chafing just a little.

She purses her lips. "It was required in school. I've been learning about how to set up a successful colony since I was five."

"Schooling ain't life."

"*Ain't* it?" she says, her eyebrows raising in a mock.

"*What did I say before?*" I snap back. "Some of us were busy surviving and couldn't learn about subdivided farming."

"*Subsistence.*"

"Don't care." I get myself moving again on the road.

Viola stomps after me. "We're going to be teaching you lot a thing or two when my ship arrives," she says. "You can be sure of that."

"Well, won't we dumb hicks be queuing up to kiss yer behinds in thankfulness?" I say, my Noise buzzing and not saying "behinds".

"Yes, you *will* be." She's raising her voice. "Trying to turn back the clock to the dark ages has really worked out for you, hasn't it? When we get here, you'll see how people are *supposed* to settle."

"That's *seven months* from now," I seethe at her. "You'll have plenty of time to see how the other half live."

"Todd!" Manchee barks, making us jump again, and suddenly he takes off down the road ahead of us.

"Manchee!" I yell after him. "Get back here!"

And then we both hear it.

22

WILF AND THE SEA
OF THINGS

IT'S WEIRD, Noise, but almost wordless, cresting the
hill in front of us and rolling down, single-minded but talking
in legions, like a thousand voices singing the same thing.

Yeah.

Singing.

"What is it?" Viola asks, spooked as I am. "It's not the
army, is it? How could they be in front of us?"

"Todd!" Manchee barks from the top of the small hill.
"Cows, Todd! Giant cows!"

Viola's mouth twists. "Giant cows?"

"No idea," I say and I'm already heading up the little hill.

Cuz the sound–

How can I describe it?

Like how stars might sound. Or moons. But not mountains. Too floaty for mountains. It's a sound like one planet
singing to another, high and stretched and full of different
voices starting at different notes and sloping down to other

different notes but all weaving together in a rope of sound that's sad but not sad and slow but not slow and all singing one word.

One word.

We reach the top of the hill and another plain unrolls below us, the river tumbling down to meet it and then running thru it like a vein of silver thru a rock and all over the plain, walking their way from one side of the river to the other, are creachers.

Creachers I never seen the like of in my life.

Massive, they are, four metres tall if they're an inch, covered in a shaggy, silvery fur with a thick, fluffed tail at one end and a pair of curved white horns at the other reaching right outta their brows and long necks that stretch down from wide shoulders to the grass of the plain below and these wide lips that mow it up as they trudge on dry ground and drink water as they cross the river and there's *thousands* of 'em, thousands stretching from the horizon on our right to the horizon on our left and the Noise of them all is singing one word, at different times in different notes, but one word binding 'em all together, knitting 'em as a group as they cross the plain.

"*Here,*" Viola says from somewhere off to my side. "They're singing *here.*"

They're singing **Here**. Calling it from one to another in their Noise.

Here I am.

Here we are.

Here we go.

Here is all that matters.

Here.

It's—

Can I say?

It's like the song of a family where everything's always all right, it's a song of belonging that makes you belong just by hearing it, it's a song that'll always take care of you and never leave you. If you have a heart, it breaks, if you have a heart that's broken, it fixes.

It's—

Wow.

I look at Viola and she has her hand over her mouth and her eyes are wet but I can see a smile thru her fingers and I open my mouth to speak.

"Ya won't get ver far on foot," says a completely other voice to our left.

We spin round to look, my hand going right to my knife. A man driving an empty cart pulled by a pair of oxes regards us from a little side path, his mouth left hanging open like he forgot to close it.

There's a shotgun on the seat next to him, like he just put it there.

From a distance, Manchee barks "Cow!"

"They's all go round carts," says the man, "but not safe on foot, no. They's squish ya right up."

And again leaves his mouth open. His Noise, buried under all the **Here**s from the herd, seems to pretty much be saying exactly what his mouth is. I'm trying so hard not to think of certain words I'm already getting a headache.

"Ah kin give y'all a ride thrus," he says. "If ya want."

He raises an arm and points down the road, which

disappears under the feet of the herd crossing it. I hadn't even thought about how the creachers'd be blocking our way but you can see how you wouldn't wanna try walking thru them.

I turn and I start to say something, *anything*, that'll be the fastest way to get away.

But instead the most amazing thing happens.

Viola looks at the man and says, "Ah'm Hildy." She points at me. "At's Ben."

"What?" I say, barking it almost like Manchee.

"Wilf," says the man to Viola and it takes a second to realize he's saying his name.

"Hiya, Wilf," Viola says and her voice ain't her own, ain't her own at all, there's a whole new voice coming outta her mouth, stretching and shortening itself, twisting and unravelling and the more she talks the more different she sounds.

The more she sounds like Wilf.

"We're all fra Farbranch. Where yoo from?"

Wilf hangs his thumb back over his shoulder. "Bar Vista," he says. "I'm gone Brockley Falls, pick up s'plies."

"Well, at's lucky," Viola says. "We're gone Brockley Falls, too."

This is making my headache worse. I put my hands up to my temples, like I'm trying to keep my Noise inside, trying to keep all the wrong things from spilling out into the world. Luckily, the song of **Here** has made it like we're already swimming in sound.

"Hop on," Wilf says with a shrug.

"C'mon, Ben," Viola says, walking to the back of the cart and hoisting her bag on top. "Wilf's gone give us a ride."

She jumps on the cart and Wilf snaps the reins on his

oxes. They take off slowly and Wilf don't even look at me as he passes. I'm still standing there in amazement when Viola goes by, waving her hand frantically to me to get on beside her. I don't got no choice, do I? I catch up and pull myself up with my arms.

I sit down next to her and stare at her with my jaw down around my ankles. *"What are you doing?"* I finally hiss in what's sposed to be a whisper.

"Shh!" she shushes, looking back over her shoulder at Wilf, but he could've already forgotten he picked us up for all that's going on in his Noise. "I don't know," she whispers by my ear, "just play along."

"Play along with what?"

"If we can get to the other side of the herd, then it's between us and the army, isn't it?"

I hadn't thought about that. "But what are you doing? What do Ben and Hildy gotta do with it?"

"He has a gun," she whispers, checking on Wilf again. "And you said yourself how people might react about you being from a certain place. So, it just sort of popped out."

"But you were talking in his *voice*."

"Not very well."

"Good enough!" I say, my voice going a little loud with amazement.

"Shh," she says a second time but with the combo of the herd of creachers getting closer by the second and Wilf's obvious not-too-brightness, we might as well be having a normal conversayshun.

"How do you do it?" I say, still pouring surprise out all over her.

"It's just lying, Todd," she says, trying to shush me again with her hands. "Don't you have lying here?"

Well of course we have lying here. New World and the town where I'm from (avoiding saying the name, avoiding *thinking* the name) seem to be nothing *but* lies. But that's different. I said it before, men lie all the time, to theirselves, to other men, to the world at large, but who can tell when it's a strand in all the other lies and truths floating round outta yer head? Everyone knows yer lying but everyone else is lying, too, so how can it matter? What does it change? It's just part of the river of a man, part of his Noise, and sometimes you can pick it out, sometimes you can't.

But he never stops being himself when he does it.

Cuz all I know about Viola is what she says. The only truth I got is what comes outta her mouth and so for a second back there, when she said she was Hildy and I was Ben and we were from Farbranch and she spoke just like Wilf (even tho he ain't from Farbranch) it was like all those things *became* true, just for an instant the world changed, just for a second it became made of Viola's voice and it wasn't describing a thing, it was *making* a thing, it was making us different just by saying it.

Oh, my head.

"Todd! Todd!" Manchee barks, popping up at the end of the cart, looking up thru our feet. "Todd!"

"Crap," Viola says.

I hop off the cart and sweep him up in my arms, putting one hand round his muzzle and using the other to get back on the cart. "Td?" he puffs thru closed lips.

"Quiet, Manchee," I say.

"I'm not even sure it matters," Viola says, her voice stretching out.

I look up.

"Cw," Manchee says.

A creacher is walking right past us.

We've entered the herd.

Entered the song.

And for a little while, I forget all about any kinda lies.

I've never seen the sea, only in vids. No lakes where I grew up neither, just the river and the swamp. There may have been boats once but not in my lifetime.

But if I had to imagine being on the sea, this is what I'd imagine. The herd surrounds us and takes up everything, leaving just the sky and us. It cuts around us like a current, sometimes noticing us but more usually noticing only itself and the song of **Here**, which in the midst of it is so loud it's like it's taken over the running of yer body for a while, providing the energy to make yer heart beat and yer lungs breathe.

After a while, I find myself forgetting all about Wilf and the – the other things I could think about and I'm just lying back on the cart, watching it all go by, individual creachers snuffling around, feeding, bumping each other now and again with their horns, and there's baby ones, too, and old bulls and taller ones and shorter ones and some with scars and some with scruffier fur.

Viola's laying down next to me and Manchee's little doggie brain is overwhelmed by it all and he's just watching the herd go by with his tongue hanging out and for a while, for a little while, as Wilf drives us over the plain, this is all there is in the world.

This is all there is.

I look over at Viola and she looks back at me and just smiles and shakes her head and wipes away the wet from her eyes.

Here.

Here.

We're **Here** and nowhere else.

Cuz there's nowhere else but **Here**.

"So this … Aaron," Viola says after a while in a low voice and I know exactly why it's now that she brings him up.

It's so safe inside the **Here** we can talk about any dangers we like.

"Yeah?" I say, also keeping my voice low, watching a little family of creachers waltz by the end of the cart, the ma creacher nuzzling forward a curious baby creacher who's staring at us.

Viola turns to me from where she's lying down. "Aaron was your holy man?"

I nod. "Our one and only."

"What kind of things did he preach?"

"The usual," I say. "Hellfire. Damnayshun. Judgement."

She eyes me up. "I'm not sure that's the usual, Todd."

I shrug. "He believed we were living thru the end of the world," I say. "Who's to say he was wrong?"

She shakes her head. "That's not what the preacher we had on the ship was like. Pastor Marc. He was kind and friendly and made everything seem like it was going to be okay."

I snort. "No, that don't sound like Aaron at all. He was always saying, 'God hears' and 'If one of us falls, we all fall'.

244

Like he was looking forward to it."

"I heard him say that, too." She crosses her arms over herself.

The **Here** wraps us still, flowing everywhere.

I turn to her. "Did he… Did he hurt you? Back in the swamp?"

She shakes her head again and lets out a sigh. "He ranted and raved at me, and I guess it might have been preaching, but if I ran, he'd run after me and rant some more and I'd cry and ask him for help but he'd ignore me and preach some more and I'd see pictures of myself in his Noise when I didn't even know what Noise was. I've never been so scared in my life, not even when our ship was crashing."

We both look up into the sun.

"If one of us falls, we all fall," she says. "What does that even mean?"

Which, when I really think about it, I realize I don't know and so I don't say nothing and we just sink back into the **Here** and let it take us a little farther.

Here we are.

Not nowhere else.

After an hour or a week or a second, the creachers start thinning and we come out the other side of the herd. Manchee jumps down off the cart. We're going slow enough that there's no danger of him getting left behind so I let him. We're not thru lying there on the cart just yet.

"That was amazing," Viola says quietly, cuz the song is already starting to disappear. "I forgot all about how much my feet hurt."

"Yeah," I say.

"What *were* those?"

"'Em big thangs," Wilf says, not turning round. "Jus thangs, thass all."

Viola and I look at each other, like we forgot he was even there.

How much have we given away?

"'Em thangs got a name?" Viola asks, sitting up, acting her lie again.

"Oh, sure," Wilf says, giving the oxes freer rein now that we're outta the herd. "Packy Vines or Field Baysts or Anta Fants." We see him shrug from behind. "I just call 'em thangs, thass all."

"Thangs," Viola says.

"Things," I try.

Wilf looks back over his shoulder at us. "Say what, y'all from Farbranch?" he asks.

"Yessir," Viola says with a look at me.

Wilf nods at her. "Y'all bin seen that there army?"

My Noise spikes real loud before I can quiet it but again Wilf don't seem to notice. Viola looks at me, worry on her forehead.

"And what army's that, Wilf?" she says, the voice missing a little.

"That there army from cursed town," he says, still driving along like we're talking about vegetables. "That there army come outta swamp, come takin settlements, growin as it comes? Y'all bin seen that?"

"Where'd yoo hear bout an army, Wilf?"

"Stories," Wilf says. "Stories a-come chatterin down the

river. People talkin. Ya know. Stories. Y'all bin seen that?"

I shake my head at Viola but she says, "Yeah, we seen it."

Wilf looks back over his shoulder again. "Zit big?"

"Very big," Viola says, looking at him seriously. "Ya gotta prepare yerself, Wilf. There's danger comin. Yoo need to warn Brockley Hills."

"Brockley Falls," Wilf corrects her.

"Ya gotta warn 'em, Wilf."

We hear Wilf grunt and then we realize it's a laugh. "Ain't nobody lissnen to Wilf, I tell ya what," he says, almost to himself, then strikes the reins on the oxes again.

It takes most of the rest of the afternoon to get to the other side of the plain. Thru Viola's binos we can see the herd of things still crossing in the distance, from south to north, like they're never gonna run out. Wilf don't say nothing more about the army. Viola and I keep our talking to a bare minimum so we don't give any more away. Plus, it's so hard to keep my Noise clear it's taking mosta my concentrayshun. Manchee follows along on the road, doing his business and sniffing every flower.

When the sun is low in the sky, the cart finally creaks to a halt.

"Brockley Falls," Wilf says, nodding his head to where we can see in the distance the river tumbling off a low cliff. There's fifteen or twenty buildings gathered round the pond at the bottom of the falls before the river starts up again. A smaller road turns off from this one and leads down to it.

"We're getting off here," Viola says and we hop down, taking our bags from the cart.

"Thought ya mite," Wilf says, looking back over his shoulder at us again.

"Thank ya, Wilf," she says.

"Welcome," he says, staring off into the distance. "Best take shelter 'fore too long. Gone rain."

Both Viola and me automatically look straight up. There ain't a cloud in the sky.

"Mmm," Wilf says. "No one lissnen to Wilf."

Viola looks back at him, her voice returning to itself, trying to get the point to him clearly. "You have to warn them, Wilf. Please. If you're hearing that an army's coming, then you're right and people have to be ready."

All Wilf says is "Mmm" again before snapping the reins and turning the oxes down the split road towards Brockley Falls. He don't even look back once.

We watch him go for a while and then turn back to our own road.

"Ow," Viola says, stretching out her legs as she steps forward.

"I know," I say. "Mine too."

"You think he was right?" Viola says.

"Bout what?"

"About the army getting bigger as it marches." She imitates his voice again. "Growin as it comes."

"How do you *do* that?" I ask. "Yer not even from here."

She shrugs. "A game I used to play with my mother," she says. "Telling a story, using different voices for every character."

"Can you do my voice?" I ask, kinda tentative.

She grins. *"So you can have a conversayshun with yerself?"*

I frown. "That don't sound nothing like me."

We head back down the road, Brockley Falls disappearing behind us. The time on the cart was nice but it weren't sleep. We try to go as fast as we can but most times that ain't much more than a walk. Plus maybe the army really is caught far behind, really will have to wait behind the creachers.

Maybe. Maybe not. But within the half hour, you know what?

It's raining.

"People should listen to Wilf," Viola says, looking up.

The road's found its way back down near the river and we find a reasonably sheltered spot twixt the two. We'll eat our dinner, see if the rain stops. If it don't we got no choice but to walk in it anyway. I haven't even checked to see if Ben packed me a mac.

"What's a mac?" Viola asks as we sit down against different trees.

"A raincoat," I say, looking thru my rucksack. Nope, no mac. Great. "And what did I say bout listening too close?"

I still feel a little calm, if you wanna know the truth, tho I probably shouldn't. The song of **Here** still feels like it's being sung, even if I can't hear it, even if it's miles away back on the plain. I find myself humming it, even tho it don't have a tune, trying to get that feeling of connectedness, of *belonging*, of having someone there to say that you're **Here**.

I look over at Viola, eating outta one of her packets of fruit.

I think about my ma's book, still in my rucksack.

Stories in voices, I think.

Could I stand to hear my ma's voice spoken?

Viola crinkles the fruit packet she's just finished. "That's the last of them."

"I got some of this cheese left," I say, "and some dried mutton, but we're gonna have to start finding some of our own on the way."

"You mean like stealing?" she asks, her eyebrows up.

"I mean like hunting," I say. "But maybe stealing, too, if we have to. And there's wild fruit and I know some roots we can eat if you boil 'em first."

"Mmm." Viola frowns. "There's not much call for hunting on a spaceship."

"I could show you."

"Okay," she says, trying to sound cheerful. "Don't you need a gun?"

"Not if yer a good hunter. Rabbits are easy with snares. Fish with lines. You can catch squirrels with yer knife but there ain't much meat."

"Horse, Todd," Manchee barks, quietly.

I laugh, for the first time in what seems like forever. Viola laughs, too. "We ain't hunting *horses*, Manchee." I reach out to pet him. "Stupid dog."

"Horse," he barks again, standing up and looking down the road from the direkshun we just came.

We stop laughing.

23

A KNIFE IS ONLY AS GOOD AS THE ONE WHO WIELDS IT

THERE'S HOOFBEATS ON THE ROAD, distant but approaching at full gallop.

"Someone from Brockley Hills?" Viola says, hope and doubt both in her voice.

"Brockley *Falls*," I say, standing. "We need to hide."

We repack our bags in a hurry. It's a narrow strip of trees we've managed to get ourselves stuck in twixt the road and the river. We daren't cross the road and with the river at our backs, a fallen log is the best we're gonna get. We gather the last of our things and crouch down behind it, Manchee held twixt my knees, rain splashing everywhere.

I take out my knife.

The hoofbeats keep coming, louder and louder.

"Only one horse," Viola whispers. "It's not the army."

"Yeah," I say, "but listen how fast he's riding."

Thump budda-thump budda-thump we hear. Thru the trees we can see the dot of him approaching. He's coming full out down the road, even tho it's raining and night's falling. No one'd ride like that with good news, would they?

Viola looks behind us at the river. "Can you swim?"

"Yeah."

"Good," she says. "Because I can't."

Thump budda-thump budda-thump.

I can hear the buzz of the rider's Noise starting but for a time the galloping is louder and I can't hear it clearly.

"Horse," Manchee says from down below.

It's there. Static twixt the hoofbeats. Flashes of it. Parts of words caught. Rid– and Pa– and Dark– and Stup– and more and more.

I clench the knife harder. Viola's not saying nothing now.

Thump budda-thump budda-thump budda–

Faster and Nightfall and Shot and Whatever it–

And he's coming down the road, round a little curve we took just a hundred metres back, leaning forward–

Thump budda–

The knife turns in my hand cuz–

Shot 'em all and She was tasty and Dark here–

Thump BUDDA–

I think I reckernize–

THUMP BUDDA-THUMP BUDDA–

And he's nearer and nearer till he's almost–

And then Todd Hewitt? rings out as clear as day thru the rain and the galloping and the river.

Viola gasps.

And I can see who it is.

"Junior," Manchee barks.

It's Mr Prentiss Jr.

We try to duck down farther below the log but it ain't no use cuz we already see him pulling back hard on the reins to stop his horse, causing it to rear up and nearly throw him.

But only nearly.

And not enough to make him drop the rifle he's got under one arm.

Todd BLOODY HEWITT! screams his Noise.

"Oh, shit," I hear Viola say and I know what she means.

"Well, HOOO-EEE!" Mr Prentiss Jr yells and we're close enough to see the smile on his face and hear amazement in his voice. "Yer taking the *ROAD*?! You ain't even going *OFF TRAIL*?!"

My eyes meet Viola's. What choice did we have?

"I been hearing yer Noise for almost yer whole stupid life, boy!" He turns his horse this way and that, trying to find where exactly we are in our little strip of woods. "You think I'm not gonna hear it if ya just *HIDE*?"

There's joy in his Noise. Real joy, like he can't believe his luck.

"And wait a minute," he says and we can hear him edging his horse off the road and into the woods. "Wait just a minute. What's that beside you? That empty space of *nothing*."

He says it so nasty Viola flinches. I got the knife in my hand but he's on horseback and we know he's got a gun.

"Too effing right I've got a gun, Todd boy," he calls, no longer searching round but coming straight for us, getting his horse to step over bushes and round trees. "And I got

253

another gun, too, another one special, just for yer little lady there, Todd."

I look at Viola. I know she sees what he's thinking, what's in his Noise, the pictures that ooze out of it. I know she does cuz I can see her face closing right up. I bump her arm and I flash my eyes over to our right, just about the only possibility we have for an escape.

"Oh, *please* run, boy," Mr Prentiss Jr calls. "Please give me a reason to hurt you."

The horse is so close we can hear its Noise, too, jittery and crazy.

There's no farther down we can crouch.

He's nearly on top of us.

I grip the knife and squeeze Viola's hand once, hard, for luck.

It's now or never.

And–

"NOW!" I yell.

We jump up and a gun blast rings out, splintering the branches over our heads, but we run anyway.

"GET!" Mr Prentiss Jr shouts to his horse and here they come.

In two bounds, his horse turns and jumps back to the road, following along it as we run. The strip twixt the road and the river ain't getting any thicker and we can see each other as we go. Branches snap and puddles splash and feet slip and he pounds along the road matching our every step.

We ain't gonna get away from him. We just ain't.

But we try, each of us taking a twisty path up and over logs and thru bushes and Manchee's panting and barking at our heels and the rain's splashing down on us and the road's getting closer and then it suddenly veers sharply towards the river and we got no choice but to cross it in front of him to get to the deeper woods on the other side and I can see Viola leaping over the boundary and onto the road with her arms pumping and Mr Prentiss Jr rounding the bend and he's twirling something in his hand and we make a dash for the other side but the horse is roaring down on us and suddenly I feel something grab my legs, binding 'em so fast and so tight I fall right off my feet.

"Aaagh!" I yell and I hit my face into muck and fallen leaves and the rucksack goes over my head and nearly rips my arms off as it flies off my back and Viola sees me fall and she's nearly cross the road but I see mud curling up from where her feet are digging in to stop herself and I shout, "NO! RUN! RUN!" and she locks my eyes and I see something change on her face but who knows what it means and as the horse bears down she turns and disappears into the woods and Manchee runs back to me and barks "Todd! Todd!" and I'm caught I'm caught I'm caught.

Cuz Mr Prentiss Jr is standing over me, breathing hard, high on his white horse, rifle cocked and pointed. I know what's happened. He's thrown a rope with weights at either end right at my legs and they've twisted round and caught me, expert, just like a hunter after swamp deer. I'm stuck down here in the mud on my belly, caught like an animal.

"My pa sure is gonna be glad to see you," he says, his horse nervy and stepping side to side. **Rain,** I can hear it thinking, and **Is it a snake?**

"I was just sposed to see if there were rumours of you on

the road ahead," Mr Prentiss Jr sneers, "but here you are, in the real honest-to-God flesh."

"Eff you," I say and do you think I say eff?

I've still got the knife in my hand.

"And it sure is making me quake with fear," he says, moving the rifle so I'm looking right down the barrel. "Drop it."

I hold my arm out away from me and drop the knife. It splashes in the mud and I'm still on my belly.

"Yer little lady sure didn't show you no loyalty, now did she?" he says, hopping off his horse, calming it with his free hand. Manchee growls at him but Mr Prentiss Jr just laughs. "What happened to its tail?"

Manchee jumps, his teeth bared, but Mr Prentiss Jr is faster, kicking him away with a vicious boot to the face. Manchee yelps and cowers into the bushes.

"Friends abandoning you right and left, Todd." He walks over to me. "But that's the lesson you learn, eh? Dogs is dogs and women turn out to be dogs, too."

"You *shut* up," I say, clenching my teeth.

His Noise goes all fake sympathy and triumph. "Poor, poor Toddy. All this time travelling with a woman and I'm guessing you never figured out what to do with one."

"You stop talking bout her," I spit. I'm still on my belly and my legs are still tied.

But I find I can bend my knees.

His Noise gets uglier, louder, but his face is all blank like a terror from a dream. "What you do, Todd," he says, squatting down to get closer to me, "is you keep the ones that're whores and you shoot the ones that're not."

He leans even closer. I can see the pathetic hairs on his upper lip, not even made darker by the rain coming down. He's only two years older than me. Only two years bigger.

Snake? thinks the horse.

I put my hands slowly down on the ground.

I push a little into the mud.

"After I tie you up," he says, turning it into a whispering taunt, "I'll go find yer little lady and let you know which kind she is."

Which is when I jump.

I push up with my hands and kick forward hard with my legs, launching myself right at his face. The top of my head hits his nose with a crunch and he falls backwards, me coming down right on top of him. I hit him hard in the face with each fist while he's still too surprised to react and then ram my knee into the man's place twixt his legs.

He curls up like a bug and lets out a low, angry moan and I roll off him back over to my knife, picking it up and getting to my feet and I kick the gun away and I jump in front of the horse screaming "Snake! Snake!" and waving my arms which does the trick instantly and it turns and runs back down the road with a terrified whinny, riderless into the rain.

I look round and *BAM!* Mr Prentiss Jr hits me across the bridge of the nose with his fist but I don't fall and he yells "You piece of–" and I swing my arm out with the knife in it and I make him jump back and I swing it again, water pouring outta my eyes from both the punch and the rain and he steps away from me, looking for his gun and limping a little and he sees it in the mud and he turns his body to fetch it and I'm not thinking at all and I jump on him, knocking him back down and he hits me with his elbow but I don't fall off and my Noise is screaming and his Noise is screaming.

And I don't even know how but I've got him on his back and the point of my knife held up under his chin.

We both stop struggling.

"Why are you after us?!" I shout into his face. "Why are you chasing us?!"

And him and his stupid pathetic non-moustache *smile*.

I knee him again twixt his legs.

He groans again and spits at me but I've still got the knife which has now made a little cut.

"My father wants you," he finally says.

"Why?" I say. "Why does he want us?"

"*Us?*" His eyes go wide. "There's no effing *us*. He wants you, Todd. Just you."

I can't believe this. "What?" I say. "*Why?*"

But he's not answering. He's looking into my Noise. He's looking and searching.

"Hey!" I say, slapping him cross the face with the back of my hand. "Hey! I'm asking you an asking!"

But the smile's back. I can't effing believe it but the smile's back.

"You know what my father always says, Todd Hewitt?" he leers up at me. "He says a knife is only as good as the one who wields it."

"Shut up," I say.

"Yer a fighter, I'll give you that." Still smiling, still bleeding a little below his chin. "But you ain't no killer."

"Shut *up!*" I yell but I know he can see in my Noise that I heard those exact words from Aaron.

"Oh, yeah?" he says. "Whaddya gonna do about it? *Kill* me?"

"I WILL," I shout. "I'll *KILL* you!"

He just licks some rain from his lips and laughs. I have him pinned to the ground with a knife up under his chin and he's *laughing.*

"STOP IT!" I scream at him and I raise the knife.

He keeps on laughing and then he looks at me and he says—

He says—

He says *this*—

"You wanna hear how Ben and Cillian screamed for mercy before I shot 'em twixt the eyes?"

And my Noise buzzes red.

And I clench the knife to strike at him.

And I'm going to kill him.

I'm going to *kill* him.

And—

And—

And—

And right at the top of my swing—

Right at the moment when I start to bring it down—

Right at the moment when the power is mine to command and do with as I please—

I hesitate—

Again—

I hesitate—

Only for a second—

But goddam me–

Goddam me forever and forever–

Cuz in that second he kicks up his legs, throws me off him and elbows me in the throat. I lean over choking and I can only feel his hand wrench the knife away from my own.

As easy as candy from a baby.

"Now, Todd," he says, standing over me, "let me show you a thing or two about wielding."

24

THE DEATH OF
THE WORTHLESS COWARD

I DESERVE IT. I've done everything wrong. I deserve it. If I had the knife back I'd kill myself with it. Except I'd probably be too much of a coward to do that, too.

"Yer some piece of work, Todd Hewitt," Mr Prentiss Jr says, examining my knife.

I'm kneeling now, knees in the mud, hand at my throat, still trying to get my breath.

"You had this fight won and then you went and just threw it away." He runs a finger up the blade. "Stupid as well as yella."

"Just finish it," I mumble into the mud.

"What was that?" Mr Prentiss Jr says, the smile back, his Noise bright.

"Just FINISH IT!" I shout up to him.

"Oh, I'm not gonna kill you," he says, his eyes flashing. "My pa wouldn't be too happy with that, now would he?"

He steps up to me and holds the knife near my face. He

puts the tip of it into my nose so I have to hold my head back farther and farther.

"But there's lots of things you can do with a knife," he says, "without killing a man."

I'm not even looking round no more for ways to get away.

I'm looking right into his eyes which are awake and alive and about to win, his Noise the same, pictures of him in Farbranch, pictures from back at my farm, pictures of me kneeling in front of him.

There ain't nothing in my Noise but a pit full of my stupidity and worthlessness and hate.

I'm sorry, Ben.

I'm so, so sorry.

"But then again," he says, "you *ain't* a man, are ya?" He lowers his voice. "And you never will be."

He moves the knife in his hand, turning the blade towards my cheek.

I close my eyes.

And I feel a wash of silence flow over me from behind.

My eyes snap open.

"Well, looky here," Mr Prentiss Jr says, glancing up over the top of my head. My back is to the deeper woods opposite the river and I can feel the quiet of Viola standing there as clearly as if I could see her.

"Run!" I yell, without turning round. "Get away from here."

She ignores me. "Step back," I hear her say to Mr Prentiss Jr. "I'm warning you."

"Yer warning *me*?" he says, pointing to himself with the knife, the smile back on his face.

Then he jumps a little as something smacks him in the chest and sticks there. It looks like a bunch of little wires with a plastic bulb on the end. Mr Prentiss Jr puts the knife underneath it and tries to flick it off but it stays stuck. He looks up at Viola, smirking. "Whatever this is sposed to be, sister," he says, "it didn't work."

And *SMACKFLASH!!*

There's a huge clap of light and I feel a hand on the back of my collar yank me back to the point of choking. I fall back and away as Mr Prentiss Jr's body jerks into a spasm, flinging the knife out to one side, sparks and little flashes of lightning flying out of the wires and into his body. Smoke and steam comes from everywhere, his sleeves, his collar, his pantlegs. Viola's still pulling me back outta the way by my neck when he falls to the ground, face first in the muck, right on top of his rifle.

She lets go and we tumble together on a little bank by the side of the road. I grab my neck again and we lay there breathing heavily for a second. The sparks and flashes stop and Mr Prentiss Jr twitches in the mud.

"I was afraid –" Viola says twixt deep breaths "– all this water around –" breath "– that I might take you and me with him –" breath "– but he was about to cut–"

I stand without saying nothing, my Noise focused, my eyes on the knife. I go right to it.

"Todd–" Viola says.

I pick it up and stand over him. "Is he dead?" I ask without looking at Viola.

"Shouldn't be," she says. "It was just the voltage from a–"

I raise the knife.

"Todd, no!"

"Give me one good reason," I say, knife still hovering, eyes still on him.

"You're not a killer, Todd," she says.

I spin round to her, my Noise roaring up like a beast. "Don't SAY THAT!! Don't you EVER SAY THAT!!"

"Todd," she says, her hand out, her voice calming.

"I'M why we're in this mess! They're not looking for YOU! They're looking for *ME!*" I turn back to Mr Prentiss Jr. "And if I could kill one of them, then maybe we–"

"Todd, no, listen to me," she says, coming closer. "Listen to me!" I look at her. My Noise is so ugly and my face so twisted she hesitates a little but then she takes another step forward. "Listen to me while I tell you something."

And then out pour more words from her than I ever heard before.

"When you found me, back there in the swamp, I had been running from that man, from Aaron, for four days, and you were only the second person I'd ever seen on this planet and you came at me with that same knife and for all I knew you were exactly like him."

Her hands are still up, like I'm Mr Prentiss Jr's long-gone horse in need of calming.

"But before I even understood what was going on with the Noise and with Prentisstown and with whatever your story was, I could tell about you. People can tell, Todd. We can see that you won't hurt us. That that's not you."

"You hit me in the face with a branch," I say.

She puts her hands on her hips. "Well, what did you expect? You came at me with a knife. But I didn't hit you

264

hard enough to hurt you badly, did I?"

I don't say nothing.

"And I was right," she says. "You bandaged my arm. You rescued me from Aaron when you didn't have to. You took me out of the swamp where I would have been killed. You stood up for me to that man in the orchard. You came with me when we needed to leave Farbranch."

"No," I say, my voice low, "no, yer not reading the story right. We're only having to run cuz I couldn't–"

"I think I'm finally *understanding* the story, Todd," she says. "Why are they coming after you so fiercely? Why is a whole army chasing you across towns and rivers and plains and the whole stupid planet?" She points to Mr Prentiss Jr. "I heard what he said. Don't you wonder why they want you so badly?"

The pit in me is just getting blacker and darker. "Cuz I'm the one who don't fit."

"Exactly!"

My eyes go wide. "Why is that good news? I have an army who wants to kill me cuz I'm not a killer."

"Wrong," she says. "You have an army who wants to *make* you a killer."

I blink. "Huh?"

She takes another step forward. "If they can turn you into the kind of man they want–"

"Boy," I say. "Not a man yet."

She waves this away. "If they can snuff out that part of you that's good, the part of you that won't kill, then they win, don't you see? If they can do it to you, they can do it to anyone. And they win. They *win*!"

265

She's near me now and she reaches out her hand and puts it on my arm, the one still holding the knife.

"We beat them," she says, "*you* beat them by not becoming what they want."

I clench my teeth. "He killed Ben and Cillian."

She shakes her head. "No, he *said* he did. And you believed him."

We look down at him. He's not twitching no more and the steam is starting to lessen.

"I know this kind of boy," she says. "We have this kind of boy even on spaceships. He's a liar."

"He's a man."

"How can you keep *saying that*?" she asks, her voice finally snappy. "How can you keep saying that he's a man and you're not? Just because of some stupid *birthday*? If you were where I came from you'd already be fourteen and a month!"

"I'm not where yer from!" I shout. "I'm from *here* and that's how it works here!"

"Well, how it works here is *wrong*." She lets go of my arm and kneels down by Mr Prentiss Jr. "We'll tie him up. We'll tie him up good and tight and we'll get the heck out of here, all right?"

I don't let go of the knife.

I will never let go of this knife, no matter what she says, no matter how she says it.

She looks up and around. "Where's Manchee?"

Oh, no.

We find him in the bushes. He growls at us without words, just animal growls. He's holding his left eye shut and there's blood around his mouth. It takes a bunch of tries but I finally catch him while Viola takes out her medipak-of-wonders. I hold him down as she forces him to swallow a pill that makes him go floppy and then she cleans out his broken teeth and puts a cream in his eye. She tapes a bandage to it and he looks so small and beaten that when he says "Thawd?" thru one-eyed grogginess I just hug him to me and sit for a bit, under the bushes, outta the rain, while Viola repacks everything and gets my rucksack outta the mud.

"Your clothes are all wet," she says after a while. "And the food is smashed. But the book's still in the plastic. The book's all right."

And the thought of my ma knowing what a coward her son would be one day makes me want to throw the book in the river.

But I don't.

We go to tie up Mr Prentiss Jr with his own rope and find that the electric shock has blown the wooden stock right off of his rifle. Which is a shame cuz it coulda come in handy.

"What was that you shocked him with?" I ask, huffing and puffing as we drag him to the side of the road. Knocked out people are *heavy*.

"A device for telling the ship in space where I am on the planet," she says. "It took forever to pull apart."

I stand up. "How will yer ship know where you are now?"

She shrugs. "We just have to hope that Haven'll have something."

I watch her go to her own bag and pick it up. I sure hope Haven has half what she's expecting.

We leave. Mr Prentiss Jr was right about the stupidity of staying on the road, so we keep twenty or thirty metres away from it on the non-river side, trying to keep it in sight as best we can. We take turns carrying Manchee as the night passes.

We don't talk much neither.

Cuz she might have a point, right? Yeah, okay, maybe that's what the army's after, maybe if they can make me join, they can make anyone join. Maybe I'm their test, who knows, the whole town's crazy enough to believe something like that.

If one of us falls, we all fall.

But for one that don't explain why Aaron's after us and for two I've heard her lie now, ain't I? Her words sound good but who's to know if she's making truth up rather than just saying it?

Cuz I'm *never* going to join the army and Mayor Prentiss must know that, not after what they did to Ben and Cillian, the truth of Mr Prentiss Jr's Noise or not, so that's where she's dead wrong. Whatever they want, whatever the weakness is in me that I can't kill a man even when he deserves it, it's got to change for me to be a man. It's *got* to or how can I hold my head up?

Midnight passes and I'm twenty-five days and a million years from becoming a man.

Cuz if I'd killed Aaron, he couldn't've told Mayor Prentiss where he'd seen me last.

If I coulda killed Mr Prentiss Jr back at the farm,

he wouldn't've led the Mayor's men to Ben and Cillian and wouldn't've lived to harm Manchee so.

If I'd been any kinda killer, I coulda stayed and helped Ben and Cillian defend themselves.

Maybe if I was a killer, they wouldn't be dead.

And that's a trade I'd make any day.

I'll be a killer, if that's what it takes.

Watch me.

The terrain's getting rougher and steeper as the river starts making canyons again. We rest for a while under a rocky outcropping and eat the last of the food that didn't get ruined by the fight with Mr Prentiss Jr.

I lay Manchee across my lap. "What was in that pill?"

"It was just a little crumb of a human painkiller," she says. "I hope it's not too much."

I run my hand over his fur. He's warm and asleep so at least still living.

"Todd–" she says, but I stop her.

"I wanna keep moving as long as we can," I say. "I know we should sleep but let's go till we can't go no more."

She waits a minute and then she says, "Okay", and we don't say nothing more, just finish the last of the food.

The rain keeps up all night as we go and there's no racket like rainfall in the woods, a billion drops pattering down a billion leaves, the river swelling and roaring, the squish of the mud under our feet. I hear Noise now and again in the distance, probably from woodland creachers but always outta sight, always gone when we get near.

"Is there anything out here that could harm us?" Viola asks me, having to raise her voice over the rain.

"Too many to count," I say. I gesture to Manchee in her arms. "He awake yet?"

"Not yet," she says, worry in her voice. "I hope I–"

And that's how unprepared we are when we step round another rocky outcropping and into the campsite.

We both stop immediately and take in what's in front of our eyes, all in a flash.

A fire burning.

Freshly caught fish hanging from a spit over it.

A man leaning over a stone, scraping scales from another fish.

That man looking up as we step into his campsite.

In an *instant*, like knowing Viola was a girl even tho I'd never seen one, I know in the second it takes me to reach for my knife, I know that he's not a man at all.

He's a Spackle.

25

KILLER

THE WORLD STOPS SPINNING.

The rain stops falling, the fire stops burning, my heart stops beating.

A Spackle.

There ain't no more Spackle.

They all died in the wars.

There ain't no more Spackle.

And here's one standing right in front of me.

He's tall and thin like in the vids I remember, white skin, long fingers and arms, the mouth mid-face where it ain't sposed to be, the ear flaps down by the jaw, eyes blacker than swamp stones, lichen and moss growing where clothes should be.

Alien. As alien as you can be.

Holy crap.

You might as well just crumple up the world I know and throw it away.

"Todd?" Viola says.

"Don't move," I say.

Cuz thru the sound of the rain I can hear the Spackle's *Noise*.

No words come out clear, just pictures, skewed up strange and with all the wrong colours, but pictures of me and Viola standing in front of him, looking shocked.

Pictures of the knife now outstretched in my hand.

"Todd," Viola says, a small warning in her voice.

Cuz his Noise has more in it. It's got feelings, washing up in a buzz.

Feelings of fear.

I feel his fear.

Good.

My Noise turns red.

"Todd," Viola says again.

"Quit saying my name," I say.

The Spackle pulls himself slowly upright from where he's skinning the fish. He's made his camp underneath another rocky outcropping down the slope of a small hill. A good part of it's dry and I see bags and a roll of moss that might be a bed.

There's also something shiny and long resting against the rock.

I can see the Spackle picture it in his Noise.

It's the spear he's been using to catch fish in the river.

"*Don't*," I say to him.

I think for a second, but *only* for a second, how clear I understand all this, how clear I can see him standing in the river, how easy he is to read, even tho it's all pictures.

But the second passes in a flash.

Cuz I see him thinking about making a leap for the spear.

"Todd?" she says. "Put the knife down."

And he makes his leap.

I leap at the same time.

(Watch me.)

"No!" I hear Viola scream but my Noise is roaring way too loud for me to hear it as more than a whisper.

Cuz all I'm thinking as I take running steps across the campsite, knife up and ready, bearing down on the Spackle, all skinny knees and elbows as he stumbles heading for his spear, all I'm thinking and sending forward to him in my red, red Noise are images and words and feelings, of all I know, all that's happened to me, all the times I failed to use the knife, every bit of me screaming–

I'll show you who's a killer.

I get to him before he gets to the spear, barrelling into him with my shoulder. We fall to the less muddy dirt with a thud and his arms and legs are all over me, long, like wrestling with a spider, and he's striking me about the head but they're little more than slaps really and I realize and I realize and I realize–

I realize he's weaker than me.

"Todd, stop it!" I hear Viola call.

He scrabbles away from me and I thump him on the side of his head with a fist and he's so light it topples him over onto a pile of rocks and he looks back up at me and his mouth is making a hissing sound and there's terror and panic flying outta his Noise.

273

"STOP IT!" Viola screams. "Can't you see how scared he is?"

"And well he should be!" I yell back.

Cuz there ain't no stopping my Noise now.

I step towards him and he tries to crawl away but I grab him by his long white ankle and drag him off the rocks back onto the ground and he's making this horrible *keening* sound and I ready my knife.

And Viola must've put Manchee down somewhere cuz she grabs my arm and she pulls it back to stop me cutting down the spack and I push into her with my body to shake her off but she won't let go and we go stumbling away from the Spackle who cowers down by a rock, his hands in front of his face.

"Let go of me!" I yell.

"Please, Todd!" she yells back, pulling and twisting my arm. "Stop this, please!"

I twist my arm around and use my free one to push her away and when I turn the Spackle's skittered along the ground–

Heading for his spear–

Has his fingers on the end–

And all my hate erupts into me like a volcano at full bright red—

And I fall on him–

And I punch the knife into his chest.

It crunches as it goes in, turning to the side as it hits a bone and the Spackle screams the most terrible, terrible sound and dark red blood (red, it's red, they bleed *red*) sprays outta the wound and he brings a long arm up and scratches across my face and I pull back my arm and I stab him again and a long screeching breath comes outta his mouth with a loud gurgle and his arms and legs still scramble around him and he looks at me with his black, black eyes and his Noise filled with pain and bafflement and fear–

And I twist the knife–

And he won't die and he won't die and he won't die–

And in a moan and a shudder he dies.

And his Noise stops altogether.

I gag in my throat and I yank out the knife and paddle my way back along the mud.

I look at my hands, at the knife. There's blood all over everything. The knife is covered with it, even all over the handle, and both my hands and arms and the front of my clothes and a splash on my face that I wipe away mingling with my own blood from the scratch.

Even with the rain coming down on me now there's more of it than seems possible.

The Spackle lays where I–

Where I killed him.

I hear Viola make a choking and gasping sound and I look up to her and when I do she flinches back from me.

"You don't know!" I shout at her. "You don't know anything! They started the war. They killed my ma! All of it, everything that's happened, is their fault!"

And then I throw up.

And I keep throwing up.

And when my Noise starts to calm I throw up all over again.

I keep my head to the ground.

The world has stopped.

The world is still stopped.

I don't hear nothing from Viola but her silence. I feel my rucksack digging into the back of my neck as I lean forward. I don't look over at the Spackle.

"He woulda killed us," I finally say, talking into the ground.

Viola don't say nothing.

"He woulda killed us," I say again.

"He was *terrified*!" Viola cries, her voice breaking. "Even I could see how scared he was."

"He went for his spear," I say, lifting my head.

"Because you came after him with a knife!" I can see her now. Her eyes are wide and growing more blank, like they did when she closed up on herself and started rocking.

"They killed everyone on New World," I say.

She shakes her head, fiercely. "You idiot! You stupid fucking IDIOT!"

She don't say effing.

"How many times have you found out that what you've been told isn't true?" she says, backing away from me even further, her face twisting. "How many times?"

"Viola–"

"Weren't all the Spackle killed in the war?" she says and my God how I hate how frightened her voice sounds. "Huh? *Weren't they*?"

And the last of my anger drops outta my Noise as I

realize how I've been the fool again–

And I turn round to the Spackle–

And I see the campsite–

And I see the fish on the lines–

And (no no no no no) I see the fear that was coming from his Noise–

(No no no, please no.)

And there's nothing left for me to throw up but I heave anyway–

And I'm a killer–

I'm a killer–

I'm a killer–

(Oh, please no) I'm a killer.

I start to shake. I start to shake so bad I can't stand up. I find I'm saying "No" over and over again and the fear in his Noise keeps echoing around mine and there's nowhere to run from it, it's just there and there and there and I'm shaking so bad I can't even stay on my hands and knees and I fall into the mud and I can still see the blood everywhere and the rain's not washing it off.

I squeeze my eyes shut tight.

And there's only blackness.

Only blackness and nothing.

One more time, I've ruined everything. One more time, I've done everything wrong.

From a long way away I can hear Viola saying my name.

But it's so far away.

And I'm alone. Here and always, alone.

I hear my name again.

From a far, far distance I feel a pull on my arm.

It's only when I hear a squib of Noise not my own that I open my eyes.

"I think there's more of them out there," Viola whispers down near my ear.

I raise my head. My own Noise is so filled with junk and horror that it's hard to hear clearly and the rain is still falling, heavy as ever, and I take a stupid moment to wonder if we'll ever get dry again and then I hear it, murmuring and indistinct in the trees, impossible to pin down but definitely out there.

"If they didn't want to kill us before," Viola says, "they'll sure want to do it now."

"We need to go." I try to get to my feet. I'm still shaking and it takes a try or two, but I do.

I'm still holding the knife. It's sticky with blood.

I throw it to the ground.

Viola's face is a terrible thing, grieved and scared and horrified, all at me, all at me, but as ever we ain't got no choice so I just say again, "We need to go," and I go to pick up Manchee from where she'd set him down in the dry lee of the Spackle's outcropping.

He's still sleeping and shivering from the cold when I pick him up and I bury my face in his fur and breathe in his familiar doggy stink.

"*Hurry*," Viola says.

And I turn back to her to see her looking all around, the Noise still whispering all around thru the woods and the rain, the fear still on her face.

She returns her gaze to me and I find it impossible to hold and so I look away.

But as I'm looking away, I see movement behind her.

I see the bushes part behind where she's standing.

And I see her see my face changing.

And she turns in time to see Aaron coming outta the woods behind her.

And he's grabbing her by the neck with one hand and smashing a cloth over her nose and mouth with the other and as I call out and take a step forward I hear her scream from beneath it and she tries to fight with her hands but Aaron's holding her tight and by the time I've taken my second and third steps she's already swooning from whatever's on the cloth and on my fourth and fifth steps he's dropping her to the ground and Manchee is still in my arms and on my sixth step he's reaching behind his back and I don't have my knife and I have Manchee with me and I can only run towards him and on my seventh step I see him bring around a wooden staff that's been strapped to his back and it swings thru the air and strikes me full on the side of my head with a

CRACK

and I fall and Manchee tumbles from my arms and I crash into the ground on my belly and my head is ringing so hard I can't even catch myself and the world goes wobbly and grey and full of only pain and I'm on the ground and everything is tilting and sliding and my arms and legs weigh too much to lift and my face is half in the mud but half turned up and I can see Aaron watching me on the ground and I see his Noise and Viola in it and I see him see my knife shining red in the mud and he picks it up and I try to crawl away but the weight of my body sticks me to the spot and I can only watch as he stands over me.

"I have no further use for you, boy," he says and he raises the knife over his head and the last thing I see is him bringing it down with the full force of his arm.

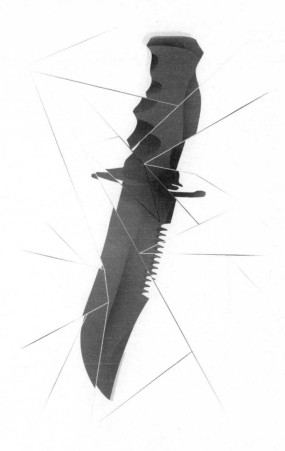

PART V

26

THE END OF ALL THINGS

FALLING NO FALLING no please *help me Falling* The Knife *The Knife* Spackle spacks are dead, all spacks dead *VIOLA* sorry, please, sorry *he's got a spear* FALLING Please please *Aaron, behind you! He's coming!* no further use to me, boy *Viola falling*, Viola Eade spackle *the screaming and the blood and no* WATCH ME watch me no *please* watch me he woulda killed us *Ben* please I'm sorry *Aaron! Run!* E-A-D-E More of them *we have to get outta here* FALLING falling dark blood *The Knife* dead run *I'm a killer please no* SPACKLE *Viola Viola Viola*–

"Viola!" I try and scream but it's blackness, it's blackness with no sound, blackness and I've fallen and I have no voice–

"Viola," I try again and there's water in my lungs and an ache in my gut and pain, pain in my–

"Aaron," I whisper to myself and no one. "Run, it's Aaron."

And then I fall again and it's blackness…

…

…

"Todd?"

…

"Todd?"

Manchee.

"Todd?"

I can feel a dog's tongue on my face which means I can feel my face which means I can tell where it is and with a rush of air clanging into me, I open my eyes.

Manchee's standing right by my head, shifting from foot to foot, licking his lips and nose nervously, the bandage still over his eye, but he's all blurry and it's hard to–

"Todd?"

I try to say his name to calm him but all I do is cough and a sharp pain soars thru my back. I'm still down on my belly in the muck, where I fell when Aaron–

Aaron.

When Aaron hit me in the head with his staff. I try to raise my head and a blinding ache stretches over the right side of my skull all the way down to my jaw and I have to lie there gritting my teeth for a minute just letting it hurt and blaze before I can even try speaking again.

"Todd?" Manchee whimpers.

"I'm here, Manchee," I finally mutter but it comes up outta my chest like a growl held back by goo and it sets off more coughing–

Which I have to cut short cuz of the sharp pain in my back.

My back.

I stifle another cough and a horror feeling spreads out from my gut into the rest of me.

The last thing I saw before–

No.

Oh, no.

I cough a little in my throat, trying not to move any muscle at all, failing at it and surviving the pain till it ebbs as far as it's gonna and then I work on making my mouth move without killing me.

"Is there a knife in me, Manchee?" I rasp.

"Knife, Todd," he barks and there's worry all over him. "Back, Todd."

He comes forward to lick my face again, the dog way of trying to make it better. All I do is breathe and not move for a minute. I close my eyes and pull air inside, despite how my lungs are complaining and already seem full.

I am Todd Hewitt, I think, which is a mistake, cuz here comes all of it back, falling on me, dragging me down and the Spackle's blood and Viola's face frightened of me and Aaron coming outta the woods and taking her–

I start to weep but the pain from the grip of the weep is so bad that for a minute I feel paralysed and a living fire burns thru my arms and back and there's nothing to do but suffer it till it goes.

Slowly, slowly, slowly, I start to uncurl one arm from beneath me. My head and back hurt so bad I think I pass out for a minute but I wake again and slowly, slowly, slowly reach my hand up and behind me, crawling my fingers up my wet filthy shirt and up the wet filthy rucksack which unbelievably I'm still wearing and up and back till there it is under my fingertips.

The handle of the knife. Sticking outta my back.

But I'd be dead.

I'd be *dead*.

Am I dead?

"Not dead, Todd," Manchee barks. "Sack! Sack!"

The knife is sticking in me, up high twixt my shoulder blades, the pain's telling me all about it very specifically, but the knife's gone thru the rucksack first, something in the rucksack's stopped the knife from going all the way in–

The book.

My ma's book.

I feel with my fingers again, slowly as I can, but yes, Aaron raised his arm and brought it down thru the book in the rucksack and it's stopped it from going all the way thru my body.

(Like it did thru the Spackle.)

I close my eyes again and try to take as deep a breath as possible which ain't too deep and then I hold it till I can get my fingers round the knife and then I have to breathe and wait till the pain passes and then I try to pull but it's the heaviest thing in the world and I have to wait and breathe and try again and I pull and the pain in my back increases like a gun firing and I scream out uncontrollably as I feel the knife come outta my back.

I gasp and pant for a minute and try to stop from weeping again, all the while holding the knife away from me, still stuck thru the book and the rucksack.

Manchee licks my face once more.

286

"Good boy," I say, tho I don't know why.

It takes what feels like a lifetime to get the rucksack straps off my arms and finally be able to cast the knife and the whole mess aside. Even then, I can't come near standing up and I must pass out again cuz Manchee's licking my face and I'm having to open my eyes and cough in my breath all over again.

As I lay there, still in the muck, I wish to myself more than anything in the whole world that Aaron's knife had gone thru me, that I was as dead as the Spackle, that I could finish falling down that pit, down down down till there's only blackness, down into the nowhere where there's no more Todd to blame or screw things up or fail Ben or fail Viola, and I could fall away forever into nothingness and never have to worry no more.

But here's Manchee, licking away.

"Get off." I reach up an arm to push him away.

Aaron coulda killed me, coulda killed me so easy.

The knife thru my neck, the knife in my eye, the knife across my throat. I was his for the killing and he didn't kill me. He musta known what he was doing. He *musta*.

Was he leaving me for the Mayor to find? But why was he so far ahead of the army? How could he have come all this way without a horse like Mr Prentiss Jr? How long had he been following us?

How long before he stepped outta the bushes and took Viola away?

I let out a little moan.

That's why he left me alive. So I could live knowing that he took Viola. That's how he wins, ain't it? That's how he makes me suffer. Living and having the sight of him taking her forever in my Noise.

A new kinda energy runs thru me and I make myself sit up, ignoring the pain and bringing myself forward and breathing till I can think about standing. The rattle in my lungs and the pain in my back make me cough more but I grit my teeth and get thru it.

Cuz I have to find her.

"Viola," Manchee barks.

"Viola," I say and I grit my teeth even harder and try to get to my feet.

But it's too much, the pain takes my legs from me and I topple back in the mud and I just lay there pulled tight from it all and struggling to breathe and my mind goes all woozy and hot and in my Noise I'm running and I'm running and I'm running towards nothing and I'm hot all over and I'm sweating and I'm running in my Noise and I can hear Ben from behind the trees and I'm running towards him and he's singing the song, he's singing the song from my bedtimes, the song that's for boys and not men but when I hear it my heart stretches and it's *early one morning just as the sun was rising*.

I come back to myself. The song comes with me.

Cuz the song goes:

> *Early one morning just as the sun was rising,*
> *I heard a maiden call from the valley below.*
> *"Oh don't deceive me, oh never leave me."*

I open my eyes.

Don't deceive me. Never leave me.

I have to find her.

I have to find her.

I look up. The sun is in the sky but I have no idea how much time has passed since Aaron took Viola. That was just before dawn. It's cloudy but bright now and so it could be late morning or early afternoon. It might not even be the same day, a thought I try to push away. I close my eyes and I try to listen. The rain's stopped so there's none of that clatter but the only Noise I can hear belongs to me and to Manchee and the distant wordless chatter of woodland creachers getting on with their lives that ain't got nothing to do with mine.

No sound of Aaron. No space of silence for Viola.

I open my eyes and I see her bag.

Dropped in the struggle with Aaron, of no use or interest to him and just left on the ground like it don't belong to no one, like it don't matter that it's Viola's.

That bag so full of stupid and useful things.

My chest clenches and I cough painfully.

I can't seem to stand so I crawl forward, gasping at the pain in my back and head but still crawling, Manchee barking, worried, "Todd, Todd," all the time, and it takes forever, it takes *too effing long* but I get to the bag and I have to lean hunched with the pain for a minute before I can do anything with it. When I can breathe again I open it and fish around till I find the box with the bandages. There's only one left but it'll have to do. Then I start on the process of taking off my shirt which requires more stopping, more breathing, inch by inch, but finally it's off my burning back and over my burning head and I can see blood and mud everywhere on it.

I find the scalpel in her medipak and cut the bandage in two. I put one part on my head, holding it till it sticks, and reach around slowly and put the other on my back. For a minute it hurts even more as the bandage material, the human cell whatever the hell she talked about, crawls into the wounds and makes a bind. I clench my teeth thru it but then the medicine starts to work and a flush of cool flows into my bloodstream. I wait for it to work enough till I can stand up. I'm wobbly when I first get to my feet but I can manage to just stand for a minute.

After another I can take a step. And then another.

But where do I go?

I've no idea where he took her. I've no idea how much time has passed. He could already be all the way back to the army by now.

"Viola?" Manchee barks, whimpering.

"I don't know, fella," I say. "Let me think."

Even with the bandages doing their thing I can't stand up straight all the way but I do my best and look around. The Spackle's body is on the edge of my vision but I turn myself so I can't see it.

Oh don't deceive me. Oh never leave me.

I sigh and I know what I have to do.

"There ain't nothing for it," I say to Manchee. "We have to go back to the army."

"Todd?" he whines.

"There ain't nothing for it," I say again and I put everything outta my head but moving.

First things first I need a new shirt.

I keep the Spackle to my back and turn to the rucksack.

The knife is still thru the cloth of the rucksack and the book inside. I don't really wanna touch it and even in my haze I don't wanna see what's become of the book but I have to get the knife out so I brace the sack with my foot and pull hard. It takes a few tugs but it comes out and I drop it to the ground.

I look at it on the wet moss. There's blood all over it still. Spackle blood mostly but my blood brighter red at the tip. I wonder if that means that Spackle blood got into my blood when Aaron stabbed me. I wonder if there are extra special viruses you can catch directly from Spackle.

But there's no time for further wondering.

I open the rucksack and take out the book.

There's a knife-shaped hole all the way thru and out the other side. The knife is so sharp and Aaron must be so strong that it's hardly ruined the book at all. The pages have a slit running thru them all the way thru the book, my blood and Spackle blood staining the edges just a little, but it's still readable.

I could still read it, still have it read.

If I ever deserve to.

I push that thought away too and take out a clean shirt. I cough as I do and even with the bandages it hurts so I have to wait till I stop. My lungs feel filled with water, like I'm carrying a pile of river stones in my chest, but I put the shirt on, I gather what useable things I can still get from my rucksack, some clothes, my own medipak, what ain't been ruined by Mr Prentiss Jr or the rain and I take them and my ma's book over to Viola's bag and put them inside cuz there's no way I can carry a rucksack on my back no more.

And then there's still the asking, ain't there?

Where do I go?

I follow the road back to the army, that's where I go.

I go to the army and somehow I save her, even if it's changing my place for hers.

And for that I can't go unarmed, can I?

No, I can't.

I look at the knife again, sitting there on the moss like a thing without properties, a thing made of metal as separate from a boy as can be, a thing which casts all blame from itself to the boy who uses it.

I don't wanna touch it. Not at all. Not never again. But I have to go over and I have to clean off the blood as best I can on some wet leaves and I have to sheath it behind me in the belt that's still around my waist.

I have to do these things. There ain't no choice.

The Spackle hovers on the edge of my vision but I do not look at it as I handle the knife.

"C'mon, Manchee." I loop Viola's bag as gingerly as I can over one shoulder.

Don't deceive me. Never leave me.

Time to go.

"We're gonna find her," I say.

I keep the campsite behind me and head off in the direkshun of the road. Best to just get on it and walk back to 'em as fast as I can. I'll hear 'em coming and can get outta the way and then I guess I'll see if there's any way I can save her.

Which might mean meeting them head on.

I push my way thru a row of bushes when I hear Manchee bark, "Todd?"

I turn, trying to keep from seeing the campsite. "C'mon, boy."

"Todd!"

"I said, c'mon, now. I mean it."

"This way, Todd," he barks and wags his half-tail.

I turn more fully to him. "What'd you say?"

He's pointing his nose in another direkshun altogether from the one I'm going. "This way," he barks. He rubs at the bandage over his eye with a paw, knocking it off and squinting at me with the injured eye.

"What do you mean 'This way'?" I ask, a feeling in my chest.

He's nodding his head and pushing his front feet in a direkshun not only away from the road but in the opposite direkshun from the army. "Viola," he barks, turning round in a circle and then facing that way again.

"You can smell her?" I ask, my chest rising.

He barks a bark of yes.

"You can *smell* her?"

"This way, Todd!"

"Not back to the road?" I say. "Not back to the army?"

"Todd!" he barks, feeling the rise in my Noise and getting excited himself.

"Yer sure?" I say. "You gotta be sure, Manchee. You gotta be."

"This way!" and off he runs, thru the bushes and off on a track parallel to the river, away from the army.

And towards Haven.

Who knows why and who cares cuz in the moment I'm running after him as best as my injuries will let me, in the moment I see him bounding away and ahead, I think to myself, *Good dog, good bloody dog*.

27

ON WE GO

"THIS WAY, TODD," Manchee barks, taking us round another outcropping.

Ever since we left the Spackle campsite, the terrain's been getting more and more rugged. The woods have been rising up into hills for an hour or two now and we rush up 'em and down 'em and up 'em again and sometimes it's more like hiking than running. When we get up to the top of one, I see more and more rolling away in front of me, hills under trees, a few so steep you have to go around rather than over. The road and the river twist thru 'em on snaky paths off to my right and sometimes it's all I can do to keep them in sight.

Even with the bandages doing their best to hold me together, every step I take jars my back and my head and every once in a while I can't help but stop and sometimes throw up my empty stomach.

But on we go.

Faster, I think to myself. *Go faster, Todd Hewitt.*

They've got at least half a day's march on us, maybe even a *day* and a half, and I don't know where they're going or what Aaron plans on doing when he gets there and so on we go.

"Yer sure?" I keep asking Manchee.

"This way," he keeps barking.

The thing that makes no sense is that we're pretty much on the path that Viola and I would have taken anyway, following the river, keeping back from the road, and heading east towards Haven. I don't know why Aaron's going there, I don't know why he'd head away from the army, but that's where Manchee's smelling their scents and so that's the way we go.

We keep on thru the middle of the day, up hills, down hills, and onwards, thru trees that turn from the broad leaves of the trees on the plains to more needly kinds, taller and more arrow-like. The trees even smell different, sending a sharp tang in the air I can taste on my tongue. Manchee and I hop over all manner of streams and creeks that feed the river and I stop now and then to refill the water bottles and on we go.

I try not to think at all. I try to keep my mind pointed ahead, pointed towards Viola and finding her. I try not to think about how she looked after I killed the Spackle. I try not to think about how afraid she was of me or how she backed away like I might hurt her. I try not to think about how scared she musta been when Aaron came after her and I was no use.

And I try not to think about the Spackle's Noise and the

fear that was in it or how surprised he musta been being killed for nothing more than being a fisherman or how the crunch felt up my arm when the knife went in him or how dark red his blood was flowing out onto me or the bafflement pouring outta him and into my Noise as he died as he died as he died as he–

I don't think about it.

On we go, on we go.

Afternoon passes into early evening, the forest and the hills seem never-ending, and there comes another problem.

"Food, Todd?"

"There ain't none left," I say, dirt giving way under my feet as we make our way down a slope. "I don't got nothing for myself neither."

"Food?"

I don't know how long it is since I ate last, don't know how long since I really slept, for that matter, since passing out ain't sleeping.

And I've lost track of how many days till I become a man but I can tell you it's never felt farther away.

"Squirrel!" Manchee suddenly barks and tears around the trunk of a needly tree and into a mess of ferns beyond. I didn't even see the squirrel but I can hear **Whirler dog** and "Squirrel!" and **Whirler-whirler-whirler-** and then it stops short.

Manchee jumps out with a waxy squirrel drooping in his maul, bigger and browner than the ones from the swamp. He drops it on the ground in front of me, a gristly, bloody plop, and I ain't so hungry no more.

"Food?" he barks.

"That's all right, boy." I look anywhere but the mess. "You can have it."

I'm sweating more than normal and I take big drinks of water as Manchee finishes his meal. Little gnats cloud round us in near-invisible swarms and I keep having to bat 'em away. I cough again, ignoring the pain in my back, the pain in my head, and when he's done and ready to go, I wobble just a little but on we go again.

Keep moving, Todd Hewitt. Keep going.

I don't dare sleep. Aaron may not so I can't. On and on, the clouds passing sometimes without me noticing, the moons rising, stars peeping. I come down to the bottom of a low hill and scare my way thru a whole herd of what look like deer but their horns are all different than the deer I know from Prentisstown and anyway they're off flying thru the trees away from me and a barking Manchee before I hardly register they're even there.

On we go still thru midnight (twenty-four days left? Twenty-three?). We've come the whole day without hearing no more sounds of Noise or other settlements, not that I could see anyway, even when I was close enough to see brief snatches of the river and the road. But as we reach the top of another wooded hill and the moons are directly over-head, I finally hear the Noise of men, clear as a crash.

We stop, crouching down even tho it's night.

I look out from our hilltop. The moons are high and I can see two long huts in two separate clearings on hillsides across the way. From one I can hear the murmuring ruckus of sleeping men's Noise. **Julia?** and **on horseback** and **tell him it ain't so** and **up the river past morning** and lots of things that make no sense cuz dreaming Noise is the weirdest of all. From the other hut, there's silence, the aching silence of women, I can feel it even from here, men in one hut, women in another, which I guess is one way of solving the problem of sleeping, and the touch of the silence from the women's side makes me think of Viola and I have to keep my balance against a tree trunk for a minute.

But where there's people, there's food.

"Can you find yer way back to the trail if we leave it?" I whisper to my dog, stifling a cough.

"Find trail," Manchee barks, seriously.

"Yer sure?"

"Todd smell," he barks. "Manchee smell."

"Keep quiet as we go then." We start creeping our way down the hill, moving softly as we can thru the trees and brush till we get to the bottom of a little dale with the huts above us, sleeping on hillsides.

I can hear my own Noise spreading out into the world, hot and fusty, like the sweat that keeps pouring down my sides, and I try to keep it quiet and grey and flat, like Tam did, Tam who controlled his Noise better than any man in Prentisstown–

And there's yer proof.

Prentisstown? I hear from the men's hut almost immediately.

We stop dead. My shoulders slump. It's still dream Noise I'm hearing but the word repeats thru the sleeping men like echoes down a valley. **Prentisstown?** and **Prentisstown?** and **Prentisstown?** like they don't know what the word means yet.

But they will when they wake.

Idiot.

"Let's go," I say, turning and scurrying back the way we came, back to our trail.

"Food?" Manchee barks.

"Come *on*."

And so, still, no food for me but on we go, thru the night, rushing the best we can.

Faster, Todd. Get yer bloody self moving.

On we go, on we go, up hills, grabbing onto plants sometimes to pull myself up, and down hills, holding on to rocks to keep my balance now and then, the scent keeping well clear of anywhere easy it might be to walk, like the flatter parts down by the road or riverbank, and I'm coughing and sometimes stumbling and as the sun starts to show itself there comes a time when I can't, when I just can't, when my legs crumple beneath me and I have to sit down.

I just have to.

(I'm sorry.)

My back is aching and my head is aching and I'm sweating so stinking much and I'm so hungry and I just have to sit down at the base of a tree, just for a minute, I just have to and I'm sorry, I'm sorry, I'm sorry.

"Todd?" Manchee mumbles, coming up to me.

"I'm fine, boy."

"Hot, Todd," he says, meaning me.

I cough, my lungs rattling like rocks falling down a hill.

Get up, Todd Hewitt. Get off yer goddam butt and get going.

My mind drifts, I can't help it, I try to hold on to Viola

but there my mind goes and I'm little and I'm sick in bed and I'm *real* sick and Ben's staying in my room with me cuz the fever is making me see things, horrible things, shimmering walls, people who ain't there, Ben growing fangs and extra arms, all kindsa stuff and I'm screaming and pulling away but Ben is there with me and he's singing the song and he's giving me cool water and he's taking out tabs of medicine–

Medicine.

Ben giving me medicine.

I come back to myself.

I lift my head and go thru Viola's bag, taking out her medipak again. It's got all kindsa pills in it, too many. There's writing on the little packets but the words make no sense to me and I can't risk taking the tranquilizer that knocked out Manchee. I open my own medipak, nowhere near as good as hers, but there's white tabs in it that I know are at least pain relievers, however cruddy and homemade. I chew up two and then two more.

Get up, you worthless piece of crap.

I sit and breathe for a while and fight fight fight against falling asleep, waiting for the pills to work and as the sun starts to peek up over the top of a far hill I reckon I'm feeling a little better.

Don't know if I actually am but there ain't no choice.

Get up, Todd Hewitt. Get an effing MOVE ON!

"Okay," I say, breathing heavy and rubbing my knees with my hands. "Which way, Manchee?"

On we go.

The scent carries like it did before, avoiding the road,

avoiding any buildings we might see at a distance, but always onward, always towards Haven, only Aaron knows why. Mid-morning we find another small creek heading down to the river. I check for crocs, tho it's really too small a place, and refill the water bottles. Manchee wades in, lapping it up, snapping unsuccessfully at these little brass-coloured fishes that swim by, nibbling at his fur.

I sit on my knees and wash some of the sweat from my face. The water is cold as a slap and it wakes me up a little. I wish I knew if we were even gaining on 'em. I wish I knew how far they were ahead.

And I wish he'd never found us.

And I wish he'd never found Viola in the first place.

And I wish Ben and Cillian hadn't lied to me.

And I wish Ben was here right now.

And I wish I was back in Prentisstown.

I rest back on my heels, looking up into the sun

No. No, I don't. I don't wish I was back in Prentisstown. Not no more, I don't.

And if Aaron hadn't found her then *I* might not have found her and that's no good neither.

"C'mon, Manchee," I say, turning round to pick up the bag again.

Which is when I see the turtle, sunning itself on a rock.

I freeze.

I never seen this kinda turtle before. Its shell is craggy and sharp, with a dark red streak going down either side. The turtle's got its shell all the way open to catch as much warmth as possible, its soft back fully exposed.

You can eat a turtle.

Its Noise ain't nothing but a long **ahhhhhhh** sound, exhaling under sunlight. It don't seem too concerned about us, probably thinking it can snap its shell shut and dive underwater faster than we could get to it. And even if we did get to it, we wouldn't be able to get the shell back open to eat it.

Unless you had a knife to kill it with.

"Turtle!" Manchee barks, seeing it. He keeps back cuz the swamp turtles we know have more than enough snap to get after a dog. The turtle just sits there, not taking us seriously.

I reach behind my back for the knife.

I'm halfway there when I feel the pain twixt my shoulder blades.

I stop. I swallow.

(Spackle and pain and bafflement.)

I glance down into the water, seeing myself, my hair a bird's nest, bandage across half my head, dirtier than an old ewe.

One hand reaching for my knife.

(Red blood and fear and fear and fear.)

I stop reaching.

I take my hand away.

I stand. "C'mon, Manchee," I say. I don't look at the turtle, don't even listen for its Noise. Manchee barks at it a few more times but I'm already crossing the creek and on we go, on we go, on we go.

So I can't hunt.

And I can't get near settlements.

And so if I don't find Viola and Aaron soon I'll starve to death if this coughing don't kill me first.

"Great," I say to myself and there's nothing to do but keep going as fast as I can.

Not fast enough, Todd. Move yer effing feet, you gonk.

Morning turns to another midday, midday turns to another afternoon. I take more tabs, we keep on going, no food, no rest, just forward, forward, forward. The path is starting to tend downhill again, so at least that's a blessing. Aaron's scent moves closer to the road but I'm feeling so poor I don't even look up when I hear distant Noise now and then.

It ain't his and there's no silence that's hers so why bother?

Afternoon turns into another evening and it's when we're coming down a steep hillside that I fall.

My legs slip out from under me and I'm not quick enough to catch myself and I fall down and keep falling, sliding down the hill, bumping into bushes, picking up speed, feeling a tearing in my back, and I reach out to stop myself but my hands are too slow to catch anything and I judder judder judder along the leaves and grass and then I hit a bump and skip up into the air, tumbling over onto my shoulders, pain searing thru them, and I call out loud and I don't stop falling till I come to a thicket of brambles at the bottom of the hill and ram into 'em with a thump.

"Todd! Todd! Todd!" I hear Manchee, running down after me, but all I can do is try and withstand the pain again and the tired again and the gunk in my lungs and the hunger gnawing in my belly and bramble scratches all over me and I think I'd be crying if I had any energy left at all.

"Todd?" Manchee barks, circling round me, trying to find a way into the brambles.

"Gimme a minute," I say and push myself up a little. Then I lean forward and fall right over on my face.

Get up, I think. *Get up, you piece of filth, GET UP!*

"Hungry, Todd," Manchee says, meaning me that's hungry. "Eat. Eat, Todd."

I push with hands on the ground, coughing as I come up, spitting up handfuls of gunk from my lungs. I get to my knees at least.

"Food, Todd."

"I know," I say. "I know."

I feel so dizzy I have to put my head back down on the ground. "Just gimme a sec," I say, whispering it into the leaves on the ground. "Just a quick sec."

And I fall again into blackness.

I don't know how long I'm out but I wake to Manchee barking. "People!" he's barking. "People! Todd, Todd, Todd! People!"

I open my eyes. "What people?" I say.

"This way," he barks. "People. Food, Todd. Food!"

I take shallow breaths, coughing all the way, my body weighing ninety million pounds, and I push my way out the other side of the bramble. I look up and over.

I'm in a ditch right by the road.

I can see carts up ahead on the left, a whole string of 'em, pulled by oxes and by horses, disappearing round a bend.

"Help," I say, but my voice comes out like a gasp with not near enough volume.

Get up.

"Help," I call again, but it's only to myself.

Get up.

It's over. I can't stand no more. I can't move no more. It's over.

Get up.

But it's over.

The last cart disappears round the bend and it's over.

… give up.

I put my head down, right down, on the roadside, grit and pebbles digging into my cheek. A shiver shakes me and I roll to my side and pull myself to myself, curling my legs to my chest, and I close my eyes and I've failed and I've failed and please won't the darkness just take me please please please–

"That you, Ben?"

I open my eyes.

It's Wilf.

28

THE SMELL OF ROOTS

"Y'ALL RIGHT, BEN?" he asks, putting a hand under my armpit to help me up but even with that I can't barely stand nor even raise my head much and so I feel his other hand under my other armpit. That don't work neither so he goes even further than that and lifts me over his shoulder. I stare down at the back of his legs as he carries me to his cart.

"Hoo is it, Wilf?" I hear a woman's voice ask.

"'s Ben," Wilf says. "Lookin poorly."

Next thing I know he's setting me down on the back of his cart. It's piled rag-tag with parcels and boxes covered in leather skins, bits of furniture and large baskets, all tumbled together, almost overflowing with itself.

"It's too late," I say. "It's over."

The woman's walked over the back of the cart from the seat and hops down to face me. She's broad with a worn dress and flyaway hair and lines at the corners of her eyes and her voice is quick, like a mouse. "What's over, young'un?"

"She's gone." I feel my chin crumpling and my throat pulling. "I lost her."

I feel a cool hand on my forehead and it feels so good I press into it. She takes it away and says, "Fever," to Wilf.

"Yup," Wilf says.

"Best make a poultice," the woman says and I think she heads off into the ditch but that don't make no sense.

"Where's Hildy, Ben?" Wilf says, trying to get his eyes to meet mine. Mine are so watery it's hard to even see him.

"Her name ain't Hildy," I say.

"Ah know," Wilf says, "but at's whatcha call her."

"She's gone," I say, my eyes filling. My head falls forward again. I feel Wilf put a hand on my shoulder and he squeezes it.

"Todd?" I hear Manchee bark, unsure, a ways off the road.

"I ain't called Ben," I say to Wilf, still not looking up.

"Ah know," Wilf says again. "But at's what we're callin ya."

I look up to him. His face and his Noise are as blank as I remember but the lesson of forever and ever is that knowing a man's mind ain't knowing the man.

Wilf don't say nothing more and goes back to the front of the cart. The woman comes back with a seriously foul-smelling rag in her hands. It stinks of roots and mud and ugly herbs but I'm so tired I let her tie it round my forehead, right over the bandage that's still stuck on the side of my head.

"At should work onna fever," she says, hopping back up. We both lurch forward a little bit as Wilf snaps the rein on his oxes. The woman's eyes are wide open, looking into mine like searching for exciting news. "Yoo runnin from the army, too?"

Her quiet next to me reminds me so much of Viola it's all I can do not to just lean against her. "Kinda," I say.

"Yoo's what told Wilf about it, huh?" she says. "Yoo's and a girl told Wilf bout the army, told him to tell people, tell people they had to gettaway, dincha?"

I look up at her, smelly brown root water dripping down my face, and I turn back to look at Wilf, up there driving his cart. He hears me looking. "They lissened to Wilf," he says.

I look up and past him to the road ahead. As we go round a bend, I can hear not only the rush of the river to my right again, like an old friend, an old foe, I can see a line of carts stretching on up ahead of us on the road at least as far as the next bend, carts packed with belongings just like Wilf's and all kindsa people straggled along the tops, holding on to anything that won't knock 'em off.

It's a caravan. Wilf is taking the rear of a long caravan. Men and women and I think even children, too, if I can see clearly thru the stink of the thing tied round my head, their Noise and silence floating up and back like a great, clattery thing all its own.

Army I hear a lot. **Army** and **army** and **army**.

And **cursed town**.

"Brockley Falls?" I ask.

"Bar Vista, too," the woman says, nodding her head fast. "And others. Rumour's been flyin up the river and road. Army from cursed town comin and comin, growin as it comes, with men pickin up arms to join in."

Growing as it comes, I think.

"Thousands strong, they say," says the woman.

Wilf makes a scoffing sound. "Ain't no thousand people 'tween here and cursed town."

The woman twists her lips. "Ah'm only sayin what people are sayin."

I look back at the empty road behind us, Manchee panting along a little distance away, and I remember Ivan, the man in the barn at Farbranch, who told me that not everyone felt the same about history, that Pren– that my town had allies still. Maybe not thousands, but still maybe growing. Getting bigger and bigger as it marches on till it's so big how can anyone stand against it?

"We're going to Haven," the woman says. "They'll pruhtekt us there."

"Haven," I mumble to myself.

"Say they even got a cure for Noise in them there parts," the woman says. "Now there's a thing Ah'd like to see." She laughs out loud at herself. "Or *hear*, Ah guess." She slaps her thigh.

"They got Spackle there?" I ask.

The woman turns to me surprised. "Spackle don't come near people," she says. "Not no more, not since the war. They's keep to theirselves and we's keep to ourselves and such is the peace kept." It sounds like she's reciting the last part. "Tain't hardly none left anyway."

"I gotta go." I put my hands down and try to lift myself up. "I gotta find her."

All that happens is that I lose my balance and fall off the end of the cart. The woman calls to Wilf to stop and they both lift me back up on it, the woman getting

Manchee up top, too. She clears a few boxes away to lay me down and Wilf gets the cart going again. He snaps the oxes a bit harder this time and I can feel us moving along faster – faster than I could walk at least.

"Eat," the woman says, holding up some bread to my face. "Yoo can't go nowhere till yoo eat."

I take the bread from her and eat a bite, then tear into the rest so hungrily I forget to give some to Manchee. The woman just takes out some more and gives some to both of us, watching wide-eyed at every move I make.

"Thanks," I say.

"Ah'm Jane," she says. Her eyes are still way open, like she's just bursting to say stuff. "Didja see the army?" she asks. "With yer own eyes?"

"I did," I say. "In Farbranch."

She sucks in her breath. "So it's true." Not an asking, just saying it.

"*Told* yoo it were true," Wilf says from up front.

"Ah hear they're cuttin off people's heads and boilin their eyes," Jane says.

"Jane!" Wilf snaps.

"Ah'm just *sayin*."

"They're killing folk," I say, low. "Killing's enough."

Jane's eyes dart all over my face and Noise but all she says after a bit is, "Wilf told me all bout yoo," and I can't figure out at all what her smile means.

A drip from the rag makes it to my mouth and I gag and spit and cough some more. "What *is* this?" I say, pressing the rag with my fingers and wincing from the smell.

"Poultice," Jane says. "For fevers and ague."

"It *stinks*."

"Evil smell draws out evil fever," she says, as if telling me a lesson everyone knows.

"Evil?" I say. "Fever ain't evil. It's *fever*."

"Yeah, and this poultice treats fever."

I stare at her. Her eyes never leave me and the wide open part of them is starting to make me uncomfortable. It's how Aaron looks when he's pinning you down, how he looks when he's imparting a sermon with his fists, when he's preaching you into a hole you might never come out of.

It's a mad look, I realize.

I try to check the thought but Jane don't give no sign she heard.

"I gotta go," I say again. "Thank you kindly for the food and the poultry but I gotta go."

"Yoo can't go off in these woods here, nosirree," she says, still staring, still not blinking. "Them's dangerous woods, them is."

"What do you mean, dangerous?" I push myself away from her a little.

"Settlements up the way," she says, her eyes even wider and a smile now, like she can't wait to tell me. "Crazy as anything. Noise sent 'em wild. Hear tell of one where everyone wears masks so's no one kin see their faces. There's another where no one don't do nothing but sing all day long they gone so crazy. And one where everyone's walls are made a glass and no one wears no clothes cuz no one's got secrets in Noise, do they?"

She's closer to me now. I can smell her breath, which is worse than the rag, and I feel the silence behind all these words. How can that be so? How can silence contain so much racket?

"People can keep secrets in Noise," I say. "People can keep all kindsa secrets."

"Leave a boy alone," Wilf says from his seat.

Jane's face goes slack. "Sorry," she says, a little grudgingly.

I raise up a little, feeling the benefit of food in my belly whatever the stinking rag may or may not be doing.

We've pulled closer to the rest of the caravan, close enough for me to see the backs of a few heads and hear more closely the Noise of men chattering up and down and the silence of women twixt them, like stones in a creek.

Every now and then one of them, usually a man, glances back at us, and I feel like they're seeking me out, seeing what I'm made of.

"I need to find her," I say.

"Yer girl?" Jane asks.

"Yeah," I say. "Thank you, but I need to go."

"But yer fever! And the other settlements!"

"I'll take my chances." I untie the dirty rag. "C'mon, Manchee."

"Yoo can't go," Jane says, eyes wider than ever, worry on her face. "The army–"

"I'll worry about the army." I pull myself up, readying to jump down off the cart. I'm still pretty unsteady so I have to take a cloudy breath or two before I do anything.

"But they'll get yoo!" Jane says, her voice rising. "Yer from Prentisstown–"

I look up, sharp.

Jane slaps a hand over her mouth.

"*Wife!*" Wilf yells, turning his head round from the front of the cart.

"Ah didn't mean it," she whispers to me.

But it's too late. Already the word is bouncing up and down the caravan in a way that's become too familiar, not just the word, but what pins it to me, what everyone knows or thinks they know about me, already faces turning about to look deeper at the last cart in the caravan, oxes and horses drawing to a stop as people turn more fully to examine us.

Faces and Noise aimed right back down the road at us.

"Who yoo got back there, Wilf?" a man's voice says from just one cart up.

"Feverish boy," Wilf shouts back. "Crazy with sickness. Don't know what he's sayin."

"Yoo entirely sure about that?"

"Yessir," Wilf says. "Sick boy."

"Bring him out," a woman's voice calls. "Let's see him."

"What if he's a spy?" another woman's voice calls, rising in pitch. "Leadin the army right to us?"

"We don't want no spies!" cries a different man.

"He's Ben," Wilf says. "He's from Farbranch. Got nightmares of cursed town army killin what he loves. I vouch for him."

No one shouts nothing for a minute but the Noise of the men buzzes in the air like a swarm. Everyone's face is still on us. I try to make my own look more feverish and put the invasion of Farbranch first and foremost. It ain't hard and it makes my heart sick.

And there's a long moment where nobody says nothing and it's as loud as a screaming crowd.

And then it's enough.

Slowly but slowly the oxes and horses start moving forward again, pulling away from us, people still looking back but at least getting farther away. Wilf snaps the reins on his oxes but keeps them slower than the rest, letting a distance open between us and everyone else.

"Ah'm *sorry*," Jane says again, breathless. "Wilf told me not to say. He told me but–"

"That's okay," I say, just wanting her to stop talking already.

"Ah'm so so sorry."

There's a lurch and Wilf's stopped the cart. He waits till the caravan's off a good distance then hops down and comes back.

"No one lissens to Wilf," he says, maybe with a small smile. "But when they do, they believe him."

"I need to go," I say.

"Yup," he says. "T'ain't safe."

"Ah'm sorry," Jane keeps saying.

I jump off the cart, Manchee following me. Wilf reaches for Viola's bag and holds it open. He looks at Jane, who understands him. She takes an armful of fruits and breads and puts them in the bag, then another armful of dried meats.

"Thanks," I say.

"Hope yoo find her," Wilf says as I close the bag.

"I hope so, too."

With a nod, Wilf goes and reseats himself on the cart and snaps the reins on his oxes.

"Be careful," Jane calls after me, in the loudest whisper you ever heard. "Watch out for the crazies."

I stand for a minute and watch 'em pull away, coughing still, feverish still, but feeling better for the food if not the smell of roots and I'm hoping Manchee can find the trail again and I'm also wondering just exactly what kinda welcome I'm gonna get if I ever do get to Haven.

29

AARON IN A THOUSAND WAYS

IT TAKES A LITTLE WHILE, a horrible little while, for Manchee to find the scent again once we're back in the woods but then he barks, "This way," and we're off again.

He's a good bloody dog, have I said that?

Night's fully fallen by now and I'm still sweating and I'm still coughing enough to win a contest and my feet ain't made of nothing but blisters and my head's still buzzy with feverish Noise but I've got food in my belly and more in the bag to see me thru a coupla days and so all that matters is still ahead of us.

"Can you smell her, Manchee?" I ask, as we balance on a log across a stream. "Is she still alive?"

"Smell Viola," he barks, jumping off the other side. "Viola fear."

Which hits me a little and I quicken my step. Another midnight (twenty-two days? Twenty-one?) and my torch battery gives out. I take out Viola's but it's the last we got. More hills and steeper, too, as we go on thru the night, harder to climb up, dangerous to climb down but we go and go and go, Manchee sniffing away, eating Wilf's dried meat as we stumble forward, me coughing away, taking the shortest rests possible, usually bent double against trees, and the sun starts coming up over a hill so it's like we're walking up into the sunrise.

And it's when light hits us full that I see the world start to shimmer.

I stop, hanging on to a fern to keep my balance against the steepness of the hill. Everything's woozy for a second and I close my eyes but it don't help as there's just a wash of colours and sparkles behind my eyelids and my body is jelly-like and waving in the breeze I can feel coming off the hilltop and when it passes, it don't really pass altogether, the world keeping its weird brightness, like I've woke up in a dream.

"Todd?" Manchee barks, worry there, no doubt from seeing who knows what in my Noise.

"The fever," I say, coughing again. "I shouldn't've thrown away that filthy rag."

Ain't nothing for it.

I take the last of the pain tabs from my medipak and we gotta keep going.

We get to the top of the hill and for a minute all the other hills in front of us and the river and the road down below rumble up and down like they're on a blanket someone's shaking and I do my best to blink it away till it calms down enough to keep walking. Manchee whines by my feet.

I nearly tip over when I try and scratch him so instead I focus on getting down the hill without falling.

I think again of the knife at my back, of the blood that was on it when it went into my body and my blood mixed with the Spackle's and who knows what now spinning round my insides since Aaron stabbed me.

"I wonder if he knew," I say, to Manchee, to myself, to no one, as we get to the bottom of the hill and I lean against a tree to make the world stop moving. "I wonder if he killed me slow."

"*Course I did,*" Aaron says, leaning out from behind the tree.

I yell out and fall back away from him and fling my arms in front of me trying to slap him away and I hit the ground on my butt and start scampering back before I look up–

And he's gone.

Manchee's got his head cocked at me. "Todd?"

"Aaron," I say, my heart thundering, my breath catching and turning into meatier and meatier coughs.

Manchee sniffs the air again, sniffs the ground around him. "Trail this way," he barks, shifting from foot to foot.

I look around me, coughing away, the world spotty and wavy.

No sign of him, no Noise other than mine, no silence of Viola. I close my eyes again.

I am Todd Hewitt, I think against the swirling. *I am Todd Hewitt.*

Keeping my eyes shut, I feel for the water bottle and take a swig and I tear a piece from Wilf's bread and chew it down. Only then do I open my eyes again.

Nothing.

Nothing but woods and another hill to climb.

And sunlight that shimmers.

The morning passes and at the bottom of yet another hill there's yet another creek. I refill the water bottles and take a few drinks from the cold water with my hands.

I feel *bad*, ain't no two ways about it, my skin's tingling and sometimes I'm shivering and sometimes I'm sweating and sometimes my head weighs a million pounds. I lean into the creek and splash myself with the cold.

I sit up and Aaron is reflected in the water.

"*Killer*," he says, a smile across his torn-up face.

I jump back, scrabbling away for my knife (and feeling the pain shoot thru my shoulders again) but when I look up he ain't there and Manchee's made no sign of stopping his fish-chasing.

"I'm coming to find you," I say to the air, air that's started to move more and more with the wind.

Manchee's head pops up from the water. "Todd?"

"I'll find you if it's the last thing I do."

"*Killer*," I hear again, whispered along the wind.

I lay for a second, breathing heavy, coughing but keeping my eyes peeled. I go back to the creek and I splash so much cold water on myself it makes my chest hurt.

I pick myself up and we carry on.

The cold water does the trick for a little while and we manage a few more hills as the sun gets to midday in the sky with minimal shimmer. When things do start to wobble again I stop us and we eat.

"*Killer*," I hear from the bushes around us and then

again from another part of the forest. *"Killer."* And again from somewhere else. *"Killer."*

I don't look up, just eat my food.

It's just the Spackle blood, I tell myself. Just the fever and the sickness and that's all.

"Is that all?" Aaron says from across the clearing. *"If that's all I am, why you chasing me so bad?"*

He's wearing his Sunday robes and his face is all healed up like he's back in Prentisstown, his hands clasped in front of him like he's ready to lead us in prayer and he's glowing in the sun and he's smiling down at me.

The smiling fist I remember so well.

"The Noise binds us all, young Todd," he says, his voice slithering and shiny like a snake. *"If one of us falls, we all fall."*

"You ain't here," I say, clenching my teeth.

"Here, Todd," Manchee barks.

"Ain't I?" Aaron says and disappears in a shimmer.

My brain knows this Aaron ain't real but my heart don't care and it's beating in my chest like a race. It's hard to catch my breath and I waste more time waiting just to be able to stand up and move on into the afternoon.

The food's helping, God bless Wilf and his crazy wife, but sometimes we can't go much faster than a stumble. I start to see Aaron outta the corner of my eye pretty much all the time, hiding behind trees, leaning against rocks, standing on top of woodfall, but I just turn my head away and keep stumbling.

And then, from a hilltop, I see the road cross the river again down below. The landscape's moving in a way that turns my stomach but I can definitely see a bridge down there, taking the road to the other side so there's nothing now twixt me and the river.

I wonder for a minute about that other fork we never took back in Farbranch. I wonder where *that* road is in the middle of all this wilderness. I look from the hilltop to my left but there's just woods as far as I can see and more hills that move like hills shouldn't. I have to close my eyes for a minute.

We make our way down, too slow, too *slow*, the scent taking us close to the road and towards the bridge, a high rickety one with rails. Water's gathered where the road turns into it, filling it with puddles and muck.

"Did he cross the river, Manchee?" I put my hands on my knees to catch my breath and cough.

Manchee sniffs the ground like a maniac, crossing the road, re-crossing it, going to the bridge and back to where we stand. "Wilf smell," he barks. "Cart smell."

"I can see the tracks," I say, rubbing my face with my hands. "What about Viola?"

"Viola!" Manchee barks. "This way."

He heads away from the road, keeping to this side of the river and following it. "Good dog," I say twixt raggedy breaths. "Good dog."

I follow him thru branches and bushes, the river rushing closer to my right than it's been in days.

And I step right into a settlement.

I stand up straight and cough in surprise.

It's been destroyed.

The buildings, eight or ten of them, are charcoal and ash and there ain't a whisper of Noise nowhere.

For a second I think the army's been here but then I see plants growing up in the burnt-out buildings and no smoke is rising from any fire and the wind just blows thru it like only the dead live here. I look round and there's a few decrepit docks on the river, just down from the bridge, one lonely old boat knocking against it in the current and a few more half-sunk boats piled halfway up the riverbank along from what may have been a mill before it became a pile of burnt wood.

It's cold and it's long dead and here's another place on New World that never made it to subdivided farming.

And I turn back round and in the centre of it stands Aaron.

His face is back to how it was when the crocs tore it open, peeled half away, his tongue lolling out the side of the gash in his cheek.

And he's still smiling.

"*Join us, young Todd,*" he says. "*The church is always open.*"

"I'll kill you," I say, the wind stealing my words but I know he can hear me cuz I can hear every last thing he's saying.

"*You won't,*" he says, stepping forward, his fists clenched by his sides. "*Cuz I says you ain't a real killer, Todd Hewitt.*"

"Try me," I say, my voice sounding strange and metallic.

He smiles again, his teeth poking out the side of his face, and in a wash of shimmer he's right in front of me. He puts his cut up hands to the opening of his robe and pulls it apart enough to show his bare chest.

"*Here's yer chance, Todd Hewitt, to eat from the Tree of Knowledge.*" His voice is deep in my head. "*Kill me.*"

The wind's making me shiver but I feel hot and sweaty at the same time and I can't get no more than a third of a breath down my lungs and my head is starting to ache in a way that food ain't helping and whenever I look anywhere fast everything I see has to slide into place to catch up.

I clench my teeth.

I'm probably dying.

But he's going first.

I reach behind me, ignoring the pain twixt my shoulders, and I grab the knife outta the sheath. I hold it in front of me. It's shiny with fresh blood and glinting in sunlight even tho I'm standing in shadow.

Aaron pulls his smile wider than his face can really go and he pushes his chest out to me.

I raise the knife.

"Todd?" Manchee barks. "Knife, Todd?"

"Go ahead, Todd," Aaron says and I swear I smell the dankness of him. *"Cross over from innocence to sin. If you can."*

"I've done it," I say. "I've already killed."

"Killing a Spackle ain't killing a man," he says, grinning away at how stupid I am. *"Spackles are devils put here to test us. Killing one's like killing a turtle."* He widens his eyes. *"'Cept you can't do that neither now, can ya?"*

I grip the knife hard and I make a snarling sound and the world wavers.

But the knife still ain't falling.

There's a bubbling sound and gooey blood pours outta the gash in Aaron's face and I realize he's laughing.

"It took a long, long time for her to die," he whispers.

And I call out from the pain–

And I raise the knife higher–

And I aim it at his heart–

And he's still smiling–

And I bring the knife down–

And stab it right into Viola's chest.

"No!" I say, in the second that it's too late.

She looks up from the knife and right at me. Her face is filled with pain and confused Noise spills from her just like the Spackle that I–

(That I killed.)

And she looks at me with tears in her eyes and she opens her mouth and she says, "*Killer*".

And as I reach out for her, she's gone in a shimmer.

And the knife, clean of all blood, is still in my hand.

I fall onto my knees and then pitch forward and lie on the ground in the burnt-out settlement, breathing and coughing and weeping and wailing as the world melts around me so bad I don't feel like it's even solid no more.

I can't kill him.

I want to. I want to *so bad*. But I can't.

Cuz it ain't me and cuz I lose her.

I can't. I can't I can't I can't.

I give in to the shimmering and I disappear for a while.

It's good old Manchee, the friend who's proved truest, who wakes me up with licks to my face and a worried murmured word coming thru his Noise and his whines.

"Aaron," he's yelping, quiet and tense. "Aaron."

"Leave off, Manchee."

"Aaron," he whimpers, licking away.

"He ain't really there," I say, trying to sit up. "It's just something–"

It's just something Manchee can't see.

"Where is he?" I say, getting up too fast, causing everything to swirl bright pink and orange. I reel back from what's waiting for me.

There are a hundred Aarons at a hundred different places, all standing round me. There are Violas, too, frightened and looking to me for help, and Spackles with my knife sticking outta their chests and there're all talking at once, all talking to me in a roar of voices.

"Coward," they're saying. All of 'em. "Coward" over and over again.

But I wouldn't be a Prentisstown boy if I couldn't ignore Noise.

"Where, Manchee?" I say, getting to my feet, trying not to see how everything's pitching and sliding.

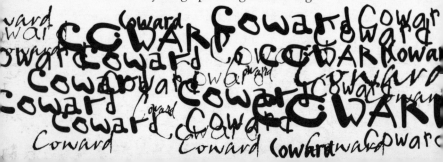

"This way," he barks. "Down the river."

I follow him thru the burnt-out settlement.

He leads me past what musta been the church and I
don't look at it as we go by and he runs up a small bluff and
the wind's getting howlier and the trees are bending and I
think it's not just how I'm seeing them and Manchee has to
bark louder to let me know.

"Aaron!" he barks, sticking his nose in the air. "Upwind."

Thru the trees on the little bluff I can see downriver. I
can see a thousand Violas looking frightened of me.

Coward Coward
ward
ward

I can see a thousand Spackle with my knife killing them.

Coward Coward Coward
Coward Coward Coward Cowar
Coward Coward Coward war
Coward Coward
Coward

I can see a thousand Aarons looking back at me and calling me "Coward" with the worst smile you ever seen.

Coward Coward Coward Coward
Coward Coward Coward Coward
Coway Coward Coward Coward
Coward

And beyond them, in a camp by the side of the river, I see an Aaron who ain't looking back at me at all.

COWARD Coward Coward Coward
Coward Coward Coward Coward
Coward Coward Coward
Coward

I see an Aaron kneeling down in prayer.

Coward Coward Coward Coward
Coward Coward Coward
Coward Coward Coward Coward

And I see Viola on the ground in front of him.

Coward Coward Coward Coward
Coward Coward Coward Coward
Coward

"Aaron," Manchee barks.

Coward
Coward Coward Coward Coward
Coward Coward Coward

"Aaron," I say.

Coward.

30

A BOY CALLED TODD

"WHAT ARE WE GONNA DO?" says the boy, creeping up to my shoulder.

I raise my head from the cold river water and let it splash down my back. I stumbled back down from the bluff, elbowing my way thru crowds all calling me coward, and I got to the riverbank and I plunged my head straight in and now the cold is making me shake violently but it's also calming the world down. I know it won't last, I know the fever and spack blood infection will win in the end, but for now, I'm gonna need to see as clearly as possible.

"*How are we gonna get to them?*" the boy asks, moving round to my other side. "*He'll hear our Noise.*"

The shivering makes me cough, *everything* makes me cough, and I spit out handfuls of green goo from my lungs, but then I hold my breath and plunge in my head again.

The cold of the water feels like a vice but I hold it there, hearing the bubbling of the water rushing by and the wordless barks of a worried Manchee hopping around my feet. I can feel the bandage on my head detach and wash away in the current. I think of Manchee wriggling the bandage off his tail in a different part of the river and I forget and I laugh underwater.

I lift my head up, choking and gasping and coughing more.

I open my eyes. The world shines like it shouldn't and there are all kindsa stars out even tho the sun is still up but at least the ground has stopped floating and all the excess Aarons and Violas and Spackles are gone.

"*Can we really do it alone?*" asks the boy.

"Ain't no choice," I say to myself.

And I turn to look at him.

He's got a brown shirt like mine, no scars on his head, a rucksack on his back, a book in one hand and a knife in the other. I'm shaking from the cold still and it's all I can do to stand but I breathe and cough and shake and look at him.

"C'mon, Manchee," I say and I head back across the burnt-out settlement, back to the bluff. Just walking is tough, like the ground could cave away at any minute, cuz I weigh more than a mountain but less than a feather, but I'm walking, I'm keeping walking, I'm keeping the bluff in sight, I'm reaching it, I'm taking the first steps up it, I'm taking the next steps, I'm grabbing on to branches to pull myself along, I'm reaching the top, I'm leaning against a tree at the top, and I'm looking out.

"*Is it really him?*" says the boy behind my ear.

I squint out across the trees, tracing my eye down the river.

And there's still a campsite, still at the river's edge, so far

330

away they're just specks against other specks. I still have Viola's bag around my shoulders and I reach for her binos, holding 'em up to my eyes but shaking so much it's hard to get a clear image. They're far enough away that the wind's covering up his Noise but I'm sure I feel her silence out there.

I'm sure of it.

"Aaron," Manchee says. "Viola."

So I know it's not a shimmer and in the shakiness I can just about catch him still kneeling, praying some prayer, and Viola laid out on the ground in front of him.

I don't know what's happening. I don't know what he's doing.

But it's really them.

All this walking and stumbling and coughing and dying and it's really really them, by God it's really them.

I may not be too late and it's only how my chest rises and my throat grips that I realize all along I've thought I *was* too late.

But I'm not.

I lean down again and (shut up) I cry, I cry, I'm *crying* but it has to pass cuz I have to figure it out, I have to figure it out, it's down to me, there's only me, I have to find a way, I have to save her, I have to save–

"What are we gonna do?" the boy asks again, standing a little way away, book still in one hand, knife in the other.

I put my palms into my eyes and rub hard, trying to think straight, trying to concentrate, trying not to listen–

"What if this is the sacrifice?" says the boy.

I look up. "What sacrifice?"

"*The sacrifice you saw in his Noise*," he says. "*The sacrifice of–*"

"Why would he do it here?" I say. "Why would he come all this way and stop in the middle of a stupid forest and do it here?"

The boy's expression doesn't change. "*Maybe he has to,*" he says, "*before she dies.*"

I step forward and have to catch my balance. "Dies of what?" I say, my voice snappy, my head aching and buzzy again.

"*Fear,*" says the boy, taking a step backwards. "*Disappointment.*"

I turn away. "I ain't listening to this."

"Listening, Todd?" Manchee barks. "Viola, Todd. This way."

I lean back again against the tree. I've got to think. I've got to ruddy *think*.

"We can't approach," I say, my voice thick. "He'll hear us coming."

"*He'll kill her if he hears us,*" says the boy.

"Ain't talking to you." I cough up more gunk, which makes my head spin, which makes me cough more. "Talking to my dog," I finally choke out.

"Manchee," Manchee says, licking my hand.

"And I can't kill him," I say.

"*You can't kill him,*" says the boy.

"Even if I want to."

"*Even if he deserves it.*"

"And so there has to be another way."

"*If she's not too scared to see you.*"

I look at him again. Still there, still book and knife and rucksack.

"You need to leave," I say. "You need to go away from me and never come back."

"*Yer probably too late to save her.*"

"Yer of no use to me at all," I say, raising my voice.

"*But I'm a killer,*" he says and the knife has blood on it.

I close my eyes and grit my teeth. "You stay behind," I say. "You stay *behind.*"

"Manchee?" Manchee barks.

I open my eyes. The boy isn't there. "Not you, Manchee," I say, reaching out and rubbing his ears.

Then I regard him, Manchee. "Not you," I say again.

And I'm thinking. In the clouds and the swirls and the shimmers and the lights and the ache and the buzz and the shaking and the coughing, I'm thinking.

And I'm thinking.

I rub the ears of my dog, my stupid goddam ruddy *great* dog that I never wanted but who hung around anyway and who followed me thru the swamp and who bit Aaron when he was trying to choke me and who found Viola when she was lost and who's licking my hand with his little pink tongue and whose eye is still mostly squinted shut from where Mr Prentiss Jr kicked him and whose tail is way way shorter from when Matthew Lyle cut it off when my dog – *my dog* – went after a man with a machete to save me and who's right there when I need pulling back from the darkness I fall into and who tells me who I am whenever I forget.

"Todd," he murmurs, rubbing his face into my hand and

thumping his back leg against the ground.

"I got an idea," I say.

"What if it don't work?" says the boy from behind the tree.

I ignore him and I pick up the binos again. Shaking still, I find Aaron's campsite one more time and look at the area around it. They're near the river's edge and there's a forked tree just this side of them along the riverbank, bleached and leafless, like it maybe once got struck by lightning.

It'll do.

I put down the binos and take Manchee's head in both hands. "We're gonna save her," I say, right to my dog. "Both of us."

"Save her, Todd," he barks, wagging his little stump.

"It won't work," says the boy, still outta sight.

"Then you should stay behind," I say to the air, riding thru a cough while I send pictures of Noise to my dog to tell him what he needs to do. "It's simple, Manchee. Run and run."

"Run and run!" he barks.

"Good boy." I rub his ears again. "Good boy."

I pull myself to my feet and half-walk, half-slide, half-stumble my way back down the little bluff into the burnt-out settlement. There's a thump in my head now, like I can hear my poisoned blood pumping, and everything in the world throbs with it. If I squeeze my eyes nearly shut, the swirling lights ain't so bad and everything sort of stays in its place.

The first thing I need is a stick. Manchee and I tear thru the burnt-out buildings, looking for one the right size.

Pretty much everything is black and crumbly but that suits me fine.

"Thith one, Thawd?" Manchee says, using his mouth to pull one about half the length of himself out from under what looks like a burnt-up pile of stacked chairs. What happened in this place?

"Perfect." I take it from him.

"This won't work," the boy says, hiding in a dark corner. I can see the glint of the knife in one of his hands. *"You won't save her."*

"I will." I break off some larger splinters from the stick. Only one end is blackened charcoal but that's exactly what I want. "Can you carry this?" I say to Manchee, holding it out.

He takes it in his mouth, tosses it a little to get it comfortable, but then it rests just fine. "Yeth!" he barks.

"Great." I stand up straight and nearly fall over. "Now we need a fire."

"You can't make a fire," the boy says, already outside waiting for us. *"Her fire-making box is broken."*

"You don't know nothing," I say, not looking at him. "Ben taught me."

"Ben's dead," says the boy.

"Early one mor-r-ning," I sing, loud and clear, making the whirly shapes of the world go spangly and weird, but I keep on singing. "Just as the sun was ri-i-sing."

"Yer not strong enough to make a fire."

"I heard a maiden call from the val-l-ley below." I find a long, flat piece of wood and use the knife to carve a little hollow in it. "Oh, don't dece-e-ive me." I carve a rounded

335

end to another smaller stick. "Oh, never le-e-ave me."

"How could you use a poor maiden so?" the boy finishes.

I ignore him. I put the rounded end of the stick into the little hollow and start spinning it twixt my hands, pressing hard into the wood. The rhythm of it matches the thumping in my head and I start to see me in the woods with Ben, him and me racing to see who could get the first smoke. He always won and half the time I could never get any sorta fire at all. But those were times.

Those were times.

"C'mon," I say to myself. I'm sweating and coughing and woozy but I'm making my hands keep on spinning. Manchee's barking at the wood to try and help it along.

And then a little finger of smoke rises from the hollow.

"Ha!" I cry out. I protect it from the wind with my hand and blow on it to make it catch. I use some dried moss as kindling and when the first little flame shoots out it's as near as I've come to joy since I don't know when. I throw some small sticks on it, wait for them to catch, too, then some larger ones, and pretty soon there's a real fire burning in front of me. A real one.

I leave it to burn for a minute. I'm counting on us being downwind to keep the smoke from Aaron.

And I'm counting on that wind for other reasons, too.

I lurch my way towards the riverbank, using tree trunks to keep me upright, till I make it to the dock. "C'mon, c'mon," I say under my breath as I steady myself to walk down it. It creaks under my feet and once I nearly pitch over into the river but I do finally make it to the boat still tied there.

"It'll sink," says the boy, standing knee-high in the river.

I hop in the little boat and after a lot of wobbling and coughing, I stand up in it. It's rickety and narrow and warping.

But it floats.

"You don't know how to steer a boat."

I get out and cross the dock and make my way back to the settlement and search round till I find a flat enough piece of wood to use as an oar.

And that's all I need.

We're ready.

The boy's standing there, holding the things of mine in each hand, rucksack on his back, no real nothing on his face, no Noise that I can hear.

I stare him down. He don't say nothing.

"Manchee?" I call but he's already at my feet.

"Here, Todd!"

"Good boy." We go to the fire. I take the stick he found and put the already burnt end into it. After a minute, the end is red hot and smoky, with flames catching on the new wood. "You sure you can hold this?" I say.

He takes the non-burning end into his maul and there he is, best ruddy dog in the universe, ready to carry fire to the enemy.

"Ready, friend?" I say.

"Weddy, Thawd!" he says, mouth full, tail wagging so fast I see it as a blur.

"He'll kill Manchee," the boy says.

I stand, world spinning and shining, my body barely my own, my lungs coughing up bits of themselves, my head thumping, my legs shaking, my blood boiling, but I stand.

I ruddy well stand.

"I am Todd Hewitt," I say to the boy. "And I am leaving you here."

"You can't never do that," he says, but I'm already turning to Manchee and saying "Go on, boy," and he takes off back up the bluff and down the other side, burning stick in his mouth, and I count to a hundred, loud, so's I can't hear no one say nothing and then I make myself count to a hundred again and that's enough and I lurch as fast as I can back to the dock and the boat and I get myself in and I take the oar onto my lap and I use the knife to cut away the last of the raggedy rope tying the little boat in place.

"You can't never leave me behind," the boy says, standing on the dock, book in one hand, knife in the other.

"Watch me," I say and he gets smaller and smaller in the shimmering and fading light as the boat pulls away from the dock and starts making its way downstream.

Towards Aaron.

Towards Viola.

Towards whatever waits for me down the river.

31

THE WICKED ARE PUNISHED

THERE'S BOATS IN PRENTISSTOWN but no one's used 'em since I can remember. We got the river, sure, this same one that's sloshing me back and forth, but our stretch is rocky and fast and when it does slow down and spread out, the only peaceful area is a marsh full of crocs. After that, it's all wooded swamp. So I ain't never been on a boat and even tho it looks like it should be easy to steer one down a river, it ain't.

The one bit of luck I got is that the river here is pretty calm, despite some splashing from the wind. The boat drifts out into the current and is taken and moves its way downriver whether I do anything or not so I can put all my coughing energy into trying to keep the boat from spinning around as it goes.

It takes a minute or two before I'm successful.

"Dammit," I say under my breath. "Effing thing."

But after some splashing with the oar (and one or two

full spins, shut up) I'm figuring out how to keep it more or less pointed the right way and when I look up, I realize I'm probably already halfway there.

I swallow and shake and cough.

This is the plan. It's probably not a very good one but it's all that my shimmering, flickering brain's gonna let me have.

Manchee'll take the burning stick upwind of Aaron and drop it somewhere to catch fire and make Aaron think I've lit up my own campsite. Then Manchee'll run back to *Aaron's* campsite, barking up a storm, pretending he's trying to tell me he's found Aaron. This is simple since all he has to do is bark my name, which is what he does all the time anyway.

Aaron'll chase him. Aaron'll try to kill him. Manchee'll be faster (Run and run, Manchee, run and run). Aaron'll see the smoke. Aaron, who fears me not one tiny little bit, will go off into the woods towards the smoke to finish me off once and for all.

I'll float downstream, come upon his campsite from the riverside while he's out in the woods looking for me, and I'll rescue Viola. I'll pick up Manchee there, too, when he circles back round ahead of a chasing Aaron (run and run).

Yeah, okay, that's the plan.

I know.

I *know*, but if it don't work, then I'll have to kill him.

And if it comes to that, it can't matter what I become and it can't matter what Viola thinks.

It can't.

It'll have to be done and so I'll have to do it.

I take out the knife.

The blade still has dried blood smeared on it here and there, my blood, Spackle blood, but the rest of it still shines, shimmering and flickering, flickering and shimmering. The tip of it juts out and up like an ugly thumb and the serrashuns along one side spring up like gnashing teeth and the blade edge pulses like a vein full of blood.

The knife is alive.

As long as I hold it, as long as I use it, the knife lives, lives in order to take life, but it has to be commanded, it has to have me to tell it to kill, and it wants to, it wants to plunge and thrust and cut and stab and gouge, but I have to want it to as well, my will has to join with its will.

I'm the one who allows it and I'm the one responsible.

But the knife wanting it makes it easier.

If it comes to it, will I fail?

"*No*," whispers the knife.

"*Yes*," whispers the wind down the river.

A drop of sweat from my forehead splashes on the blade and the knife is just a knife again, just a tool, just a piece of metal in my hand.

Just a knife.

I lay it on the floor of the boat.

I'm shaking again, still. I cough up more goo. I look up and around me, ignoring the waviness of the world and letting the wind cool me down. The river's starting to bend and I keep on floating down it.

Here it comes, I think. Ain't no stopping it.

I look up and over the trees to my left.

My teeth are chattering.

I don't see no smoke yet.

C'mon, boy, it's the next thing that has to happen.

And no smoke.

And no smoke.

And the river's bending more.

C'mon, Manchee.

And no smoke.

And *chatter chatter chatter* go my teeth. I huddle my arms to myself—

And *smoke*! The first small puffs of it, coming up like cotton balls farther down the river.

Good dog, I think, holding my teeth together. *Good dog*.

The boat's tending a bit mid-river so I row as best I can and guide it back to the river's edge.

I'm shaking so bad I can barely hang on to the oar.

The river's bending more.

And there's the forked tree, the tree struck by lightning, coming up on my left.

The sign that I'm almost there.

Aaron'll be just beyond it.

Here it comes.

I cough and sweat and tremble but I'm not letting go of the oar. I row some more, closer to the edge. If Viola can't run for any reason, I'm gonna have to beach it to go get her.

I keep my Noise as blank as I can but the world's closing up in folds of light and shimmer so there's no chance of that. I'll just have to hope the wind's loud enough and that Manchee—

"Todd! Todd! Todd!" I hear from a distance. My dog, barking my name to lure Aaron away. "Todd! Todd! Todd!"

The wind's keeping me from hearing Aaron's Noise so I don't even know if this is working but I'm moving past the forked tree so there's nothing for it now–

"Todd! Todd!"

C'mon, *c'mon*–

The forked tree passing by–

I crouch down in the boat–

"Todd! Todd!" getting fainter, moving back–

Snappings of branches–

And then I hear "TODD HEWITT!!" roared loud as a lion–

As a lion *moving away*–

"C'mon," I whisper to myself, "c'mon, c'mon, c'mon–"

My clenched fists trembling around the oar and–

Round the bend and–

Past the tree and–

The campsite comes and–

There she is.

There she is.

Aaron's gone and there she is.

Lying on the ground in the middle of his campsite.

Not moving.

My heart ratchets up and I cough without even noticing and I say, "Please, please, please," under my breath and I paddle the board furiously and get the boat closer and closer to the river's edge and I stand and leap out into the water and I fall on my rump but I still catch the front of the boat in my hands and "please, please, please" and I get up and I drag the boat far enough up the riverbank and I let go and I run and stumble and run to Viola Viola Viola–

"Please," I say as I run, my chest clenching and coughing and hurting, "*Please*."

I get to her and there she is. Her eyes are closed and her mouth is open a little and I put my head to her chest, shutting out the buzz of my Noise and the shouting of the wind and the barking and yelling versions of my name coming outta the woods around me.

"Please," I whisper.

And *thump, thump*.

She's alive.

"Viola," I whisper fiercely. I'm starting to see little flashing spots before my eyes but I ignore them. "Viola!"

I shake her shoulders and take her face in my hand and shake that, too.

"Wake up," I whisper. "Wake up, wake up, wake up!"

I can't carry her. I'm too shaking and lopsided and weak.

But I'll ruddy well carry her if I have to.

"Todd! Todd! Todd!" I hear Manchee barking from deep in the woods.

"Todd Hewitt!" I hear Aaron yell as he chases my dog.

And then, from below me, I hear, "Todd?"

"Viola?" I say and my throat is clenching and my eyes are blurring.

But she's looking back at me.

"You don't look too good," she says, her voice slurring and her eyes sleepy. I notice some bruising underneath her eyes and my stomach clenches in anger.

"Ya gotta get up," I whisper.

"He drugged..." she says, closing her eyes.

"Viola?" I say, shaking her again. "He's coming back,

Viola. We gotta get outta here."

I can't hear no more barking.

"We gotta go," I say. "Now!"

"I weigh too much," she says, her words melting together.

"Please, Viola," I say and I'm practically *weeping* it. "*Please*."

She blinks open her eyes.

She looks into mine.

"You came for me," she says.

"I did," I say, coughing.

"You came for me," she says again, her face crumpling a little.

Which is when Manchee comes flying outta the bushes, barking my name like his life depended on it.

"TODD! TODD! TODD!" he yelps, running towards us and past. "Aaron! Coming! Aaron!"

Viola lets out a little cry and with a push that nearly knocks me over she gets to her feet and catches me as I fall and we steady ourselves against each other and I manage to point to the boat.

"There!" I say, trying hard to catch my breath.

And we run for it–

Across the campsite–

Towards the boat and the river–

Manchee bounding on ahead and clearing the front of the boat with a leap–

Viola's stumbling ahead of me–

And we're five–

Four–

Three steps away–

And Aaron comes pounding outta the woods behind us–

His Noise so loud I don't even need to look–

"TODD HEWITT!!"

And Viola's reached the front of the boat and is falling in–

And two steps–

And one–

And I reach it and push with all my strength to get it back into the river–

And "TODD HEWITT!!"

And he's closer–

And the boat don't move–

"I WILL PUNISH THE WICKED!"

And closer still–

And the boat don't move–

And his Noise is hitting me as hard as a punch–

And the boat *moves*–

Step and step and my feet are in the water and the boat's moving–

And I'm falling–

And I don't have the strength to get in the boat–

And I'm falling into the water as the boat moves away–

And Viola grabs my shirt and yanks me up till my head and shoulders are over the front–

"NO, YOU DON'T!" Aaron roars–

And Viola calls out as she pulls me again and my front's in the boat–

And Aaron's in the water–

And he's grabbing my feet–

"No!" Viola screams and grips me harder, pulling with all her strength–

And I'm lifted in the air–

And the boat stops–

And Viola's face is twisted in the effort–

But it's a tug of war which only Aaron's ever gonna win–

And then I hear "TODD!" barked in a voice so ferocious I wonder for a minute if a croc's raised outta the water–

But it's Manchee–

It's Manchee–

It's my dog my dog my dog and he's leaping past Viola and I feel his feet hit my back and leave it again as he launches himself at Aaron with a snarl and a howl and a "TODD!" and Aaron calls out in anger–

And he lets go of my feet.

Viola lurches back but she don't let go and I go tumbling into the boat on top of her.

The lurch pushes us farther out into the river.

The boat is starting to pull away.

My head tips and whirls as I spin round and I have to stay on my hands and knees for balance but I'm up as much I can and leaning out the boat and I'm calling, "Manchee!"

Aaron's fallen back into the soft sand at the river's edge, his robe getting tangled up in his legs. Manchee's going for his face, all teeth and claws, growls and roars. Aaron tries to shake him off but Manchee gets a bite either side of Aaron's nose and gives his head a twist.

He rips Aaron's nose clean away from his face.

Aaron yells out in pain, blood shooting everywhere.

"Manchee!" I scream. "Hurry, Manchee!"

"Manchee!" Viola yells.

"C'mon, boy!"

And Manchee looks up from Aaron to see me calling him–

And that's where Aaron takes his chance.

"*No!*" I scream.

He grabs Manchee violently by his scruff, lifting him off the ground and up in one motion.

"Manchee!"

I hear splashing and I'm dimly aware that Viola's got the oar and is trying to stop us going any farther into the river and the world is shimmering and throbbing and–

And Aaron has my dog.

"GET BACK HERE!" Aaron yells, holding Manchee out at arm's length. He's too heavy to be picked up by his scruff and he's yelping from the pain but he can't quite get his head round to bite Aaron's arm.

"Let him go!" I yell.

Aaron lowers his face–

There's blood pouring outta the hole where his nose used to be and tho the gash in his cheek is healed you can still see his teeth and it's this mess that repeats, almost calmly this time, burbling thru the blood and gore, "Come back to me, Todd Hewitt."

"Todd?" Manchee yelps.

Viola's rowing furiously to keep us outta the current but she's weak from the drugs and we're getting farther and farther away. "No," I can hear her saying. "No."

"Let him go!" I scream.

"The girl or the dog, Todd," Aaron calls, still with the

calm that's so much scarier than when he was shouting. "The choice is yers."

I reach for the knife and I hold it out in front of me but my head spins too much and I fall off my hands and smack my teeth on the boat seat.

"Todd?" Viola says, still rowing against the current, the boat twisting and turning.

I sit up tasting blood and the world waves so much it nearly knocks me over again.

"I'll kill you," I say, but so quietly I might as well be talking to myself.

"Last chance, Todd," Aaron says, no longer sounding so calm.

"Todd?" Manchee's still yelping. "Todd?"

And no–

"I'll kill you," but my voice is a whisper–

And no–

And there ain't no choice–

And the boat's out in the current–

And I look at Viola, still rowing against it, tears dripping off her chin–

She looks back at me–

And there ain't no choice–

"No," she says, her voice choking. "Oh, no, Todd–"

And I put my hand on her arm to stop her rowing.

Aaron's Noise roars up in red and black.

The current takes us.

"I'm sorry!" I cry as the river takes us away, my words ragged things torn from me, my chest pulled so tight I can't barely breathe. "I'm sorry, Manchee!"

"Todd?" he barks, confused and scared and watching me leave him behind. *"Todd?"*

"Manchee!" I scream.

Aaron brings his free hand towards my dog.

"MANCHEE!"

"Todd?"

And Aaron wrenches his arms and there's a CRACK and a scream and a cut-off yelp that tears my heart in two forever and forever.

And the pain is too much it's too much it's too much and my hands are on my head and I'm rearing back and my mouth is open in a never-ending wordless wail of all the blackness that's inside me.

And I fall back into it.

And I know nothing more as the river takes us away and away and away.

PART VI

32

DOWNRIVER

THE SOUND OF WATER.

And bird noise.

Where's my safety? they sing. **Where's my safety?**

Behind it, there's music.

I swear there's music.

Layers of it, flutey and strange and familiar–

And there's light against the darkness, sheets of it, white and yellow.

And warmth.

And softness on my skin.

And a silence there next to me, pulling against me as strong as it ever did.

I open my eyes.

I'm in a bed, under a cover, in a small square room with white walls and sunlight pouring in at least two open windows with the sound of the river rushing by outside and birds flitting in the trees (and music, is that music?) and for a minute it's not just that I don't know where I am, I also don't know *who* I am or what's happened or why there's an ache in my–

I see Viola, curled up asleep on a chair next to the bed, breathing thru her mouth, her hands pressed twixt her thighs.

I'm still too groggy to make my own mouth move and say her name just yet but my Noise must say it loud enough cuz her eyes flutter open and catch mine and she's outta her seat in a flash with her arms wrapped around me and squishing my nose against her collarbone.

"Oh, Jesus, *Todd*," she says, holding so tight it kinda hurts.

I put one hand on her back and I inhale her scent.

Flowers.

"I thought you were never coming back," she says, squeezing tight. "I thought you were dead."

"Wasn't I?" I croak, trying to remember.

"You were sick," Viola says, sitting back, knees still on my bed. "*Really* sick. Doctor Snow wasn't sure you'd ever wake up and when a doctor admits *that* much–"

"Who's Doctor Snow?" I ask, looking round the little room. "Where are we? Are we in Haven? And what's that music?"

"We're in a settlement called Carbonel Downs," she says. "We floated down the river and–"

She stops cuz she sees me looking at the foot of the bed.

At the space where Manchee ain't.

I remember.

My chest closes up. My throat clenches shut. I can hear him barking in my Noise. *"Todd?"* he's saying, wondering why I'm leaving him behind. *"Todd?"* with an asking mark, just like that, forever asking where I'm going without him.

"He's gone," I say, like I'm saying it to myself.

Viola seems like she's about to say something but when I glance up at her, her eyes are shiny and all she does is nod, which is the right thing, the thing I'd want.

He's gone.

He's gone.

And I don't know what to say about that.

"Is that Noise I hear?" says a loud voice, preceded by its own Noise thru a door opening itself at the foot of the bed. A man enters, a *big* man, tall and broad with glasses that make his eyes bug out and a flip in his hair and a crooked smile and Noise coming at me so filled with relief and joy it's all I can do not to crawl out the window behind me.

"Doctor Snow," Viola says to me, scooting off the bed to make way.

"Pleased to finally meet you, Todd," Doctor Snow says, smiling big and sitting down on the bed and taking a device outta his front shirt pocket. He sticks two ends of it into his ears and places the other end on my chest without asking. "Could you take a deep breath for me?"

I don't do nothing, just look at him.

"I'm checking if your lungs are clear," he says and I realize what it is I'm noticing. His accent's the closest to Viola's I ever heard on New World. "Not exactly the same," he says, "but close."

"He's the one who made you well," Viola says.

I don't say nothing but I take a deep breath.

"Good," Doctor Snow says, placing the end of the device on another part of my chest. "Once more." I breathe in and out. I find that I *can* breathe in and out, all the way down to the bottom of my lungs.

"You were a very sick boy," he says. "I wasn't sure we were going to be able to beat it. You weren't even giving off Noise until yesterday." He looks me in the eye. "Haven't seen that sort of sickness for a long time."

"Yeah, well," I say.

"Haven't heard of a Spackle attack for a *very* long time," he says. I don't say nothing to this, just breathe deep. "That's great, Todd," the doctor says. "Could you take off your shirt, please?"

I look at him, then over to Viola.

"I'll wait outside," she says and out she goes.

I reach behind me to pull my shirt over my head and as I do I realize there's no pain twixt my shoulderblades.

"Took some stitches, that one," Doctor Snow says, moving around behind me. He puts the device against my back.

I flinch away. "That's cold."

"She wouldn't leave your side," he says, ignoring me and checking different places for my breath. "Not even to sleep."

"How long I been here?"

"This is the fifth morning."

"*Five days?*" I say and he barely has a chance to say yes before I'm pulling back the covers and getting outta the bed. "We gotta get outta here," I say, a little unsteady on my feet but standing nonetheless.

Viola leans back in the doorway. "I've been trying to tell them that."

"You're safe here," Doctor Snow says.

"We've heard that before," I say. I look to Viola for support but all she does is stifle a smile and I realize I'm standing there in just a pair of holey and seriously worn-out underpants that ain't covering as much as they should. "Hey!" I say, moving my hands down to the important bits.

"You're safe as you're going to be anywhere," Doctor Snow says behind me, handing me a pair of my trousers from a neatly washed pile by the bed. "We were one of the main fronts in the war. We know how to defend ourselves."

"That was Spackle." I turn my back to Viola and shove my legs in the trousers. "This is men. A *thousand* men."

"So the rumours say," Doctor Snow says. "Even though it's not actually numerically possible."

"I don't know nothing from numerickly," I say, "but they got guns."

"*We* have guns."

"And horses."

"We've got horses."

"Do you have men who'll join them?" I say, challenging him.

He don't say nothing to that, which is satisfying. Then again, it ain't satisfying at all. I button up my trousers. "We need to go."

"You need to rest," the doctor says.

"We ain't staying and waiting for the army to show up." I turn to include Viola, turn without thinking to the space where my dog'd be waiting for me to include him too.

There's a quiet moment when my Noise fills the room with Manchee, just fills it with him, side to side, barking and barking and needing a poo and barking some more.

And dying.

I don't know what to say about that neither.

(He's gone, he's gone.)

I feel empty. All over empty.

"No one's going to make you do anything you don't want to, Todd," Doctor Snow says gently. "But the elder-men of the village would like to talk to you before you leave us."

I tighten my mouth. "Bout what?"

"About anything that might help."

"How can I *help?*" I say, grabbing a washed shirt to put on. "The army will come and kill everyone here who don't join it. That's it."

"This is our home, Todd," he says. "We're going to defend it. We have no choice."

"Then count me out–" I start to say.

"Daddy?" we hear.

There's a little boy standing in the doorway next to Viola.

An actual boy.

He's looking up at me, eyes wide open, his Noise a funny, bright, roomy thing and I can hear myself described as skinny and scar and sleeping boy and at the same time there are all kindsa warm thoughts towards his pa with just the word daddy repeated over and over again, meaning everything you'd want it to: askings about me, identifying his daddy, telling him he loves him, all in one word, repeated forever.

"Hey, fella," Doctor Snow says. "Jacob, this is Todd. All woke up."

Jacob looks at me solemnly, a finger in his mouth, and gives a little nod. "Goat's not milking," he says quietly.

"Is she not?" Doctor Snow says, standing up. "Well, we'd better go see if we can talk her into it, hadn't we?"

Daddy daddy daddy says Jacob's Noise.

"I'll see to the goat," Doctor Snow is saying to me, "and then I'll go round up the rest of the eldermen."

I can't stop staring at Jacob. Who can't stop staring at me.

He's so much closer than the kids I saw at Farbranch.

And he's so *small*.

Was I that small?

Doctor Snow's still talking. "I'll bring the eldermen back here, see if you can't help us." He leans down till I'm looking at him. "And if we can't help you."

His Noise is sincere, truthful. I believe he means what he says. I also believe he's mistaken.

"Maybe," he says, with a smile. "Maybe not. You haven't even seen the place yet. Come on, Jake." He takes his son's hand. "There's food in the kitchen. I'll bet you're starved. Be back within the hour."

I go to the door to watch them leave. Jacob, finger still in his mouth, looks back at me till he and his pa disappear outta the house.

"How old is that?" I ask Viola, still looking down the hallway. "I don't even know how old that is."

"He's four," she says. "He's told me about 800 times. Which seems kind of young to be milking goats."

"Not on New World, it ain't," I say. I turn back to her and her hands are on her hips and she's giving me a serious look.

"Come and eat," she says. "We need to talk."

33

CARBONEL DOWNS

SHE LEADS ME TO A KITCHEN as clean and bright as the bedroom. River still rushing by outside, birds still Noisy, music still–

"What *is* that music?" I say, going to the window to look out. Sometimes it seems like I reckernize it but when I listen close, it's voices changing over voices, running around itself.

"It's from loudspeakers up in the main settlement," Viola says, taking a plate of cold meat outta the fridge.

I sit down at the table. "Is there some kinda festival going on?"

"No," she says, in a way that means *just wait*. "Not a festival." She gets out bread and some orange fruit I ain't never seen before and then some red-coloured drink that tastes of berries and sugar.

I dig into the food. "Tell me."

"Doctor Snow is a good man," she says, like I need to

know this first. "Everything about him is good and kind and he worked so hard to save you, Todd, I mean it."

"Okay. So what's up?"

"That music plays all day and all night," she says, watching me eat. "It's faint here at the house, but in the settlement, you can't hear yourself think."

I pause at a mouthful of bread. "Like the pub."

"What pub?"

"The pub in Prent–" I stop. "Where do they think we're from?"

"Farbranch."

I sigh. "I'll do my best." I take a bite of the fruit. "The pub where I come from played music all the time to try and drown out the Noise."

She nods. "I asked Doctor Snow why they did it here, and he said, 'To keep men's thoughts private'."

I shrug. "It makes an awful racket, but it kinda makes sense, don't it? One way to deal with the Noise."

"*Men's* thoughts, Todd," she says. "*Men*. And you notice he said he was going to ask the elder*men* to come seek out your advice?"

I get a horrible thought. "Did the women all die here, too?"

"Oh, there's women," she says, fiddling with a butter knife. "They clean and they cook and they make babies and they all live in a big dormitory outside of town where they can't interfere in men's business."

I put down a forkful of meat. "I saw a place like that when I was coming to find you. Men sleeping in one place, women in another."

"Todd," she says, looking at me. "They wouldn't listen to me. Not one thing. Not a word I said about the army. They kept calling me *little girl* and practically patting me on the bloody head." She crosses her arms. "The only reason they want to talk to you about it now is because caravans of refugees started showing up on the river road."

"Wilf," I say.

Her eyes scan over me, reading my Noise. "Oh," she says. "No, I haven't seen him."

"Wait a minute." I swallow some more drink. It feels like I haven't drunk anything for years. "How did we get so far ahead of the army? How come if I've been here five days we ain't been overrun yet?"

"We were in that boat for a day and a half," she says, running her nail at something stuck on the table.

"A day and a half," I repeat, thinking about this. "We musta come miles."

"Miles and miles," she says. "I just let us float and float and float. I was too afraid to stop at the places I passed. You wouldn't believe some of the things…" She drifts off, shaking her head.

I remember Jane's warnings. "Naked people and glass houses?" I ask.

Viola looks at me strange. "No," she says, curling her lip. "Just poverty. Just horrible, horrible poverty. Some of those places looked like they would have eaten us so I just kept on and on and you got sicker and sicker and then on the second morning I saw Doctor Snow and Jacob out fishing and I could see in his Noise he was a doctor and as weird as this place is about women, it's at least clean."

I look around the clean, clean kitchen. "We can't stay," I say.

"No, we can't." She puts her head in her hands. "I was so worried about you." There's feeling in her voice. "I was so worried about the army coming and nobody *listening* to me." She smacks the table in frustration. "And I was feeling so bad about–"

She stops. Her face creases and she looks away.

"Manchee," I say, out loud, for the first time since–

"I'm so sorry, Todd," she says, her eyes watery.

"Ain't yer fault." I stand up fast, scooting my chair back.

"He would have killed you," she says, "and then he would have killed Manchee just because he could."

"Stop talking about it, please," I say, leaving the kitchen and going back to the bedroom. Viola follows me. "I'll talk to these elder folks," I say, picking up Viola's bag from the floor and stuffing the rest of the washed clothes in it. "And then we'll go. How far are we from Haven, do you know?"

Viola makes a tiny smile. "Two days."

I stand up straight. "We came that far downriver?"

"We came that far."

I whistle quietly to myself. Two days. Just two days. Till whatever there is in Haven.

"Todd?"

"Yeah?" I say, putting her bag round my shoulders.

"Thank you," she says.

"For what?"

"For coming after me."

Everything's gone still.

"Ain't nothing," I say, feeling my face get hot and looking

away. She don't say nothing more. "You all right?" I ask, still not looking at her. "From when he took you?"

"I don't really–" she starts to say but we hear a door close and a sing-song daddy daddy daddy floating down the hall towards us. Jacob hugs the door frame of the room rather than come on in.

"Daddy sent me to fetch you," he says.

"Oh?" I raise my eyebrows. "I'm meant to come to *them* now, am I?"

Jacob nods, very serious.

"Well, in that case, we're coming," I rearrange the sack and looking at Viola. "And then we're going."

"Too right," Viola says and the way she says it makes me glad. We head out into the hallway after Jacob but he stops us at the door.

"Just you," he says, looking at me.

"Just me what?"

Viola crosses her arms. "He means just you to talk to the eldermen."

Jacob nods, again very serious. I look at Viola and back to Jacob. "Well now," I say, squatting down to his level. "Why don't you just go tell yer daddy that both me and Viola will be along in a minute. Okay?"

Jacob opens his mouth. "But he said–"

"I don't really care what he said," I say gently. "Go."

He gives a little gasp and runs out the door.

"I think I'm maybe thru of men telling me what to do," I say and I'm surprised at the weariness in my voice and suddenly I feel like I wanna get back in that bed and sleep for another five days.

"You going to be all right to walk to Haven?" Viola says.

"Try and stop me," I say and she smiles again.

I head on out the front door.

And for a third time I'm expecting Manchee to come bounding out with us.

His absence is so big it's like he's there and all the air goes outta my lungs again and I have to wait and breathe deep and swallow.

"Oh, man," I say to myself.

His last *Todd?* hangs in my Noise like a wound.

That's another thing about Noise. Everything that's ever happened to you just keeps right on talking, for ever and ever.

I see the last of Jacob's dust as he runs on up the trail thru some trees towards the rest of the settlement. I look round. Doctor Snow's house ain't too big but it stretches out to a deck overlooking the river. There's a small dock and a really low bridge connecting the wide path that comes from the centre of Carbonel Downs to the river road that carries along on the other side. The road across the river, the one we spent so much time coming down, is almost hidden behind a row of trees as it carries on past the settlement on the final two days towards Haven.

"God," I say. "It's like paradise compared to the rest of New World."

"There's more to paradise than nice buildings," Viola says.

I look round some more. Doctor Snow's got a well-kept front garden on the path to the settlement. Looking up the path, I can see more buildings thru the trees and hear that music playing.

That weird music. Constantly changing to keep you from getting used to it, I guess. It's nothing I reckernize but it's louder out here and I guess on one level you ain't *sposed* to reckernize it but I swear I heard something in it when I was waking up–

"It's almost unbearable in the middle of the settlement," Viola says. "Most of the women don't even bother coming in from the dormitory." She frowns. "Which I guess is the whole point."

"Wilf's wife told me bout a settlement where everyone–"

I stop cuz the music changes.

Except it don't change.

The music from the settlement stays the same, messy and wordy and bending around itself like a monkey.

But there's more.

There's more music than just it.

And it's getting louder.

"Do you hear that?" I say.

I turn.

And turn again. Viola, too.

Trying to figure out what we're hearing.

"Maybe someone's set up another loudspeaker across the river," she says. "Just in case the women were getting any uppity ideas about leaving."

But I ain't listening to her.

"No," I whisper. "No, it can't be."

"What?" Viola says, her voice changing.

"Shh." I listen close again, trying to calm my Noise so I can hear it.

"It's coming from the river," she whispers.

"Shh," I say again, cuz my chest is starting to rise, my Noise starting to buzz too loud to be of any use at all.

Out there, against the rush of the water and the Noise of the birdsong, there's—

"A song," Viola says, real quiet. "Someone's singing."

Someone's singing.

And what they're singing is:

Early one mor-r-ning, just as the sun was ri-i-sing...

And my Noise surges louder as I say it.

"Ben."

34

OH NEVER LEAVE ME

I RUN DOWN TO THE RIVER'S EDGE and stop and listen again.

Oh don't deceive me.

"Ben?" I say, trying to shout and whisper at the same time.

Viola comes thumping up behind me. "Not *your* Ben?" she says. "Is it your Ben?"

I shush her with my hand and listen and try to pick away the river and the birds and my own Noise and there, just there under it all–

Oh never leave me.

"Other side of the river," Viola says and takes off across the bridge, feet smacking against the wood. I'm right behind her, passing her, listening and looking and listening and looking and there and there and there–

There in the leafy shrubs on the other side of the water–

It's Ben.

It really is Ben.

He's crouched down behind leafy greenery, hand against a tree trunk, watching me come to him, watching me run across the bridge, and as I near him, his face relaxes and his Noise opens up as wide as his arms and I'm flying into 'em both, leaping off the bridge and into the bushes and nearly knocking him over and my heart is busting open and my Noise is as bright as the whole blue sky and–

And everything's gonna be all right.

Everything's gonna be all right.

Everything's gonna be all right.

It's Ben.

And he's gripping me tight and he's saying, "Todd," and Viola's standing back a ways, letting me greet him, and I'm hugging him and hugging him and it's Ben, oh Christ Almighty, it's Ben Ben Ben.

"It's me," he says, laughing a little cuz I'm crushing the air outta his lungs. "Oh, it's good to see ya, Todd."

"Ben," I say, leaning back from him and I don't know what to do with my hands so I just grab his shirt front in my fists and shake him in a way that's gotta mean love. "Ben," I say again.

He nods and smiles.

But there's creases round his eyes and already I can see the beginnings of it, so soon it's gotta be right up front in his Noise, and I have to ask, "Cillian?"

He don't say nothing but he shows it to me, Ben running back to a farmhouse already in flames, already burning down, with some of the Mayor's men inside but with Cillian, too, and Ben grieving, grieving still.

"Aw, no," I say, my stomach sinking, tho I'd long guessed it to be true.

But guessing a thing ain't knowing a thing.

Ben nods again, slow and sad, and I notice now that he's dirty and there's blood clotted on his nose and he looks like he ain't eaten for a week but it's still Ben and he can still read me like no other cuz his Noise is already asking me bout Manchee and I'm already showing him and here at last my eyes properly fill and rush over and he takes me in his arms again and I cry for real over the loss of my dog and of Cillian and of the life that was.

"I left him," I say and keep saying, snot-filled and coughing. "I left him."

"I know," he says and I can tell it's true cuz I hear the same words in his Noise. **I left him,** he thinks.

But after only a minute I feel him gently pushing me back and he says, "Listen, Todd, there ain't much time."

"Ain't much time for what?" I sniffle but I see he's looking over at Viola.

"Hi," she says, eyes all alert.

"Hi," Ben says. "You must be her."

"I must be," she says.

"You been taking care of Todd?"

"We've been taking care of each other."

"Good," Ben says, and his Noise goes warm and sad. "Good."

"C'mon," I say, taking his arm and trying to pull him back towards the footbridge. "We can get you something to eat. And there's a doctor–"

But Ben ain't moving. "Can you keep an eye out for us?"

he asks Viola. "Let us know if you see anything, anything at all. Either from the settlement or the road."

Viola nods and catches my eye as she steps outta the green and back to the path.

"Things have escalated," Ben says to me, low, serious as a heart attack. "You gotta get to a place called Haven. Fast as you can."

"I *know* that, Ben," I say, "why do you–?"

"There's an army after you."

"I know that, *too*. *And* Aaron. But now that yer here we can–"

"I can't come with you," he says.

My mouth hangs open. "What? *Course* you can–"

But he's shaking his head. "You know I can't."

"We can find a way," I say, but already my Noise is whirling, thinking, remembering.

"Prentisstown men ain't welcome anywhere on New World," he says.

I nod. "They ain't too happy bout Prentisstown *boys*, neither."

He takes my arm again. "Has anyone hurt you?"

I look at him quietly. "Lots of people," I say.

He bites his lip and his Noise gets even sadder.

"I looked for you," he says. "Day and night, following the army, getting round it, ahead of it, listening for rumours of a boy and a girl travelling alone. And here you are and yer okay and I knew you would be. I knew it." He sighs and there's so much love and sadness in it I know he's about to say the truth. "But I'm a danger to you in New World." He gestures at the bush we're hiding in, hiding in like thieves.

"Yer gonna have to make it the rest of the way alone."

"I ain't alone," I say, without thinking.

He smiles, but it's still sad. "No," he says. "No, yer not, are ya?" He looks around us again, peering thru the leaves and over the river to Doctor Snow's house. "Were you sick?" he asks. "I heard yer Noise yesterday morning coming down the river but it was feverish and sleeping. I been waiting here ever since. I was worried something was really wrong."

"I was sick," I say and shame starts to cloud my Noise like a slow fog.

Ben looks at me close again. "What happened, Todd?" he says, gently reading into my Noise like he always could. "What's happened?"

I open up my Noise for him, all of it from the beginning, the crocs that attacked Aaron, the race thru the swamp, Viola's ship, being chased by the Mayor on horseback, the bridge, Hildy and Tam, Farbranch and what happened there, the fork in the road, Wilf and the things that sang *Here*, Mr Prentiss Jr and Viola saving me.

And the Spackle.

And what I did.

I can't look at Ben.

"Todd," he says.

I'm still looking at the ground.

"Todd," he says again. "Look at me."

I look up at him. His eyes, blue as ever, catching mine and holding them. "We've all made mistakes, Todd. All of us."

"I killed it," I say. I swallow. "I killed *him*. It was a him."

"You were acting on what you knew. You were acting on what you thought best."

"And that *excuses* it?"

But there's something in his Noise. Something off and telling.

"What is it, Ben?"

He lets out a breath. "It's time you knew, Todd," he says. "Time you knew the truth."

There's a snap of branches as Viola comes rushing back to us.

"Horse on the road," she says, outta breath.

We listen. Hoofbeats, down the river road, coming fast. Ben slinks back a little farther into the bushes. We go with him but the horseman is coming so quick he ain't interested in us at all. We hear him thunder by on the road and turn up the bridge that heads straight into Carbonel Downs, hooves clattering on boards and then on dirt till they're swallowed up by the loudspeaker sounds.

"That can't be good news," Viola says.

"It'll be the army," Ben says. "By now they're probably not more than a few hours from here."

"What!?" I say, rearing back. Viola jumps, too.

"I told you we don't have much time," Ben says.

"Then we gotta *go!*" I say. "You gotta come with us. We'll tell people–"

"No," he says. "No. You get yerselves to Haven. That's all there is to it. It's yer best chance."

We pelt him with sudden askings.

"Is Haven safe then?" Viola asks. "From an army?"

"Is it true they have a cure for the Noise?" I ask.

"Will they have communicators? Will I be able to contact my ship?"

"Are you sure it's safe? Are you *sure*?"

Ben raises his hands to stop us. "I don't know," he says. "I haven't been there in twenty years."

Viola stands up straight.

"Twenty years?" she says. "Twenty *years*?" Her voice is rising. "Then how can we know what we'll find when we get there? How do we know it's even still *there*?"

I rub my hand across my face and I think it's the emptiness where Manchee used to be that makes me realize, realize what we never wanted to know.

"We don't," I say, only saying the truth. "We never did."

Viola lets out a little sound and her shoulders slump down. "No," she says. "I guess we didn't."

"But there's always hope," Ben says. "You always have to hope."

We both look at him and there must be a word for how we're doing it but I don't know what it is. We're looking at him like he's speaking a foreign language, like he just said he was moving to one of the moons, like he's telling us it's all just been a bad dream and there's candy for everybody.

"There ain't a whole lotta hope out here, Ben," I say.

He shakes his head. "What d'you think's been driving you on? What d'you think's got you this far?"

"Fear," Viola says.

"Desperayshun," I say.

"No," he says, taking us both in. "No, no, no. You've come farther than most people on this planet will do in their lifetimes. You've overcome obstacles and dangers and things that should've killed you. You've outrun an army and a madman and deadly illness and seen things most people will never see. How do you think you could have possibly come this far if you didn't have hope?"

Viola and I exchange a glance.

"I see what yer trying to say, Ben—" I start.

"Hope," he says, squeezing my arm on the word. "It's hope. I am looking into yer eyes right now and I am telling you that there's hope for you, hope for you both." He looks up at Viola and back at me. "There's hope waiting for you at the end of the road."

"You don't know that," Viola says and my Noise, as much as I don't want it to, agrees with her.

"No," Ben says, "but I believe it. I believe it for you. And that's why it's hope."

"Ben—"

"Even if you don't believe it," he says, "believe that I do."

"I'd believe it more if you were coming with us," I say.

"He ain't coming?" Viola says, surprised, then corrects herself. "*Isn't* coming?"

Ben looks at her, opens his mouth and closes it again.

"What's the truth, Ben?" I ask. "What's the truth we need to know?"

Ben takes a long slow breath thru his nose. "Okay," he says.

But then a loud and clear "Todd?" comes calling from across the river.

And that's when we notice the music of Carbonel Downs is competing with the Noise of men now crossing the bridge.

Many men.

That's the other purpose of the music, I guess. So you can't hear men coming.

"Viola?" Doctor Snow is calling. "What are you two doing over there?"

I stand up straight and look over. Doctor Snow is crossing the bridge, little Jacob's hand in his, leading a group of men who look like less friendly versions of himself and they're eyeing us up and they're seeing Ben and seeing me and Viola talking to him.

And their Noise is starting to turn different colours as what they're seeing starts making sense to them.

And I see that some of 'em have rifles.

"Ben?" I say quietly.

"You need to run," he says, under his breath. "You need to run *now*."

"I ain't leaving you. Not again."

"Todd–"

"Too late," Viola says.

Cuz they're on us now, past the end of the bridge and heading towards the bushes where we're not really hiding no more.

Doctor Snow reaches us first. He looks Ben up and down. "And who might this be then?"

And the sound of his Noise ain't happy at all.

35

THE LAW

"THIS IS BEN," I say, trying to raise my Noise to block all the askings coming from the men.

"And who's Ben when he's at home?" Doctor Snow asks, his eyes alert and looking.

"Ben's my pa," I say. Cuz it's true, ain't it? In all that's important. "My father."

"Todd," I hear Ben say behind me, all kindsa feelings in his Noise, but warning most of all.

"Your father?" says a bearded man behind Doctor Snow, his fingers flexing along the stock of his rifle, tho not lifting it.

Not yet.

"You might want to be careful who you start claiming as a parent, Todd," Doctor Snow says slowly, pulling Jacob closer to him.

"You said the boy was from Farbranch," says a third man with a purple birthmark under his eye.

378

"That's what the girl told us." Doctor Snow looks at Viola. "Didn't you, Vi?"

Viola holds his look but don't say nothing.

"Can't trust the word of a woman," says the beard. "This is a Prentisstown man if I ever saw one."

"Leading the army right to us," says the birthmark.

"The boy is innocent," says Ben and when I turn I can see his hands are in the air. "I'm the one you want."

"Correction," says the beard, his voice angry and getting angrier. "You're the one we *don't* want."

"Hold on a minute, Fergal," Doctor Snow says. "Something's not right here."

"You know the law," says the birthmark.

The law.

Farbranch talked about the law, too.

"I also know these aren't normal circumstances," Doctor Snow says, then turns back to us. "We should at least give them a chance to explain themselves."

I hear Ben take a breath. "Well, I–"

"Not you," the beard interrupts.

"What's the story, Todd?" Doctor Snow says. "And it's become really important you tell us the truth."

I look from Viola to Ben and back again.

Which side of the truth do I tell?

I hear the cock of a rifle. The beard's raised his gun. And so have one or two of the men behind him.

"The longer you wait," the beard says, "the more you look like spies."

"We ain't spies," I say in a hurry.

"The army your girl's been talking about has been spotted

marching down the river road," Doctor Snow says. "One of our scouts just reported them as less than an hour away."

"Oh, no," I hear Viola whisper.

"She ain't my girl," I say, low.

"What?" Doctor Snow says.

"What?" Viola says.

"She's her own girl," I say. "She don't belong to anyone."

And does Viola ever *look* at me.

"Whichever," the birthmark says. "We've got a Prentisstown army marching on us and a Prentisstown man hiding in our bushes and a Prentisstown boy who's been in our midst for the last week. Looks mighty fishy if you ask me."

"He was sick," Doctor Snow says. "He was out cold."

"So you say," says the birthmark.

Doctor Snow turns to him real slow. "Are you calling me a liar now, Duncan? Remember, please, that you're talking to the head of the council of eldermen."

"You telling me you're not seeing a plot here, Jackson?" says the birthmark, not backing down and raising his own rifle. "We're sitting ducks. Who knows what they've told their army?" He aims his rifle at Ben. "But we'll be putting an end to that right now."

"We ain't *spies*," I say again. "We're running from the army just as hard as you should be."

And the men look at each other.

In their Noise, I can hear just these thoughts about the army, about running from it instead of defending the town. I can also see anger bubbling, anger at having to make this choice, anger at not knowing the best way to protect their families. And I can see the anger focussing itself, not on the army, not on themselves for being unprepared despite Viola warning 'em for days, not at the world for the state it's in.

They're focussing their anger on Ben.

They're focussing their anger on Prentisstown in the form of one man.

Doctor Snow kneels down to get to Jacob's level. "Hey, fella," he says to his son. "Why don't you run on back to the house now, okay?"

Daddy daddy daddy I hear in Jacob's Noise. "Why, Daddy?" he says, staring at me.

"Well, I'll betcha the goat's getting lonely," Doctor Snow says. "And who wants a lonely goat, huh?"

Jacob looks at his father, back at me and Ben, then to the men around him. "Why is everyone so upset?" he says.

"Oh," Doctor Snow says, "we're just figuring some things out, is all. It'll all be right soon enough. You just run on back home, make sure the goat's okay."

Jacob thinks about this for a second, then says, "Okay, Daddy."

Doctor Snow kisses him on the top of the head and ruffles his hair. Jacob goes running back over the bridge towards Doctor Snow's house. When Doctor Snow turns back to us, a whole raft of pointed guns accompany him.

"You can see how this doesn't look good, Todd," he says, and there's real sadness in his voice.

"He doesn't know," Ben says.

"Shut your hole, murderer!" says the beard, gesturing with his rifle.

Murderer?

"Tell me true," Doctor Snow says to me. "Are you from Prentisstown?"

"He *saved* me from Prentisstown," Viola speaks up. "If it hadn't been for him–"

"Shut up, girl," says the beard.

"Now's not really the time for women to be talking, Vi," Doctor Snow says.

"But–" Viola says, her face getting red.

"Please," Doctor Snow says. Then he looks at Ben. "What have you told your army? How many men we have? What our fortifications are like–"

"I've been *running* from the army," Ben says, hands still in the air. "Look at me. Do I look like a well-tended soldier? I haven't told them anything. I've been on the run, looking for my…" He pauses and I know the reason. "For my son," he says.

"You did this knowing the law?" Doctor Snow asks.

"I know the law," Ben says. "How could I possibly not know the law?"

"What ruddy LAW?" I yell. "What the hell is everyone talking about?"

"Todd is innocent," Ben says. "You can search his Noise for as long as you like and you won't find anything to say I'm lying."

"You can't trust them," says the beard, still looking down his gun. "You know you can't."

"We don't know anything," Doctor Snow says. "Not for ten years or more."

"We know they've raised themselves into an army," says the birthmark.

382

"Yes, but I don't see any crime in this boy," Doctor Snow says. "Do you?"

A dozen different Noises come poking at me like sticks.

He turns to Viola. "And all the girl is guilty of is a lie that saved her friend's life."

Viola looks away from me, face still red with anger.

"And we've got bigger problems," Doctor Snow continues. "An army coming that may or may not know all about how we're preparing to meet them."

"We ain't SPIES!" I shout.

But Doctor Snow is turning to the other men. "Take the boy and the girl back into town. The girl can go with the women and the boy is well enough to fight alongside us."

"Wait a minute!" I yell.

Doctor Snow turns to Ben. "And though I do believe you're just a man out looking for his son, the law's the law."

"Is that your final ruling?" the beard says.

"If the eldermen agree," Doctor Snow says. There's a general but reluctant nodding of heads, all serious and curt. Doctor Snow looks at me. "I'm sorry, Todd."

"Hold on!" I say, but the birthmark's is already stepping forward and grabbing my arm. "Let go of me!"

Another man's grabbing on to Viola and she's resisting just as much as I am.

"Ben!" I call, looking back at him. "*Ben!*"

"Go, Todd," he says.

"No, Ben!"

"Remember I love you."

"What're they gonna do?" I say, still pulling away from

the birthmark's hand. I turn to Doctor Snow. "What're you gonna do?"

He don't say nothing but I can see it in his Noise.

What the law demands.

"The HELL you are!" I yell and with my free arm I'm already reaching for my knife and bringing it round towards the birthmark's hand, slicing it across the top. He yelps and lets go.

"Run!" I say to Ben. "Run, already!"

I see Viola biting the hand of the man who's grabbing her. He calls out and she stumbles back.

"You, too!" I say to her. "Get outta here!"

"I wouldn't," says the beard and there are rifles cocking all over the place.

The birthmark is cursing and he raises his arm to strike but I've got my knife out in front of me. "Try it," I say thru my teeth. *"Come on!"*

"ENOUGH!" Doctor Snow yells.

And in the sudden silence that follows, we hear the hoofbeats.

Thump budda-thump budda-thump.

Horses. Five of 'em. Ten. Maybe even fifteen.

Roaring down the road like the devil hisself is on their tail.

"Scouts?" I say to Ben tho I know they ain't.

He shakes his head. "Advance party."

"They'll be armed," I say to Doctor Snow and the men, thinking fast. "They'll have as many guns as you."

Doctor Snow's thinking, too. I can see his Noise whirring, see him thinking how much time they've got before the horses get here, how much trouble me and Ben and Viola are going to cause, how much time we'll waste.

I see him decide.

"Let them go."

"What?" says the beard, his Noise itching to shoot *something*. "He's a traitor and a murderer."

"And we've got a town to protect," Doctor Snow says firmly. "I've got a son to keep safe. So do you, Fergal."

The beard frowns but says nothing more.

Thump budda-thump budda-thump comes the sound from the road.

Doctor Snow turns to us. "Go," he says. "I can only hope you haven't sealed our fate."

"We haven't," I say, "and that's the truth."

Doctor Snow purses his lips. "I'd like to believe you." He turns to the men. "Come on!" he shouts. "Get to your posts! Hurry!"

The group of men breaks up, scurrying back to Carbonel Downs, the beard and the birthmark still seething at us as they go, looking for a reason to use their guns, but we don't give 'em one. We just watch 'em go.

I find I'm shaking a little.

"Holy crap," Viola says, bending at the waist.

"We gotta get outta here," I say. "The army's gonna be more interested in us than it is in them."

I still have Viola's bag with me, tho all it's got in it any more are a few clothes, the water bottles, the binos and my ma's book, still in its plastic bag.

All the things we got in the world.

Which means we're ready to go.

"This is only gonna keep happening," Ben says. "I can't come with you."

"Yes, you can," I say. "You can leave later but we're going now and yer coming with us. We ain't leaving you to be caught by no army." I look over to Viola. "Right?"

She puts her shoulders back and looks decisive. "Right," she says.

"That's settled then," I say.

Ben looks back and forth twixt the two of us. He furrows his brow. "Only till I know yer safe."

"Too much talking," I say. "Not enough running."

36

ANSWERS TO ASKINGS

WE STAY OFF THE RIVER ROAD for obvious reasons and tear thru the trees, heading, as always, towards Haven, snapping thru twigs and branches, getting away from Carbonel Downs as fast as our legs can carry us.

It's not ten minutes before we hear the first gunshots.

We don't look back. We don't look back.

We run and the sounds fade.

We keep running.

Me and Viola are both faster than Ben and sometimes we have to slow down to let him catch up.

We run past one, then two small, empty settlements, places that obviously heeded the rumours about the army better than Carbonel Downs did. We keep to the woods twixt the river and the road but we don't even see any caravans. They must be high-tailing it to Haven.

On we run.

Night falls and we keep on running.

"You all right?" I ask Ben, when we stop by the river to refill the bottles.

"Keep on going," he says, gasping. "Keep on going."

Viola sends me a worried look.

"I'm sorry we don't got food," I say, but he just shakes his head and says, "Keep going."

So we keep going.

Midnight comes and we run thru that, too.

(Who knows how many days? Who cares any more?)

Till finally, Ben says, "Wait," and stops, hands on his knees, breathing hard in a real unhealthy way.

I look around us by the light of the moons. Viola's looking, too. She points. "There."

"Up there, Ben," I say, pointing up the small hill Viola's seen. "We'll be able to get a view."

Ben don't say nothing, just gasps and nods his head and follows us. There's trees all the way up the side but a well-tended path and a wide clearing at the top.

When we get there, we see why.

"A sematary," I say.

"A what?" Viola says, looking round at all the square stones marking out their graves. Must be a hundred, maybe two, in orderly rows and well-kept grass. Settler life is hard and it's short and lotsa New World people have lost the battle.

"It's a place for burying dead folk," I say.

Her eyes widen. "A place for doing *what*?"

"Don't people die in space?" I ask.

"Yeah," she says. "But we burn them. We don't put them in *holes*." She crosses her arms around herself, mouth and forehead frowning, peering around at the graves. "How can this be sanitary?"

Ben still hasn't said anything, just flopped down by a gravestone and leant against it, catching his breath. I take a swig from a water bottle and then hand it to Ben. I look out and around us. You can see down the road for a piece and there's a view of the river, too, rushing by us on the left now. It's a clear sky, the stars out, the moons starting to crescent in the sky above us.

"Ben?" I say, looking up into the night.

"Yeah?" he says, drinking down his water.

"You all right?"

"Yeah." His breath's getting back to normal. "I'm built for farm labour. Not sprinting."

I look at the moons one more time, the smaller one chasing the larger one, two brightnesses up there, still light enough to cast shadows, ignorant of the troubles of men.

I look into myself. I look deep into my Noise.

And I realize I'm ready.

This is the last chance.

And I'm ready.

"I think it's time," I say. I look back at him. "I think now's the time, if it's ever gonna be."

He licks his lips and swallows his water. He puts the cap back on the bottle. "I know," he says.

"Time for what?" Viola asks.

"Where should I start?" Ben asks.

I shrug. "Anywhere," I say, "as long as it's true."

I can hear Ben's Noise gathering, gathering up the whole story, taking one stream out of the river, finally, the one that tells what really happened, the one hidden for so long and so deep I didn't even know it was there for my whole up-growing life.

Viola's silence has gone more silent than usual, as still as the night, waiting to hear what he might say.

Ben takes a deep breath.

"The Noise germ wasn't Spackle warfare," he says. "That's the first thing. The germ was here when we landed. A naturally occurring phenomenon, in the air, always had been, always will be. We got outta our ships and within a day everyone could hear everyone's thoughts. Imagine our surprise."

He pauses, remembering.

"Except it *wasn't* everyone," Viola says.

"It was just the men," I say.

Ben nods. "No one knows why. Still don't. Our scientists were mainly agriculturalists and the doctors couldn't find a reason and so for a while, there was chaos. Just ... *chaos*, like you wouldn't believe. Chaos and confusion and Noise Noise Noise." He scratches underneath his chin. "A lotta men scattered theirselves into far communities, getting away from Haven as fast as roads could be cut. But soon folk realized there was nothing to be done about it so for a while we all tried to live with it the best we could, found different ways to deal with it, different communities taking their own paths. Same as we did when we realized all our livestock were talking, too, and pets and local creachers."

He looks up into the sky and to the sematary around us and the river and road below.

"Everything on this planet talks to each other," he says.

"Everything. That's what New World is. Informayshun, all the time, never stopping, whether you want it or not. The Spackle knew it, evolved to live with it, but we weren't equipped for it. Not even close. And too much informayshun can drive a man mad. Too much informayshun becomes just Noise. And it never, never stops."

He pauses and the Noise is there, of course, like it always is, his and mine and Viola's silence only making it louder.

"As the years went by," he goes on, "times were hard all over New World and getting harder. Crops failing and sickness and no prosperity and no Eden. Definitely no Eden. And a preaching started spreading in the land, a poisonous preaching, a preaching that started to blame."

"They blamed the aliens," Viola says.

"The Spackle," I say and the shame returns.

"They blamed the Spackle," Ben confirms. "And somehow preaching became a movement and a movement became a war." He shakes his head. "They didn't stand a chance. We had guns, they didn't, and that was the end of the Spackle."

"Not all," I say.

"No," he says. "Not all. But they learned better than to come too near men again, I tell you that."

A brief wind blows across the hilltop. When it stops, it's like we're the only three people left on New World. Us and the sematary ghosts.

"But the war's not the end of the story," Viola says quietly.

"No," Ben says. "The story ain't finished, ain't even *half* finished."

And I know it ain't. And I know where it's heading.

And I changed my mind. I don't want it to finish.

But I do, too.

I look into Ben's eyes, into his Noise.

"The war didn't stop with the Spackle," I say. "Not in Prentisstown."

Ben licks his lips and I can feel unsteadiness in his Noise and hunger and grief at what he's already imagining is our next parting.

"War is a monster," he says, almost to himself. "War is the devil. It starts and it consumes and it grows and grows and grows." He's looking at me now. "And otherwise normal men become monsters, too."

"They couldn't stand the silence," Viola says, her voice still. "They couldn't stand women knowing everything about them and them knowing nothing about women."

"*Some* men thought that," Ben says. "Not all. Not me, not Cillian. There were good men in Prentisstown."

"But enough thought it," I say.

"Yes," he nods.

There's another pause as the truth starts to show itself.

Finally. And forever.

Viola is shaking her head. "Are you saying...?" she says. "Are you really saying...?"

And here it is.

Here's the thing that's the centre of it all.

Here's the thing that's been growing in my head since I left the swamp, seen in flashes of men along the way, most clearly in Matthew Lyle's but also in the reakshuns of everyone who even hears the word Prentisstown.

Here it is.

The truth.

And I don't want it.

But I say it anyway.

"After they killed the Spackle," I say, "the men of Prentisstown killed the women of Prentisstown."

Viola gasps even tho she's got to have guessed it, too.

"Not *all* the men," Ben says. "But many. Allowing themselves to be swayed by Mayor Prentiss and the preachings of Aaron, who used to say that what was hidden must be evil. They killed all the women and all the men who tried to protect them."

"My ma," I say.

Ben just nods in confirmayshun.

I feel a sickness in my stomach.

My ma dying, being killed by men I probably saw every day.

I have to sit down on a gravestone.

I have to think of something else, I just do. I have to put something else in my Noise so I can stand it.

"Who was Jessica?" I say, remembering Matthew Lyle's Noise back in Farbranch, remembering the violence in it, the Noise that now makes sense even tho it don't make no sense at all.

"Some people could see what was coming," Ben says. "Jessica Elizabeth was our Mayor and she could see the way the wind was blowing."

Jessica Elizabeth, I think. New Elizabeth.

"She organized some of the girls and younger boys to flee across the swamp," Ben continues. "But before she could go herself with the women and the men who hadn't lost their minds, the Mayor's men attacked."

"And that was that," I say, feeling numb all over. "New Elizabeth becomes Prentisstown."

"Yer ma never thought it would happen," Ben says, smiling sadly to himself at some memory. "So full of love that woman, so full of hope in the goodness of others." He stops smiling. "And then there came a moment when it was too late to flee and you were way too young to be sent away and so she gave you to us, told us to keep you safe, no matter what."

I look up. "How was staying in Prentisstown keeping me safe?"

Ben's staring right at me, sadness everywhere around him, his Noise so weighted with it, it's a wonder he can stay upright.

"Why didn't you leave?" I ask.

He rubs his face. "Cuz we didn't think the attack would really happen either. Or I didn't, anyway, and we had put the farm together and I thought it would blow over before anything really bad happened. I thought it was just rumours and paranoia, including on the part of yer ma, right up to the last." He frowns. "I was wrong. I was stupid." He looks away. "I was wilfully blind."

I remember his words comforting me about the Spackle. *We've all made mistakes, Todd. All of us.*

"And then it was too late," Ben says. "The deed was done and word of what Prentisstown had done spread like wildfire, starting with the few who'd managed to escape it. All men from Prentisstown were declared criminals. We couldn't leave."

Viola's arms are still crossed. "Why didn't someone come and get you? Why didn't the rest of New World come after you?"

"And do what?" Ben says, sounding tired. "Fight another war but this time with heavily armed men? Lock us up in a giant prison? They laid down the law that if any man from Prentisstown crossed the swamp, he'd be executed. And then they left us to it."

"But they must have…" Viola says, holding her palms to the air. "Something. I don't know."

"If it ain't happening on yer doorstep," Ben says, "it's easier to think, *Why go out and* find *trouble?* We had the whole of the swamp twixt us and New World. The Mayor sent word that Prentisstown would be a town in exile. Doomed, of course, to a slow death. We'd agree never to leave and if we ever did, he'd hunt us down and kill us himself."

"Didn't people try?" Viola says. "Didn't they try and get away?"

"They *tried*," Ben says, full of meaning. "It wasn't uncommon for people to disappear."

"But if you and Cillian were innocent–" I start.

"We *weren't* innocent," Ben says strongly, and suddenly his Noise tastes bitter. He sighs. "We weren't."

"What do you mean?" I ask, raising my head. The sickness in my stomach ain't leaving. "What do you mean you weren't innocent?"

"You let it happen," Viola says. "You didn't die with the other men who were protecting the women."

"We didn't fight," he says, "and we didn't die." He shakes his head. "Not innocent at all."

"Why didn't you fight?" I ask.

"Cillian wanted to," Ben says quickly. "I want you to know that. He wanted to do whatever he could to stop them. He would have given his life." He looks away once more. "But I wouldn't let him."

"Why not?"

"I get it," Viola whispers.

I look at her, cuz I sure don't. "Get what?"

Viola keeps looking at Ben. "They either die fighting for what's right and leave you an unprotected baby," she says, "or they become complicit with what's wrong and keep you alive."

I don't know what complicit means but I can guess.

They did it for me. All that horror. They did it for me.

Ben and Cillian. Cillian and Ben.

They did it so I could live.

I don't know how I feel about any of this.

Doing what's right should be easy.

It shouldn't be just another big mess like everything else.

"So we waited," Ben says. "In a town-sized prison. Full of the ugliest Noise you ever heard before men started denying their own pasts, before the Mayor came up with his grand plans. And so we waited for the day you were old enough to get away on yer own, innocent as we could keep you." He rubs a hand over his head. "But the Mayor was waiting, too."

"For me?" I ask, tho I know it's true.

"For the last boy to become a man," Ben says. "When boys became men, they were told the truth. Or a version of it, anyway. And then they were made complicit themselves."

I remember his Noise from back on the farm, about my birthday, about how a boy becomes a man.

About what complicity really means and how it can be passed on.

How it was waiting to be passed on to me.

And about the men who–

I put it outta my head.

"That don't make no sense," I say.

"You were the last," Ben says. "If he could make every single boy in Prentisstown a man by his own meaning, then he's God, ain't he? He's created all of us and is in complete control."

"*If one of us falls*," I say.

"*We all fall*," Ben finishes. "That's why he wants you. Yer a symbol. Yer the last innocent boy of Prentisstown. If he can make you fall, then his army is complete and of his own perfect making."

"And if not?" I say, tho I'm wondering if I've already fallen.

"If not," Ben says, "he'll kill you."

"So Mayor Prentiss is as mad as Aaron, then," Viola says.

"Not quite," Ben says. "Aaron is mad. But the Mayor knows enough to use madness to achieve his ends."

"Which are what?" Viola says.

"This world," Ben says calmly. "He wants all of it."

I open my mouth to ask more stuff I don't wanna know but then, as if there was never gonna be anything else that could ever happen, we hear it.

Thump budda-thump budda-thump. Coming down the road, relentless, like a joke that ain't ever gonna be funny.

"You've *got* to be kidding," Viola says.

Ben's already back on his feet, listening. "It sounds like just one horse."

We all look down the road, shining a little in the moonlight.

"Binos," Viola says, now right by my side. I fish 'em out without another word, click on the night setting and look, searching out the sound as it rings thru the night air.

Budda-thump budda-thump.

I search down the road farther and farther back till–

There it is.

There *he* is.

Who else?

Mr Prentiss Jr, alive and well and untied and back on his horse.

"Damn," I hear from Viola, reading my Noise as I hand her the binos.

"*Davy Prentiss?*" Ben says, also reading my Noise.

"The one and only." I put the water bottles back in Viola's bag. "We gotta go."

Viola hands the binos to Ben and he looks for himself. He takes them away from his eyes and gives the binos a quick once over. "Nifty," he says.

"We need to go," Viola says. "As always."

Ben turns to us, binos still in his hand. He's looking from one of us to the other and I see what's forming in his Noise.

"Ben–" I start.

"No," he says. "This is where I leave you."

"*Ben–*"

"I can handle Davy bloody Prentiss."

"He has a gun," I say. "You don't."

Ben comes up to me. "Todd," he says.

"No, Ben," I say, my voice getting louder. "I ain't listening."

He looks me in the eye and I notice he don't seem to be having to bend down any more to do it.

"Todd," he says again. "I atone for the wrong I've done by keeping you safe."

"You can't leave me, Ben," I say, my voice getting wet (shut up). "Not again."

He's shaking his head. "I can't come to Haven with you. You know I can't. I'm the enemy."

"We can *explain* what happened."

But he's still shaking his head.

"The horse is getting closer," Viola says.

Thump budda-thump budda-thump.

"The only thing that makes me a man," Ben says, his voice steady as a rock, "is seeing you safely into becoming a man yerself."

"I ain't a man yet, Ben," I say, my throat catching (shut *up*). "I don't even know how many days I got left."

And then he smiles and it's the smile that tells me it's over.

"Sixteen," he says. "Sixteen days till yer birthday." He takes my chin and lifts it. "But you've been a man for a good while now. Don't let *no one* tell you otherwise."

"Ben–"

"Go," he says and he comes up to me and hands Viola the binos behind my back and takes me in his arms. "No father could be prouder," I hear him say by my ear.

"No," I say, my words slurring. "It ain't fair."

"It ain't." He pulls himself away. "But there's hope at the end of the road. You remember that."

"Don't go," I say.

"I have to. Danger's coming."

"Closer and closer," Viola says, binos to her eyes.

Budda-thump budda-THUMP.

"I'll stop him. I'll buy you time." Ben looks at Viola. "You take care of Todd," he says. "I have yer word?"

"You have my word," Viola says.

"Ben, please," I whisper. "Please."

He grips my shoulders for a last time. "Remember," he says. *"Hope."*

And he don't say nothing more and he turns and runs down the hill from the sematary to the road. When he gets to the bottom, he looks back and sees us still watching him.

"What are you waiting for?" he shouts. "Run!"

37

WHAT'S THE POINT?

I WON'T SAY WHAT I FEEL when we run down the other side of the hill and away from Ben, for ever this time cuz how is there any life after this?

Life equals running and when we stop running maybe that's how we'll know life is finally finished.

"Come on, Todd," Viola calls, looking back over her shoulder. "Please, hurry."

I don't say nothing.

I run.

We get down the hill and back by the river. Again. With the road on our other side. *Again.*

Always the same.

The river's louder than it was, rushing by with some force, but who cares? What does it matter?

Life ain't fair.

It ain't.

Not never.

It's pointless and stupid and there's only suffering and pain and people who want to hurt you. You can't love nothing or no one cuz it'll all be taken away or ruined and you'll be left alone and constantly having to fight, constantly having to run just to stay alive.

There's nothing good in this life. Not nothing good nowhere.

What's the effing point?

"The point is," Viola says, stopping halfway thru a dense patch of scrub to hit me *really hard* on the shoulder, "he cared enough about you to maybe sacrifice himself and if you just GIVE UP" – she shouts that part – "then you're saying that the sacrifice is worth *nothing!*"

"Ow," I say, rubbing my shoulder. "But why should he have to sacrifice himself? Why should I have to lose him *again*?"

She steps up close to me. "Do you think you're the only person who's lost someone?" she says in a dangerous whisper. "Do you forget that my parents are dead, too?"

I did.

I did forget.

I don't say nothing.

"All I've got now is you," she says, her voice still angry. "And all you've got now is *me*. And I'm mad he left, too, and I'm mad my parents died and I'm mad we ever thought of coming to this planet in the first place but that's how it is and it's crap that it's just us but we can't do anything about it."

I still don't say nothing.

But there she is and I look at her, *really* look at her, for probably the first time since I saw her cowering next to a log back in the swamp when I thought she was a Spackle.

A lifetime ago.

She's still kinda cleaned up from the days in Carbonel Downs (only yesterday, only just yesterday) but there's dirt on her cheeks and she's skinnier than she used to be and there are dark patches under her eyes and her hair is messy and tangled and her hands are covered in sooty blackness and her shirt has a green stain of grass across the front from when she once fell and there's a cut on her lip from when a branch smacked her when we were running with Ben (and no bandages left to stitch it up) and she's looking at me.

And she's telling me she's all I've got.

And that I'm all *she's* got.

And I feel a little bit how that feels.

The colours in my Noise go different.

Her voice softens but only a little. "Ben's gone and Manchee's gone and my mother and father are gone," she says. "And I hate all of that. I *hate* it. But we're almost at the end of the road. We're almost there. And if you don't give up, I don't give up."

"Do you believe there's hope at the end?" I ask.

"No," she says simply, looking away. "No, I don't, but I'm still going." She eyes me. "You coming with?"

I don't have to answer.

We carry on running.

But.

"We should just take the road," I say, holding back yet another branch.

"But the army," she says. "And the horses."

"They know where we're going. We know where they're going. We all seem to have taken the same route to get to Haven."

"And we'll hear them coming," she agrees. "And the road's fastest.

"The road's fastest."

And she says, "Then let's just take the effing road and get ourselves to Haven."

I smile, a little. "You said *effing*," I say. "You actually said the word *effing*."

So we take the effing road, as fast as our tiredness will let us. It's still the same dusty, twisty, sometimes muddy river road that it was all those miles and miles ago and the same leafy, tree-filled New World all around us.

If you were just landing here and didn't know nothing about nothing you really might think it was Eden after all.

A wide valley is opening up around us, flat at the bottom where the river is but distant hills beginning to climb up on either side. The hills are lit only by moonlight, no sign of distant settlements or anyway of ones with lights still burning.

No sign of Haven ahead neither but we're at the flattest point of the valley and can't see much past the twists in the road either before us or back. Forest still covers both sides of the river and you'd be tempted to think that all of New World had closed up and everyone left, leaving just this road behind 'em.

We go on.

And on.

Not till the first stripes of dawn start appearing down

the valley in front of us do we stop to take on more water.

We drink. There's only my Noise and the river rushing by.

No hoofbeats. No other Noise.

"You know this means he succeeded," Viola says, not meeting my eye. "Whatever he did, he stopped the man on the horse."

I just *mm* and nod.

"And we never heard gunshots."

I *mm* and nod again.

"I'm sorry for shouting at you before," she says. "I just wanted you to keep going. I didn't want you to stop."

"I know."

We're leaning against a pair of trees by the riverbank. The road is to our backs and across the river is just trees and the far side of the valley rises up and then only the sky above, getting lighter and more blue and bigger and emptier till even the stars start leaving it.

"When we left on the scout ship," Viola says, looking up across the river with me, "I was really upset leaving my friends behind. Just a few kids from the other caretaker families, but still. I thought I'd be the only one my age on this planet for seven whole months."

I drink some water. "I didn't have friends back in Prentisstown."

She turns to me. "What do you mean, no friends? You had to have friends."

"I had a few for a while, boys a coupla months older than me. But when boys become men they stop talking to boys," I shrug. "I was the last boy. In the end there was just me and Manchee."

She gazes up into the fading stars. "It's a stupid rule."

"It is."

We don't say nothing more, just me and Viola by the riverside, resting ourselves as another dawn comes.

Just me and her.

We stir after a minute, get ourselves ready to go again.

"We could reach Haven by tomorrow," I say. "If we keep on going."

"Tomorrow," Viola nods. "I hope there's food."

It's her turn to carry the bag so I hand it to her and the sun is peeking up over the end of the valley where it looks like the river's running right into it and as the light hits the hills across the river from us, something catches my eye.

Viola turns immediately at the spark in my Noise. "What?"

I shield my eyes from the new sun. There's a little trail of dust rising from the top of the far hills.

And it's moving.

"What is that?" I say.

Viola fishes out the binos and looks thru 'em. "I can't see properly," she says. "Trees in the way."

"Someone travelling?"

"Maybe that's the other road. The fork we didn't take."

We watch for a minute or two as the dust trail keeps rising, heading towards Haven at the slow speed of a distant cloud. It's weird seeing it without any sound.

"I wish I knew where the army was," I say. "How far they were behind us."

"Maybe Carbonel Downs put up too good a fight." Viola points the binos upriver to see the way we came but it's too flat, too twisty. All there is to be seen is trees. Trees and sky and quiet and a silent trail of dust making its way along the far hilltops.

"We should go," I say. "I'm starting to feel a little spooked."

"Let's go then," Viola says, quiet-like.

Back on the road.

Back to the life of running.

We have no food with us so breakfast is a yellow fruit that Viola spies on some trees we pass that she swears she ate in Carbonel Downs. They become lunch, too, but it's better than nothing.

I think again of the knife at my back.

Could I hunt, if there was time?

But there ain't no time.

We run past midday and into afternoon. The world is still abandoned and spooky. Just me and Viola running along the valley bottom, no settlements to be seen, no caravans or carts, no other sound loud enough to be heard over the rushing of the river, getting bigger by the hour, to the point where it's hard even to hear my Noise, where even if we want to talk, we have to raise our voices.

But we're too hungry to talk. And too tired to talk. And running too much to talk.

And so on we go.

And I find myself watching Viola.

The trail of dust on the far hilltop follows us as we run, pulling ahead slowly as the day gets older and finally disappearing in the distance and I watch her checking it as we hurry on. I watch her run next to me, flinching at the aches in her legs. I watch her rub them when we rest and watch her when she drinks from the water bottles.

Now that I've seen her, I can't stop seeing her.

She catches me. "What?"

"Nothing," I say and look away cuz I don't know either.

The river and the road have straightened out as the valley gets steeper and closer on both sides. We can see a little bit back the way we came. No army yet, no horsemen neither. The quiet is almost scarier than if there was Noise everywhere.

Dusk comes, the sun setting itself in the valley behind us, setting over wherever the army might be and whatever's left of New World back there, whatever's happened to the men who fought against the army and the men who joined.

Whatever's happened to the women.

Viola runs in front of me.

I watch her run.

Just after nightfall we finally come to another settlement, another one with docks on the river, another one abandoned. There are only five houses in total along a little strip of the road, one with what looks like a small general store tacked onto the front.

"Hold on," Viola says, stopping.

"Dinner?" I say, catching my breath.

She nods.

It takes about six kicks to open the door of the general store and tho there clearly ain't no one here at all, I still look round expecting to be punished. Inside, it's mostly cans but we find a dry loaf of bread, some bruised fruit and a few strips of dried meat.

"These aren't more than a day or two old," Viola says, twixt mouthfuls. "They must have fled to Haven yesterday or the day before."

"Rumours of an army are a powerful thing," I say, not chewing my dried meat well enough before I swallow and coughing up a little bit of it.

We fill our bellies as best we can and I shove the rest of the food into Viola's bag, now hanging round my shoulders. I see the book when I do. Still there, still wrapped in its plastic bag, still with the knife-shaped slash all the way thru it.

I reach in thru the plastic bag, rubbing my fingers across the cover. It's soft to the touch and the binding still gives off a faint whiff of leather.

The book. My ma's book. It's come all the way with us. Survived its own injury. Just like us.

I look up at Viola.

She catches me again.

"*What?*" she says.

"Nothing." I put the book back in the bag with the food. "Let's go."

Back on the road, back down the river, back towards Haven.

"This should be our last night, you know," Viola says. "If Doctor Snow was right, we'll be there tomorrow."

"Yeah," I say, "and the world will change."

"Again."

"Again," I agree.

We go on a few more paces.

"You starting to feel hope?" Viola asks, her voice curious.

"No," I say, fuddling my Noise. "You?"

Her eyebrows are up but she shakes her head. "No, no."

"But we're going anyway."

"Oh, yeah," Viola says. "Hell or high water."

"It'll probably be both," I say.

The sun sets, the moons rise again, smaller crescents than the night before. The sky is still clear, the stars still up, the world still quiet, just the rush of the river, getting steadily louder.

Midnight comes.

Fifteen days.

Fifteen days till–

Till what?

We carry on thru the night, the sky falling slowly past us, our words stopping a little as dinner wears off and tiredness takes hold again. Just before dawn we find two overturned carts in the road, grains of wheat spilled everywhere and a few empty baskets rolled on their sides across the road.

"They didn't even take the time to save everything," Viola says. "They left half of it on the ground."

"Good a place as any for breakfast." I flip over one of the baskets, drag it over to where the road overlooks the river and sit down on it.

Viola picks up another basket, brings it over right next to me and sits down. There are glimmers of light in the sky as the sun gets set to rise, the road pointing right towards it, the river, too, rushing towards the dawn. I open up the bag and take out the general store food, handing some to Viola and eating what I've got. We drink from the water bottles.

The bag is open on my lap. There are our remaining clothes and there are the binos.

And there's the book again.

I feel her silence next to me, feel the pull of it on me and the hollows in my chest and stomach and head and I remember the ache I used to feel when she got too close, how it felt like grief, how it felt like a loss, like I was falling, falling into nothing, how it clenched me up and made me want to weep, made me actually *weep*.

But now–

Now, not so much.

I look over to her.

She's gotta know what's in my Noise. I'm the only one around and she's got better and better at reading it despite how loud the river's getting.

But she sits there, quietly eating, waiting for me to say.

Waiting for me to ask.

Cuz this is what I'm thinking.

When the sun comes up, it'll be the day we get to Haven, the day we get to a place filled with more people than I've ever seen together in my life, a place filled with so much Noise you can't never be alone, unless they found a cure, in which case I'll be the only Noisy one which would actually be worse.

We get to Haven, we'll be part of a city.

It won't just be Todd and Viola, sitting by a river as the sun comes up, eating our breakfast, the only two people on the face of the planet.

It'll be everyone, all together.

This might be our last chance.

I look away from her to speak. "You know that thing with voices that you do?"

"Yeah," she says, quiet.

I take out the book.

"D'you think you could do a Prentisstown voice?"

38

I HEARD A MAIDEN CALL

"*MY DEAREST TODD,*" Viola reads, copying Ben's accent as best she can. Which is pretty ruddy good. "*My dearest son.*"

My ma's voice. My ma speaking.

I cross my arms and look down into the wheat spilled across the ground.

"*I begin this journal on the day of yer birth, the day I first held you in my arms rather than in my belly. You kick just as much outside as in! And yer the most beautiful thing that's ever happened in the whole entire universe. Yer easily the most beautiful thing on New World and there's no contest in New Elizabeth, that's for sure.*"

I feel my face getting red but the sun's still not high enough for anyone to see.

"*I wish yer pa were here to see you, Todd, but New World and the Lord above saw fit to take him with the sickness five months ago and we'll both just have to wait to see him in the next world.*"

413

"You look like him. Well, babies don't look much like anything but babies but I'm telling you you look like him. Yer going to be tall, Todd, cuz yer pa was tall. Yer going to be strong, cuz yer pa was strong. And yer going to be handsome, oh, are you ever going to be handsome. The ladies of New World won't know what hit them."

Viola turns a page and I don't look at her. I sense she's not looking at me neither and I wouldn't wanna see a smile on her face right about now.

Cuz that weird thing's happening too.

Her words are not her words and they're coming outta her mouth sounding like a lie but making a new truth, creating a different world where my ma is talking directly to me, Viola speaking with a voice not her own and the world, for a little while at least, the world is all for me, the world's being made just for me.

"Let me tell you bout the place you've been born into, son. It's called New World and it's a whole planet made entirely of hope–"

Viola stops, just for a second, then carries on.

"We landed here almost exactly ten years ago looking for a new way of life, one clean and simple and honest and good, one different from Old World in all respects, where people could live in safety and peace with God as our guide and with love for our fellow man.

"There've been struggles. I won't begin this story to you with a lie, Todd. It ain't been easy here–

"Oooh, listen to me, writing down 'ain't' when addressing my son. That's settler life for you, I spose, not much time for niceties and it's easy to sink to the level of people who revel in

squandering their manners. But there's not much harm in 'ain't', surely? Okay, that's decided then. My first bad choice as a mother. Say 'ain't' all you like, Todd. I promise not to correct you."

Viola purses her lips but I don't say nothing so she continues.

"So there's been hardship and sickness on New World and in New Elizabeth. There's something called the Noise here on this planet that men have been struggling with since we landed but the strange thing is you'll be one of the boys in the settlement who won't know any different and so it'll be hard to explain to you what life was like before and why it's so difficult now but we're managing the best we can.

"A man called David Prentiss, who's got a son just a bit older than you, Todd, and who's one of our better organizers – I believe he was a caretaker on the ship over, if memory serves me correct–"

Viola pauses at this, too, but this time it's me who waits for her to say something. She don't.

"He convinced Jessica Elizabeth, our Mayor, to found this little settlement on the far side of an enormous swamp so that the Noise of the rest of New World can't never reach us unless we allow it to. It's still Noisy as anything here in New Elizabeth but at least it's people we know, at least it's people we trust. For the most part.

"My role here is that I farm several fields of wheat up north of the settlement. Since yer pa passed, our close friends Ben and Cillian have been helping me out since theirs is the next farm over. I can't wait for you to meet them. Well wait, you already have! They've already held you and said hello so look at *that, one day in the world and you've already made two friends. It's a good way to start, son.*

"In fact, I'm sure you'll do fine cuz you came out two weeks early. Clearly you'd decided you'd had enough and wanted to see what this world had to offer you. I can't blame you. The sky is so big and blue and the trees so green and this is a world where the animals talk to you, really talk, and you can even talk back and there's so much wonder to be had, so much just waiting for you, Todd, that I almost can't stand that it's not happening for you right now, that yer going to have to wait to see all that's possible, all the things you might do."

Viola takes a breath and says, "There's a break in the page here and a little space and then it says *Later* like she got interrupted." She looks up at me. "You okay?"

"Yeah, yeah," I nod real fast, my arms still crossed. "Carry on."

It's getting lighter, the sun truly coming up. I turn away from her a little.

She reads.

"Later.

"Sorry, son, had to stop for a minute for a visit from our holy man, Aaron."

Another pause, another lick of the lips.

"We've been lucky to have him, tho I must admit of late he's not been saying things I exactly agree with about the natives of New World. Which are called the Spackle, by the way, and which were a BIG surprise, since they were so shy at first neither the original planners back on Old World or our first scout ships even knew they were here!

"They're very sweet creachers. Different and maybe primitive and no spoken or written language that we can really find but I don't agree with some of the thinking of the people here that the Spackle are animals rather than intelligent beings. And Aaron's been preaching lately about how God has made a dividing line twixt us and them and—

"Well that's not really something to discuss on yer first day, is it? Aaron believes what he believes devoutly, has been a pillar of faith for all of us these long years and should anyone find this journal and read it, let me say here for the record that it was a privilege to have him come by and bless you on yer first day of life. Okay?

"But I will say also on yer first day that the attractiveness of power is something you should learn about before you get too much older, it's the thing that separates men from boys, tho not in the way most men think.

"And that's all I'll say. Prying eyes and all that.

"Oh, son, there's so much wonder in the world. Don't let no one tell you otherwise. Yes, life has been hard here on New World and I'll even admit to you here, cuz if I'm going to start out at all it has to be an honest start, I'll tell you that I was nearly given to despair. Things in the settlement are maybe more complicated than I can quite explain right now and there's things you'll learn for yerself before too long whether I like it or not and there've been difficulties with food and with sickness and it was hard enough even before I lost yer pa and I nearly gave up.

"But I didn't give up. I didn't give up cuz of you, my beautiful, beautiful boy, my wondrous son who might make something better of this world, who I promise to raise only

417

with love and hope and who I swear will see this world come good. I swear it.

"*Cuz when I held you for the first time this morning and fed you from my own body, I felt so much love for you it was almost like pain, almost like I couldn't stand it one second longer.*

"*But only almost.*

"*And I sang to you a song that my mother sang to me and her mother sang to her and it goes,*"

And here, amazingly, Viola sings.

Actually *sings*.

My skin goes gooseflesh, my chest crushes. She musta heard the whole tune in my Noise and of course Ben singing it cuz here it comes, rolling outta her mouth like the peal of a bell.

The voice of Viola making the world into the voice of my ma, singing the song.

"*Early one morning, just as the sun was rising,*
I heard a maiden call from the valley below,
'*Oh don't deceive me, oh never leave me,*
How could you use a poor maiden so?'"

I can't look at her.

I can't look at her.

I put my hands to my head.

"*And it's a sad song, Todd, but it's also a promise. I'll never deceive you and I'll never leave you and I promise you this so you can one day promise it to others and know that it's true.*

"*Oh, ha, Todd! That's you crying. That's you crying from yer cot, waking up from yer first sleep on yer first day, waking up and asking the world to come to you.*

"And so for today I have to put this aside.

"Yer calling for me, son, and I will answer."

Viola stops and there's only the river and my Noise.

"There's more," Viola says after a while when I don't raise my head, flipping thru the pages. "There's a lot more." She looks at me. "Do you want me to read more?" She looks back at the book. "Do you want me to read the end?"

The end.

Read the last thing my ma wrote in the last days before–

"No," I say quickly.

Yer calling for me, son, and I will answer.

In my Noise forever.

"No," I say again. "Let's leave it there for now."

I glance over at Viola and I see that her face is pulled as sad as my Noise feels. Her eyes are wet and her chin shakes, just barely, just a tremble in the dawn sunlight. She sees me watching, feels my Noise watching her, and she turns away to face the river.

And there, in that morning, in that new sunrise, I realize something.

I realize something important.

So important that as it dawns fully I have to stand up.

I know what she's thinking.

I *know* what she's thinking.

Even looking at her back, I know what she's thinking and feeling and what's going on inside her.

The way she's turned her body, the way she's holding her head and her hands and the book in her lap, the way she's stiffening a little in her back as she hears all this in my Noise.

I can read it.

I can read *her*.

Cuz she's thinking about how her own parents also came here with hope like my ma. She's wondering if the hope at the end of our road is just as false as the one that was at the end of my ma's. And she's taking the words of my ma and putting them into the mouths of her own ma and pa and hearing them say that they love her and they miss her and they wish her the world. And she's taking the song of my ma and she's weaving it into everything else till it becomes a sad thing all her own.

And it hurts her, but it's an okay hurt, but it hurts still, but it's good, but it hurts.

She hurts.

I know all this.

I *know* it's true.

Cuz I can read her.

I can read her Noise even tho she ain't got none.

I know who she is.

I know Viola Eade.

I raise my hands to the side of my head to hold it all in.

"Viola," I whisper, my voice shaking.

"I know," she says quietly, pulling her arms tight around her, still facing away from me.

And I look at her sitting there and she looks across the river and we wait as the dawn fully arrives, each of us knowing.

Each of us knowing the other.

39

THE FALLS

THE SUN CREEPS UP into the sky and the river is loud as we look across it and we can now see it rushing fast down towards the valley's end, throwing up whitewater and rapids.

It's Viola who breaks the spell that's fallen twixt us. "You know what it has to be, don't you?" she says. She takes out the binos and looks downriver. The sun is rising at the end of the valley. She has to shield the lenses with her hand.

"What is it?" I say.

She presses a button or two and looks again.

"What do you see?" I ask.

She hands the binos to me.

I look downriver, following the rapids, the foam, right to—

Right to the end.

A few kilometres away, the river ends in mid-air.

"Another falls," I say.

"Looks way bigger than the one we saw with Wilf," she says.

"The road'll find a way past it," I say. "Shouldn't bother us."

"That's not what I mean."

"What then?"

"I mean," she says, frowning a bit at my denseness, "that falls that big're bound to have a city at the bottom of them. That if you had to choose a place anywhere on a planet for first settlement, then a valley at the base of a waterfall with rich farmland and ready water might just look perfect from space."

My Noise rises a little but only a little.

Cuz who would dare to think?

"Haven," I say.

"I'll bet you anything we've found it," she says. "I'll bet you when we get to that waterfall we'll be able to see it below us."

"If we run," I say, "we could be there in an hour. Less than"

She looks me in the eye for the first time since my ma's book.

And she says, "*If* we run?"

And then she smiles.

A genuine smile.

And I know what that means, too.

We grab up our few things and go.

Faster than before.

My feet are tired and sore. Hers must be, too. I've got blisters and aches and my heart hurts from all I miss and all that's gone. And hers does, too.

But we run.

Boy, do we run.

Cuz maybe (shut up)–

Just maybe (don't think it)–

Maybe there really *is* hope at the end of the road.

The river grows wider and straighter as we rush on and the walls of the valley move in closer and closer, the one on our side getting so close the edge of the road starts to slope up. Spray from the rapids is floating in the air. Our clothes get wet, our faces, too, and hands. The roar becomes thunderous, filling up the world with itself, almost like a physical thing, but not in a bad way. Like it's washing you, like it's washing the Noise away.

And I think, *Please let Haven be at the bottom of the falls. Please.*

Cuz I see Viola looking back to me as we run and there's brightness on her face and she keeps urging me on with tilts of her head and smiles and I think how hope may be the thing that pulls you forward, may be the thing that keeps you going, but that it's dangerous, too, that it's painful and risky, that it's making a dare to the world and when has the world ever let us win a dare?

Please let Haven be there.

Oh please oh please oh please.

The road finally starts rising a bit, pulling up above the river slightly as the water starts really crashing thru rocky rapids. There ain't no more wooded bits twixt us and it now at all, just a hill climbing up steeper and steeper on our right side as the valley closes in and then nothing but river and the falls ahead.

"Almost there," Viola calls from ahead of me, running, her hair bouncing off the back of her neck, the sun shining down on everything.

And then.

And then, at the edge of the cliff, the road comes to a lip and takes a sudden angle down and to the right.

And that's where we stop.

The falls are huge, half a kilometre across easy. The water roars over the cliff in a violent white foam, sending spray hundreds of metres out into the sheer drop and above and all around, soaking us in our clothes and throwing rainbows all over the place as the rising sun lights it.

"Todd," Viola says, so faintly I can barely hear it.

But I don't need to.

I know what she means.

As soon as the falls start falling, the valley opens up again, wide as the sky itself, taking the river that starts again at the base of the falls, which crashes forward with whitewater before it pools and calms down and becomes a river again.

And flows into Haven.

Haven.

Gotta be.

Spread out below us like a table full of food.

"There it is," Viola says.

And I feel her fingers wrap around my own.

The falls to our left, spray and rainbows in the sky, the sun rising ahead of us, the valley below.

And Haven, sitting waiting.

It's three, maybe four kilometres away down the farther valley.

But there it is.

There it ruddy well is.

I look round us, round to where the road has taken a sharp turn at our feet, sloping down and cutting into the valley wall to our right but then zig-zagging its way steeply down in a twisty pattern so even it's like a zipper running down the hillside to where it picks up the river again.

And follows it right into Haven.

"I want to see it," Viola says, letting go of my hand and taking out the binos. She looks thru them, wipes spray off the lenses, and looks some more. "It's beautiful," she says and that's all she says and she just looks and wipes off more spray.

After a minute and without saying nothing more, she hands me the binos and I get my first look at Haven.

The spray is so thick, even wiping it down you can't see details like people or anything but there are all kindsa different buildings, mostly surrounding what looks like a big church at the centre, but other big buildings, too, and proper roads curling outta the middle thru trees to more groups of buildings.

There's gotta be at least fifty buildings in all.

Maybe a *hundred*.

It's the biggest thing I've ever seen in my entire life.

"I've got to say," Viola shouts, "it's kind of smaller than I expected."

But I don't really hear her.

With the binos, I follow the river road back from it and I see what's probably a roadblock with what might be a fortified fence running away from it and to either side.

"They're getting ready," I say. "They're getting ready to fight."

Viola looks at me, worried. "You think it's big enough? You think we're safe?"

"Depends on if the rumours of the army are true or not."

I look behind us, by instinct, as if the army was just waiting there for us to move on. I look up the valley hill next to us. Could be a good view.

"Let's find out," I say.

We run back down the road a piece, looking for a good climbing spot, find one and make our way up. My legs feel light as I climb, my Noise clearer than it's been in days. I'm sad for Ben, I'm sad for Cillian, I'm sad for Manchee, I'm sad for what's happened to me and Viola.

But Ben was right.

There's hope at the bottom of the biggest waterfall.

And maybe it don't hurt so much after all.

We climb up thru the trees. The hill is steep above the river and we have to pull on vines and hang on to rocks to make our way up high enough to look back down the road, till the valley is stretching out beneath us.

I still have the binos and I look downriver and down the road and over the treetops. I keep having to wipe spray away.

I look.

"Can you see them?" Viola asks.

I look, the river getting smaller into the far distance, back and back and back.

"No," I say.

I look.

And again.

And–

There.

Down in the deepest curve of the road in the deepest part of the valley, in farthest shadow against the rising sun, there they are.

A mass that's gotta be the army, marching its way forward, so far away I can only tell it's them at all cuz it looks like dark water flowing into a dry riverbed. It's hard to get detail at this distance but I can't see individual men and I don't think I can see horses.

Just a mass, a mass pouring itself down the road.

"How big is it?" she asks. "How big has it grown?"

"I don't know," I say. "Three hundred? Four? I don't know. We're too far to really–"

I stop.

"We're too far to really tell." I crack another smile. "Miles and miles."

"We beat them," Viola says, a smile coming, too. "We ran and they chased us and we beat them."

"We'll get to Haven and we'll warn whoever's in charge," I say, talking faster, my Noise rising with excitement. "But they've got battle lines and the approach is real narrow and the army's at *least* the rest of the day away, maybe even tonight, too, and I swear that can't be a thousand men."

I swear it.

(But.)

Viola's smiling the tiredest, happiest smile I ever saw. She takes my hand again. "We beat them."

But then the risks of hope rise again and my Noise greys

a little. "Well, we ain't there yet and we don't know if Haven can–"

But she's shaking her head. "Nuh-uh," she says. "We beat them. You listen to me and you be happy, Todd Hewitt. We've spent all this time outrunning an army and guess what? We outran them."

She looks at me, smiling, expecting something from me.

My Noise is buzzing and happy and warm and tired and relieved and a little bit worried still but I'm thinking that maybe she's right, maybe we did win and maybe I should put my arms round her if it didn't feel weird and I find that in the middle of it all I do actually agree with her.

"We beat them," I say.

And then she does stick her arms round me and pulls tight, like we might fall down, and we just stand there on the wet hillside and breathe for a little bit.

She smells a little less like flowers but it's okay.

And I look out and the falls are below us, charging away, and Haven glitters thru the sunlit spray and the sun is shining down the length of the river above the falls, lighting it up like a snake made of metal.

And I let my Noise bubble with little sparks of happy and my gaze flow back along the length of the river and–

No.

Every muscle in my body jolts.

"What?" Viola says, jumping back.

She whips her head round to where I'm looking.

"*What?*" she says again.

And then she sees.

"No," she says. "No, it can't be."

Coming down the river is a boat.

Close enough to see without binos.

Close enough to see the rifle and the robe.

Close enough to see the scars and the righteous anger.

Rowing his way furiously towards us, coming like judgement itself.

Aaron.

40

THE SACRIFICE

"HAS HE SEEN US?" Viola asks, her voice pulled taut.

I point the binos. Aaron rears up in them, huge and terrifying. I press a few buttons to push him back. He's not looking at us, just rowing like an engine to get the boat to the side of the river and the road.

His face is torn and horrible, clotted and bloody, the hole in his cheek, the new hole where his nose used to be, and still, underneath all that, a look feroshus and devouring, a look without mercy, a look that won't stop, that won't never, never stop.

War makes monsters of men, I hear Ben saying.

There's a monster coming towards us.

"I don't think he's seen us," I say. "Not yet."

"Can we outrun him?"

"He's got a gun," I say, "and you can see all the way down that road to Haven."

"Off the road then. Through the trees."

"There ain't that many twixt us and the road down. We'll have to be fast."

"I can be fast," she says.

And we jump on down the hill, skidding down leaves and wet vines, using rocks as handholds best we can. The tree cover is light and we can still see down the river, see Aaron as he rows.

Which means he can see us if he looks in the right place.

"Hurry!" Viola says.

Down–

And down–

And sliding to the road–

And squelching in the mud at the roadside–

And as we get to the road he's outta sight again, still up the river–

But only for a second–

Cuz there he is–

The current bringing him fast–

Coming down the river–

In full view–

Looking right at us.

The roar of the falls is loud enough to eat you, but I still hear it.

I'd hear it if I was on the other side of the planet.

"TODD HEWITT!"

And he's reaching for his rifle.

"Go!" I shout.

Viola's feet hit the ground running and I'm right behind

her, heading for the lip of the road that goes down to the zigzags.

It's fifteen steps, maybe twenty till we can disappear over the edge–

We run like we've spent the last two weeks resting–

Pound pound pound against the road–

I check back over my shoulder–

To see Aaron try to take the rifle in one hand–

Try to balance it while keeping the boat steady–

It's bouncing in the rapids, knocking him back and forth–

"He won't be able to," I yell to Viola. "He can't row and fire at the same–"

CRACK!

A pop of mud flies up outta the road next to Viola's feet ahead of me–

I cry out and Viola cries out and we both instinctively flinch down–

Running faster and faster–

Pound pound pound–

Run run run run run my Noise chugs like a rocket–

Not looking back–

Five steps–

Run run–

Three–

CRACK!

And Viola falls–

"NO!" I shout–

And she's falling over the lip of the road, tripping down the other side and crashing down in a roll–

"NO!" I shout again and leap after her–

Stumbling down the steep incline–

Pounding down to where she's rolling–

No–

Not this–

Not now–

Not when we're–

Please no–

And she tumbles to some low shrubs at the side of the road and keeps going into them–

And stops face down.

And I'm racing towards her and I'm barely in control of my own standing up and I'm kneeling down already in the brush and I'm grabbing her and rolling her over and I'm looking for the blood and the shot and I'm saying, *"No no no no no–"*

And I'm almost blinded by rage and despair and the false promise of hope and no no no–

And she opens her eyes–

She's opening her eyes and she's grabbing me and she's saying, "I'm not hit, I'm not hit."

"Yer not?" I say, shaking her a little. "Yer sure?"

"I just fell," she says. "I swear I felt the bullet fly right by my eyes and I fell. I'm not hurt."

And I'm breathing heavy and heavy and heavy.

"Thank God," I say. "Thank God."

And the world spins and my Noise whirls.

And she's already getting to her feet and I'm up after her standing in the scrub and looking at the road around and below us.

The falls are crashing over the cliff to our left and the twisting road is both behind us and in front of us as it starts doubling back on itself and making the steep zipper down to the bottom of the falls.

It's a clear shot all the way.

No trees, just low scrub.

"He'll pick us off," Viola says, looking back up to the top of the road, to where we can't see Aaron no doubt making his way to the river's edge, stomping thru roaring water, *walking* on it for all I know.

"TODD HEWITT!" we hear again, faint over the roar of the water but loud as the whole entire universe.

"There's nowhere to hide," Viola says, looking around us and down. "Not till we get to the bottom."

I'm looking round, too. The hillsides are too steep, the road too open, the areas between the road's double-backs too shallow with shrubs.

Nowhere to hide.

"TODD HEWITT!"

Viola points up. "We could get up to those trees on top of the hill."

But it's so steep, I can already hear the hope failing in her voice.

And I spin round, looking still–

And then I see.

A little faint trail, skinny as anything, hardly even there, leading away from the first turn of the road and towards the falls. It disappears after a few metres but I follow it to where it might have gone.

Right to the cliffside.

Right down sharp to a place almost below the falls.

Right to a ledge that's almost hidden.

A ledge underneath the waterfall itself.

I take a few steps outta the scrub and back onto the road. The little trail disappears.

So does the ledge.

"What is it?" Viola asks.

I go back into the scrub again.

"There," I say, pointing. "Can you see it?"

She squints where I'm pointing. The fall is casting a little shadow on the ledge, darkening where the little trail ends.

"You can see it from here," I say, "but you can't see it from the road." I look at her. "We'll hide."

"He'll hear you," she says. "He'll come after us."

"Not over this roar, not if I don't shout in my Noise."

Her forehead creases and she looks down at the road to Haven and up to where Aaron's gotta be coming any second.

"We're so close," she says.

I take her arm and start pulling on it. "Come on. Just till he passes. Just till dark. With luck he'll think we doubled back into the trees above."

"If he finds us, we're trapped."

"And if we run for the city, he shoots us." I look in her eyes. "It's a chance. It gives us a *chance*."

"Todd–"

"Come with me," I say, looking right into her as hard as I can, pouring out as much hope as I can muster. *Oh never leave me.* "I promise I'll get you to Haven tonight." I squeeze her arm. *Oh don't deceive me.* "I promise you."

She looks right back at me, listening to it all, and then gives a single, sharp nod and we run to the little trail and down to where it ends and jump over the scrub to where it should continue and–

"TODD HEWITT!"

He's almost to the falls–

And we scrabble down a steep embankment next to the edge of the water, the steepness of the hill rearing above us–

And slide down and over to the edge of the cliff–

The falls straight ahead–

And I get to the edge and I suddenly have to lean back into Viola cuz the drop goes straight down–

She grabs onto my shirt and holds me up–

And the water is smashing down right in front of us to the rocks below–

And the ledge leading under it all is just there–

Needing a jump over emptiness to get to it–

"I didn't see this part," I say, Viola grabbing at my waist to keep us from tumbling over.

"TODD HEWITT!"

He's close, he's so close–

"Now or never, Todd," she says in my ear–

And she lets go of me–

And I jump across–

And I'm in the air–

And the edge of the falls is shooting over my head–

And I land–

And I turn–

And she's jumping after me–

And I grab her and we fall backwards onto the ledge together–

And we lay there breathing–

And listening–

And all we hear for a second is the roar of the water over us now–

And then, faint, against it all–

"TODD HEWITT!"

And he suddenly sounds miles away.

And Viola's on top of me and I'm breathing heavy into her face and she's breathing heavy into mine.

And we're looking in each other's eyes.

And it's too loud to hear my Noise.

After a second, she puts her hands on either side of me and pushes herself away. She looks up as she does and her eyes go wide.

I can just hear her say, "Wow."

I roll away and look up.

Wow.

The ledge is more than just a little ledge. It carries on till it's back, *way* back under the waterfall. We're standing at the beginning of a tunnel with one wall made of rock and another made of pure falling water, roaring past white and clean and so fast it looks almost solid.

"Come on," I say and head on down the ledge, my shoes slipping and sliding under me. It's rocky and wet and slimy and we lean as close as we can to the rock side, away from the thundering water.

The noise is just tremendous. All-consuming, like a real thing you could taste and touch.

So loud, Noise is obliterated.

So loud, it's the quietest I've ever felt.

We scramble on down the ledge, under the falls, making our way over rocky bumps and little pools with green goop growing in them. There are roots, too, hanging down from the rocks above, belonging to who knows what kinda plant.

"Do these look like steps to you?" Viola shouts, her voice small in the roar.

"TODD HEWITT!!" we hear from what sounds like a million miles away.

"Is he finding us?" Viola asks.

"I don't know," I say. "I don't think so."

The cliff face isn't even and the ledge curves round it as it stretches forward. We're both soaking wet and the water is cold and it's not easy grabbing onto the roots to keep our balance.

Then the ledge suddenly drops down and widens out, carved steps becoming more obvious. It's almost a stairway down.

Someone's been here before.

We descend, the water thundering inches away from us.

We get to the bottom.

"Whoa," Viola says behind me and I just know she's looking up.

The tunnel opens up abruptly and the ledge widens at the same time to become a cavern made of water, the rocks stretching up way over our heads, the falls slamming down past them in a wall curving way out like a moving, living sail, enclosing the wall and the shelf under our feet.

But that's not the whoa.

"It's a church," I say.

It's a church. Someone has moved or carved rocks into four rows of simple pews with an aisle down the middle, all facing a taller rock, a pulpit, a pulpit with a flat surface which a preacher could stand on and preach with a blazing white wall of water crashing down behind him, the morning sun lighting it up like a sheet of stars, filling the room with shimmering sparkles on every shiny wet surface, all the way back to a carved circle in the stone with two smaller carved circles orbiting it to one side, New World and its moons, the settler's new home of hope and God's promise somehow painted a waterproof white and practically *glowing* on the rock wall, looking down and lighting up the church.

The church underneath a waterfall.

"It's beautiful," Viola says.

"It's abandoned," I say, cuz after the first shock of finding a church I see where a few of the pews have been knocked from their places and not replaced and there's writing all over the walls, some of it carved in with tools, some of it written in the same waterproof paint as the New World carving, most of it nonsense. *P.M.+M.A.* and *Willz & Chillz 4Ever* and *Abandon All Hope Ye Who* something something.

"It's kids," Viola says. "Sneaking in here, making it their own place."

"Yeah? Do kids do that?"

"Back on the ship we had an unused venting duct that we snuck into," she says, looking around. "Marked it up worse than this."

We wander in, looking round us, mouths open. The point of the roof where the water leaves the cliff must be a good ten metres above us and the ledge five metres wide easy.

"It musta been a natural cavern," I say. "They musta found it and thought it was some kinda miracle."

Viola crosses her arms against herself. "And then they found it wasn't very practical as a church."

"Too wet," I say. "Too cold."

"I'll bet it was when they first landed," she says, looking up at the white New World. "I'll bet it was in the first year. Everything hopeful and new." She turns round, taking it all in. "Before reality set in."

I turn slowly, too. I can see exactly what they were thinking. The way the sun hits the falls, turning everything bright white, and it's so loud and so silent at the same time that even without the pulpit and the pews it would have felt like we'd somehow walked into a church anyway, like it'd be holy even if no man had ever seen it.

And then I notice that at the end of the pews, there's nothing beyond. It stops and it's a fifty-metre drop to the rocks below.

So this is where we're gonna have to wait.

This is where we're gonna have to hope.

In the church under water.

"Todd Hewitt!" barely drifts in down the tunnel to us.

Viola visibly shivers. "What do we do now?"

"We wait till nightfall," I say. "Sneak out and hope he don't see us."

I sit down on one of the stone benches. Viola sits down next to me. She lifts the bag over her head and sets it on the stone floor.

440

"What if he finds the trail?" she asks.

"We hope he don't."

"But what if he does?"

I reach behind me and take out the knife.

The knife.

Both of us look at it, the white water reflecting off of it, droplets of spray already catching and pooling on its blade, making it shine like a little torch.

The knife.

We don't say nothing about it, just watch it gleam in the middle of the church.

"Todd Hewitt!"

Viola looks up to the entrance and puts her hands to her face and I can see her clench her teeth. "What does he even *want*?" she suddenly rages. "If the army's all about you, what does he want with me? Why was he shooting at me? I don't understand it."

"Crazy people don't need an explanayshun for nothing," I say.

But my Noise is remembering the sacrifice that I saw him making of her way back in the swamp.

The sign, he called her.

A gift from God.

I don't know if Viola hears this or if she remembers it herself cuz she says, "I don't think I'm the sacrifice."

"What?"

She turns to me, her face perplexed. "I don't think it's me," she says. "He kept me asleep almost the entire time I was with him and when I did wake up, I kept seeing confusing things in his Noise, things that didn't make sense."

441

"He's mad," I say. "Madder than most."

She don't say nothing more, just looks out into the waterfall.

And reaches over and takes my hand.

"TODD HEWITT!"

I feel her hand jump right as my heart leaps.

"That's closer," she says. "He's getting closer."

"He won't find us."

"He will."

"Then we'll deal with it."

We both look at the knife.

"TODD HEWITT!"

"He's found it," she says, grabbing my arm and squeezing into me.

"Not yet."

"We were almost there," she says, her voice high and breaking a little. "Almost there."

"We'll get there."

"TODD HEWITT!"

And it's definitely louder.

He's found the tunnel.

I grip my knife and I look over to Viola, her face looking straight back up the tunnel, so much fear on it my chest begins to hurt.

I grip the knife harder.

If he *touches* her–

And my Noise reels back to the start of our journey, to Viola before she said anything, to Viola when she told me her name, to Viola when she talked to Hildy and Tam, to when she took on Wilf's accent, to when Aaron grabbed her and stole her away, to waking up to her in Doctor Snow's house, to her promise to Ben, to when she took on my ma's voice and made the whole world change, just for a little while.

All the things we've been thru.

How she cried when we left Manchee behind.

Telling me I was all she had.

When I found out I could read her, silence or not.

When I thought Aaron had shot her on the road.

How I felt in those few terrible seconds.

How it would feel to lose her.

The pain and the unfairness and the injustice.

The rage.

And how I wished it was me.

I look at the knife in my hand.

And I realize she's right.

I realize what's been right all along, as insane as it is.

She's not the sacrifice.

She's not.

If one of us falls, we all fall.

"I know what he wants," I say, standing up.

"What?" Viola says.

"TODD HEWITT!"

Definitely coming down the tunnel now.

Nowhere to run.

He's coming.

She stands, too, and I move myself twixt her and the tunnel.

"Get down behind one of the pews," I say. "Hide."

"Todd–"

I move away from her, my hand staying on her arm till I'm too far away.

"Where are you going?" she says, her voice tightening.

I look back the way we came, up the tunnel of water.

He'll be here any second.

"TODD HEWITT!"

"He'll *see* you!" she says.

I hold up the knife in front of me.

The knife that's caused so much trouble.

The knife that holds so much power.

"Todd!" Viola says. "What are you *doing*?"

I turn to her. "He won't hurt you," I say. "Not when he knows I know what he wants."

"What does he want?"

I search her out, standing among the pews, the white planet and moons glowing down on her, the water shining watery light over her, I search out her face and the language of her body as she stands there watching me, and I find I still know who she is, that she's still Viola Eade, that silent don't mean empty, that it *never* meant empty.

I look right into her eyes.

"I'm gonna greet him like a man," I say.

And even tho it's too loud for her to hear my Noise, even tho she can't read my thoughts, she looks back at me.

And I see her understand.

She pulls herself up a little taller.

"I'm not hiding," she says. "If you're not, I'm not."

And that's all I need.

I nod.

"Ready?" I ask.

She looks at me.

She nods once, firmly.

I turn back to the tunnel.

I close my eyes.

I take a deep breath.

And with every bit of air in my lungs and every last note of Noise in my head, I rear up–

And I shout, as loud as I can–

"AARON!!!!!!"

And I open my eyes and I wait for him to come.

41

IF ONE OF US FALLS

I SEE HIS FEET FIRST, slipping down the steps some but not hurrying, taking his time now that he knows we're here.

I hold the knife in my right hand, my left hand out and ready, too. I stand in the aisle of the little pews, as much in the centre of the church as I can get. Viola's back behind me a bit, down one of the rows.

I'm ready.

I realize I *am* ready.

Everything that's happened has brought me here, to this place, with this knife in my hand, and something worth saving.

Someone.

And if it's a choice twixt her and him, there is no choice, and the army can go sod itself.

And so I'm ready.

As I'll ever be.

Cuz I know what he wants.

"Come on," I say, under my breath.

Aaron's legs appear, then his arms, one carrying the rifle, the other holding his balance against the wall.

And then his face.

His terrible, terrible face.

Half torn away, the gash in his cheek showing his teeth, the hole where his nose used to be open and gaping, making him look barely human.

And he's smiling.

Which is when I feel all the fear.

"Todd Hewitt," he says, almost as a greeting.

I raise my voice over the water, willing it not to shake. "You can put the rifle down, Aaron."

"Oh, can I, now?" he says, eyes widening, taking in Viola behind me. I don't look back at her but I know she's facing Aaron, I know she's giving him all the bravery she's got.

And that makes me stronger.

"I know what you want," I say. "I figured it out."

"Have you, young Todd?" Aaron says and I see he can't help himself, he looks into my Noise, the little he can hear over the roar.

"She's not the sacrifice," I say.

He says nothing, just takes the first steps into the church, eyes glancing up at the cross and the pews and the pulpit.

"And I'm not the sacrifice neither," I say.

His evil smile draws wider. A new tear opens up at the edge of his gash, blood waving down it in the spray. "A clever mind is a friend of the devil," he says, which I think is his way of saying I'm right.

I steady my feet and turn with him as he steps round towards the pulpit half of the church, the half nearer the edge.

"It's you," I say. "The sacrifice is you."

And I open my Noise as loud as it'll go so that both he and Viola can see I'm telling the truth.

Cuz the thing Ben showed me back when I left our farm, the way that a boy in Prentisstown becomes a man, the reason that boys who've become men don't talk to boys who are still boys, the reason that boys who've become men are *complicit* in the crimes of Prentisstown is—

It's—

And I make myself say it—

It's by killing another man.

All by theirselves.

All those men who disappeared, who *tried* to disappear.

They didn't disappear after all.

Mr Royal, my old schoolteacher, who took to whisky and shot himself, *didn't* shoot himself. He was shot by Seb Mundy on his thirteenth birthday, made to stand alone and pull the trigger as the rest of the men of Prentisstown watched. Mr Gault, whose sheep flock we took over when he disappeared two winters ago, only *tried* to disappear. He was found by Mayor Prentiss running away thru the swamp and Mayor Prentiss was true to his agreement with the law of New World and executed him, only he did it by waiting till Mr Prentiss Jr's thirteenth birthday and having his son torture Mr Gault to death without the help of no one else.

And so on and so on. Men I knew killed by boys I knew to become men theirselves. If the Mayor's men had a captured escapee hidden away for a boy's thirteenth, then fine. If not, they'd just take someone from Prentisstown who they didn't like and *say* he disappeared.

One man's life was given over to a boy to end, all on his own.

A man dies, a man is born.

Everyone complicit. Everyone guilty.

Except me.

"Oh my God," I hear Viola say.

"But I was gonna be different, wasn't I?" I say.

"You were the last, Todd Hewitt," Aaron says. "The final soldier in God's perfect army."

"I don't think God's got nothing to do with yer army," I say. "Put down the rifle. I know what I have to do."

"But are you a messenger, Todd?" he asks, cocking his head, pulling his impossible smile wider. "Or are you a deceiver?"

"Read me," I say. "Read me if you don't believe I can do it."

He's at the pulpit now, facing me down the centre aisle, reaching out his Noise over the sound of the falls, pushing it towards me, grabbing at what he can, and **the sacrifice** and **God's perfect work** and **the martyrdom of the saint** I hear.

"Perhaps, young Todd," he says.

And he sets the rifle down on the pulpit.

I swallow and grip the knife harder.

But he looks over at Viola and laughs a little laugh. "No," he says. "Little girls will try to take advantage, won't they?"

And, almost casually, he tosses the rifle off the ledge into the waterfall.

It goes so fast, we don't even see it disappear.

But it's gone.

And so there's just me and Aaron.

And the knife.

He opens his arms and I realize he's assuming his preacher's pose, the one from his own pulpit, back in Prentisstown. He leans against the pulpit stone here and holds his palms up and raises his eyes to the white shining roof of water above us.

His lips move silently.

He's *praying*.

"Yer mad," I say.

He looks at me. "I'm blessed."

"You want me to kill you."

"Wrong, Todd Hewitt," he says, taking a step forward down the aisle towards me. "Hate is the key. Hate is the driver. Hate is the fire that purifies the soldier. The soldier must *hate*."

He takes another step.

"I don't want you to kill me," he says. "I want you to *murder* me."

I take a step back.

The smile flickers. "Perhaps the boy promises bigger than he can deliver."

"Why?" I say, stepping back some more. Viola moves back, too, behind and around me, underneath the carving of New World. "Why are you doing this? What possible sense does this make?"

"God has told me my path," he says.

"I been here for almost thirteen years," I say, "and the only thing I ever heard was *men*."

"God works thru men," Aaron says.

"So does evil," Viola says.

"Ah," Aaron says. "It speaks. Words of temptayshun to lull–"

"Shut up," I say. "Don't you talk to her."

I'm past the back row of pews now. I move to my right, Aaron follows till we're moving in a slow circle, Aaron's hands still out, my knife still up, Viola keeping behind me, the spray covering everything. The room slowly turns around us, the ledge still slippery, the wall of water shining white with the sun.

And the roar, the constant roar.

"You were the final test," Aaron says. "The last boy. The one that completes us. With you in the army, there's no weak link. We would be truly blessed. If one of us falls, we all fall, Todd. And all of us have to fall." He clenches his fists and looks up again. "So we can be reborn! So we can take this cursed world and remake it in–"

"I wouldn't've done it," I say and he scowls at the interrupshun. "I wouldn't've killed anyone."

"Ah, yes, Todd Hewitt," Aaron says. "And that's why yer so very very special, ain't ya? The boy who can't kill."

I sneak a glance back to Viola, off to my side a little. We're still going round in the little circle.

And Viola and I are reaching the side with the tunnel in it.

"But God demands a sacrifice," Aaron's saying. "God

demands a martyr. And who better for the special boy to kill than God's very own mouthpiece?"

"I don't think God tells you anything," I say. "Tho I can believe he wants you dead."

Aaron's eyes go so crazy and empty I get a chill. "I'll be a saint," he says, a small fire burning in his voice. "It is my destiny."

He's reached the end of the aisle and is following us past the last row of benches.

Viola and I are backing up still.

Almost to the tunnel.

"But how to motivate the boy?" Aaron continues, eyes like holes. "How to bring him into manhood?"

And his Noise opens up to me, loud as thunder.

My eyes widen.

My stomach sinks to my feet.

My shoulders hunch down as I feel weakness on me.

I can see it. It's a fantasy, a lie, but the lies of men are as vivid as their truths and I can see every bit of it.

He was going to murder Ben.

That's how he was going to force me to kill him. That's how they woulda done it. To perfect their army and make me a killer, they were going to murder Ben.

And make me watch.

Make me hate enough to kill Aaron.

My Noise starts to rumble, loud enough to hear. "*You effing piece of–*"

"But then God sent a sign," Aaron says, looking at Viola, his eyes even wider now, the blood pouring from the gash, the hole where his nose used to be stretching taut. "The girl," he says. "A gift from the heavens."

"Don't you look at her!" I yell. "Don't you even *look at her!*"

Aaron turns back to me, the smile still there. "Yes, Todd, yes," he says. "That's yer path, that's the path you'll take. The boy with the soft heart, the boy who couldn't kill. What would he kill for? Who would he protect?"

Another step back, another step nearer the tunnel.

"And when her cursed, evil silence polluted our swamp, I thought God had sent me a sacrifice to make myself, one last example of the evil that hides itself which I could destroy and purify." He cocks his head. "But then her true purpose was revealed." He looks at her and back at me. "Todd Hewitt would protect the helpless."

"She ain't helpless," I say.

"And then you *ran.*" Aaron's eyes widen, as if in false amazement. "You ran rather than fulfil yer destiny." He lifts his eyes to the church again. "Thereby making victory over you all the sweeter."

"You ain't won yet," I say.

"Haven't I?" He smiles again. "Come, Todd. Come to me with hate in yer heart."

"I *will*," I say. "I'll do it."

But another step back.

"You've been near before, young Todd," Aaron says. "In the swamp, the knife raised, me killing the girl, but no. You hesitate. You injure but you do not kill. And then I steal her from you and you hunt her down, as I knew you would, suffering from the wound I gave you, but again, not enough. You sacrifice yer beloved dog rather than see her come to harm, you let me break his very body rather than serve yer proper purpose."

"You shut up!" I say.

He holds his palms up to me.

"Here I am, Todd," he says. "Fulfil yer purpose. Become a man." He lowers his head till his eyes are looking up at me. "*Fall*."

I curl my lip.

I stand up straighter.

"I already *am* a man," I say.

And my Noise says it, too.

He stares at me. As if staring thru me.

And then he *sighs*.

Like he's *disappointed*.

"Not yet a man," he says, his face changing. "Perhaps not ever."

I don't step back.

"Pity," he says.

And he leaps at me—

"Todd!" Viola yells—

"Run!" I scream—

But I'm not stepping back—

I'm moving forward—

And the fight is on.

I'm charging at him and he's throwing himself at me and I'm holding the knife but at the last second, I leap to the side, letting him slam hard into the wall—

He whirls around, face in a snarl, swinging an arm round to hit me and I duck and slash at it with the knife, cutting across his forearm, and it don't even slow him down—

And he's swinging at me with his other arm and he's catching me just under the jaw–

Knocking me back–

"Todd!" Viola calls again–

I tumble backwards onto the last pew, falling hard–

But I'm looking up–

Aaron's turning to Viola–

She's at the bottom of the stairs–

"Go!" I yell–

But she's got a big flat stone in her hands and launches it at Aaron with a grimace and an angry grunt and he ducks and tries to deflect it with one hand but it catches him cross the forehead, causing him to stumble away from both her and me, towards the ledge, towards the front of the church–

"Come on!" Viola yells to me–

I scramble to my feet–

But Aaron's turned, too–

Blood running down his face–

His mouth open in a yell–

He jumps forward like a spider, grabbing Viola's right arm–

She punches fiercely with her left hand, bloodying it on his face–

But he don't let go–

I'm yelling as I fly at them–

Knife out–

But again I turn it at the last minute–

And I just knock into him–

We land on the upslope of the stairs, Viola falling back, me on top of Aaron, his arms boxing my head and he reaches forward with his horrible face and *takes a bite* out of an exposed area of my neck–

I yell and jerk back, punching him with a backhand as I go–

Scooting away from him back into the church, holding my neck–

He comes at me again, his fist flying forward–

Catching me on the eye–

My head jerks back–

I stumble thru the rows of pews, back to the centre of the church–

Another punch–

I raise my knife hand to block it–

But keep the knife edge sideways–

And he hits me again–

I scrabble away from him on the wet stone–

Up the aisle towards the pulpit–

And a third time his fist reaches my face–

And I feel two teeth tear outta their roots–

And I nearly fall–

And then I do fall–

My back and head hitting the pulpit stone–

And I drop the knife.

It clatters away towards the edge.

Useless as ever.

"*Yer Noise reveals you!*" Aaron screams. "*Yer Noise reveals you!*" He's stepping forward to me now, standing over me. "*From the moment I stepped into this sacred place, I knew it*

456

would be thus!" He stops at my feet, staring down at me, his fists clenched and bloody with my blood, his face bloody with his own. "You will *never* be a man, Todd Hewitt! *Never!"*

I see Viola outta the corner of my eye frantically looking for more rocks–

"I'm already a man," I say, but I've fallen, I've dropped the knife, my voice is faltering, my hand over the bleeding from my neck.

"You rob me of my sacrifice!" His eyes have turned to burning diamonds, his Noise blazing a red so fierce it's practically steaming the water away from him. "I will kill you." He bows his head to me. "And you will die knowing that I killed her slowly."

I clench my teeth together.

I start to pull myself to my ruddy feet.

"Come on if yer coming," I growl.

Aaron yells out and takes a step towards me–

Hands reaching out for me–

My face rising to meet him–

And Viola *CLUMPS* him on the side of the head with a rock she can barely lift–

He stumbles–

Leaning towards the pews and catching himself–

And he stumbles again–

But he doesn't fall.

He *doesn't ruddy fall.*

He staggers but he stands, twixt me and Viola, uncurling himself, his back to Viola but towering over her, a whole rivulet of blood spouting from the side of his head now, but he's effing well tall as a nightmare–

He really is a monster.

"You ain't human," I say.

"I have told you, young Todd," he says, his voice low and monstrous, his Noise glowering at me with a fury so pure it nearly knocks me back. "I am a saint."

He lashes his arm out in Viola's direkshun without even looking her way, catching her square on the eye, knocking her back as she calls out and falls falls falls, tripping over a pew, hitting her head hard on the rocks–

And not rising.

"Viola!" I yell–

And I leap past him–

He lets me go–

I reach her–

Her legs are up on the stone bench–

Her head's on the stone floor–

A little stream of blood running from it–

"Viola!" I say and I lift her–

And her head falls back–

"VIOLA!" I yell–

And I hear a low rumble from behind me–

Laughter.

He's laughing.

"You were always going to betray her," he says. "It was foreseen."

"You SHUT UP!"

"And do you know *why*?"

"I'll KILL YOU!"

He lowers his voice to a whisper–

But a whisper I can feel shiver thru my entire body–

"You've already fallen."

And my Noise blazes red.

Redder than it's ever been.

Murderous red.

"Yes, Todd," Aaron hisses. "Yes, that's the way."

I lay Viola gently down and I stand and face him.

And my hate is so big, it fills the cavern.

"Come on, boy," he says. "Purify yerself."

I look at the knife–

Resting in a puddle of water–

Near the ledge by the pulpit behind Aaron–

Where I dropped it–

And I hear it calling to me–

Take me, it says–

Take me and use me, it says–

Aaron holds open his arms.

"Murder me," he says. "Become a man."

Never let me go, says the knife–

"I'm sorry," I whisper under my breath tho I don't know who to or what for–

I'm sorry–

And I leap–

Aaron doesn't move, arms open as if to embrace me–

I barrel into him with my shoulder–

He doesn't resist–

My Noise screams red–

We fall past the pulpit to the ledge–

I'm on top of him–

He still doesn't resist–

I punch his face–

Over–

And over–

And over–

Breaking it further–

Breaking it into bloody messy pieces–

Hate pouring outta me thru my fists–

And still I pound him–

Still I hit–

Thru the breaking of bone–

And the snapping of gristle–

And an eye crushed under my knuckles–

Till I can no longer feel my hands–

And still I hit–

And his blood spills on me and over–

And the red of it matches the red of my Noise–

And then I lean back, still on him, covered in his blood–

And he's laughing, he's laughing *still*–

And he's gurgling "Yes" thru broken teeth, "Yes–"

And the red rises in me–

And I can't hold it back–

And the hate–

And I look over–

At the knife–

Just a metre away–

On the ledge–

By the pulpit–

Calling for me–

Calling–

And this time I know–

This time I know–

I'm going to use it.

And I jump for it–
My hand outstretched–
My Noise so red I can barely see–
Yes, says the knife–

Yes.

Take me.
Take the power in yer hand–

But another hand is there first–

Viola.

And as I fall towards it there's a rush in me–
A rush in my Noise–
A rush from seeing her there–
From seeing her alive–
A rush that rises higher than the red–
And "Viola," I say–
Just "Viola".

And she picks up the knife.

My momentum is tumbling me towards the edge and
I'm turning to try and catch myself and I can see her lifting
the knife and I can see her stepping forward and I'm falling

into the ledge and my fingers are slipping on wet stone and I can see Aaron sitting up and he's only got one eye now and it's staring at Viola as she's raising the knife and she's bringing it forward and I can't stop her and Aaron is trying to rise and Viola's moving towards him and I'm hitting the ledge with my shoulder and stopping just short of falling over and I'm watching and what's left of Aaron's Noise is radiating anger and fear and it's saying *No*–

It's saying *Not you*–

And Viola's raising her arm–

Raising the knife–

And bringing it down–

And down–

And down–

And plunging it straight into the side of Aaron's neck–

So hard the point comes out the other side–

And there's a crunch, a crunch I remember–

Aaron falls over from the force of it–

And Viola lets go of the knife–

She steps back.

Her face is white.

I can hear her breathing over the roar.

I lift myself with my hands–

And we watch.

Aaron's pushing himself up.

He's pushing himself up, one hand clawing at the knife, but it stays in his neck. His remaining eye is wide open, his tongue lolling outta his mouth.

He gets to his knees.

And then to his feet.

Viola cries out a little and steps back.

Steps back till she's next to me.

We can hear him trying to swallow.

Trying to breathe.

He steps forward but stumbles against the pulpit.

He looks our way.

His tongue swells and writhes.

He's trying to say something.

He's trying to say something to me.

He's trying to make a word.

But he can't.

He can't.

His Noise is just wild colours and pictures and things I won't ever be able to say.

He catches my eye.

And his Noise stops.

Completely stops.

At last.

And gravity takes his body and he slumps sideways.

Away from the pulpit.

And over the edge.

And disappears under the wall of water.

Taking the knife with him.

42

LAST ROAD TO HAVEN

VIOLA SITS DOWN NEXT TO ME so hard and fast it's like she fell there.

She's breathing heavy and staring into the space where Aaron was. The sunlight thru the falls casts waves of watery light over her face but that's the only thing on it that moves.

"Viola?" I say, leaping up into a squat next to her.

"He's gone," she says.

"Yeah," I say. "He's gone."

And she just breathes.

My Noise is rattling like a crashing spaceship full of reds and whites and things so different it's like my head is being pulled apart.

I woulda done it.

I woulda done it for her.

But instead–

"I woulda done it," I say. "I was ready to do it."

She looks at me, her eyes wide. "Todd?"

"I woulda killed him myself." I find my voice raising a little. "I was ready to do it!"

And then her chin starts shaking, not as if she's going to cry, but actually *shaking* and then her shoulders, too, and her eyes are getting wider and she's shaking harder and nothing leaves my Noise and it's all still there but something else enters it and it's for her and I grab her and hold her to me and we rock back and forth for a while so she can just shake all she wants to.

She don't speak for a long time, just makes little moaning sounds in her throat, and I remember just after I killed the Spackle, how I could feel the crunch running down my arm, how I could keep seeing his blood, how I saw him die again and again.

How I do still.

(But I woulda.)

(I was ready.)

(But the knife is gone.)

"Killing someone ain't nothing like it is in stories," I say into the top of her head. "Ain't nothing at all."

(But I woulda.)

She's still shaking and we're still right next to a raging, roaring waterfall and the sun's higher in the sky and there's less light in the church and we're wet and bloody and bloody and wet.

And cold and shaking.

"Come on," I say, making to stand. "First thing we need to do is get dry, okay?"

I get her to her feet. I go get the bag, still on the floor twixt two pews and go back to her and hold out my hand.

"The sun is up," I say. "It'll be warm outside."

She looks at my hand for a minute before taking it.

But she takes it.

We make our way round the pulpit, unable to keep from looking where Aaron was, his blood already washed away by the spray.

(I woulda done it.)

(But the knife.)

I can feel my hand shaking in hers and I don't know which one of us it is.

We get to the steps and it's halfway up that she first speaks.

"I feel sick," she says.

"I know," I say.

And we stop and she leans closer to the waterfall and is sick.

A lot.

I guess this it what happens when you kill someone in real life.

She leans forward, her hair wet and tangled down. She spits.

But she don't look up.

"I couldn't let you," she says. "He would have won."

"I woulda done it," I say.

"I know," she says, into her hair, into the falls. "That's why I did it."

I let out a breath. "You shoulda let me."

"No." She looks up from being crouched over. "I *couldn't* let you." She wipes her mouth and coughs again. "But it's not just that."

"What then?" I say.

She looks into my eyes. Her own are wide and they're bloodshot from the barfing.

And they're older than they used to be.

"I *wanted* to, Todd," she says, her forehead creasing. "I *wanted* to do it. I *wanted* to kill him." She puts her hands to her face. "Oh my God," she breathes. "Oh my God, oh my God, oh my God."

"Stop it," I say, taking her arms and pulling her hands away. "Stop it. He was evil. He was *crazy* evil–"

"I know!" she shouts. "But I keep seeing him. I keep seeing the knife going into his–"

"Yeah, okay, you wanted to," I stop her before she gets worse. "So what? So did *I*. But he *made* you want to. He made it so it was him or us. That's why he was evil. Not what you did or what I did, what *he* did, okay?"

She looks up at me. "He did just what he promised," she says, her voice a little quieter. "He made me fall."

She moans again and clamps her hands over her mouth, her eyes welling up.

"No," I say strongly. "No, see, here's the thing, here's what I think, okay?"

I look up to the water and the tunnel and I don't know what I think but she's there and I can see it and I don't know what she's thinking but *I know what she's thinking* and I can see her and she's teetering on the edge and she's looking at me and she's asking me to save her.

Save her like she saved me.

"Here's what I think," I say and my voice is stronger and thoughts are coming, thoughts that trickle into my Noise like whispers of the truth. "I think maybe *everybody* falls," I say. "I think maybe we all do. And I don't think that's the asking."

I pull on her arms gently to make sure she's listening.

"I think the asking is whether we get back up again."

And the water's rushing by and we're shaking from the cold and everything else and she stares at me and I wait and I hope.

And I see her step back from the edge.

I see her come back to me.

"Todd," she says and it ain't an asking.

It's just my name.

It's who I am.

"Come on," I say. "Haven's waiting."

I take her hand again and we make our way up the rest of the steps and back to the flatter part of the ledge, following the curves out from the centre, steadying ourselves again on the slippery stones. The jump back to the embankment is harder this time cuz we're so wet and weak but I take a running go at it and then catch Viola as she comes tumbling after me.

And we're in sunlight.

We breathe it in for a good long while, getting the wettest of the wet off of us before we gather up and climb the little embankment, pushing ourselves thru the scrub to the trail and back to the road.

We look down the hill, down the zigzag trail.

It's still there. Haven's still there.

"Last bit," I say.

Viola rubs her arms to dry herself a little more. She

squints at me, looking close. "You get hit in the face a lot, you know that?"

I bring my fingers up. My eye is starting to swell some and I notice a gap on the side of my mouth where I lost a few teeth.

"Thanks," I say. "It wasn't hurting till you said that."

"Sorry." She smiles a little and puts her hand up to the back of her own head and winces.

"How's yers?" I ask.

"Sore," she says, "but I'll live."

"Yer indestructible, you," I say.

She smiles again.

And then there's a weird *zipSNICK* sound in the air and Viola lets out a little gasp, a little *oh* sound.

We look each other in the eyes for a second, in the sunshine, both of us surprised but not sure why.

And then I follow her glance down her front.

There's blood on her shirt.

Her own blood.

New blood.

Pouring out a little hole just to the right of her belly button.

She touches the blood and holds up her fingers.

"Todd?" she says.

And then she falls forward.

I catch her, stumbling back a bit from the weight.

And I look up behind her.

Up to the clifftop, right where the road begins.

Mr Prentiss Jr.

On horseback.

469

Hand outstretched.

Holding a pistol.

"Todd?" Viola says against my chest. "I think someone *shot* me, Todd."

There are no words.

No words in my head or my Noise.

Mr Prentiss Jr kicks his horse and edges him down the road towards us.

Pistol still pointed.

There's nowhere to run.

And I don't got my knife.

The world unfolds as clear and as slow as the worst pain, Viola starting to pant heavy against me, Mr Prentiss Jr riding down the road, and my Noise rising with the knowledge that we're finished, that there's no way out this time, that if the world wants you, it's gonna keep on coming till it gets you.

And who am I that can fix it? Who am I that can change this if the world wants it so badly? Who am I to stop the end of the world if it keeps on coming?

"I think she wants you *bad*, Todd," Mr Prentiss Jr sneers.

I clench my teeth.

My Noise rises red and purple.

I'm Todd bloody Hewitt.

That's who I effing well am.

I look him right in the eye, sending my Noise straight for him, and I spit out in a rasp, "I'll thank you to call me *Mr Hewitt*."

Mr Prentiss Jr flinches, actually *flinches* a little and pulls his reins involuntarily, making his horse rear up for a second.

"Come on, now," he says, his voice slightly less sure.

And he knows we both can hear it.

"Hands up," he says. "I'm taking you to my father."

And I do the most amazing thing.

The most amazing thing I ever did.

I ignore him.

I kneel Viola down to the dirt road.

"It burns, Todd," she says, her voice low.

I set her down and drop the bag and slip my shirt off my back, crumpling it up and holding it against the bullet hole. "You hold that tight, you hear me?" I say, my anger rising like lava. "This won't take a second."

I look up at *Davy* Prentiss.

"Get up," he says, his horse still jumpy and edgy from the heat coming off me. "I ain't telling you twice, Todd."

I stand.

I step forward.

"I said put yer hands up," Davy says, his horse whinnying and bluffing and clopping from foot to foot.

I march towards him.

Faster.

Till I'm running.

"I'll shoot you!" Davy shouts, waving the gun, trying to control his horse which is sending **Charge! Charge!** all over the place in its Noise.

"No, you won't!" I yell, running right up to the horse's head and sending a crash of Noise right at it.

SNAKE!

The horse rears up on its back legs.

"Goddammit, Todd!" Davy yells, wheeling and whirling,

trying to control his horse with the one hand that's not holding the pistol.

I jump in, slap the horse's front quarters and jump back. The horse whinnies and rears up again.

"Yer a dead man!" Davy shouts, going in a full circle with the horse jumping and rearing.

"Yer *half* right," I say.

And I'm seeing my chance–

The horse neighs loudly and shakes its head back and forth–

I wait–

Davy pulls on the reins–

I dodge–

I wait–

"Effing horse!" Davy shouts–

He tries to jerk the reins again–

The horse is twisting round one more time–

I wait–

The horse brings Davy round to me, careening him low in the saddle–

And there's my chance–

My fist is back and waiting–

BOOM!

I catch him cross the face like a hammer falling–

I swear I feel his nose break under my fist–

He calls out in pain and falls from the saddle–

Dropping the pistol in the dust–

I jump back–

Davy's foot catches in the stirrup–

The horse rears round again–

I smack its hindquarters as hard as I can–

And the horse has had enough.

It charges back up the hill, back up the road, Davy's foot still caught, making him bounce hard against rocks and dirt as he's dragged, fast, up the incline–

The pistol's in the dust–

I move for it–

"Todd?" I hear.

And there's no time.

There's no time at all.

Without hardly thinking, I leave the pistol and I run back down to Viola at the edge of the scrub.

"I think I'm dying, Todd," she says.

"Yer not dying," I say, getting an arm under her shoulders and another under her knees.

"I'm cold."

"Yer *not effing dying!*" I say. "Not today!"

And I stand, with her in my arms, and I'm at the top of the zigzag that goes down into Haven.

And that's not going to be fast enough.

I plunge straight down. Straight down thru the scrub.

"Come on!" I say out loud as my Noise forgets itself and all there is in the universe is my legs moving.

Come on!

I run.

Thru scrub–

And across road–

Thru more scrub–

Across road again as it doubles back–

Down and down–

Kicking up clods of earth and jumping over bushes–

Stumbling over roots–

Come on.

"Hang on," I say to Viola. "You hang on, you hear me?"

Viola grunts every time we land hard–

But that means she's still breathing.

Down–

And down–

Come on.

Please.

I skid on some bracken–

But I do not fall–

Road and scrub–

My legs aching at the steepness–

Scrub and road–

Down–

Please–

"Todd?"

"Hang on!"

I reach the bottom of the hill and I hit it running.

She's so light in my arms.

So light.

I run to where the road rejoins the river, the road into Haven, trees springing up again all around us, the river rushing on.

"Hang on!" I say again, running down the road, fast as my feet will carry me.

Come on.

Please.

Round curves and corners–

Under trees and by the riverbank–

Up ahead I see the battlement I spotted with the binos from the hill above, huge wooden Xs piled up in a long row out to either side with an opening across the road.

"HELP!" I'm shouting as we come to it. "HELP US!"

I run.

Come on.

"I don't think I can–" Viola says, her voice breathless.

"Yes you CAN!" I shout. "Don't you DARE give up!"

I run.

The battlement's coming–

But there's no one.

There's no one there.

I run thru the opening on the road and to the other side.

I stop long enough to take a turn round.

There's *no one*.

"Todd?"

"We're almost there," I say.

"I'm losing it, Todd–"

And her head rolls back.

"No, yer NOT!" I shout at her face. "You WAKE UP, Viola Eade! You keep yer ruddy eyes open."

And she tries. I see her try.

And her eyes open, only a little, but open.

And I run again as fast as I can.

And I'm shouting "HELP!" as I go.

"HELP!"

Please.

"HELP!"

And her breath is starting to gasp.

"HELP US!"

Please no.

And I'm not seeing NO ONE.

The houses I pass are shut up and empty. The road turns from dirt to paved and still no one out and about.

"HELP!"

My feet slam against the pavement–

The road is leading to the big church up ahead, a clearing of the trees, the steeple shining down onto a town square in front of it.

And no one's there neither.

No.

"HELP!"

I race on to the square, crossing it, looking all around, listening out–

No.

No.

It's empty.

Viola's breathing heavy in my arms.

And Haven is empty.

I reach the middle of the square.

I don't see nor hear a soul.

I spin around again.

"HELP!" I cry.

But there's no one.

Haven is completely empty.

There ain't no hope here at all.

Viola slips a little from my grasp and I have to kneel to catch her. My shirt has dropped from her wound and I use one hand to hold it in place.

There ain't nothing left. The bag, the binos, my ma's book, I'm realizing it's all left up on the hillside.

Me and Viola are all we got, everything we have in the world.

And she's bleeding *so much*–

"Todd?" she says, her voice low and slurring.

"Please," I say, my eyes welling, my voice cracking. "Please."

Please please please please please–

"Well, since you asked so nicely," comes a voice across the square, hardly even raising itself to a shout.

I look up.

Coming round the side of the church is a single horse.

With a single rider.

"No," I whisper.

No.

No.

"Yes, Todd," says Mayor Prentiss. "I'm afraid so."

He rides his horse almost lazily across the square towards me. He looks as cool and unruffled as ever, no sweat marking his clothes, even wearing riding gloves, even clean boots.

This ain't possible.

This ain't possible at all.

"How can you be here?" I say, my voice rising. "How–?"

"Even a simpleton knows there's two roads to Haven," he says, his voice calm and silky, almost smirking but not quite.

The dust we saw. The dust we saw moving towards Haven yesterday.

"But *how*?" I say, so stunned I can barely get the words out. "The army's a day away at least–"

"Sometimes the rumour of an army is just as effective as the army itself, my boy," he says. "The terms of surrender were most favourable. One of which was clearing the streets so I could welcome you here myself." He looks back up towards the falls. "Tho I was of course expecting my son to bring you."

I look around the square and now I can see faces, faces peering outta windows, outta doors.

I can see four more men on horseback coming round the church.

I look back at Mayor Prentiss.

"Oh, it's *President* Prentiss now," he says. "You'll do well to remember that."

And then I realize.

I can't hear his Noise.

I can't hear *anyone's*.

"No," he says. "I imagine you can't, tho that's an interesting story and not what you might–"

Viola slips a little more from my hands, the shift of it making her give a pained gasp. "Please!" I say. "Save her! I'll do anything you say! I'll join the army! I'll–"

"All good things to those who wait," the Mayor says, finally looking a little annoyed.

He dismounts in one easy movement and starts taking off his gloves one finger at a time.

And I know we've lost.

Everything is lost.

Everything is over.

"As the newly appointed President of this fair planet of ours," the Mayor says, holding out his hand as if to show me the world for the first time, "let me be the very first to welcome you to its new capital city."

"Todd?" Viola whispers, her eyes closed.

I hold her tightly to me.

"I'm sorry," I whisper to her. "I'm so sorry."

We've run right into a trap.

We've run right off the end of the world.

"Welcome," says the Mayor, "to New Prentisstown."

END OF BOOK ONE

MORE CHAOS WALKING

A BONUS SHORT STORY BY PATRICK NESS

THE
NEW
WORLD

"There it is," my mother says, and what she means is that the dot we've been nearing for weeks, the one that's been growing into a larger dot with two smaller dots circling it, has now become even larger than that, growing from a dot to a disc, shining back the light from its sun, until you can see the blue of its oceans, the green of its forests, the white of its polar caps, a circle of colour against the black beyond.

Our new home, the one we've been travelling towards since way before I was even born.

We're the first ones to see it for real, not through telescopes, not through computer mapping, not even in my own drawings in the art classes I take on the *Beta* with Bradley Tench, but through just the couple centimetres of glass in the cockpit viewscreen.

We're the first ones to see it with our own eyes.

"The New World," my father says, putting a hand on my shoulder. "What do you think we'll find there?"

I cross my arms and pull away from him.

"Viola?" he asks.

"I've seen it already," I say, walking out of the cockpit. "It's wonderful. Hooray. Can't wait to get there."

"*Viola*," my mother says sharply, as I shut the cockpit door behind me. It's a slotted door, so I can't even slam it.

I keep going to my small bedroom and barely shut my own door before there's a knock on it. "Viola?" my father says from the other side.

"I'm tired," I say. "I want to sleep."

"It's one o'clock in the afternoon."

I don't say anything.

"We'll be entering orbit in four hours," he says, his voice calm, not rising to my attitude at all. "There'll be work for you to do starting in two."

"I know my duties," I say, still not opening the door.

There's a pause. "It's going to be all right, Viola," he says, his voice even kinder. "You'll see."

"How do you know?" I say back. "You've never lived on a planet either."

"Well," he says, brightening up, "I've got lots of hope."

And there it is. That word I'm so completely sick of.

"It's us," my father said on the day they told me the news, and though he was trying to look serious, I could tell he was hiding a smile. We were having dinner, and under the table, his leg was bouncing up and down.

"It's us what?" I said, though I could easily guess.

"We've been selected," my mother said. "We're the landing party."

"We leave in 91 days," my father said.

I looked down at my plate, which suddenly held a bunch of food I didn't want to eat. "I thought it was going to be Steff Taylor's parents."

My father stifled a laugh. Steff Taylor's father was such a bad pilot he could barely fly from ship to ship in the convoy without wrecking a shuttle.

"It's us, sweetheart," my mother said, my mother the pilot, my mother who was so much better at it than Steff Taylor's father that she was almost certainly the reason we'd been chosen. "Remember we talked about this. You were excited."

And that's true. I was excited when they'd first told me they were going to put themselves forward. I was even *more* excited when Steff Taylor started bragging that her father was *obviously* going to be chosen.

The job was vital. We'd leave the sleeping settlers and the other caretaker families behind, speeding into the empty black beyond in a small scout ship. The convoy was still twelve months from the planet. We'd make the journey in five and spend seven months there – not just my parents, I'd have work to do, too – finding the best landing site for the five big settler ships and starting to prepare the ground for the first landings.

But it was more exciting when it *could* have been us. It was surprisingly less so when it was *actually* us.

"You'll get more training," my mother said. "You'll learn a *lot* more, just like you wanted."

"It's an honour, Viola," my father said. "We'll be the first ones to see our new home."

"Unless the original settlers are still there," I said.

They exchanged a glance.

"Are you unhappy with this, Viola?" my mother asked, her face serious.

"Would you not go if I was?" I asked.

And they exchanged another glance.

And I knew what that meant.

"Thirty minutes to orbital," my mother is saying as I step back into the cockpit, only a little bit late. She's the only one there. My father must have gone down to the engine room already, prepping them for orbital entry. My mother glances up at my reflection in her screens. "And she rejoins us."

"It's my job," I say, sitting down at a terminal ninety degrees from her. And it *is* my job, one I trained for on the convoy and in the five months I've been here. My mother will pilot us into orbit, my father will ready the thrusters that will carry us down into the planet's atmosphere, and I'll be monitoring for possible landing sites.

"There's been something new while you pouted," my mother says.

"I wasn't pouting–"

"Look," she says, bringing up a box on the viewscreen showing the larger of the two northern continents.

"What *is* that?"

There's a stretch of river that heads east towards the ocean on the night side of the planet. It's impossible to tell from this distance, even with the ship's scanners, but there's an emptier space up the river a ways, possibly a valley, where the forest breaks open a bit and what looks like might even be lights.

"The other settlers?" I ask.

The other settlers are almost a ghost story to us. We've had no communications from them either in my lifetime or my parents', so we always figured they didn't make it. It's a long, long trip from Old World to New, decades and decades, and so they were still on their way when our convoy left. But we heard nothing from them. Even our deepest space probes only caught distant glimpses of them as they travelled. Then after the time came when they would have landed, still years before I was born, it was hoped that we could communicate with them on the planet as we got closer, let them know we were coming, asking what it was like, what we should prepare ourselves for.

But either no one was listening, or no one was there anymore. And it was the second possibility that got everyone worried.

If they didn't make it, what would become of us?

My father says they were idealistic settlers, leaving Old World to start a simpler, low-technology, farming kind of life with religion and all that. Which seems both stupid to me and also seems to have failed completely. But we were already so far out by the time whatever happened to them happened, there was no turning back, just the same course to the same place where we'll find our own doom, no doubt.

"How didn't we see it before?" I say, leaning closer to the screen.

"No real energy signatures," my mum says. "If they're powering themselves, it's not through a big reactor like we'd expect."

"There's a river," I say. "Maybe it's hydro-electric."

"Or maybe it's empty." My mum's voice is quiet as we watch the screen. "It's hard to tell if those are even actual lights or just blips in the readings."

The little patch by the river starts getting farther away. We're entering orbit the other direction, heading west, circling the planet once as we enter the atmosphere, and coming back round the other side to land.

"Is that where we're going?" I say.

"It's as good a place to start as any," my mother says. "If they didn't last, then the first thing we need to do is learn from their mistakes."

"Or get killed the same way."

"We've got better technology," my mother says. "And from what we know, they shunned what they had anyway, which could very easily have been why they failed." She looks at me. "That's not going to happen to us."

You *hope*, I think to myself.

We both watch as the continent rolls away from under us.

"Ready," my father calls over the comm system.

"Then let's call that ten minutes mark," my mother says, pressing a countdown button.

"Everyone up there excited?" my father's voice says.

"Some of us are," my mother says, frowning at me.

"I'm *so* glad we're not going," Steff Taylor said the first time I saw her in class after it was announced it was my parents who were the landing party and not hers. It was actually my favourite class, art with Bradley on the *Beta*. Bradley also taught us maths and agriculture, and was pretty much my favourite person on the whole convoy, even though he made me sit next to Steff Taylor since we were the only girls our age in all of the caretaker families.

Lucky us.

"It'll be *so* boring," Steff said, twisting her hair in her fingers. "Five *months* on that *little* ship with just your mum and dad for company."

"I can vid back to friends and classes," I said. "And I like my mum and dad."

She sneered at me. "Not after five months you won't."

"Steff, you used to brag about how your father–"

"And then when you *land*, you've got to live there with who knows what kinds of scary animals and hoping your food rations last and there's going to be *weather* there, Viola. Actual *weather*."

"We'll be the first people to see it."

"Oh, whoopee," she said. "First people to see a deserted mudhole." She twisted her hair a little harder. "First people to die there more like."

"Steff Taylor!" Bradley said from the front of the class. All the other kids huddled over their interactive art vids were suddenly looking up.

"I'm working," Steff said, running her hands over her artpad.

"Is that so?" Bradley said. "Then perhaps you can come up here and show the rest of us what you're working on."

Steff frowned, hard, a frown I knew covered the latest grudge she was adding to her long, long list. As slowly as she could get away with, she got to her feet.

"Thirteenth birthday," she whispered to me. "All alone."

And I could tell by the satisfied look on her face that I reacted just exactly how she wanted.

"120 seconds to orbital," my mother says.

"Ready here," my father says over the comm, and I hear the engines change their pitch as we prepare to stop falling out of the black beyond and power our way through the atmosphere of the planet.

"Ready here, too," I say, opening up screens that I won't really use until we're closer to the ground, looking for a clearing big enough to put down. A clearing, if I'm good enough at my job, where we might actually grow our first town.

"90 seconds," my mother says.

"Engines opening," my father says, and there's another change in pitch. "Oxygenating the fuel."

"Buckle up," my mother says.

"I *am* buckled," I say, then turn my chair so I can buckle into it without her seeing.

"60 seconds," my mum says.

"One more minute and we're the first ones there!" my dad shouts over the comm.

My mother laughs. I don't.

"Oh, come on, Viola," she says. "It really *is* exciting." She checks one of her screens, dials on it with her fingertips, then says, "30 seconds."

"I was happy on the ship," I say, quietly but so seriously my mother turns to look. "I don't want to live down there."

My mother frowns. "15 seconds."

"Fuel ready!" my father says. "Let's go atmo-surfing!"

"Ten," my mother says, still looking at me. "Nine."

And that's when things go really, really wrong.

"But it's a whole *year*," I said to Bradley in one of my training tutorials less than a month before we left. "A year away from my friends, a year away from schoolwork–"

"And if you stayed," he said, "it would be a year away from your parents."

I looked back into the empty classroom. It was usually filled with the other caretaker families' children, learning our lessons, talking to our friends. But today it was just me and Bradley, going over some of the science tech for the trip. Tomorrow, Simone from the *Gamma* – who I think Bradley secretly fancies – would be teaching me emergency survival skills, just in case the worst happened. But it would still just be me and her in this room, separated out from everybody else.

"Why does it have to be us, though?" I said.

"Because you're the best ones for the job," Bradley said. "Your mother is probably our best pilot, your father is a highly skilled engineer–"

"And what about me? Why do I have to pay for what they're good at?"

He smiled. "You're hardly just some girl. You're tops in maths. You're the younger ones' favourite tutor in music–"

"And for that, I should be punished by being dragged away from everyone I know for a year?"

He gave me a look, then he dialled so quickly on the training pads in front of us that I could barely see what he was doing. "Name this," he said, in a teacherly tone that made me answer immediately.

"Hardpan," I said, looking at the simulated landscape he'd chosen. "Good drainage, but dry. Irrigation for at least five to eight years before suitable for crops."

"And this?" he said, dialling again.

"Temperate forest. Limited clearing needed, potentially good for cattle, but strong environmental concerns."

"This one?"

"Near desert. Subsistence farming only. Bradley–"

"You've got skills, Viola. You're bright and resourceful and even at your age, you'll be a vital part of the mission."

I didn't answer because for some stupid reason, I could feel my eyes getting wetter.

"What are you really frightened of?" Bradley asked, so gently I looked up into his brown eyes, into the kindness of the smile across his brown skin, the small grey curls just starting to show in the hair at his temples. I saw nothing but warmth.

"Everyone keeps talking about *hope*," I said, swallowing.

Bradley's voice was too tender to bear. "Viola–"

"I'm not afraid," I lied, swallowing again. "It's just I'm going to miss my thirteenth birthday party, and the graduation ceremony to the upper fifth–"

"But you'll be seeing things no one else will. Heck, you'll be an *expert* by the time everyone else gets there, the one everyone turns to for an opinion."

I pulled my arms to myself. "They'll just think I'm a show-off."

"They think that now," he said, but he was smiling.

And I didn't want to smile back.

But I did. A little.

There's a small banging sound from the bottom of the ship as we hit the first turbulence of the atmosphere.

But my mother and I both look up immediately. It's the wrong kind of bang.

"What was that?" my mother says.

"I think—" my father's voice says—

And there's a sudden *ROARING* sound over the comm and a yelp of alarm from my father—

"Thomas!" my mum yells.

"Look!" I shout, pointing at the display pads, which are lighting up, one after the other.

The engine room is filling with fire and the exits are sealing shut to contain it.

And they're doing it with my father inside.

"*Dad!*" I scream—

And that fast, everything changes.

My mother frantically presses her displays, trying to open the engine vents to blow the fire out of the ship—

"They're not responding!" she yells. "Thomas, can you hear me?!"

"What's happening?" I shout, because the roar of the atmosphere is getting so much louder than in our simulations.

"It shouldn't be this *thick*," my mother shouts back, meaning the atmosphere, and I have a sinking feeling in my stomach as I wonder if this is what happened to the original settlers. Maybe they never even made it to the surface.

"I'm going down to find Dad," I say, unbuckling from my chair and standing–

But there's another *bang* and the ship lists badly to one side. I fall, hanging on to the chair by my fingers. My mother grabs the manual controls with both hands and wrestles us back in position. "Viola, I need you to find us a landing spot! Now!"

"But Dad–"

"I can't get us back up, so we're going to have to go down! *Now*, Viola!"

I sit down and buckle back in, my hands shaking.

"Find that stretch of ground by the river!" she says.

"It's on the other side of the planet," I say, but I know from the shuddering of the ship that we're tearing through the atmosphere *way* faster than we should.

"Just find it!" my mother shouts. "If there are people there–"

And I can see from her face how worried she is about my father, and I know that if she's battling with the ship instead of going down to find him, then we're in even worse trouble than I thought–

"I'll *miss* you," Steff Taylor said at our going away party, her voice twisting up high, making it sound even more insincere than it was.

All the caretaker families had gathered in the conference room of the *Delta* for the party, happy for any excuse to get drunk and say goodbye. Steff swept me into her arms in a hug angled so that everyone around us would see *her* face, how sad *she* was that I was going away for a year. Then she let me go and collapsed into her mother's arms with a wailing that was louder than anything else in the room.

Bradley came over with an amused look. "I'm sure Steff will cope with her grief better than I will," he said, handing me a wrapped gift. "Don't open it until you've landed."

"'Til we've *landed*?" I said. "That's five months from now."

He smiled and lowered his voice. "Do you know what separates us from the beasts, Viola?"

I frowned, sensing a lesson. "The ability to wait to open a present?"

He laughed. "Fire," he said. "The ability to make fire at will. It allowed us light to see in the darkness, warmth against the cold, a tool to cook our food." He gestured vaguely in the direction of the *Delta*'s engines. "Fire is what eventually led to travel across the black beyond, the ability to start a new life on a New World."

I looked down at the present.

"You're frightened," he said. This time, it wasn't an asking.

I shrugged. "A little."

He leaned down to whisper to me. "I'm frightened, too."

"You are?"

He nodded. "My grandfather was the last of the original caretakers on the convoy to die, the last one of us who'd actually breathed the air of a planet and not of a ship."

I waited for him to go on. "And?"

"He didn't have anything good to say about it," he said. "Old World was polluted and crowded and dying from its own poisons. That's why we left, to find a better place, one we could do our very best not to wreck like we had Old World."

"I know all this–"

"But the rest of us are just like you, Viola. We've never seen any space bigger than the cargo bay on the *Gamma*. I don't know what fresh air smells like either except what they've got on the immersive vids, and that's not the real thing. I mean, can you imagine what a real *ocean* is like, Viola? How big it must seem? How small we are compared to it?"

"Is this supposed to make me feel better?"

"Actually, yes." He smiled and tapped the present I was holding. "Because you'll have something to help you against the darkness."

The present was small in my hand, but heavy, substantial. "But I can't open it 'til I get there."

"How would I know?" he asked. "I'll just have to trust you."

I looked back up. "I'll wait," I said. "I promise."

"And I'm going to miss her *birthday*!" Steff Taylor wailed loudly, shooting me a look, and I could see that her eyes, at least, weren't wailing.

"I'll see you in twelve months, Viola," Bradley said. "And when I get there, make sure I'm the first one you tell what the night looks like by firelight."

The scout ship feels like it's going to fly apart at any second. The atmosphere is bashing us around and it's all my mother can do to keep us upright.

She calls occasionally for my dad, but there's still no answer.

"Viola, where are we?!" she shouts, wrestling with the controls.

"We're coming back around!" I shout over the roar of it all. "We're going too fast, though. I think we're going to over-shoot it."

"I'll try to get us down as best I can. Can you see anything on the scanners? Anything beyond that bit of the river where we can land?"

I press through my screens but they're jumping around as much as everything else on the ship. The engines are still firing us forward and so we're pretty much *falling* towards the planet, too fast, with no way to slow ourselves down. We're zooming over a *huge* ocean right now and I can tell my mother is worried that we'll have to put down in the middle of it–

But the continent's coming up on our screens now, looming dark as night and way too fast and suddenly we're over it, the ground whipping by down below us.

"Are we near it?!" my mum yells.

"Hold on!" I check the mapping. "We're south of it! About 15ks!"

She wrestles with the manual controls, trying to turn us a bit more north. "Dammit!" The ship lists and I slam my elbow into the control panel, losing my maps for second.

"Mum?" I say, worry and fright in my voice as I try to bring the maps up again.

"I know, sweetheart," she says, grunting with the controls.

"What about Dad?"

She doesn't say anything but I can see it all on her face. "We've got to find a place to put down, Viola! And then we'll do everything we can to save him!"

I turn back to my maps. "Looks like a prairie of some kind first," I say, "but we'll probably overshoot that." I dial through some more scans. "A swamp!" I say. My mother's got us heading north again, back towards that river we saw, which seems to peter out into swampland.

"Will we be low enough?" my mother yells.

I dial through a few more screens and projected landing arcs. "It'll be close."

The ship gives a huge jolt.

And then there's an eerie quiet.

"We've lost the engines," my mother says. "The vents never opened. The fire choked out." She turns to me. "We're gliding in. Program me a flightpath and hold on tight."

I dial quickly through a few more screens, locking in a landing arc into what I'm hoping will be a nice soft swamp.

My mother pulls the manual controls hard with her fists, lining up her screen with the path I've laid out. Out the portholes I can see the ground far too clearly now, treetops getting closer and closer below us.

"Mum?" I say, watching as we get lower in the sky.

"Hang on!" she says.

"MUM!"

And we hit.

"Happy birthday!" they shouted on the big day, ambushing me at breakfast with the least surprising surprise party in the history of the universe.

"Thanks," I mumbled.

We'd left the convoy three months earlier, watching it blink out of sight behind us as we sped away fast, fast, fast. We were still eight weeks away from the new planet, eight long weeks in a ship that was beginning to smell a bit, no matter how much the air got filtered.

"Presents!" my father said, sweeping his hand over the wrapped boxes on the table.

"You could at least *try* to look pleased, Viola," my mother said.

"Thanks," I said again, a bit louder. I opened the first present, a new pair of boots, meant for hiking through rough terrain, completely the wrong colour, but I made sort of fake thankful sounds for them anyway.

I opened the second.

"Binos," my father said as I took them out. "Your mother had them upgraded by Eddie, the engineer on the *Alpha* before we left. These do things you wouldn't even believe. Night vision, in-screen zoom..."

I looked through them and found a giant version of my father's left eye looking back at me.

"She's smiling," my father said and his own giant grin filled the binos.

"I am *not*," I said.

My mother left the room and came back with my favourite breakfast, a stack of pancakes, this time with thirteen motion-activated fibre-optic lights glittering on the top. They sang me the song, and it took four goes moving my hands before I got all the lights to go off.

"What'd you wish for?" my father asked.

"If you tell," I said. "It doesn't come true."

"Well, we're not turning the ship around," my mother said, "so I hope it wasn't that."

"Hope!" my father said, too loud, covering up my mother's

words with forced enthusiasm. "That's what we should all wish for. Hope!"

I frowned because there was that word again.

"We brought this out, too," my father said, touching Bradley's still-wrapped present. "Just in case you wanted to open it now."

I looked at my parents' faces, my father bright and happy, my mother annoyed with all my moaning but trying to make me have a good birthday anyway. And for a brief second, I saw their worry about me, too.

Their worry that I didn't seem to have any hope at all.

I looked at Bradley's present. *A light against the darkness*, he'd said.

"He said it was for when we got there," I said. "I'll wait until then."

The sound when we crash is so loud it's almost impossible.

The ship smashes through trees, snapping them into bits, and then hits the ground with a jolt so violent I knock my head against the control panel and pain rips through it but I'm still awake, awake enough to hear the ship start to break apart, awake enough to hear every *crash* and *snap* and *grind* as we carve out a long ditch through the swamp, awake as the ship rolls over again and again, which can only mean the wings have broken off, and everything in the cabin falls to the ceiling and back down again and then there's an actual crack in the structure of the cockpit and water rushes in from the swamp but then we're rolling again–

And we're slowing–

The roll is slowing down–

The grinding of metal is deafening and the main lights cut off as we take another roll, replaced immediately by the quivery battery lights–

And the roll keeps slowing–

Slowing until–

It stops.

And I'm still breathing. My head is spinning and aching and I'm hanging almost upside down from my buckle in my seat.

But I'm breathing.

"Mum?" I say, looking down and around. "*Mum?*"

"Viola?" I hear.

"Mum?" I twist round to where her seat should be–

But it's not there–

I twist round some more–

And there she is, resting against the ceiling, her chair ripped from the floor–

And the way she's lying there–

The way she's lying there *broken*–

"Viola?" she says again.

And the way she says it makes my chest grip tight as a fist.

No, I think. *No.*

And I start the struggle to get out of my chair to get to her.

"Big day tomorrow, Skipper," my dad said, coming into the engine room, where I was replacing tubes of coolant, one of about a million chores they'd come up with in the past five months to keep me busy. "We'll finally be entering orbit."

I clicked in the last coolant tube. "Terrific."

He paused. "I know this hasn't been easy for you, Viola."

"Why do you care if it wasn't?" I said. "I didn't have any say in the matter."

He came closer. "Okay, what are you *really* frightened of, Viola?" he said, and it's so exactly the question Bradley asked me that I look back at him. "Is it what we could find there? Or is it just that it's change?"

I sighed heavily. "No one ever seems to wonder what happens if it turns out we *hate* living on a planet. What if the sky's too big? What if the air stinks? What if we go hungry?"

"And what if the air tastes of honey? What if there's so much food we all get too fat? What if the sky is so beautiful we don't get any work done because we're all looking at it too much?"

I turned and closed up the coolant tube cases. "But what if it isn't?"

"But what if it is?"

"What if it *isn't?*"

"What if it *is?*"

"Yeah, this is getting us somewhere."

"Haven't we raised you to be hopeful?" he said. "Wasn't that the whole point of your great-grandmother agreeing to be a caretaker on this ship, so that one day *you* could have a better life? *She* was full of hope. Your mum and I are full of hope." He was close enough now for a hug, if I wanted it. "Why can't you share some of that?"

And he was looking so caring, so worried, that how could

I tell him? How could I tell him how much I hate even the sound of the word?

Hope. That's all anyone ever talked about on the convoy, especially as we got closer. Hope, hope, hope.

As in, "I hope the weather's good." This from people who'd never actually experienced weather except in immersive vids.

Or, "I hope there's interesting wildlife." From people who'd only ever met Scampus and Bumpus, the ship's cats on the *Delta*. 10,000 frozen sheep and cow embryos didn't count.

Or, "I hope the natives are friendly." This always said with a laugh because there aren't supposed to *be* any natives, at least according to the deep space probes.

Everybody was hoping for something, talking about our new life to come and all that they *hoped* from it. Fresh air, whatever that's supposed to mean. Real gravity, instead of the fake kind that broke every now and then (even though no one over fifteen would admit that it was actually really fun when it did). All the wide open spaces we'd have, all the new people we'd meet when we woke them up, ignoring completely what happened to the original settlers, super-confident that we were *so* much better equipped that nothing bad could possibly happen to us.

All this hope, and here I was, right at the very edge of it, looking out into the darkness, the first to see it coming, the first to greet it when we found out what it *really* looked like.

But what if?

"Is it because hope is scary?" my father asked.

I looked back at him, startled. "You think so, too?"

He smiled, full of love. "Hope is *terrifying*, Viola," he said. "No one wants to admit it, but it is."

I feel my eyes go wet again. "Then how can you *stand* it? How can you bear even *thinking* it? It feels so dangerous, like you'll be punished for even thinking you deserved it."

He touched my arm, just lightly. "Because, Viola, life is so much *more* terrifying without it."

I swallowed away my tears again. "So you're telling me the only choice I have is which way I'm going to be terrified for the rest of my life?"

He laughed and opened his arms. "And at last a smile," he said.

And he did hug me.

And I let him.

But in my chest, there was still fear, and I didn't know which kind it was. Fear with hope, or fear without it.

It takes what seems like forever to unbuckle my belt, hard to do when you're hanging upside down against it. When it finally comes undone, I fall away from the seat, sliding down the wall of the cockpit, which seems to have folded into itself.

"Mum?" I say, scooting over to her.

She's face down on what used to be the ceiling, her legs twisted in a way I can't really look at–

"Viola?" she says again.

"I'm here, Mum." I push away the things that have fallen on her, all the files and screenpads, everything broken as we tumbled, everything that wasn't fastened down broken to pieces–

I pull up a large metal plate off her back–

And I see it–

The pilot's chair was torn from the floor, tearing away the back panel of it, turning the backrest into a shard of metal–

A shard that's gone right into my mother's spine–

"Mum?" I say, my voice tight, trying to lift it further off her–

But when I move it more, she screams, screams like I'm not even there–

I stop.

"Viola?" she says one more time, gasping. Her voice is high, broken. "Is that you?"

"I'm here, Mum," I say, lying down next to her so I can get close to her face. I push away a last bit of glass that's covering her cheek and see her eye looking wildly around–

"Sweetheart?" she says.

"Mum?" I say, crying, brushing away more glass. "Tell me what to do, Mum."

"Sweetheart, are you hurt?" she says, high and fluttery again, like she can't really take a breath.

"I don't know," I say. "Mum, can you move?"

I put a hand under her shoulder to lift her, but she screams again, which makes me scream, too, and I let her go back to how she was lying, on her stomach, on the ceiling, the metal shard in her back, blood coming out of it slowly like it was no big deal, and everything around us broken, broken, broken.

"Your father," she gasps.

"I don't know," I say. "The *fire*–"

"Your father loved you," she says.

I stop and look at her. "What?"

I see her moving her hand, trying to worm it out from under herself and I take it gently, holding it with my own. "I love you, too, Viola," she says.

"*Mum?* Don't *say* that–"

"Listen, sweetheart, listen to me."

"Mum!"

"No, *listen*–"

And she coughs and the pain of it causes her to scream again and I hold her hand tighter and I barely even notice that I'm screaming along with her.

She stops, gasping again, and her eye looks up at me, more focussed this time, like she's trying really hard, like she's never tried harder to do anything in her entire life. "They'll come for you, Viola."

"Mum, stop, *please*–"

"You've been trained," she says. "You stay alive. You stay *alive*, Viola Eade, do you hear me?" Her voice is getting louder, even though I can hear the pain in it.

"Mum, you're not *dying*–"

"Take my hope, Viola," she says. "Take your father's, too. I'm giving it to you, okay? I'm giving you my hope."

"Mum, I don't understand–"

"Say you'll take it, sweetheart. Say it to me."

My throat is choking and I think I'm crying but nothing feels attached to anything and I'm here holding my mother's hand in a wrecked spaceship on the first planet I've ever been to, in the middle of a night I can see through a crack in the ship's hull and she's dying, she's *dying*, and I've been so horrible to her for months–

"Say it, Viola," my mother whispers. "Please."

"I'll take it," I say. "I'll take your hope. I've got it, okay? *Mum?*"

But I don't know if she hears me–

Because her hand isn't gripping back any more.

And that's when something happens, something that makes everything *now*, something that cuts all the past away, the convoy and everyone on it gone and past, and it's just me, here, *now*, so fast, it doesn't seem real.

My father. The crash. My mother. It's not real.

It's like I'm watching it all, including myself, from somewhere else.

I watch myself stand up next to my mother.

I watch myself wait there in the wreckage for a while not knowing what to do.

Until enough time passes that *something* has to be done, so I watch as I climb to where the wall of the cockpit has come apart and look out into the planet for the first time.

Look out into the darkness. Darkness upon further darkness. Darkness that hides things.

Things I can hear.

Animal noises that almost sound like words.

I watch myself step back into the ship, away from the darkness, my heart beating heavy.

And then I seem to blink and the next thing I see is myself pulling back a broken panel to the engine room.

From even farther away, I see myself finding my father, burnt in a nightmarish way from the chest down, a terrible wound on his forehead that would have killed him anyway.

I watch myself as coldness flows through me, watch as I'm so cold I'm unable to even cry at my father's body.

I blink again and then I'm seeing myself back next to my mother in the cockpit, my arms pulled tight around my knees, the battery lights in the panels flickering and slowly getting dimmer.

And then there's a birdcall or something from outside, louder than the rest, a weird one that almost sounds like the word *Prey* or *Pray*.

And I'm back behind my eyes.

Because I've seen something, tumbled there.

Something my mother must have taken from my room and brought into the cockpit, something to give to me as soon as we landed, which hurts me somewhere in a far, far off place.

There, in the wreckage.

Bradley's present.

It's still wrapped, after all these months, after even my birthday. And everything still feels impossible and like a dream, so why shouldn't I open it? If that's what my mother and father wanted, why shouldn't that be the first thing I do on this planet?

I pick it up, sliding off the torn paper and opening it just as the last of the battery power cuts out, leaving me in total darkness.

But it's okay.

It's okay because I've already seen what it is.

The darkness is so thick I have to feel my way out of the wreckage, still feeling dazed, still feeling dreamy, the blanket of darkness so complete, it's almost like I'm sleeping. But I'm holding Bradley's gift.

I step out onto the planet and my foot sinks in about ten centimetres of water.

A swamp.

That's right. We were aiming for a swamp.

I keep walking, my feet sticking in the mud sometimes, but I keep walking.

Keep walking until the ground gets more solid, a little way from the ship.

My eyes are adjusting and I can see a little clearing, surrounded by trees, the sky above us filled with all the stars I was just flying through.

I'm hearing more animals, too, but I swear it sounds like they're actually *talking* so I figure it must still be the shock.

Mostly there's just darkness.

There's just darkness closing me in.

And that's exactly what Bradley's gift was for.

There's a dry enough spot in the middle of the raised clearing, not great, not perfect, but enough. I set down the gift and feel around for some twigs and leaves, getting a few damp handfuls and piling them on top.

I press a button on the gift and step back.

The damp leaves and twigs burst immediately into flame.

And there's light.

Light across the little clearing, light reflecting on the metal of the ship, light that includes me in it, standing here.

Light from a fire.

Bradley gave me a fire box. One that will start a fire nearly anywhere, in nearly any condition, with nearly any fuel.

Start it to give a light against the darkness.

And for a while it's all I can do just to stare at it until I feel myself shivering, and I sit down closer to the fire until I stop.

Which takes a long, long time.

The fire for now is all I can see.

Soon, I'll need to see what supplies I have left to live off. Soon, I'll need to see if any of the communications equipment survived so I can try and contact the convoy.

Soon, I'll need to take the bodies of my father and my mother and–

But that's soon, that's not now–

Now there's only fire from the fire box.

Now there's only a tiny light against the darkness.

Whatever's going to happen next can wait.

I don't really know what my mother was saying, I don't know that hope is something you can give to someone else, something that you can *take*.

But I said I would, I said I *did*.

And so I sit in front of Bradley's fire, on the surface of a dark, dark planet, and I have their hope, if not any of mine.

Except the hope that it'll be enough.

And then I see a lightening in the air, in the sky above and behind me. I turn to watch this planet's sun rising, and I realize it's morning, that I've made it to morning.

That I've had enough hope to make it to morning.

Okay, I think to myself.

Okay.

And I begin to think of what I need to do next.

ALSO BY PATRICK NESS

A MONSTER CALLS

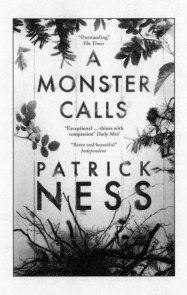

"Outstanding… Gripping, moving, brilliantly crafted."
The Times

"Brave and beautiful."
Independent

"Brilliant and elegant."
Guardian

"Electrifying."
Telegraph

"Exceptional … shines with compassion."
Daily Mail